GILBERT MORRIS

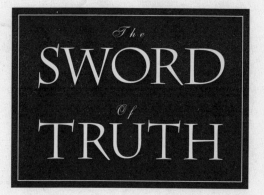

TYNDALE HOUSE PUBLISHERS, INC.
Wheaton, Illinois

Library of Congress Cataloging-in-Publication Data

Morris, Gilbert.
      The sword of truth / Gilbert Morris.
         p.   cm. — (The Wakefield dynasty ; 1)
      ISBN 0-8423-6228-2
       1. Great Britain—History—Tudors, 1485-1603—Fiction.   I. Title.
    II. Series: Morris, Gilbert. Wakefield dynasty ; 1.
    PS3563.08742S9   1994
    813′.54—dc20   94-7013

Printed in the United States of America

02 01 00
9 8 7 6

THE WAKEFIELD DYNASTY

1

To my wife, Johnnie—
Almost half a century has passed since we stood
together in a small church
and made promises.
I've enjoyed every second of it!

CONTENTS

PART FOUR: THE FUGITIVE—1530–1534

EPILOGUE

THE GENEALOGY OF THE WAKEFIELDS

Margred Morgan
(1491–1522)——————— Myles
Sir Robert Wakefield   (1507–)
(1470–)
married 1506
Jane Harwich
(1485–)

THE COURT OF HENRY VIII

Catherine of Aragon
1485–1536)
married 1509 —————— Mary I
divorced 1533   (1516–)
King Henry VIII
(1491–)
married 1533 —————— Elizabeth I
Anne Boleyn (1507–)   (1533–)

The

Part
ONE

1 5 1 3   1 5 2 2

Serf

DANGEROUS JOURNEY

The shrill clarion call of a cock somewhere off in the barnyard drew Margred out of a fitful sleep. She shivered and tried to burrow deeper underneath the thin blankets. Despite her efforts, the cold seemed to penetrate, and she could draw no warmth from the frigid air of the shack in which she lived. She slipped an arm around the sleeping form of her six-year-old son, Myles, noting that he was warmer than she, and she was glad for that. For a few moments she lay there, dreading to leave the warmth, meager though it was, of her bed. Then, hearing the lowing of the heifer, she reluctantly slipped out of the pallet, pausing to draw the thin, scanty rags of blankets around Myles's curled-up body.

Shivering almost violently, Margred slipped into her rough woolen dress and quickly pulled the only outer garment she owned over her head. It was a rough-woven garment of wool, sewn together from remnants of other garments. The shoes she put on her feet were made of raw untanned cowhide, and though they did little to keep her feet warm, they protected against the sharp stones.

As she opened the door quietly and headed across the open space toward the barn, she noticed that the sky in the east had just begun to lighten. She paused a moment, enjoying the faint, almost buttermilk quality of the dawn. *It'll be cold today,* she thought, padding across the bare ground. *I wouldn't be surprised if it snowed.*

Stepping into the barn, which was a small frame building no more than fifteen feet square, she opened the shutters on the windows to let in the faint light of the dawn. Then she picked up the milk pail and walked over to the cow, who lowed at her and lifted her head to watch Margred's approach.

"Good morning, Lady," Margred murmured, rubbing her hand across the animal's velvet nose. She led the cow to a feed rack, put a few handfuls of the feed inside, then sat down on a low stool and began to milk. Her hands were stiff and cold but soon grew warm with the work. There was something pleasant about the hissing of the milk as it began to fill up the small pail. Hunger caused Margred's stomach to twist as the aroma of the fresh milk drifted about her, and it took a determined act of will not to lift the bucket and sample the liquid. To do so would bring the wrath of Ianto Motshill, the owner of the manor, upon her. Neither the cow nor its milk were Margred's to enjoy.

I'll have to take at least a little for Myles, she thought. *He's always so hungry.*

When the cow was stripped, she rose and pushed the stool back under the feed trough. Then she released the calf, who had been penned up, to have his share of the milk. The eager beast butted against her, ran over to his mother, and immediately began his morning meal. Margred smiled in amusement and stood for a moment, watching the calf feeding greedily.

She was attractive, this Margred Morgan, blonder than most women of Welsh blood, with large blue eyes set in an oval face. She was not tall, but even the rough garments she wore could not conceal her pleasing form. There was something almost mystical in her expression—which was not misleading, for she was a woman of spirit, as were many of the Welsh women. Even as she watched the calf, she was able to put aside the hard physical conditions around her, as well as the cold and hunger that pulled at her, and think about the things of the Spirit. But she was rudely pulled back to the world around her by a hard, cold voice.

"So, here you are!"

She whirled and saw the large, bulky form of Ianto Motshill. He had stepped inside and was blocking the door—and even by the dim light of dawn, she could clearly see the dark desire on his face. For one moment, fear rippled through her, and she moved instinctively to pass by him. But he was too quick for her.

"Don't be in such a hurry, girl!" he said huskily, reaching out to take hold of her arm in a viselike grip. "Give a man a kiss, can't you?" He swung her around, holding her effortlessly as she struggled. He pinned her arms to her sides, then laughed roughly. "I never seen such a girl for running away from a man! What's the matter? You're no innocent, you had a husband—" He broke off and laughed. "Or at least, a man. You've got that boy, haven't you? You didn't find him under a gorseberry bush!"

"Let me go!" she cried, struggling to break the grip of his massive hands. He had been watching her for weeks now, and the times he'd actually come after her, she had managed to escape— something some of the other women on the manor had not been able to accomplish.

Margred knew Motshill viewed the women who worked on his place in almost the same light as the animals he owned: they were his property, to do with as he willed. When his attention had turned to her, she had been tempted more than once to take Myles and leave. But she had nowhere else to go. Famine had held Wales in its grasp for two years now, and it was only growing worse. Were she to leave this place of security—pitiful though it might be—she feared what would happen to her son.

Silently she struggled, but she was like a small bird in the manor owner's massive hands. He was strong beyond belief, and suddenly she knew that there was little hope for her.

Oh God, help me to get away! Help me!

Motshill seemed to enjoy her struggles. He loosened his grip on one of her arms and began to caress her, saying, "Now then, girl, don't take on so! You needs a man, and I needs a woman, and that's all there be to it!" He held her tightly and began to kiss her, his huge lips sliding over her cheek as she turned her head frantically, his hand pulling at her outer garment.

God! Help me!

Suddenly Margred reached up to rake her nails down his face with a vicious jerk. Motshill let out a shrill cry, then a curse, and let her go. She leaped across the room as he put a hand to his face. Quickly she snatched up a pitchfork and held it with both hands, aiming it directly at the man's face. She might be cornered, but she was not defenseless!

"Ye'll leave me alone!" she said in cold fury. "Ere I run this through your throat!"

Motshill took in the woman's flashing blue eyes and the weapon poised to strike. He stepped back, blinked at her, then said angrily, "What kind of a woman are ye?" He started to come at her, but stopped when she lifted the fork, putting the points on level with his face. With a frustrated snarl, he backed off. "Ye're not worth the fight!" he threw at her as he reached up to touch his face gingerly. When he saw blood on his fingers, a fierce anger leaped into his piggish eyes.

"There's plenty o' women looking for a good place, Margred Morgan! So make up your mind! Tonight ye'll be with me, or ye'll be out in the cold with the sky for a roof. And there'll be no more clawing like a wild beast! So make up your mind to it." He turned and walked quickly out of the stable.

As soon as he was gone, Margred began to shake. Laying the fork to one side, she sagged against the wall and began drawing in great gusts of air, as though she'd been running hard. She had known, deep down, that this was coming. And now . . . now she had no choice.

She sank to her knees, and for a long time, she stayed there, silent and unmoving. The sun rose higher in the sky, and still she did not move. But her stillness was not that of fear. Margred Morgan was a woman with a profound faith in God, and now she was deep in prayer. She grew unaware of the barn, the stable, and the calf that came over to nuzzle her. Everything seemed to fade as she sought God.

Finally she gave a sudden deep sigh, opened her eyes, and a trace of a smile touched her lips. Her course was clear. "Thank you, Lord God!" she whispered, then rose, got the milk pail, and left the barn.

She went at once back to the hovel where she had been assigned a place to sleep with Myles. Entering, she saw that he was beginning to awaken. Setting the pail on the ground, she smiled affectionately, then her face sobered. It was good the boy had gotten so much sleep this morning. He would need it.

She went to him as he sat up and threw her arms around him. "How's the old man this morning?" she whispered, her voice gentle as he turned at once to wrap his young arms around her in a hug.

"Good morning, Mother," he said cheerfully.

"It's time to get up."

Scrambling out of the ragged blankets, he slipped into his rough cotton trousers, pulled a shirt over his head that was much too big for him, and then pulled on the woolen shirt he used for a coat. Margred tucked the sleeves up so that his hands were free, then reached behind her and picked up the milk pail. "Here's your breakfast, old man," she said, smiling again as she considered her son. She had started calling him "old man" because he so often seemed like an adult. Many a time he would stare at her studiously and thoughtfully, pondering some deep issue.

He picked up the small bucket, looked in it, then his blue-gray eyes fell on her. "How much may I drink, Mother?"

"All ye can hold," she said reassuringly. "Drink 'til your little stomach is full." She saw wonder come to his eyes—he had never had such an offer before. Without further invitation, he lifted the pail and began to drink. She could almost hear the milk hitting the bottom of his empty stomach, and she put her hand on his shaggy auburn hair. When at last he lowered the pail, his smile of contentment was a blessing to behold.

"Now I'll have a drink of my own," she said, and she too drank the still-warm liquid until she could hold no more.

She put the pail down, then turned and put her hands on his shoulders. Carefully she wiped the white mustache of milk from his lips, smiled at him, and said, "Guess what? We're going on a long trip, Myles."

"Are we, Mother?" he asked, and a smile came to his lips. "That will be fun, won't it!"

"It'll be hard, old man," she answered. "But the good Lord will keep us. We'll have to wrap up with all the clothes we have, so let's get ready. I want to be on our way soon."

He scrambled around, finding his meager belongings, and she did the same. It did not take long to gather them. She made one trip to the barn and found a coarse feed sack, then hesitated for one moment. Shaking her head, she thought, *The good Lord knows I've earned it!* She scooped some of the dried corn, which was kept for the cow, into a smaller bag, then put it into the larger sack. She counted out ten of the potatoes drying in the loft, then went to the smokehouse and helped herself to some of the meat. It would not be enough, she knew, for their journey would be long. But it was all the resources she had.

Back at the shack she found that Myles had strapped his cowhide shoes onto his feet. He looked up as she entered and said cheerfully, "I'm ready, Mother."

Margred put their thin blankets into the sack, gathered their few pitiful clothes and stuffed them inside, then reached underneath the straw they slept on and pulled out the single package—a small pouch of deerhide that contained her only personal possessions. Placing that and some of the food inside, she drew the string of the sack tight. As she secured it, she noted dispassionately how small the package was, even with all their belongings in it. Then she found a smaller sack for Myles and filled it with the rest of the food, saying, "There. This is yours to carry."

He lifted it. "I can take more than this, Mother."

"It's all we have," she said. "Now, we have a long way to go, and do you know who's going to help us?"

"Who?"

"God. He's going to be with us. So let's pray that he will give us a safe journey." Immediately the boy bowed his head, and Margred put her arms around him and began to pray.

Myles listened carefully. He was accustomed to this, for his mother prayed about everything. Or so it seemed to him. When she was through, he said, "Amen!" brightly.

She laughed and gave him a quick hug. "Come now, we have a long way to go."

They left the shack and, a few minutes later, were out of sight of Ianto Motshill's farm. Margred did not look back. She kept her eyes fixed on the horizon far ahead, where the mountains of Wales rose. Across them lay England—the place she had seen as she had prayed in the barn.

Though there had been no audible voice, no great booming command, she had seen clearly the image of a house situated in a valley, near a river. And then a voice . . . no, an impression . . . *something* had told her, "Go to the River Severn. There will be a place for you."

As they trudged along over the cold broken ground, Margred knew that God had spoken to her. This was not surprising, for she had learned to listen to God. She looked up at the sun, which now was sending scarlet beams over the trees in the east, and smiled. "Isn't it good that the Lord is going to be with us all the way, Myles?"

"Yes, it is good, Mother," he replied cheerfully.

⁕⁕⁕

The afternoon sun grew warm as the two travelers trudged along the road that was little more than a beaten path. It was made up of two ruts worn on the path through the woods, so narrow that two wagons could not meet. Margred and Myles passed few people on the road, for the cold weather had kept most near their hearthfires. What's more, travel through Wales was dangerous, especially in the mountains. People traveled in large groups or not at all.

Once they passed an old man driving a cart along, and he merely gave them a look, saying not a word. They paused a few hours after noon, and Margred opened their food sack and removed one of the potatoes. She built a small fire, roasted it, then, when it was hot and smoking, raked it from the ashes.

"Here, Myles," she said, "eat your lunch."

He ate his portion of the potato, almost burning his lips, and laughed. "That's hot, Mother! But it's good!" She knew he was far from full, but they had to ration their supplies carefully. They found a stream and drank deeply, then continued their walk.

All afternoon they followed the winding road. Margred was glad to see that Myles, young as he was, could keep up. She looked at him more than once, admiring his lean but sturdy figure and the beauty of his auburn hair, which caught the red-gold lights of the sun. *He's a handsome boy,* she thought. *I never saw a lad of better appearance.*

When the sun dipped into the west, she began to look about but found no sign of a shelter of any kind. At least, not in the form of a house. Off to one side of the road she spotted a series of bluffs. She would find something there. They left the road and came

10

upon a small cave—an indentation in the bluff that went back for five feet and closed around itself.

"Here's our house for the night, old man," Margred said with a smile. "Why don't you find us some firewood? Soon we'll be snug as if in a castle of our own!"

Myles quickly found enough dry wood to get the fire started. Using flint and steel as she had been taught as a child, Margred soon had a cheery blaze going. They huddled around it, watching the yellow flames flicker. Carefully she pulled out some of the meat, hesitated, then took another of the potatoes, and they had their supper. She put some of the heavier chunks of wood onto the fire, then made a pallet on the ground next to the wall of the cave. Pulling the cover back she said, "Come now. Let's say our prayer and have a good night's sleep. We have a long, long way to go tomorrow."

Margred looked out the cave mouth, up at the night sky. As she watched the stars twinkle coldly far overhead, the wisdom of her Welsh forefathers cautioned her, *"There's snow in that sky. Maybe not tomorrow, but soon."*

Myles came sleepily to the pallet, snuggling close to her, and she arranged the thin blankets around them. When he was still, she prayed her nightly prayer, and soon the two of them were fast asleep. Once, when an animal came sniffing and grunting close to the edge of the cave, Margred woke instantly and waited almost breathlessly. But it came no closer, and she fell back asleep.

The snow had begun as a mere sensation of intense cold in the air. Within an hour, as Margred trudged along, she felt a flake touch her cheek. She glanced sharply at the gray sky. She had been dreading this for the last three days, and now it had come. Apprehensively she looked down at Myles, at his thin clothes, and wondered how they would weather a snowstorm. Soon the flakes were floating down, laying strips of white along the broken land and making fantastic shapes out of the bushes and twisted trees that lined the road.

Myles looked up at her and shivered. "It's cold, isn't it, Mother?" But his eyes held a merriment. "Look!" he said happily, looking down at his feet. "Look at how I can leave footprints. See?"

"I see, Myles," she said. It was only two o'clock, and she knew that soon the snow would be deep enough to overflow their flimsy shoes. She scanned the area, searching for a shelter. She had avoided travelers on the road—a woman was at the mercy of any man that happened along. Several times, upon seeing a group coming, she had taken to the brush and waited until they passed, warning Myles to be still. He had made a game out of it, his eyes sparkling—and she had been grateful he did not understand the danger.

But now as they trudged along, she knew they could not stand the cold for very long. Their food was almost gone. She prayed as they passed silently through the swirling flakes that they would find a place.

Two hours later, the piled snow made for slow going, especially for Myles, who had to lift his knees to clear the snow. The flakes fell so thickly that Margred could not see more than a few yards ahead. The sky was gray as a coffin; dark was coming on.

Myles, she saw, was trembling fiercely. She stopped and pulled the blankets out of her sack, then wrapped one around him and the other around her own shoulders, covering her head as with a hood. Taking Myles's hand, she stumbled on.

Half an hour later, she saw a building of some kind off to one side and whispered, "There, Myles! Quickly!"

Stumbling, the two struggled toward the building. She could see now that it was a crude farm, similar to those she had seen all of her life. In fact, she had grown up on a farm such as this in

South Wales. The snow was piled up around the door, and there was a single window in the front through which she could see a light burning. She knocked on the door, her hand so numb she could not even feel the wood.

Instantly a voice called out, "Who's there?"

"A traveler," she whispered hoarsely. "Me and my son."

The door opened a crack, and she saw a white-haired man peering out. His eyes were narrow, and he said suspiciously, "What are ye doin' here?"

"We're on our way to England. There's no harm in us."

Margred watched as he looked intently over her shoulder, then his face relaxed. He opened the door. "Well, then, come in. And quickly! I don't need ye to bring the cold in with ye."

Margred, still holding to Myles's hand, all but fell inside, and the blessed warmth of the room enveloped her. There was a fireplace, and a woman who was sitting by it suddenly rose. Margred was so tired she could barely think, and all that registered in her mind was the warmth and the fact that these were poor people.

The woman came over to stand beside her husband and said, "You must be near froze to death, lass. Come over and sit by the fire." She reached out as Myles staggered forward, and she touched his face. "Why, the poor lad's almost blue with cold!" she exclaimed. "Samuel, heat some water. We'll make some gruel for these two."

"Yes, Betty," he said. He was a small man, no taller than Margred. He glanced at her, suspicion crossing his face again. "The law is not after you, is it, woman?"

"No," Margred said through chattering teeth. "We're just trying to get to England."

"All right then. Sit yourself down."

Thirty minutes later, their stomachs full of gruel made from ground corn with a bit of salt pork added, Margred and Myles sat as she explained to their benefactors where they were going. The old people listened incredulously, and when the old man said he'd never heard of the Severn River, Margred nodded. "I don't know it, either, but God has told us to go there."

Betty looked at her, wonder in her faded eyes. "Is that so, now? You've never heard of the place, but ye're goin' there because God's told you to?" She took a deep breath and went on. "I never heard of such in my whole life."

Margred did not argue; she didn't have the energy. She was so sleepy and tired that she could barely keep awake. When the old woman looked closer at her and Myles, she ordered, "Come now, Samuel, fix a place for these two."

Soon Margred and Myles were fast asleep, lying under heavy blankets. Watching them, Betty said slowly, "Samuel, I never heard of such a thing. But it may be that God sent them to us, so we'll have to do our best for them."

"As you say, woman," the frail old man muttered.

The storm went on for two days, during which time Margred and Myles rested and were filled with all the food they could eat. It was plain, simple fare, but it was nourishing and filling. The weather kept them inside, and Myles and his mother slept much of the time. The two days went by quickly, and both of them felt well and strong again by the time the storm abated and the sun came out.

"We must leave," Margred said, smiling at their two new friends. "God bless you both and grant you mercy for being so kind to a woman and her child."

Samuel looked embarrassed and said, "We fixed up some things for you to take."

Betty came forward with a bundle. "Here are some warmer clothes. They belonged to my daughter, who died in childbirth. I'm of a mind they'll fit you, and they'll be much warmer. I even cut down some things of Samuel's here, for the boy."

Samuel said, "And I made up a pack of food that will last until you get to this River Severn, wherever it is."

Tears came to Margred's eyes, and she dropped her head, unable to speak for a moment. Finally she drew Myles to her, put her arm around his shoulders, and looked at the two dear people. "God reward you richly," she said, her voice husky. Tears glittered in her fine eyes as she and Myles shouldered the two packs that the old people had put together.

"It's a fine morning," she said to Myles as they went outside. "And you see how God has helped us? Now, we'll be on our way." She turned to Betty and Samuel, then went to them and—to their surprise—embraced them both. Upon seeing this, Myles came forward and offered his hand, which they both took.

"God be with you," he said brightly.

Margred turned and Myles followed, and they walked away from the little farm, down the icy road, stopping only to wave just before they moved beyond a bend in the road.

The weather was warmer, and they had better clothing now— even stockings!—which helped keep their feet warm and dry. They made good time that day, and Margred noted gratefully that the snow appeared to be melting.

Later that night, as they started walking down out of the mountains, Margred looked around, then glanced at Myles. "Well, old man, I'm thinking we'll be soon out of Wales and into England."

"And the river you've talked of, Mother?" he demanded.

Margred looked ahead into the distance and shifted the bundle she carried. "It'll be a long way yet." But she laughed and ordered, "Come along, old man! God will be with us, and we will find the River Severn. And the house I told you of."

And so the two forged ahead, Margred sometimes singing one of the songs in the old Welsh tongue that she had learned as a girl, Myles looking up at her and joining in from time to time.

Nob, who had kept the falcons and hawks for the Bourneville family for fifteen years, moved around the mews, checking the birds carefully. He was a small, lean man—almost as lean as the hounds and the hawks that he kept for Sir Geoffrey Bourneville. He had gray hair, sharp features, and amazingly blue eyes. He moved slowly, checking his equipment, looking in on a tiercel goshawk that had been ailing. Reaching over, he ruffled the feathers on the raptor's chest and saw the fierce eyes light up and the beak open. Taking a bit of meat out of his pocket, he gave it to the hawk and murmured, "Ye'll be all right, me lad. Just need a little exercise is me thought."

He turned then and left the mews, going toward the manor house to give Sir Geoffrey a report. But a movement to his left caught his eye, and he blinked with surprise as he saw two figures, one large and one small, emerge from over the hill. His eyes narrowed with suspicion—strangers did not come to Harrow in the dead of winter. Then he saw that it was a woman and a child, and he relaxed.

The woman was staring at the big house, fixed and still, almost as though frozen. Finally she moved, and the pair made their way toward Nob.

He waited until they came close, and he saw that they were having a heavy go of it, the woman holding the boy to keep him from falling. He moved forward rapidly and stopped in front of them saying, "Where be ye going?"

The woman lifted her face to him, and he saw that her lips were blue with cold, her cheeks sunken. She was, he noted, fairly young, and would be quite attractive if she were not so lean. Her lips moved, and he could barely make out her words.

"My son and I, we are seeking the river."

"The river?" Nob asked, perplexed. "You mean the Severn?"

16

Her eyes lit up, and she nodded eagerly. "Yes, the Severn!"

Nob waved his hand to his right. "It lies over that way, about two miles," he said. "An' what would you be wanting with the river in the dead of winter?"

He peered at her closely and then looked down at the boy, whose eyes were closed. He was shivering with cold and fatigue. "Od's tooth, woman! What be ye doing with a child out in the middle of winter like this? What are ye thinking of, woman?" He was half angry with her, but when she only shook her head, he said in disgust, "Then come in, and let's see if we can get the lad thawed out."

He led the way to a small room that was attached to the mews. This was the room he shared, more or less, with his hounds. There was no chimney or fireplace—a hole in the ceiling let out the smoke—so the room was rather smoky from a fire that had almost gone out. Throwing a few fagots on it, he blew on the embers and soon had a cheerful enough blaze going. Then he turned to look at the woman, who was standing silently, weaving with fatigue. He said quickly, "There. Put yourself down."

She collapsed, saying weakly, "Thank you," and drew the boy to her. At once he lay down with his head in her lap.

Nob stared at the woman, more perplexed than ever, but he was a practical man and could see that she was exhausted. Now was not the time for questions. "Here. I'll be finding something to eat. And I've got a bit of beer that will do you good." He rummaged around on a shelf, found the jug, and poured it into the single cup that he possessed. "Get this down the boy, then drink some for yourself. I'll cook a piece of meat for you."

As the man scurried around, cutting off a hunk of meat and putting it on a sharp stick to roast over the fire, Margred pulled Myles into a sitting position in the crook of her arm and put the cup to his lips. "Drink it, Myles," she whispered. She watched as he came slowly out of the exhausted sleep and then drank almost the whole cup. She drank the rest, and the falconer, seeing the drink was gone, came with the jug and refilled the cup.

"Help yourself, Miss," he said. "What's your name?"

"Margred Morgan, and this is Myles."

Nob stared at her. "Might be you come from Wales?"

"Yes."

"So do I." He nodded energetically. "A long time ago, when I was a boy. I still remember the mountains, though." He had seared some of the meat and, taking his knife from his scabbard, began to slice off small bits of it into bite-sized pieces. "Let the boy chew on some of this. He looks like he needs it. And take some for yourself."

Margred shook Myles awake again, and at the smell of the cooked meat his pale face began to look more alive. She popped the morsel in his mouth, and he began to chew vigorously. He swallowed and instantly opened his mouth again for another bite.

Nob grinned, "Just like a young sparrow in the nest, ain't he now? But don't let him eat too much right off, or he'll be sick. He can have more later."

Margred fed Myles, then ate some herself, feeling her energy return as she did so. She studied the small man standing on the other side of the fire. "Thank you," she said gravely. "We've had not a bite to eat for the last two days."

"You've come a long way?" he inquired. "Not all the way from Wales?"

"Yes. It's been a long journey," she sighed. The food and drink had brought some color into her cheeks, and Nob saw that she was a very pretty woman indeed.

"You're looking for the Severn, you say. What will you be doing there?"

Margred hesitated. She was hesitant to mention God and her vision, but the man had been kind and there was, despite the roughness of his dress and a tough-looking face, a goodness in his eyes. After a moment, she nodded.

"We had to leave Wales because of . . . well, we had to leave. And I prayed, and God seemed to put it into my heart to come to England. He told me to come to the River Severn, and he showed me the big house that stands here. It's just the same as I saw in a dream."

"God told you, eh?" Nob said, then compressed his lips. "Well, God has never told me nothing, but sometimes I'm wishing he would." He studied the pair, then asked curiously, "You've no kin? No place to go, no work?"

"No, we have nothing."

Again his sharp eyes grew stormy at what he perceived to be her carelessness. "And didn't you pick a fine time to come? In winter, when there's little work!" He began to pace back and forth, then he saw that Margred was growing very sleepy. The boy had promptly gone back to sleep after eating a few bites of meat, and the mother wasn't far behind. "Sleep over there," he said gruffly. "When you wake, you can have more to eat."

He turned and walked out of the shed, and Margred pulled Myles into her embrace. She fell asleep at once beside the warm fire.

Several times that day Nob went back to his little dwelling, only to find that the woman and boy were still sleeping soundly. He said nothing to anyone about the visitors. No one ever came to the mews—at least not in the winter—so he felt safe enough.

While he could understand leaving a place to find a better life, he could not understand the woman and her talk of God. "She don't look like a lunatic," he muttered to himself. "But don't she talk like one, now! A pity it is, an' her having that likely-looking boy." Nob had no family—the plague had taken his wife and children—and he remembered his boy had a look about him such as this one. With a shake of his head, he went about his work.

He checked on the two travelers at about three that afternoon and found them awake, so he built up the fire and cooked more of the meat.

Watching them intently he said, "I don't know what to do with you. You'll freeze to death or starve if you try to go on to the next town." He added wryly, "You can't live on that River Severn. People drown themselves in it, even in the summertime. What are you going to do?"

Margred said, "I don't know. We've done what God said." Her lips curved upward in a faint smile. "I sound like a madwoman, don't I?"

Nob ducked his head, scratched his pate, then shrugged. "I've seen crazier in my time." They sat staring into the fire, neither saying much as they tried to decide what to do.

At length Nob seemed to come to a decision. "I'll ask the master if ye can stay. Will you work?" he demanded. "And the boy too?"

"Oh yes!" Margred replied instantly. "I'm a good worker. I can cook and clean and milk and do anything else on the farm." She looked at Myles and smiled. "And the boy here, he can learn, too."

Nob considered them silently, then rose to his feet and left the shed abruptly. He walked to the manor house, around to the back, and asked a woman who had come out with a pail of slops, "Is the master here?"

She looked at him with a bleary eye and grunted, "Yes," then went on her way.

Nob looked at the house almost fearfully. He did not enter the manor house often, the master usually came to him when he needed him. Nob was a man of the wood, a man for the dogs, a man for the birds. . . . It made him nervous to be confined inside the big house. He stood staring balefully at the door, then decided he would wait for Sir Geoffrey to come out. Maybe the master would feel a little more charitable after eating.

"Well, what's this? Who are you, and what are you doing here?"

Margred looked up, startled by the man who had entered. He was short, fat, and dressed in a very heavy fur coat. He had tow-colored hair and light blue eyes that were examining her closely. "My name is Margred Morgan. This is my son, Myles. Are you the master?"

"Yes. I am Sir Geoffrey Bourneville. And this is Harrow you are on now." He waited, looking the two strangers up and down as they scrambled to their feet. He had been approached by Nob, who now stood just inside the door watching carefully, regarding the homeless pair.

At first he had told Nob to get rid of them, but Nob had said, "Aye, sir, it's as you say. But one of the maids said Lady Mary had been complaining about not having enough help. I think this lass might make a good house servant. And she's got a boy that I could use with the hounds. He's young, but I like 'em young so I can teach them in the right manner."

Sir Geoffrey had listened carelessly. He was in a good mood, for he had won a large sum at dice the previous evening and had just enjoyed a good lunch.

Now, looking at the two who stood before him, he saw that the woman looked neat enough and the boy seemed bright. He said rather roughly, "Can't afford idle hands here. You will work for your keep. And that is what it will be, your keep—a place to sleep, food to eat, and clothes for your back. What do you say to it?"

"Thank you, sir," Margred curtseyed gracefully. "We'll work very hard, won't we, Myles?"

"Yes sir!" The boy was looking up, and Sir Geoffrey thought he resembled a bird with his bright eyes and his reddish hair.

The master nodded abruptly. "That's all right, then. Come up to the house later in the day and I'll see you're taught what to do. Nob, you teach the boy to be of some help with the birds and the hounds."

"Aye, sir, I'll do that."

As soon as Sir Geoffrey left, Margred walked over and hugged Myles, her face alight with pleasure. "You see, old man, how God looks after us? He brought us all the way from the mountains of Wales to the River Severn, and now he's got us a fine place to work and live! Isn't the good Lord fine to such as us?"

"Yes, he is, Mother," Myles agreed. He looked up at Nob and asked eagerly, "I'm to help you? With birds? And dogs?"

"That's right, boy," Nob nodded. "And a hard enough master you'll find me if I catch you mistreating one of my animals!" He watched the mother and son as they hugged, discovering as he did so that somehow a good feeling had come to him. *Well, if God brought her here, maybe God put me here to see that she had a place. About time God said something to me, after all this time.*

"So, come now and let's have a bit more of that meat. Then later on you can go up to the big house." With that he began to slice off more of the roasted meat, finding great enjoyment in watching the young woman and the boy as they eagerly sat down in front of the fire.

Two

THE KING'S WAR

Sir Robert Wakefield passed through the great hall strewn with rushes, making a mental note as he did so to tell the servants to change the plants. They were rank and filthy. He passed out of the hall, passing through several rooms, thinking of the newer houses in Tudor England that had incorporated corridors. Since he had a logical mind, this new method of construction made sense to him. His manor, Wakefield, was an old structure, and corridors were unheard of when it was built. Consequently, one room opened into the next in a way that gave occupants no way to shut the door and achieve some privacy without disrupting traffic. Occasionally a room was built off the mainstream that might be closed off, and these were called "closets."

In most of the rooms he walked through, people stopped to bow or curtsey respectfully, but he paid no attention. Finally he passed ,through a great, eight-foot oaken door and entered his own chamber.

"You're late, Robert," said the woman sitting in the huge bed, which took up a great deal of the space in the room. The bed was made out of carved oak and was spacious enough for half a dozen people at least. Lady Jane Wakefield lifted her warm brown eyes and smiled at her husband. "I waited up for you." She was a small and delicate woman, with the look of an invalid, though she was not confined to her bed. A series of miscarriages in her youth had wrecked her health, and now she was unable to carry out most of the activities enjoyed by ladies of her station. She was, however, cheerful and never complained about her lot. As her husband came over to stand beside the bed, reaching out his hand, she took it and kissed the back of it asking, "What have you been doing?"

Sir Robert Wakefield looked down at her from his height of six feet. He was a strongly built man with dark red hair and blue-gray eyes. He had a stubborn, squarish face and a scar that ran down his left cheek—a memento of his days in the army. His short beard and trim mustache were the same reddish color of his hair and contributed to what many felt were his good looks. He did not give the appearance of being forty-three years old. One had to look closely at him to see the beginnings of fine lines in his face and the few gray hairs that had begun to show on his head.

Now he smiled down at his wife, squeezed her hand, then sank wearily into the chair beside the bed. Staring up at the ceiling, he explained, "I've been making some arrangements." His clear tenor voice could carry a good distance in the open air—which was useful when one hunted with the hounds. He lolled in the chair for a moment, then sat up straight and twisted around so he could face Jane. "My dear," he said slowly, "I've made up my mind about Ralph. I'm going to adopt him as my heir."

His words brought a sudden tightening to Lady Jane's lips, and her soft eyes grew watchful. She said nothing for a moment, only looked down at her hands. Knowing she was not one to speak quickly, he waited. At length she lifted her face and said in a low voice, "I've failed you, Robert."

He knew immediately what she meant. He had fallen in love with Lady Jane Harwich the first time he had seen her. After a whirlwind courtship, they had married and then had settled down with the idea of raising a large family. The years had passed, and child after child had been born lifeless. Robert Wakefield had never reproached his wife for their lack of children, but he knew that it grieved her deeply. He looked at her and, knowing her so well, was aware of the sorrow in her that she had not borne him a child.

He leaned over and took her hand again, gently squeezing it and smiling as best he could. "God settles these things," he murmured.

She shook her head slightly, and he knew that she was not convinced. He got up, bent and kissed her, then began to speak with an enthusiasm that she had not seen for a long time. "Now, my dear, we'll have a young man in Ralph. He'll be our son, someone to take over. He'll marry and have children, and we'll have little ones around."

Lady Jane listened and tried to show a proper attitude. She did not like Ralph Geddes. True, he was a relative, a distant cousin of Robert's, and sometimes she felt guilty for her distrust of him. There was nothing in Geddes's manner—indeed, nothing in his life—that she could put her finger on. The most she could count against him was that he was not warmhearted and open, at least not with her. She knew he seemed so to Robert, but to her that was another evidence of his lack of honesty. She knew he was not by nature an outgoing young man, and his actions with Robert seemed . . . calculated.

When Robert came and sat beside her, she knew he was waiting for her approval.

"I understand that you need an heir, dear," she said. "And nothing would please me more than to see a young bride coming to Wakefield, to see babies being born." A wistful longing came into her eyes, and she went on, "If I could just hold a child in my arms, I think I'd ask nothing more of earth or heaven." She paused thoughtfully. "But it's such a final thing, taking someone for an heir. It isn't like anything else. . . ."

"It is very serious," he agreed, "and I've thought about it long."

"Why don't you wait for a while? Bring the young man to Wakefield. Let him live here, and we shall see how we get on. After all, you can always go through the formalities, the legal business, later. Once you do so, there'll be no taking it back."

Robert gave her a searching glance. He had sensed her reluctance to accept Geddes, but she had never been outspoken about it. He had great respect for her judgment, however, and he felt there was wisdom in what she said. He thought for a moment, then nodded firmly. "You're right, I think. I'll talk to him at once, and we shall see."

"I think that might be best, dear." She smiled at him brilliantly. It was one thing to put on an act occasionally, but to maintain it every day . . . surely if Ralph Geddes were to live here he would eventually expose what he really was. Lady Jane herself was not sure what that was and wondered if perhaps she had misjudged him . . . but she could not deny the relief she felt because her husband had agreed to wait.

"I have other news which won't be to your liking," he said with a slight grimace.

"Yes, dear?"

"A messenger from the king came this morning." He ran his fingers through his thick reddish hair in an impatient gesture. "He wants me to go to this fool war with him, against France."

"Oh, I hoped that he wouldn't ask that!"

"Well, he has, and I'll have to go, of course." Wakefield rose and began to strip off his clothes, letting them lie as they fell. He walked over and blew out the candles, then slipped in between the bedcovers. Lying together, he reached out and held her gently, stroking her hair. Even after these years, and in spite of her barrenness, he was still very much in love with his wife.

"I have to go," he repeated softly.

She reached up and put her hand on his cheek. "How long will it take?"

26

"I've no idea. And it's the wrong thing to do. But you know Henry. He's gotten this in his head and nothing on earth will stop him." He fell silent, thinking as he stroked her arm, marveling as always at the smoothness of her skin. Then he continued, "I don't think it will be long. I think we're in for a battle at the negotiating table." A thought struck him then, and he said, "I'll take the boy with me. We can get acquainted."

She was fearful, knowing the fortunes of war, and put her arms around him to draw him close. "Oh, Robert. Oh, be careful!"

At seven o'clock on Thursday, June the 30th, 1513, Sir Robert Wakefield and Ralph Geddes stood on board one of the warships that had brought the army of England to Calais. It had been an exciting time for young Geddes. He stood beside Wakefield, his dark eyes searching the shore, excitement stiffening his back. He was of medium height but seemed taller because of his erect posture. He was trim, and his black hair and eyebrows went well with his dark complexion. He had a black mustache that covered a rather weak mouth, and his eyes were a trifle close together. Aside from this, he was a handsome man, an excellent swordsman, and a fine rider. By all accounts, he was a shrewd young man for his eighteen years.

"Well, sir, we are here at last! I thought we should never get across the Channel!"

Wakefield turned to smile at the young man. "I thought so myself, Ralph." He looked out over the harbor that was filled with the ships being unloaded. "It takes time to move thirty to forty thousand men in full harness. 'Tis a wonder we ever got here at all!" He scanned the shoreline. "I'm thinking we'd better go ashore. We'll meet with the king this afternoon and see what his battle plan is." He hesitated, then said in a low voice, "If he has one."

Geddes shot him a keen look. "What is this war all about, sir? I don't seem to understand it."

"It's not a thing one really understands, Ralph," Sir Robert said dryly. He tried to explain by saying, "It is all tied in somehow with Henry's marriage to Catherine. You understand that she was his brother Arthur's wife, though some say the marriage was never consummated. In any case, after Arthur's death, England got Henry VIII instead of Arthur I for a ruler."

"Don't you think he's a good ruler?"

"He's capable enough. I doubt that England ever saw a king with more potential," Sir Robert admitted. "But three years ago, Pope Julius formed a Holy League with Maximilian, the emperor of the German states, and with Ferdinand, king of Spain. He wanted to stop Louis XII of France." Sir Robert's face grew grim as he went on. "Henry was so galled at being left out that he volunteered England to whip Louis all by himself. I think he sees himself as sort of a Robin Hood, with the pope as the oppressed and King Louis of France as the Sheriff of Nottingham." He walked slowly along the deck, pressing through the swarm of soldiers preparing to disembark, and added, "This kingly invasion is designed to prove that Henry is the king of England and the world had better take note!"

The two men clambered into a small, crowded boat and were ferried to shore along with a load of archers and their officers. When they got ashore, they moved among the teeming mass of troops that seemed to be no more purposeful than a bunch of ants on an anthill. The uniformed soldiers swarmed here and there, moving equipment, shouting, cursing, jostling one another. Eventually Sir Robert found an officer and asked, "Which way to the king's pavilion?"

"Over there, just at the top of the knoll," the lieutenant said, nodding toward the structure.

"Come along, Ralph. We shall see what we can find out."

They pressed their way through the milling crowd of men, cleared the beach, and found a huge tent set up and surrounded by a uniformed guard. An officer came forward and smiled. "Good morning, Sir Robert. The king has been asking for you. You'd better go in. Sir Thomas Wolsey is already with him."

"Thank you, Lieutenant," Robert said, then turned to Ralph. "Wait out here. I'll be back as soon as I can."

He entered the large tent and found it more ornate than any room in his whole manor house. Persian rugs had been thrown on the floor and large pieces of furniture set in place. Standing beside a large table were the two men who ruled England: Henry and Sir Thomas Wolsey. They both turned, and Henry came forward, crying out as Sir Robert started to kneel, "No ceremony! No ceremony, Robert! Come over here and help Wolsey and me decide how to demolish this rotten French king."

Henry VIII was clearly a king in appearance, Robert thought again, as he did each time he met the king. Six feet three inches tall, broad-shouldered, blessed with light golden hair that boasted a reddish tinge, a short red beard—everything about the man bespoke nobility. Burly and strong enough to win a joust with some of the best of his own soldiers, there was arrogance in every move Henry made. Though he had a tendency to be condescending to his advisers, Sir Robert had yet to see the king decree anything that he did not fully believe in.

Now Sir Robert stepped up to the table and looked at the map. A smile crossed his lips. "I suppose you and Sir Thomas have done all the planning already."

Wolsey gave him a very slight smile. "His Majesty has pretty well taken care of that, Robert." Wolsey was a man of middle age, the son of a butcher from Ipswich. He had become chaplain to the archbishop of Canterbury, then later a chaplain to Henry VII. A man of incredible capacity and stamina, Wolsey had practically bulled his way into a position of power in the court of Henry VIII. This war might be the king's, but it was Wolsey who supervised everything, from the number of tent pegs to the color of the king's satin robe for each occasion.

Wolsey had heavy features, yet to Robert's mind there was something feral about the man. He knew that Sir Thomas, though a priest of the church, could be a carnivore, who would devour anyone who stood in his way and stop at nothing to achieve ultimate power.

"See this, Robert?" Henry burst out, pointing a blunt finger down at the map stretched out on the table. "This is where we strike."

Sir Robert looked down at the map and said, "Therouanne?" He looked up, startled, and saw that discussion would not be possible. So he said only, "It seems, Your Majesty, that Bologne, being a natural stronghold, might be more advantageous."

"No, it is Therouanne. We shall move the army instantly and besiege it. That will bring Louis to his knees!"

"Yes, Your Majesty," Sir Robert said, suppressing a shrug. He saw no sense at all in the battle plan, but he knew enough of Henry VIII to know that one did not argue with the king when he had made up his mind. "What are your instructions, sire?"

He listened as the king reeled off a long list of orders, then said, "If we are to start so soon, I had better get the men organized." He turned to ask Sir Thomas, "Is there anything especial you would have me do?"

Wolsey waved his fat hand in the air saying, "Certainly not, Sir Robert. You have more military experience than I. We trust you to see that the expedition is carried out quickly and with dispatch."

"Yes, my lord."

Sir Robert left and went back out to where Ralph was waiting. Immediately the young man asked, "What are we to do?"

"The impossible," Sir Robert said grimly. He looked at the

aimless movements of the men, saw the mass of materials, weapons, and gear being unloaded, and shook his head. "We are to attack Therouanne." Then he added sarcastically, "At once. And with great dispatch."

A smile touched Geddes's thin lips, and he said, "King Henry does not wish to be bothered with details, does he, sir?"

"No, that is our job. So, Ralph, let us see what we can do to pull this army together."

⚜

The "instant and with dispatch" attack of the English army did not take place. The forces were divided into three sections: the forward, middleward, and rearward. The king was in the middle, of course, and his part of the force contained about sixteen thousand men, of which over two thousand were there solely to wait upon His Majesty. The king's wardrobe staff numbered forty-nine, with another fifteen to look after his beds. There were one hundred and fifteen on his chapel staff, and five hundred seventy-nine ushers, grooms, pages, and general servants. Eight trumpeters and ten minstrels and players were added. And, presumably in case the king came too close to the battle, thirty-one of His Majesty's physicians, surgeons, and their assistants were along as well.

Upon observing the king and his entourage, Sir Robert remarked, "The king is safe enough, virtually impregnable. He wears sixty pounds of ornamental steel, and at night he sleeps in a portable prefabricated house."

And so he did. The house had two rooms, the larger measuring twenty-seven feet by fourteen feet by eight feet high, and was complete with fireplace and chimney. It was red outside and hung with golden tapestry inside. Twelve wagons were required to transport this palace.

Sir Robert shook his head and sighed. "What a way to go to war!"

"Thomas Wolsey doesn't do badly, either, does he, sir?" Geddes remarked. He was looking at the line of wagons carrying that honored gentleman's trappings. Wolsey had ordered the slaughter of twenty-five thousand oxen for the occasion, supplemented by one thousand sheep. With a beer allowance of almost a gallon per man per day and a food allowance of ten pounds of meat and drink for each man, Wolsey required a fleet of wagons for provisions alone.

Sir Robert was more concerned about the weapons than he was about the sleeping comfort of Henry and Wolsey. He walked along, examining some of the new cannons, or "bombards," as they were called. Europe was realizing the bow and arrow were rapidly becoming obsolete, and Wakefield studied the enormous cannons with a deep appreciation as they were dragged along by teams of oxen. Twenty-four Flemish mares were required to pull each cannon; the heaviest cannon required thirty horses. Each weapon had the disadvantages of a massive recoil and problems with overheating, which made it so that they could only be fired five times a day. Named after the twelve apostles, the cannons were capable of firing twenty-pound iron balls. In addition, the army carried five hundred and ten tons of powder.

As the days went by and the army progressed at the same slow pace, Sir Robert became frantic. "We must do better!" he said to the officers.

But they merely looked at him stubbornly, one of them saying, "Sir Robert, no one on earth can move this mountain of equipment and gear any faster than we are going. In three days we've come twelve miles, and it looks like we'll be slowing down from here on."

"Kill the horses if you must, we have to make better time!" Sir Robert gave the officer a meaningful look, adding, "You know how His Majesty is when he is frustrated."

A pallor came over the officer's face and he said promptly, "Yes, Sir Robert! We will step up the pace as much as possible."

Later that evening, when the army had stopped for the night, Robert received a summons from Wolsey. He went to the pavilion tent and found the man sitting in a chair, seemingly half drunk, though whether it was from wine or fatigue, Wakefield could not tell.

"Sit down, Sir Robert, sit down," Sir Thomas said. "Help yourself to the wine." He waited until Robert was seated, then took a glass of wine and asked, "How long until we reach Therouanne?"

"Another month, at the rate we're traveling now," Sir Robert said glumly. "How much is all this going to cost?"

Wolsey's face grew hard. "More than England has. Although a private only receives sixpence a day and his coat money, it is the extras that are killing us." He waved toward the direction of the king's portable house. "His Majesty has a wardrobe of clothes, trimmed in ermine, that he wears but once. He has fourteen wagons loaded with gold and four with silver coin," he grunted, "and he's spending it like he is going to die tomorrow, giving away gold and jewels and coins as his whim takes him." Wolsey swilled down more of the wine and gestured toward Sir Robert. "You know how he is! We had to tax the people double to supply all of this, but Henry never thinks about that. After all," Sir Thomas said sarcastically, "this is the king's war."

That was when Sir Robert knew Wolsey was drunk, for he would never speak so lightly unless he was. He shrugged and settled back in his seat, listening patiently as Wolsey complained. Finally, Sir Thomas concluded, "The best we can hope for out of this war, Robert, is to bring Louis to the negotiating table. This army is not really a fighting army. It's Henry's personal body-guard."

"You're right about that, Your Grace," Robert agreed. He had noted from the start that the men were not in good condition. Most were untrained, and for many the journey was more a pleasurable excursion than a war.

The two men talked on until finally Wolsey waved him out wearily. "Good night, Robert. Get us to Therouanne as quickly as you can, and we shall see if we can satisfy His Majesty."

At the end of July, Henry and his army were near Therouanne. The first engagement with the French forces lasted six hours, and by its conclusion, one English soldier and twenty French lay dead on the field.

"At this rate," Sir Robert muttered under his breath, "the campaign could last a century!"

The army settled down, and the king settled himself comfortably into his apartments. No one could move him, not even King Louis of France, who was trying desperately to assemble an army large enough to dislodge the invading force.

Finally in August, Maximilian of Germany arrived. The English army had had virtually no success in breaching the town, and Louis was rapidly building his army. Despite the objections of Wolsey and Robert Wakefield, Henry charged Maximilian twenty thousand pounds plus an allowance of twenty pounds a day for the privilege of having him ride with the English army and provide a few German mercenaries. Henry and Maximilian rode out before the armies, the English king resplendent in a coat of gold cloth adorned with pearls and precious stones. He cut an impressive figure, as did the nine men-at-arms, all dressed in white and crimson, who carried the king's helmet and heavy armor. The king's horses were covered with tinkling golden bells that were dropped off during their rides and left as souvenirs for the Emperor's bodyguard.

Unfortunately, the weather spoiled the show. So Henry and the officers lived splendidly in tents and marquees, which were connected to each other by covered passages. Inside the king's marquee, which was covered from floor to roof with cloth of gold, sat a beautiful gilded sideboard with magnificent gold drinking cups.

Sir Robert and the officers of the army were at their wits' end. The king would neither attack nor retreat, so the entire army stayed camped outside the city, doing absolutely nothing. "Sooner or later," Sir Robert said in despair, "he must give up and go home."

"Not as long as he's having a good time," Captain Maddox said. He was a tall officer who was as disgusted with the "war" as Sir Robert.

The only thing that brought Wakefield any relief at all was the fact that he spent a good deal of time with Ralph Geddes and was pleased with the young man's behavior—with one exception. He noticed that Ralph took part eagerly in the orgies that went on among the lower ranks of the king's retainers.

There were plenty of camp followers and plenty of wine, and night after night, wild spectacles went on. Sir Robert never attended, but he noticed that Ralph was a regular participant. *Oh well,* he said to himself, *he's a young man. He'll outgrow such things.*

August dragged by, and early one afternoon in September, Sir Robert looked up to see a rider coming in, his horse lathered and windblown.

He walked over and watched as the rider dismounted and handed a dispatch to Wolsey, who had come out of his marquee. Wolsey read the letter and turned at once to walk over to the king's quarters. He was admitted by the soldiers, and Sir Robert strolled over to await developments. A few minutes later Wolsey came out, his face pale.

"What is it, Sir Thomas?" Robert inquired.

Wolsey looked at him, unseeing for a moment. Then he seemed to shake himself. "There has been a battle," he said, "in Flodden. The earl of Surrey has met with James IV of Scotland, who has attacked England. Surrey has won the day. The message is from

Queen Catherine." He looked reproachfully at the parchment, reading, "'This battle has been to Your Majesty and all your realm the greatest honor that could be, and more than if you should win the crown of France.'" He slapped the paper angrily with the back of a hand and glared at Sir Robert as if he had committed some fault.

"I don't understand," Robert said pensively. "This is good news, is it not? The Scots have been driven off?"

"Not to His Majesty." Wolsey ground out the words. "Here he is, trying to make a name for himself, and, in the only battle that has been fought, he was a mile behind the front lines! He is very upset, to say the least."

"Well, what will happen now?" Robert asked.

"If the city does not surrender, I suppose eventually we shall go back to England," Wolsey sighed.

However, on September 23rd, the city obligingly surrendered at nine o'clock in the morning. Henry rode on to Tournai, which was battered by the cannons and capitulated on September 25th.

Henry took that as a victory and arranged a day of splendid tournaments to convince everyone of the glory of being English. But this was spoiled by a sudden rain.

Henry called Wolsey and Robert into his tent later and said, "Well, the war is won. We return to England."

"That's well, Your Majesty," Robert said in relief. "Victory is yours." He and Wolsey spent some time bolstering up the king's opinion of himself, and they returned to England as soon as was possible.

Henry VIII returned to a plague-ridden London to be met by Catherine's miscarriage and a rousing case of the measles.

Wakefield, however, returned to a joyful wife, who threw herself into his arms and said with tears in her eyes, "Robert, I hope you never leave me again! Wars are so terrible!"

He laughed, glad to be back, and held her tight in his arms. He kissed her thoroughly, then said ironically, "With a war like that, one is safer there than here at Wakefield!"

Later she asked him of King Henry. "Was he a good soldier?" she inquired.

Sir Robert thought about the question for a few moments. "He is a man who thinks only of his own pleasures and of power. Yet he will listen to no one. That is a bad combination, my dear." A gloom settled on him. "He is going to be a hard sovereign for any of us to serve."

Lady Jane saw her husband's face grow cloudy and did not want him to think of anything unpleasant. "How did you and Ralph get on?" she asked quickly.

His face brightened. "Fine, just fine. He's come back with me. We shall begin to show him Wakefield tomorrow." He looked at her anxiously and said, "I hope you get on with him, Jane."

"I will do my best," she promised, then smiled and forgot Ralph Geddes. Her husband was home again, and she was happy.

Three

FLIGHT OF THE FALCON

arrow, Sir Geoffrey Bourneville's estate, was a thing of beauty. The castle stood in an enormous clearing, surrounded for the most part by a large forest. It had a courtyard and a moat, which was covered by a fortified stone bridge that ended halfway across it. The other half of the moat was covered by a wooden drawbridge that could be cranked up at night. Just across the drawbridge was the top of the village street—the only street in the village—which extended for about half a mile, flanked on both sides by thatched houses of wattle and daub.

The street divided the clearing into two huge fields, the left one of which was cultivated in hundreds of long narrow strips, while the right ran down to a river and was used as a pasture. Half of the right-hand field was fenced off for hay.

It was now July of the sixth year of Myles's and his mother's stay at Harrow. As on every other July, haymaking demanded that every able-bodied man and woman work in the fields. The weather was hot, and everyone turned brown from working long hours in the sun. The dogs moved about with their tongues hanging out or lay panting in bits of shade. The horses sweated through their coats and tried to kick the horseflies off their bellies with their great hind hooves. In the pasture fields, the cows could be seen galloping about with their tails in the air.

Myles had always liked haymaking, hard work though it was. As the work began, he threw himself into it. The best mowers worked away in a line where the grass was still uncut. The women raked the dry hay together in long strips with wooden rakes, and boys with pitchforks followed on either side of the strip, turning the hay well inward so that it lay in such a way as to allow for easy picking up. Finally the great carts followed, drawn by horses or slow, white oxen. One man stood on top of the cart to receive the hay from the boys, who would throw it to him with a pitchfork. When the wagon was loaded it was drawn to a rick, which was built into a small mountain. There men put each forkful of the hay in place where it could be easily taken down.

Myles, at the age of twelve, had become an expert at his job. He plunged himself into the hay and even breathed it in. Seeds stuck in his hair and mouth and nostrils and worked inside his clothes, tickling him. He laughed at Percy, the twelve-year-old son of Sir Geoffrey, who hated everything about haymaking and did all he could to get out of it. But in this one instance, Sir Geoffrey had no mercy, even on the spoiled Percy, forcing him to labor along with the rest.

All morning they worked, but in the afternoon a great storm broke. Sir Geoffrey kept at them until great lightning flashes were right overhead, and then the sky grew dark as night and the rain came pouring down upon them as though dumped from a bucket, so they were drenched all at once and could not see a hundred yards away. They all ran for shelter, and seeing his mother, Myles ran to her. The two of them crawled under a wagon to keep their wet bodies warm against the cold wind that rose up.

As they lay there, a thought came to Myles and he turned to his mother. "Who was my father?"

The question caught Margred off guard. She smoothed her wet hair down over her shoulders, her blue eyes studying the boy who lay flat beside her on the ground, observing her carefully. She was still, at the age of twenty-seven, far more attractive than most women of her station. She had never taken another man, although pursued by several. She had thrown her life into making a way at Sir Geoffrey's estate, mostly for the sake of her son. Harrow, for all its hard work and lack of luxuries, had become a sanctuary for them.

"Why do you ask me that?" Margred asked quietly. He had asked before, but it had been at least two years ago. She had put him off then but had known that, sooner or later, the question would have to be answered. Now as the rains turned the field into a small lake and glistened on the fallen hay, she waited while Myles framed his answer.

Myles fixed his blue-gray eyes on his mother. He looked older than his twelve years. He had a squarish face, a short English nose, long mobile lips, and smallish ears that lay flat against his skull. He had a pugnacious chin that reflected the stubbornness that lay within him. Tall for his age, he was lean and very strong. He would be a fine, tall man, agile and quick. Any who knew him recognized that he was stubborn, strong-willed, and very sensitive. Almost unhealthily so. Now he picked up a straw, stuck it between his lips, and said as though it didn't matter, "Oh, I just thought I'd ask." He hesitated, then looked off at the horses that were cooling off under the fresh rain. "Most boys seem to have a father. One they can see, I mean."

Margred reached out her hand to push the wet hair away from his forehead, carefully considering the answer she would give him. None came for the moment. There were many children without fathers, for legitimacy was a thing for the rich. Among the poor, many young girls bore children, some not having the slightest idea who the father was. Others knew the father's identity but kept quiet—generally because it was the lord of the manor or one of the sons, and there was nothing to be done about it.

"Are you very unhappy, not having a father, Myles?"

"Oh, no," he said, his eyes opening very wide. "I just wonder, that's all."

Margred said only, "Your father was a fine man, Myles. But he was bound by marriage to another. Do you understand that?"

Myles did not but, seeing the distress in his mother's blue eyes, said, "Oh yes." He grinned at her then, saying, "I just think about it sometimes. Don't worry about it, Mother."

The rain gave no signs of letting up, so Myles said, "I'm going to the mews, Mother." Slipping out from under the wagon, he ran along the fields, passing others on their way to their houses. He went to the mews, glancing at the nearby stables and kennels. These three locations had formed a large part of his world for the past six years. The mews faced south, and the outside windows were small, but the windows that looked inward to the courtyard were big and sunny. They had close vertical slats nailed down, but no horizontal ones. Animal horn covered the small windows, forming a nearly translucent plate over the opening.

Entering the building, Myles went to a bench and began working on a hood for one of the merlins. He had gotten to be very good at such things, and Nob now trusted him to do much of this sort of work. For the next hour he toiled steadily, working in Sir Geoffrey's colors. He would pause from time to time, admiring the white leather with blue baize at the side and a bunch of blue-gray plumes on top, made out of the hackle feathers of herons. He was happy as he worked, and only briefly did the thought come into his mind, *She didn't tell me who my father was. But she said he was a good man.*

That was as far as his thoughts had gone when suddenly Percy Bourneville entered the mews. He was a large boy with brown hair and light blue eyes. He tended to be overweight, a result of his love of food of all kinds. He was spoiled, as was natural for the oldest son of a baron. He had grown up in a world in which his father was absolute ruler and the serfs of little more import than draft animals.

The one exception in Percy's mind was Myles Morgan, for the two of them, being almost of the same age, had spent a great portion of their lives playing together. Not that there was any sense of democracy in Percy Bourneville—he simply had needed someone to play with. Since there were no boys or young people of his station close at hand, he and Myles had swum the river, hunted, and attended the various functions that came to the little town.

"The rain has stopped at last!" Percy declared, a gleam in his eyes. "Let's go before they can call us back to work!"

"Go where?" Myles asked, puzzled.

"We're going to take Thor on a hunt," he announced.

Myles looked at him doubtfully. "Do you think we ought to fly him? You know what Nob said about it. He's not ready now."

As usual Percy paid no attention to any sort of advice coming from Myles. He snorted disdainfully, walked over to where Thor, the great goshawk, was perched, and pulled on a left-hand gauntlet. Thor glared at him malevolently with a marigold eye and refused to move toward the gauntlet.

"I don't think we ought to fly him, Percy," Myles persisted, knowing his words would do little good. "What would happen if he got away and refused to come back?"

"You don't know anything about it," Percy snapped meanly. He shoved his gauntlet under the great hawk's talons, forcing him to leap on, and slipped a hood over the bird's head rather awkwardly. "You're only a serf. You have to be one of the nobility to understand hawks," he said rather grandly. This was not true, for already Myles knew more about falconry than some full-grown men who flew the birds. But he also knew better than to argue with the son of the baron. With a resigned sigh, he followed Percy from the mews. They went out across the hayfield and headed toward the forest.

The coneys had hundreds of holes and nests at the edge of the forest, so the problem was not to find a rabbit but to find one far enough away from its hole to give the hawk a chance to rise and then swoop down upon it.

They walked along until finally Percy hissed, "There's one—over there in that opening!"

Myles tried one more time. "Why don't we go over to the plain, where there's more room? This is too close to the woods."

"You don't know anything about flying a hawk. Only the man who's carrying him knows that." Percy removed the jesses and leash from the great bird, then removed the hood. The awkwardness with which he was handled confused the goshawk, and he did not rise at once when Percy lifted his wrist. Instead, he merely raised his crest and stared at the trees over to his right. Percy threw his arm upward to give the hawk a better takeoff, crying out as he did so.

The suddenness of Percy's movement caught all three of them off guard: the hawk, the rabbit, and Myles. Myles watched in anguish as the hawk went swooping like a child flung high in a swing and then flew to a tree over to their right and perched on a high branch, his beak open in a pant of failure. As for the rabbit, startled by the boy's cry, it had exploded in a gray flash. In the seconds it took for the hawk to rise into the air, the rabbit had disappeared into a thicket.

"Now you've done it!" Myles said angrily, staring up at the hawk. "We'll never get him down from there!"

"Who cares?" Percy glared at him. He knew he had handled the hawk badly, and he knew Myles could have done it much better. This did not soothe him in the least. "He's no good anyway. Come on, let's go home."

"We can't lose Thor!" Myles stared at the other boy in shock. It had never once occurred to him to walk away and leave the hawk.

"Who wants that rotten, stupid hawk?" Percy snapped. "It serves him right! He's stupid and not good for anything! You stay yourself if you're so keen about it. I'm going home!"

Myles stood there, almost trembling, as Percy stalked off without a backward glance. He looked up at the great bird and sat down beneath the tree. He knew Percy really had no heart for hawking. Were it not a popular occupation for a young man of his heritage, he probably wouldn't ever participate. But Nob had instilled into Myles some of the love of the sport. Myles knew that before Nob had started Thor's training for the hunt he had carried the young bird with him everywhere for three days and two nights until Thor finally went to sleep—which meant that the hawk had learned to trust Nob. Then Nob had spent hour after hour teaching the bird his trade.

Remembering the look in the older man's eyes as he gazed at the hawk each day, Myles could not bear to go away and leave the bird.

Time passed slowly. Myles wished more than once that Thor was hungry, but he had been well fed the night before. The hot day and Percy's handling had put Thor in a bad temper, and he began to change trees, never going far, but ever working his way inward toward the deepest part of the forest. Underneath, Myles followed until they were further from the castle than was wise. There were wild boars in that forest, and wild men, too—outlaws as cunning and bloody as the boars themselves.

As the dark began to fall, Myles grew more and more apprehensive. The forest was trackless; if Thor kept shifting from point to point, Myles would not be able to find his way home.

Longing to go back but determined to retrieve the bird and take him home even if he had to stay out all night, Myles followed Thor. He had a stout heart, this Myles Morgan. Though only a boy, there was a toughness in him that would not let him run away. He followed until dark and finally put himself under the tree where the great goshawk had at last perched and tucked his head under his wing.

Birds did not move much after dark—only owls did that—so

Myles curled up under the tree, shivering with the damp of the cool evening air, and waited for the morning.

Sir Geoffrey Bourneville, at the age of thirty-three, loved to eat and to drink. Likewise, he loved to hunt, either with his hounds or with his hawks. Nothing was more likely to put him into a vile humor than to hear that one of the dogs was injured, his horses lame, or his hawks lost.

"What do you mean you took Thor out?" He stared coldly at his son. "Nob told you he wasn't to be hunted for at least another week!"

Percy Bourneville was very much afraid of his father. He knew that there was nothing he could do to arouse the man's anger more quickly than making a mistake with one of his hawks. Being a boy who had not been taught better, he said immediately, "It was Myles's fault! He insisted on taking Thor out!"

Shame ran through him as he said this, and he felt even worse. But he had learned the art of hiding what was in his heart from his father, so he stared back at him stonily.

Sir Geoffrey's face flushed red and he thundered, "I'll have the hide off that boy! Go find 'em, Nob!" He twirled and glared at the falconer. "Bring 'em back and let me know as soon as you find 'em!"

Nob's eyes were on Percy, who could not meet his gaze, as he turned and left the manor. He knew the forest as well as he knew the inside of Sir Geoffrey's estate, having spent much more time there, thus it was not a difficult matter for him to find the boy and the hawk. So it was that, less than an hour later, he came upon a scene that brought him up to a sudden halt.

Thor, the great hawk, was perched on a limb high in the tree. On the ground below, curled between two roots, was the sleeping form of Myles Morgan.

"Rise up, boy," Nob said quietly. When Myles stirred out of his sleep, his hair in his face, his eyes confused, Nob put his gnarled finger to his lips and whispered, "We'll get him down now."

The great bird knew the sound of his master's voice. When he saw Nob lift his gauntleted hand, a piece of raw meat held high, he fluttered down from the tree at once and landed neatly on the glove, instantly snatching up the meat in his powerful beak in a blur of motion. Nob had no need to hood the bird when he held him. Thor was content as Nob drew his arm close in, bending his elbow and holding his hand straight up so Thor could perch on the highest point. Nob threaded the jesses loosely between the fingers of the gauntlet and turned to Myles.

"I'm sorry for it, Myles. But the master's going to thrash you."

Myles's eyes grew large and he cried out, "Thrash me! What for?"

"For taking Thor out before he was ready," Nob said evenly. He saw the shock hit the boy's eyes, saw the fine mouth tighten, and waited for the protest. Nob knew that Myles would never have taken Thor out, just as he knew that Percy Bourneville was a selfish, self-centered brat. Myles was silent, though, and Nob realized he would make no protest.

"I know how it was," he said quietly, "but there's nothing for it."

Myles looked up at the thin form of the falconer, his best friend in the world, and was sure that Nob spoke truthfully. Somehow that knowledge warmed him, and he said nothing as the two trudged back.

Sir Geoffrey kept his word, and instead of assigning the beating to one of the servants, he himself took Myles outside the mews and bade him strip off his shirt. Then, with a rough peach tree stick twice as big around as his thumb, the lord laid on. Margred, who was forced to watch, felt her eyes fill with tears.

When the beating was over, Sir Geoffrey threw the stick down and turned, then started when his eyes met those of the falconer. Though Nob said nothing to him, Sir Geoffrey realized he was being weighed in the balances and found wanting. He himself was fairly certain that it was his son and not this boy who had taken the hawk, but he could not make a liar out of his own son in the eyes of the serfs. He glanced back at Myles, who had risen unsteadily to his feet.

"See that you behave better next time," he snapped at the boy, then whirled and stalked off.

Myles slipped on his shirt, determined not to show the pain that simple action caused him. Margred walked up and touched his arm gently. "Does it hurt much?" she asked tremulously. It had taken all her will to not step between the big baron and the small boy, but she knew that would never do.

"Why no, Mother," Myles said cheerfully, though his face was pale and his lips trembled slightly. "It hardly hurt at all."

"Come inside and I'll put some ointment on it," she said.

"No!" he cried out, losing his composure for a moment. "I don't want it!" He took a deep breath to steady himself, then turned and walked off quickly, leaving Nob and Margred watching him with pity and regret.

"It was Percy," Nob said, his lips twisting with anger. "He's always doing something like this! Every time he gets in trouble, he sees Myles gets the blame for it."

Noting the pain in Margred's eyes, his heart went out to her. He had come to know her well over the last years—indeed, he had been her protector. He knew too well how little protection a woman alone had against men in their day. And Margred was too lovely not to draw attention.

One afternoon, Nob had returned from working the dogs to find Margred out in the fields. He had paused to watch her work, then turned to enter his house—until a motion just beyond Margred had caught his eye. Frowning, he had scanned the area until he spotted a tall, crude serving man called Poins crouching nearby, his gaze fixed on the working woman.

Poins was a thin man, with cruel hazel eyes and brown hair falling down in his face, and Nob had no trouble recognizing the wicked gleam in the man's eyes as he watched Margred. Casually, so as not to attract attention to himself, Nob had circled the field until he was standing directly behind the serving man.

Poins had uttered a cry of alarm, and Margred had spun around, her eyes widening at the picture of Nob holding a glittering knife against the throat of a man she had never seen before.

Nob had smiled at her. "Good day, Margred. Never mind me and me fine friend here. We've got a bit of discussing to do, if you'll be so kind as to excuse us?"

"Of course, Nob," Margred had said with a nod, then she turned and went toward her house.

"Don't hurt me!" Poins had cried out, "I wasn't doing nothing wrong!"

"Not doing, but surely considering," Nob had retorted, his voice low and cold. When he spoke again, it was in an almost conversational tone—and, as he did so, the falconer slowly drew his knife across Poins's throat, slicing the flesh enough to let the warm blood flow down. "I would like to let all your blood out, Poins. I've wanted to do it for a long time. And if you ever touch this woman, I promise by the saints that it's dead meat you'll be!"

Nob had watched over Margred ever since, and though he was a small man, he was deadly with a bow or a knife. Margred well understood that it was his protection that had insured her safety. She looked at him now and asked, "What will become of him, Nob?"

Nob looked after the fleeing form of the tall boy and said, "He's going to be a fine man. He works, he's smart, he's not a crybaby—" here he gave Margred a fond look—"and he's got a fine mother!" Then Nob said something he had never said before, although the thought had often been in his mind. "Will ye ever be marryin' again?"

Margred looked at him and asked, "Are you asking for yourself, Nob?"

He smiled wryly. "No, girl, marriage is not for me. But there's a man or two about that wouldn't make bad husbands. I've wondered why you didn't give the boy a father."

"He has a father," Margred said almost sharply. Realizing the tone of her voice, she amended, "No, Nob, I'll never marry." She did not answer in detail, nor did he pursue it. He was content simply to help her and, for himself, to keep the boy as close as possible, for he had grown to love Myles Morgan as though he were the son he had lost so long ago.

Myles ran down the street of the village, turned toward the church that was set far at the end of the lane, and went at once to his secret place. There was little privacy in his world. Only the wealthy people had private chambers. Most of the retainers of the wealthy families slept in common rooms, and immorality ran rife as a result of it. The daily life of the average serf was not given to privacy. He worked, slept, and ate with others.

Something in Myles demanded privacy—always had, even when he was a small boy. Not long after coming to Harrow, he had discovered, on the south side of the church next to the town wall, a small projection coming out of the main structure. Myles guessed that it once was a balcony, but that the door had been walled up. It was old and weathered, and some of the timbers were rotting. But it was readily accessible, thanks to a huge apple tree with a branch that dipped over it conveniently.

Myles climbed the tree, shinnied out on the branch, and dropped onto the balcony with the ease of long practice. There was a railing running around the balcony, though most of the palings were missing, so that, once he was inside, he had the sensation of being closed off from the world. On one side was the solid wall of the old Norman church; on the other, the wall of the city. People rarely passed beneath, so he could—and did—spend many hours alone there, just lying on his back, staring up at the sky or playing the solitary games of a boy with an active imagination.

Normally he would have lain down at once, but his smarting back would not allow that. So he just leaned on the railing and closed his eyes. It was quiet, so still, that he could hear only faint echoes of voices. The sun was still rising, and the leaves of the trees whispered to one another in the heightening breeze. It always smelled good to Myles here. The village almost always stank, since people threw garbage and waste out their windows and allowed it to rot in the street. In addition, hogs and other animals rooted around everywhere, filling the air with their stench. It was only when he came to this place, with the grass beneath and the apple tree filling the sky over his head, that Myles indulged in the luxury of inhaling deeply.

He moved to perch on the side of the old railing, unsure whether his back or his spirits smarted more. He had been beaten often enough to take such a thing philosophically, but the injustice of it gnawed at him, making him miserable and angry.

He sat nursing his injuries, reliving what had happened. The only redemption in it for him was the fact that he knew that Nob approved of what he had done. He had said as much on the way back from the woods with Thor. "If it hadn't been for you, Thor would have been lost," he'd said gravely, stroking the huge bird just under his beak, down the powerful chest. "And when a falconer loses his bird, he loses something out of his life. All the hours you put into a falcon or a hawk make them a part of you. You have invested yourself. And so when that bird is gone, part of you is gone."

Myles sat quietly, warmed by the memory of the approval on Nob's face. Then he thought again of Percy, and the corners of his mouth turned down. He started feeling sorry for himself again and began picturing himself leaping on Percy and punching him in the face. But he knew that would never happen, not unless he wanted to be whipped into a bloody pulp.

"Hello! What are you doing up there?"

Confused and startled, Myles looked down and saw a young girl looking up at him from the ground below. She was about his own age, he thought, and was very pretty, her honey-colored hair tied by a red ribbon and flowing over her shoulders. She had very light blue eyes, the lightest he had ever seen, and they almost sparkled in her oval face. He knew the people in his little world very well—even regular visitors he had known for years—but this girl was new to him.

"I-I'm . . . thinking," he stammered, feeling like a fool.

Her eyes lit up with mischief, and she smiled at him. "Oh? And haven't you found a fine place to do it, now! I wish I could get up there with you!"

"Well, you can't," he said shortly. He nodded at the branch of the tree and said, "Girls can't climb trees."

"I'll bet I can," she said and ran at once to the tree. But she was mistaken, for the first branch was too high for her. She turned to him and shrugged, saying cheerfully, "Well, I guess you're right."

Myles was intrigued by her easy acceptance. "Wait!" he said. "I'll come down." He leaped to the branch, made his way along it to the trunk, worked his way downward, then leaped to the ground, landing on his feet lightly. "I haven't seen you before, have I?"

"No," she said. "This is my first visit. My name is Hannah Kemp. What's yours?"

"Myles Morgan."

"What a pretty name!" she exclaimed. "I never heard one like that before."

He was pleased at her approval and nodded. "It's a Welsh name. My mother and I, we come from Wales. Came over the mountains," he added nonchalantly.

"I've never been that far," she said. "We live over with Sir John Walsh, on Little Sodsbury. My father is Sir John's seneschal." She looked back up to the perch and asked, "What is that? What's it for?"

"I don't know." He shrugged. "I guess it used to be a balcony, but now it's my secret place. I go there sometimes when I want to be by myself." He felt suddenly as if he had told a shameful secret, and his face grew red. "I guess that sounds crazy, doesn't it?"

"Why would that be crazy?" she asked in surprise. "I like to go off and be by myself, too. I have a little place in the woods, under a big tree, where the roots make kind of a little cradle. No one can see me there. Sometimes I take my books or my sewing and I go there and just sew or read. It's nice."

Intrigued again, Myles nodded. "Why, that's the way I feel." He was shocked to find someone else who had these notions. "What are you doing here?"

"Oh, Sir John came over to visit Sir Geoffrey, and my mother and I came along to visit with a friend of hers that she's known a long time, Lady Grace. I think she's a relative of Sir Geoffrey."

"His sister," Myles affirmed. He suddenly felt ill at ease, for he had never carried on a conversation with anyone, let alone a girl, of Hannah's station. He could tell now that she was not of his class, for her clothes were well made, woven, and very expensive. She had a gold necklace around her neck with a small green stone hanging from the fine chain. He looked down and saw that she had a book in her hand and forgot his discomfort, asking abruptly, "You say you can read?"

"Yes. The tutor of the last place where my father worked taught me how." This seemed almost a miracle to Myles. Nobody he knew could read. Nob could read almost anything in the forest, as clearly as if it were a printed page, but he could not read a book. He knew that Percy and Isabella were learning to read, but they refused to help him, saying only that such things were not for serfs.

Now he eyed the book she held and said wistfully, "It must be wonderful to be able to read a book."

Hannah looked searchingly at him and saw the hunger in his eyes. "Why yes, it is rather fun," she said gently. She hesitated for a moment, then said, "Come over here and sit down, and I'll read to you." She walked over to the base of the apple tree, sat down on the grass, and arranged her skirt. Myles came over and sat down rather warily beside her. He looked over her shoulder at the inside of the book—at the strange, meaningless black markings—and listened silently as she began to read.

She had a clear, sweet voice and read in such a way that the story of an ocean voyage seemed to come alive. She read about strange sea monsters, about storms at sea with waves as high as barns, about islands where the people wore no clothes and cut off each other's heads. Finally she looked up and saw the intensity of his face. "I'd like to go on a ship sometime, wouldn't you, Myles?"

"Yes," he agreed, still caught up in the story. "Someday I'm going to do that. I'm going to go on a ship around the world."

"You'd fall off the edge, silly!" she laughed. "Besides," she went on practically, "you'll have to stay here, won't you? Aren't you and your mother attached to this estate?"

That was the way it was in her world. People did not just move. A serf was intertwined with an estate, and it was almost as if they were as rooted as the trees that grew there. The truth of that came to Myles as he realized that none of the people in his class had ever moved away, and none of them had ever gone on any kind of a journey.

His mouth grew firm and he clenched his jaw slightly. "I'm going to see more of the world than this little place," he said stubbornly. "Somehow I'll do it!"

Hannah regarded him, fascinated by his determination, captivated by his good looks. Most of the serfs she knew were thick, both of body and brain. Somehow this boy was different. She sat beside him, talking. Though she was only eleven, she had enough discernment to draw him out and soon had found out about his mother, that he had no father that he knew of, and that he was a bright boy of high imagination.

After a while, he gave her a startled look. "I'm talking too much, aren't I?"

She shook her head. "Why no, why would you think that? I like to talk to people, and you are very interesting, Myles."

Her simple statement surprised him. No one had ever thought he was interesting before, not that he knew of. He blushed a little with pleasure. "I don't really know anything, except maybe a little about hawks and horses." His eyes fell on the book and he did not speak, though the longing was evident on his face.

Impulsively, Hannah reached out to touch his arm. "Maybe I could teach you to read." She was rewarded by a flash of light in his blue-gray eyes, and she went on. "We'll be coming over, my mother tells me, at least once a week. She's teaching the ladies here how to do a new kind of weaving. My father brought the loom today so she could teach them here instead of them coming to our village. So would you like it if I could come with her? We could meet here," she said excitedly, "and it could be our secret!"

Entranced yet doubtful, Myles stared at her. "It might be against the law. I never heard of any boys around here learning to read. And I don't think Sir Geoffrey would like it."

But Hannah was caught up with the idea. Her eyes shone and her hair glimmered in the streams of sunlight that stole down through the leaves of the apple tree. "They won't know, Myles! It'll just be my secret, and yours! Come on, we can start right now." Opening the book she pointed and said, "You see that? That is an *A*. The first letter of the alphabet. Say ay!"

Myles repeated obediently, "Ay!"

"Good! Now give me your finger." She took his finger and, holding it like a pointer, traced the shape of the *A*. "Say ay. And when I come next time, you can practice making one of these. Even if we don't have any paper, you can make it in the dust."

"Ay!" Myles said. For the next hour they sat there as Hannah took Myles through the first few letters of the alphabet, making him repeat them and trace them on the back of the book.

When at last she rose to leave, Myles scrambled to his feet. "I'll be back next week," she said, her strange, light blue eyes sparkling. "I'll be looking for you right here, at the secret place."

"I'll come if I can," he promised, and then he was tongue-tied. "I-I . . . don't know what to say," he stammered, then said gravely, "I thank you for offering to teach me how to read. 'Tis a thing I never thought I'd learn."

The gratitude in his eyes warmed her, and she said in a kindly fashion, "Oh, it's all right. It'll be fun! Well, I must go now. Good-bye! I'll see you next week!"

He watched until she disappeared around the corner of the church, standing alone and feeling a little afraid that the encounter might have been a dream. But he knew it was not. And he knew that, somehow, no matter how difficult it was to get away, he would be here in this place—their secret place—next week.

Four

IN THE STOCKS

Myles Morgan always remembered two days to the end of his life. One was the morning when he met Hannah Kemp. He remembered every detail as clearly as if it were in a painting: her face as she looked up at him as he sat on the rim of the balcony, her honey-colored hair, her amazingly bright blue eyes, and the smile on her face. Scarcely a day passed in the next three years when he did not think of that meeting, and it grew to be the center of his life—as did the days when Hannah came with her mother to Sir Geoffrey's castle. He took more than one beating for neglecting his work to meet with Hannah, and he considered it a miracle from God that during those years no one ever happened upon them or their secret place.

But the time eventually came when Hannah told Myles she would not be returning for a while. "My mother feels she is finished with her teaching here, at least for a time," she told him, struggling to keep the tremor of disappointment out of her voice.

Myles nodded, ashamed to find tears pricking at his eyes. "I'll see you again, Hannah," was all he said. And she smiled at him in her gentle way.

The other day that Myles remembered was the most bitter-sweet experience of his life. He had no notion when he rose up early that morning that the day would hold anything unusual. He washed his face in cold water and slipped into his jerkin. Eating a quick breakfast of dried venison, he hurried out, intending to spend some time hunting. But he was halted by one of the servants from the big house, whose name was Ridley.

"You there! Morgan!" the man called out, then waited until Myles came to stand before him. He was a tall, thin man of fifty and had been the seneschal for the Bournevilles since he had obtained his maturity. He knew everything about Harrow, Sir Geoffrey's estate. Sometimes it seemed almost magical to the serfs how he knew so much about their private lives, and they wondered if he knew as much about the people inside the great house.

Myles, at the age of fifteen, was approaching the height of six feet and could look the seneschal in the eye. Ridley said brusquely, "I am sending you, along with Cheval, on a short journey. You will be taking the loom back to Lady Walsh, over in the next county. 'Tis too heavy for one man, so you go along with Cheval." He paused, eyeing the boy carefully. "Cheval is not too bright, you know, and I cannot spare anyone else. Be sure you find Sir John Walsh's home and no other. And if you hurt that loom or lose it . . ." The unspoken threat was evident in the man's eyes. "Quick now, Cheval has the horses hitched."

Myles's heart began thumping wildly. He was going to Hannah's home, for her father was Sir John's seneschal!

He raced to tell his mother where he was going, then hurried back to clamber into the wagon with Cheval. "All ready!" He grinned. "Let's go!"

Cheval was a huge man, a giant, really. The horses he took care of were his pride and joy, and Myles had remarked once when describing him to Hannah, "He isn't as big as a horse, but then, he isn't much smaller, either."

Cheval had small dark eyes that were set rather close together, coarse black hair that he kept cropped short, and a mild temperament—except when his temper was aroused. "Aye, we'll have to hurry to get there before dark," he grumbled.

All day the horses plodded along, and it was meat and drink to Myles, who, since the day he and his mother had been taken in by Nob, had not been more than three miles outside the perimeter of the Bourneville lands. He chattered like a magpie all the way to Gloucestershire County. When they reached the town where Sir John lived, it was Myles who looked about, then spotted an elderly woman, her face like a dried apple, who was cooking something outside in a huge pot. And it was Myles who went to her and inquired, "Please, where will we find Sir John Walsh?"

The woman looked up at him, then pointed down the street. "Turn right past them trees," she said and went back to stirring whatever was in her black pot with a long stick.

Cheval slapped the reins, grumbling, "We got to find something for them horses to eat before we go back tomorrow."

Myles did not answer. He was looking everywhere, hoping to catch a glimpse of Hannah Kemp. When they wheeled around the grove of trees, he saw a large house that was built in a fashion unfamiliar to him. Constructed of small square stones, the house was a wonder to the boy, who had never seen a brick before. He marveled at how much trouble it must be to hew stones into such tiny shapes. It was an attractive house, with the front divided by several windows and six chimneys rising above the steep roof. A man was working on the flowerbeds outside the house, and once again it was Myles who spoke to him. "We're looking for the home of Sir John Walsh," he said.

The man, a short rotund figure with a rosy complexion and a pair of sharp dark eyes, got to his feet. "This be Sir John's house. What do you want?" he demanded.

"We've brought a loom back from Sir Geoffrey Bourneville," Myles answered.

"Oh. Well, wait here, and I'll find out what's to be done with it."

The man disappeared for a few moments, then came back, accompanied by a lady of about thirty-five. She looked at the two and said briefly, "You must bring it into the house. Be careful. I don't want it broken up."

"Yes, ma'am," Myles said, and he and Cheval hopped down from the wagon.

"Come with me and I shall show you where to bring it."

"Shall I help them, Lady Walsh?" the rotund gardener asked.

"It might be as well," she said. "'Tis very heavy."

But as it turned out, they did not need help. Cheval laughed and reached up, then picked up the loom by himself and set it on the ground. "Weighs no more'n a bird," he said.

Lady Walsh, who had come back to supervise, watched him critically, then said, "You are very strong. Very well, come back this way."

Myles grabbed one end of the loom. Cheval carried most of the weight, but he was not going to be cheated of the opportunity to see inside the Walsh home. They entered through tall oak doors in the front, made their way through the equivalent of a great hall, and wound around a corridor until they came to some stairs.

"You shall have to go up these stairs," Lady Walsh said and then led the way. It was somewhat of a struggle to get the loom up, but finally they succeeded. Lady Walsh directed them to one end of an upstairs corridor, where they entered a sparsely furnished room, and Lady Walsh said with relief, "Put it down here. Very good. Now I suppose you want something to eat. Come along and I'll tell the cook to fix you something."

She was about to leave the room when suddenly a girl came in, and Myles felt himself grow alert—it was Hannah. At fifteen she was becoming a lovely young woman. She was wearing a beautifully embroidered pale green gown, and Myles blinked, for he had never seen her dressed up before. She glanced at him but said nothing as Lady Walsh explained, "Hannah, these men have brought back my loom. Take them to the kitchen and see that they are fed, please."

"Yes, Lady Walsh," Hannah answered, then turned to Myles and Cheval. "Come this way. I'll take you to the kitchen."

She led the way down the stairs, down a corridor to the right, and then into the large kitchen. It was dominated by a huge fireplace at one end, with many hooks suspended above it on which to hang the pots and pans. A rotund woman was cleaning the room and looked up as they came in.

"Cook," Hannah said, "these men have come all the way from Sir Geoffrey Bourneville's estate in the next county. I want you to fix them something very good to eat."

The cook grunted and shuffled over near the stove, where a multitude of pots and pans lay. "It ain't ready for supper yet," she mumbled, "but I guess they can have theirs early."

Soon Myles and Cheval were eating from the wooden trenchers, and Hannah sat down on the other side of the table to watch. "You shall have to stay the night. I'll show you where when you get through eating."

"Thank you, miss," Myles said carefully. He ate his fill and watched as Cheval devoured enough for three men, then yawned hugely.

"I'll be going to bed now," the large man announced.

Hannah said, "Come along with me."

The two followed her, and she showed them a small room off the stable that was filled with saddles and gear, then motioned toward some pallets that were piled underneath a rough wooden table. "Those will do, I suppose," she said. Then she looked at Myles and said casually, "If you're not sleepy now perhaps you'd like to walk around the estate."

"Yes," Myles said eagerly. "You go on to bed, Cheval. I'll be in after a while." He turned and followed Hannah from the room, and as soon as they were outside and away from the stables he grinned at her. "Are you surprised to see me?"

"Yes," she said with a smile. "I haven't seen you in so long!"

"Two months." He nodded. "I was sorry you stopped coming. But I've kept up with my reading. I go over the books every day." She had given him two books, and he had memorized them so that, even when he was not looking at the page, he could almost quote them from memory.

"I have another one for you," she said. "Does anyone know you can read?"

"No, not even Mother. I keep the books hidden, where no one can find them, all wrapped up in a soft skin so they won't get damp. But I check them over every day."

"Do you still go to our secret place?" Hannah asked sweetly, a wistful look in her eyes. "I enjoyed that so much!"

"Why yes, I do." He thought for a moment, then said, "I get lonely for you. That was the finest part of my life, those days when you would come, and we would sneak off so you could teach me to read. I wonder what would've happened though, if you had gotten caught? I know what would have happened to me." He looked at her and raised an eyebrow. "Do they whip young ladies?"

"I don't know," she laughed. "They've never whipped me, anyway." Then she said excitedly, "Come on, I want you to meet someone."

"I'd rather not," he said hesitantly. "Let's just go for a walk."

"We can do that later. This is important." She led him back into the house and through the great hall with its tall oak beam ceilings and wooden screens at the south end, then went up two flights of stairs. On the third floor she knocked on a door, and a voice said, "Come in!"

Myles followed her into a small room with a steep, arched

ceiling, the eaves of which fell almost to the floor. The eaves, he was to discover later, were made of ship's timbers, a ship from Avonmouth. As they entered the room, Myles saw a man sitting at a desk, several books and papers in front of him and a turkey quill in his right hand.

"Here is someone I would like for you to meet, Mr. Tyndale," Hannah said politely. "This is Myles Morgan. He's come bringing the loom back. And this is Mr. William Tyndale, Myles, the tutor for Sir Walsh's children."

Tyndale remained seated but put his pen down and smiled at Myles. "Well, Myles," he said, "I have heard some little about you."

Hannah turned to Myles explaining, "I have told Mr. Tyndale how I taught you to read, Myles."

Myles gave her a worried look, wondering if she had told him any more about their secret place, but he saw that she was smiling at him reassuringly. "I'm glad to meet you, Mr. Tyndale," he said and bowed a little nervously. "Hannah has talked much about you."

Tyndale was a man of no more than twenty-seven, of medium height as far as Myles could judge. He had a small frame and was rather lean. His face was pleasant enough—he had a high domed forehead and a long nose, very deep-set brown eyes, which were dark and penetrating, and high cheekbones. His firm mouth was almost covered by a mustache and a beard. Myles noticed that the man's fingers were very long, his hands sensitive looking.

"Well now, lad, let us see how good a teacher Miss Hannah is." He reached behind him, deftly picked a book off a shelf, opened it to a passage, then reversed it and laid it across from him. "Let us hear a little of this."

Myles was embarrassed, but an encouraging smile from Hannah made him feel better. He stepped forward, leaned over, and read a few lines from the book in front of him, then looked up anxiously at William Tyndale.

"Fine, fine! Exactly right!" Tyndale nodded and smiled warmly. He looked at Hannah and said, "Please do not tell Sir John what a good teacher you are, or he'll be rid of me!"

"Oh no," Hannah said seriously. "This is a secret. Please don't ever tell anyone, Mr. Tyndale!"

"No, of course I won't." Tyndale, of course, understood the situation. He had been concerned about it when she had confided in him, but now as he looked at the boy, he saw that he was rather a finer type than he had expected, and he felt much better. "Well, well, sit down and let's talk."

Myles never forgot that first meeting with William Tyndale. The man seemed to know everything! Myles, trapped in his little world of Harrow, bound in a small county of a small country, had lived most of his life cut off from the great world. But as Tyndale sat there and began talking, Myles could envision the world itself. The teacher spoke of how a man called Magellan was sailing around the southern tip of South America with the hope of being the first man to ever sail around the world. He spoke of a man called Martin Luther, who had defied the power of the church in Rome by nailing ninety-five theses to the door of Wittenberg chapel. He somehow had heard that chocolate had been brought to Spain from Mexico for the first time and that a strange bird called a "turkey" had been introduced to Spain from America.

Myles listened avidly and then began to ask questions. He was ignorant, as were most boys his age and station, for they received no education whatsoever. But as he asked his questions, Tyndale's eyes grew sharp. He recognized that the boy had an inquisitive spirit, and he was careful to answer as fully as he could. Then Myles asked, "But, Mr. Tyndale, this Martin Luther. He's wrong, isn't he? I mean, the pope couldn't be wrong, could he? And the church?"

A sober expression touched William Tyndale's intelligent face. "Myles, my boy, you have touched upon the question that is threatening to tear the world apart." He leaned back in his chair, put his long fingers together, making a sort of cathedral, and stared at them. He was quiet for a long time, then gave the two young people a thoughtful look, saying, "I would not say these things to many people." A wry smile crossed his face. "Indeed, to do so would be to put my life at risk. However, I cannot deny you the answer you so earnestly seek, young Myles. So I will answer you and trust you—and the good Lord—to keep me safe."

He paused, then slowly went on, "Martin Luther is right. The pope and the church are wrong." He watched the shock come into their eyes and continued to observe them carefully. "I am sorry to shake your ideas so, but what Luther is protesting is the sale of 'indulgences.' Do you know what that is?"

"No, sir."

"'Tis simply the right to buy a license to sin. What I mean is," he explained, "that if you wish to commit a sin, then the present practices of the church allow you to go to a priest, pay him money, and he will hand you a piece of paper that grants you the right to commit your sin."

Myles's eyes grew wide with astonishment. "You don't mean, do you sir, that if I wanted to kill someone, I could buy the right to do it?"

"I fear that is exactly what it means," Tyndale replied with a shrug. "Although usually it is not a license to murder that people seek. Far more often, men buy the right to commit fornication or adultery, or especially to get drunk. These indulgences are hawked about Europe by monks who claim to be the servants of God." A chill look came into his eyes, and he said, "God is going to judge such a practice. And we shall see it in our lifetimes. Luther is only the first to speak out against these practices. He has already been joined by some, and sooner or later he will be joined by many. Then, young friends," he added sternly, "there will be a trying of the people of God, a crucible. Many, I fear, will not die in their beds but will have to die for the truth."

Something about Tyndale and his words frightened Myles, though he could not say why. The man was very pleasant and had a kind look in his eyes, but when he talked of death and dying and especially of the shaking up of the things in which Myles had always believed, it made him very nervous.

Seeing this, Tyndale said gently, "Well, we must talk of this again sometime. I hope you will come back, young man."

Myles, recognizing he was being dismissed, rose and bowed respectfully. "Thank you very much, Mr. Tyndale. I won't forget our visit."

When they were out of the room, he asked Hannah with some bewilderment, "What sort of man is he?"

"He is a teacher. And a preacher, too," Hannah answered rather proudly. "When he preaches, people come from all over the country to hear him. Some of the priests don't like him, though," she added. "They don't think Sir John ought to let Mr. Tyndale teach his children. But Sir John likes such things, and quite often he asks the priests to eat with the family and brings in William Tyndale—Just to torment them, I think."

They spent as much time together as possible without arousing suspicion, and all too soon it was time for bed. Early the next morning Cheval and Myles left Little Sodsbury. The last thing Myles saw was Hannah's bright honey-colored hair at the third story window, her hand outstretched. She waved frantically at him, and he waved back, then turned around and slumped in the wagon seat.

"I hate to go back," he said dispiritedly. "It was so much fun, coming here."

Cheval looked at him in surprise. "Fun? And why is it you say such, boy? Just another day's work."

But it had not been that for Myles, and he knew that he would never forget Little Sodsbury or Hannah or especially William Tyndale.

"You have been like a boy in a daze," Margred complained, standing over Myles as he sat at the rough table. He had come in to eat breakfast, which consisted of a piece of boiled mutton and some boiled wheat. But mostly he had been staring out the window.

"What's the matter with you?" she demanded. "Ever since you went to take that loom back you've been woolgathering around. What happened to you there, Myles?"

Myles flushed and took a bite of the boiled wheat. He swallowed, mumbling, "Oh, nothing." He knew he had been distracted ever since that trip. He could not decide whether it was the visit he had had with William Tyndale or the memory of Hannah that had made him absentminded in his manner and clumsy in his movements. He had been having dreams about both—one, a nightmare in which he dreamed he was being burned at the stake, as some of the heretics were, he had learned. He had awakened in a cold sweat, trembling, and could almost hear the flames crackle and feel the heat on his flesh. That had happened once. But he had dreamed of Hannah almost every night. Somehow that embarrassed him; he thought it was wrong, though he did not quite know why.

He gobbled his food down, then stood up, and, seeing that Margred was frowning at him, went over and gave her a hug. "Don't worry. Nothing is wrong with me."

She grunted as he squeezed her roughly, then smiled up at him. She was a small woman and took pride in this tall young son of hers. "All right, old man," she said, using her childhood nickname for him. "Off with you now. I'll have a bit of something good for your supper tonight."

All day Myles worked alongside Nob, putting the dogs and the hawks through training, caring for the horses, going out to work in the fields of Bourneville. At noon they came back and, feeling hot and sweaty, Myles went at once to the pump just outside the small shack where he lived with his mother. He had reached out for the handle when he heard a sharp cry inside and knew at once that it was his mother. He looked around, but Nob was not there. Quickly he ran to the door, jerked it open, and saw his mother being wrestled down to the floor by a young man that he had never seen before. Myles had learned long ago that it was Nob's protection that had kept the serfs from troubling his mother, but this man was no serf. He was, Myles knew instantly, of the upper class. He had black hair, very dark eyes, a black mustache, and wore a dagger at his side. "Get away, boy," he snarled.

Myles stepped inside saying, "Get out of here! Leave my mother alone!"

His words brought fury to the eyes of the intruder. He whipped his dagger out and screamed, "Get out of here, boy! Or I'll cut your throat!"

Margred struggled to her feet and tried to catch the man's arm. He swung his other arm and connected a sharp blow to her temple that drove her back against the wall, where she slumped helplessly.

The sudden blow drove Myles almost mad. A light of battle leaped into his eyes, and he shouted, "Get out! Get out!"

The black-haired man took one look at the tall boy, laughed harshly, and stepped forward, the dagger in his hand flashing as he made a sweep with it. The keen blade sliced into Myles's forearm, sending a cold sliver of pain along his nerves. But the thrust had thrown the man off balance and, ignoring the pain, Myles reached out and struck the man's wrist a violent blow. With a cry, the man snatched his arm back and the dagger fell to the earth floor. Like a hawk, Myles swooped and snatched it up, grabbed the man by the arm, and shoved him out the door. He followed him, holding the knife in front of him, saying through clenched teeth, "If you ever touch my mother again, I'll kill you!" His voice was a hiss, and he was unaware that people were running toward him. Anger had seized him in a steely grasp, and murder was in his eyes.

Then he heard a voice shouting, "Seize him! Grab him, you two!"

He whirled around to see Sir Geoffrey running across the yard, followed closely by several of the servants from the house. Immediately he realized what he had done, and his face turned pale. His arms were seized by two of the serfs, and Sir Geoffrey advanced and took the knife from his nerveless fingers. He glared at the boy, his face twisted with fury and rage. "You dare attack one of my guests!"

"He was—he was hurting my mother," Myles whispered.

"Shut your mouth!" Sir Geoffrey shouted. He turned to the man and asked, "Are you hurt, Ralph?"

"No, I'm all right," he answered sullenly. He turned his glittering gaze upon the boy. "I don't know what's wrong with the whelp. I just spoke to his mother, and he snatched my dagger out and came at me. Tried to kill me!"

There was another stranger there, a man who had come out with Sir Geoffrey and had stood silently watching and listening. He was about fifty and close to six feet tall. He had dark red hair and a stubborn face. A scar marked his left cheek, and a short beard and trim mustache adorned his face. He walked up and stared at Myles. He said nothing for a moment, just studied Myles's face. Then he shrugged and said, "Boy, you should know better than to do a thing like that." Then he turned and said, "Come, Ralph, we'll let Sir Geoffrey handle this."

The man called Ralph looked at Myles with bitterness burning in his eyes and said venomously, "I hope they take the skin off your back!" Then he turned on his heel and walked away with the older man.

Sir Geoffrey reached out one meaty hand and cuffed Myles across the face. He was so angry he could hardly speak. "How dare you attack a nobleman!" he spat. "Do you know what I could have done to you, boy? Do you know?"

"Please, please don't hurt him, Sir Geoffrey!" Margred came and put her arm around Myles, her eyes lifted to Sir Geoffrey's face pleadingly. "He was only trying to help me. That man lied! He was attacking me!"

Sir Geoffrey shook his head. He knew very well that what the woman said might be true, but he also knew that he had to keep the order that held his world together. If he started taking the word of a wench against the word of a knight or any of the nobility, the system would break down. Nevertheless, her words did cause him to make a quick adjustment in his mind.

"Here, here, I can't listen to that," he said hastily. "But I won't have the boy whipped." He thought for a moment, then said, "He must sit in the stocks for a few hours. And henceforth, keep yourself hid away or teach the boy better manners!" he blustered.

Instantly Myles said, "Please, Sir Geoffrey, I'd rather be whipped! Don't put me in the stocks!"

"Shut your mouth, boy," he said harshly. "It won't hurt you. You may get a few rotten tomatoes in the face, but 'tis better than having your back torn up. Besides, you wouldn't be able to work for a month if I put the cat to you!"

Later that afternoon Myles was taken by Thomas Ridley into the center of the village. The seneschal was sympathetic to the boy but didn't allow it to show in his face. When they got to the stocks, he motioned for the servants he had brought with him—two husky farmhands—to put the boy in them. Myles started to struggle, but to no avail. Soon his head, feet, and wrists were firmly secured. He was sitting on the ground, and waves of humiliation washed over him. When the two men stepped back, Ridley said coldly, "Be grateful, boy. This may hurt your feelings, but your hide will be whole. I'll be back at dusk to turn you loose."

Ridley turned and walked away, and one of the hands winked at Myles whispering, "Don't worry. They won't spoil your pretty face. It'll wash off."

They left and almost at once the villagers, always anxious for a break in the monotony, began to gather. Myles had known this would happen. He himself had stopped to look at people put in the stocks, sometimes for a simple thing such as gossiping, sometimes for breaking one of the game laws, sometimes for a more serious offense. But usually it was a minor thing that caused a man or a woman to be punished this way.

One of the small boys came up, grinning impudently into Myles's face. "Well now. I'm thinking I have just the thing for you." He walked over and picked up a flat board, then scooped some fresh manure off the ground. "How would you like to have this for supper?"

Myles kept his face impassive. He knew that nothing he could say would stop any of the abuse he was destined to suffer. Suddenly the boy flipped the odorous mass on his head so that it tumbled down over his face and ears. Laughter went up from the crowd, and ribald advice came loudly from the rougher elements.

I wish I were dead, Myles thought bitterly. *It would be better than this!* But there was no help for him. So he sat there, determined at least not to let them see how he felt.

All afternoon he bore his shame in silence. Though one or two people brought rotten vegetables to throw at his face, he was so stoic that there was no fun in it for them. Finally the sun began to go down, and Ridley appeared. He unlocked the stocks, released Myles, and said, "Now, go to the well and get yourself cleaned up. And mind you learn a lesson from this!"

Myles stumbled over to the well, drew a bucketful and dumped it over his head gratefully. He did so several times until he felt reasonably clean. Ridley was standing off to one side, and when the boy was finished, he said, "Come along now."

"I can find my way home," Myles said sullenly.

"That may be, but I have a few things to say to you."

Ridley turned and began walking toward the manor house. Myles had no choice but to follow. Ridley said nothing until they were halfway home. "I know what happened, Myles," he said. He looked down at the boy with compassion and added, "Ralph Geddes is a fornicator. Everyone knows that about him."

Myles looked up at him. "That was wrong, what he tried to do to my mother!" he blurted out.

"Yes, it was," Ridley agreed. "But it was also wrong what you did, drawing a knife on him."

"I don't think it was," Myles retorted with spirit.

"Then you had better learn to think differently, boy," Ridley snapped. "Otherwise you'll find yourself hanging from a gallows someday. Do you know how much chance you would have in a court against a man like Geddes? No more chance than a coney in an open field!" He stopped and gripped Myles by the shoulders, whipping him around. "Look, Myles! Listen to me! That is how the world is. There are men like Geddes, who have the power; there are men like you, who don't. Even my word wouldn't mean a thing against Sir Geoffrey of Bourneville. You know that, don't you? If I should pull a knife on him, for any reason, I would die for it just as surely as if I had murdered a hundred people—even if I didn't shed a drop of his blood. So make up your mind to it. You're what you are, and nothing in the world can change it."

The two stood there—the older man, his face tense, gripping Myles by the shoulders; the boy, silent, keeping his head bowed. He had been flayed to the very spirit by the humiliation of being in the stocks. Although he had known others who had laughed about such treatment, he knew he never would. Nor would he ever forget the shame he'd felt that day.

He lifted his head, and the seneschal saw there was almost a flinty quality in the boy's blue-gray eyes. "I would rather die than give in," Myles said slowly.

Ridley was disturbed. He had seen such rebels before, and every one of them had come to a bad end. He tried to think of something to say that might change the look on the boy's face, but the stubborn set of the jaw, the pugnacious chin, and the cold light of anger in his eyes convinced him it was useless.

"Think of your mother," he sighed. "You can't help her if you're a corpse dangling from a rope."

And with that, he left the boy standing there.

Five

THE KING'S
TOURNAMENT

Myles's first glimpse of London was not particularly pleasant. He was riding in a wagon at the last of the procession that had made its way to the city from Harrow, Sir Bourneville's estate. He had been surprised to be chosen as a part of the procession, for in the year that had passed since he had been clapped in the stocks, Sir Geoffrey had watched him closely. Now he was sixteen, though he looked more like twenty, and had been given the honor of accompanying the procession going to the king's tournament, which was held just outside London.

As they passed over London Bridge, Myles was shocked to see a series of poles, each of them carrying a human head. His stomach rolled over a little, and he said to Percy, "Look!"

Percy Bourneville had been to London several times and enjoyed being the sophisticate. "Oh, those are traitors' heads," he said grandly, waving a hand carelessly in the direction of the grisly artifacts. "They got a fresh one or two, I see."

Try as he might, Myles could not be quite so nonchalant, and so he fell quiet as the two rode along. Percy, now sixteen, was not quite as overweight as he had been as a boy, but still he filled his clothes out rather plumply. Myles, on the other hand, was lean and muscular. Despite his age, he was accounted a man by all and had done a man's full work for several years.

After living in the tiny village, everything about the city seemed enormous to Myles. As they left the bridge, they were caught up in a world that hummed and buzzed with activity. Carts and coaches made such a thundering that it seemed all the world was on wheels. At every corner, they encountered throngs of men and women, some in the sooty rags of chimney sweeps, others in array of gold, others wearing gaudy satin. Some of the people were carried in sedan chairs borne by lackeys with thick legs. Porters sweated under their burdens; chapmen darted from shop to shop; and tradesmen scurried along like ants, pulling at the coats of prospective buyers, who fought their way through the human tide that flowed and ebbed on the street.

"Watch yourself!" Percy shouted, hopping down out of the wagon and motioning to Myles, who followed him. "Look what they've done! They've put a drain in the street!" He pointed to a ditch about a foot wide and six inches deep in the center of the cobblestone street. "That carries all the slops and garbage away quite nicely, you know. Isn't it a wonder what a change modern improvements make! Why, most cities just let the filth pile up until it's cleared away by rain. But not London, no sir!"

All afternoon Myles worked with the other servants who had come, getting ready for the gala jousting on the following day.

And then, though he said nothing, it finally happened: He caught Isabella Bourneville's attention.

Isabella, at seventeen, was a real beauty. She had long blonde hair and green eyes and was tall like her mother and (many said) was almost as proud. Myles had watched her over the years, always admiring, always longing—for he believed her to be the most perfect girl who ever had graced the earth. But her world was far above his, and so he contented himself with merely adoring her from afar.

Now he was carrying a heavy trunk to rooms above a series of small shops, where the family was to stay during their time in

London. Isabella watched him come in, and he set the trunk down and looked at her shyly. He had been looking at her shyly for several years now. She already had more suitors than some girls had in a lifetime, and Myles was quick enough to perceive that she enjoyed it all.

"If you need help, Miss Isabella," he said lamely, "I'll be somewhere around."

Isabella smiled at him, her eyes gleaming with exhilaration. "Isn't it wonderful, Myles? Did you ever feel such excitement?" She threw herself down into a chair and clasped her hands together most passionately. "Oh, I wish we lived in London! There's nothing at all in Harrow! Nothing at all! I shall die of boredom there!"

"Well," Myles said with a shrug, "you won't die of boredom here, not with the tournament tomorrow. You'll get to see the king!"

"Yes! And some of those handsome courtiers he keeps in his court," Isabella said with rapture. She looked at Myles. "If you're to find yourself a woman, you'd better do it behind Father's back. He doesn't like servants visiting the sties, going after common women."

Myles's face flamed at her blunt speech. "I won't be doing that." He turned to leave, his face a dark red. But she caught him at the door and pulled him around, laughing.

"Oh, poor, poor Myles! I've tormented you, have I not? I always did, no?" She reached up and ran her hand through his crisp auburn hair, then pulled the front of it so it came down in a point on his forehead. "I always did love that widow's peak! I wish I had one." She searched his face and patted his cheek. "Don't be upset, Myles. I didn't mean to torment you. I know you are a good, pure, wholesome young man. Go to church every Sunday, don't you? Sometimes more than that!"

Myles gazed down at her, remembering how they had been

playmates as children. Now . . . now Isabella had gone to a sphere as far away from him as the moon in the sky. For the last several years, he had carefully hidden his adulation of her from everyone else, doing his utmost to appear diffident when she was around. When others commended her beauty or her grace, he had never added one word of approval.

Now here she was, holding onto his arm, and he thought he would explode with the emotions that swelled within his young breast. He inhaled the sweet scent she wore and wondered what it was, and he studied the smoothness of her cheeks, thinking that he had never seen anything so beautiful.

She stood placidly, watching him admire her, taking it as her due, then shoved at him. "Get out of here now, Myles. I'm going to change clothes."

He stumbled from the room and went downstairs, where he found Cheval unloading more gear. Shaking his head to clear it, he bent to pick up the heaviest burden he could find, throwing himself into the backbreaking work with a vengeance!

They finished unloading before dark, and Myles wondered what to do now. All the other servants had been to London before and were rather blasé, but he was almost dancing with excitement. The master had given them each a coin to spend, and it was burning a hole in the young man's purse. He went to find Sir Geoffrey, and when he located him, he said, "Sir Geoffrey, everything is unloaded. Would it be all right if I walked around the streets a little?"

Sir Geoffrey looked at him and grinned. Despite the incident with Ralph Geddes, he had grown fond of Myles. He knew he was a hardworking, intelligent young man. "I know what you're up to, boy," he said with a twinkle in his eye. He reached into his pocket and pulled out another coin and said, "There. And watch out you don't come down with the pox! You're no good to me lying up in a bed somewhere. Off with you now."

"Thank you, Sir Geoffrey! I'll be back pretty soon."

"I doubt that," Sir Geoffrey laughed roughly. "Just be here early in the morning. I don't want to be getting you out of jail for some stunt!"

Fingering his new wealth, Myles walked the streets of London with great anticipation. He was enthralled with the narrow structures, half-timbered and high-storied, lining the street. Pubs and shops occupied the ground floors, while innkeepers and tradesmen lived up over them for the most part. Myles walked until it grew dark and then turned to go back to where he was staying.

He was almost there when a feminine voice called out, "Hello, handsome!"

He wheeled and saw a young woman standing there. Myles had never seen a woman before with so much paint on her face or a gown cut so daringly low. He stared at her until she laughed and walked over to him. Reaching up, she pinched his earlobe sharply. "My! Aren't you the handsome one, though!"

Myles was absolutely at a loss for words. Finally he stammered, "I–I'm just a visitor. I've never been to London before."

"Is that right, ducky?" the girl said, and her crimson lips turned up in a smile. She released his ear and grabbed his arm familiarly. "Ain't it lucky now that you and me got here together! I'm a visitor meself, don't you know."

"Really?" Myles said eagerly, looking at the buildings around them. "I've never seen anything like this before. It certainly is different than the farm. Where are you from?"

"Oh, up north," the woman said airily. "Me name's Polly. What might yours be?" She chattered on, gently leading Myles, and—though he was oblivious to it—a calculating look was on her face. "Ain't that lucky, that we met? Could you do with something to drink?"

"I guess so." Myles felt the weight of the two coins in his

pocket and glanced at her. The image of Isabella flitted through his mind, and he shook it away. She was out of his reach, as unattainable as the stars. While this woman . . . this woman was of his station. *She looks like she would know places to go and things to do. I don't suppose it would hurt to have a drink.*

The girl led him to a pub, and for the next hour or so, they laughed and talked. Myles had not known he was so witty, but it seemed that the more of the strong wine he drank, the funnier he became. And the girl across from him responded with more and more raucous laughter. It wasn't long before Myles's vision grew blurred. But Polly kept saying, "Let's have us another one, Myles! After all, we're only young once, ain't we now?"

She had moved close to him at the table, and he felt her press against him. From time to time, she would turn and hug him, and when she pressed against him, his tongue became even thicker. He knew he should leave, but he was fascinated.

Finally he grew very sleepy, and Polly said, "Why, you're about to go to sleep! Tell you what," she whispered, "I've a place of me own. You can lie down there. Come along, sweetheart."

Myles remembered later stumbling along, his stomach cramping a little from the unaccustomed liquor. When the girl led him to a hovel by an alley and opened the door, he saw there was only one bed and a few articles of furniture. She stepped inside, turned up the lamp, and came toward him.

As Myles watched her approach, it seemed that the amber light of the lantern flared in her eyes and that the room was reeling. She reached over and shoved him so that he sat down abruptly on the bed.

She smiled slowly. "We'll have a good time, won't we, ducky!"

Alarmed, Myles struggled to his feet. "No!" he blurted out, then his face flamed as she stared at him in surprise. Brushing her aside, he staggered to the door and pulled it open. Turning back, he blinked his eyes, trying to see clearly. But all he could see was the blurry form of the girl, standing with her arms crossed, watching him with interest.

"I'm—I'm sorry." He forced the words past his slow tongue. "Hafta go." And with that, he stumbled from the room and out into the night. He made his way down the alley and to the street, where his groggy mind struggled to remember where he needed to go.

But the alcohol haze would not let him go, and he staggered along the dark and dirty backstreets uncertainly, until at last the world seemed to spin around him and he felt himself falling. He landed with a thud and lay there, unable to move, until the merciful darkness finally took him over.

"Where in the world did you disappear to last night?" Cheval asked the next morning. They were harnessing the horses, and though Cheval was not usually observant, he could not miss the boy's pale face and trembling hands. "You ain't coming down with the plague, are you boy?" he demanded fearfully.

"N-no," Myles muttered. "Guess I ate something that didn't suit my stomach too well." He finished harnessing the horses and tried to put the thoughts of the previous evening out of his mind. Not that he remembered much of the night, not clearly anyway. When he searched his memory, there were only flashes of Polly's face . . . and the sensation of falling. . . .

What was clear in his mind was the morning, when he had awakened in an alley outside of town with no gold coins at all, a splitting headache, and a tongue that felt like it was made out of wood. And ill-tasting wood, at that.

Myles hurried to finish his task as Sir Geoffrey came down the stairs, accompanied by Ralph Geddes. Geddes glanced at him and said nothing, but a tightening of his lips told Myles clearly that the fellow had never forgotten what had happened between them.

What Myles didn't know was that Geddes had tried several times to encourage Sir Geoffrey to get rid of him. But Bourneville was not one to so easily let go of a bargain. Since Myles had become adept at all the work of the manor, he had only laughed at Geddes, saying, "Just don't pull a knife on him, Ralph, and maybe you'll be all right."

Lady Bourneville and Isabella soon came down to the carriage, too, and the servants followed. They threaded their way through the business district and joined a stream of traffic composed of pedestrians, horsemen, and carriages and wagons of all sorts. Finally they saw the flags whipping from the poles that surrounded the jousting field.

"Now you'll see something," Cheval said to Myles. "I seen a tournament once. We came three years ago. The knights get on their horses and take long spears and ride right at each other. One of them got killed the time I seen it!"

After the Bournevilles disembarked from their carriages, Myles and Cheval took the vehicles some distance away from the field and secured the horses. Cheval said, "You go see some of it, boy, if you want to. I seen it before, and if you see one joust, you've seen them all."

"Thanks, Cheval." Myles grinned and hurried back to where the tournament was about to begin.

Tournaments were more popular with the nobility than they had ever been, but they were becoming more and more removed from the reality of war. Steps were taken to minimize the risks by dressing the jousters in heavy suits of armor, with a helmet that covered the entire face, except for narrow slits for the nose and eyes.

Myles joined the crowd of retainers and squires at one end of the field. In the center, he saw a wooden barrier, a fence about four feet high that ran the length of the field. Even as he watched, one knight approached each end, each carrying a lance.

The colors were beautiful. All of the noble houses' pennants flew in front of their seats, and the air sparkled with reds, blues, yellows, greens. The dresses of the ladies and the ornate costumes of the gentlemen sparkled in the setting. At that moment a trumpet rang out and a man rode down the line of the barrier, stopping in the middle to call out something, but Myles was too far away to hear it. The man then slowly rode away, and the two knights spurred their horses forward.

Myles watched, his breath held, as the two approached each other. He expected the spears to pierce the two riders, but suddenly they turned their spears at a right angle, and each attempted to sweep the other off his horse. Both of them were shaken by the blows they received, but neither was unhorsed.

There were many jousts and other ceremonies, and then someone cried out, "The king! It's the king!" Myles looked quickly and saw an enormous white horse being led out by a small groom. Sitting on the huge animal's back was a large man in a suit of armor that looked almost pure silver as it flashed in the sunlight.

"It's the king!" the whisper went around.

A knight dressed entirely in black appeared at the other end of the field and sat waiting. The same rider from the first game appeared in the center of the field at the barrier and announced, "And now, Our Gracious Lord and Sovereign will enter into the lists and manifest his knightly skill."

Myles watched almost with fear as the signal was given, and the king threw his horse at a fast pace toward the other knight, who was approaching in the same manner. This time, Myles saw, there would be no "sweeping." Both riders kept their lances level, and they came together with a tremendous crash in the center of the run. Both men's wooden lances shattered, and the black knight fell off his horse with a ringing clatter of armor.

The king wheeled his horse and rode back to where the

members of the court were assembled, stopped, and bowed his head as the crowd went wild.

"Well, there weren't no question about *that* match, were there now?"

Myles turned to see a tall, heavyset merchant of some sort standing directly behind him. The man, who had a smile on his face, went on, "I've been watching the king joust for several years and somehow he never loses. Doesn't it make a body think, now?"

"He's so good at it, isn't he?"

The amused brown eyes of the merchant fell on Myles, and he took in the crude clothes, which immediately identified the country origins of the boy. "Well, he's right fair. But I'm thinking that no knight with good sense would unhorse the king. Wouldn't be courtly, now would it?" The man chuckled and ambled off, leaving Myles to ponder his words.

He wandered through the crowd, thinking about what the man had said. He wanted to get closer to the nobility so he could have something to tell his mother when he got back. At length, he worked his way to the foot of the elevated seats where Queen Catherine sat with a group of courtiers and noblemen, all of whom were dressed in rich clothing. He stared at the queen in wonder, remembering what he had been told of Henry's bride. She had been married to his brother Arthur, but when Arthur died, Henry, for whatever reason, chose to marry her himself. She was an attractive woman but had not given Henry VIII the son he so desperately needed.

He remained there for a time, seeing Isabella and Percy in their seats, then went back to where the rest of the retainers were standing.

All day he was at the beck and call of Sir Geoffrey, but there was really nothing for him to do. Later he drove one of the carriages back to the inn, deposited the family, then put the carriage up. They would be leaving in a few days, and he did not know what to do with himself in the meantime. He wandered back through the city, going down the back streets, listening to the polyglot of languages. When it grew dark he started toward home.

Perhaps it was unconscious, perhaps not. In any case, he passed by the same pub where he had encountered Polly the day before. Sure enough, there she was.

"Well, ducky," she said, grinning impudently, "change yer mind, did ye?" She winked at him and posed suggestively. "What say we make a night of it?"

Myles's face flamed, and he said sharply, "I don't have any money." He knew now that she was a harlot, a fact that had left him uneasy. He had heard how many of these women carried the strange disease called "the pox"—an affliction that could kill a man—and he wondered if just being in her filthy room was enough for him to be infected.

She came to lean against him, slipping her arm through his. He tried to pull away, but she held on. "Come along, ducky. I'll show you how we might have some fun." He resisted a moment longer, then gave in. All he wanted to do was have a little fun. Surely that couldn't be wrong. He wouldn't let things get so out of hand tonight.

He followed her toward the tavern, pausing for a moment when the image of his mother flitted into his mind. Would she want him coming into a place such as this? But before he could ponder these thoughts out, Polly grasped his arm again and looked at him beseechingly.

"Come on, ducky. You wouldn't want me to have to sit alone, now would you? Nothin' worse in the world than bein' alone."

At the plaintive look on her face, Myles felt his resistance weaken. What could be wrong in keeping the woman company? Hadn't his mother always urged him to be kind to those he met? So thinking, he allowed Polly to lead him into the tavern.

They found a table and sat down. Since he had no money,

Myles reluctantly took the ale that Polly bought for him and drank it slowly. *I won't get drunk tonight,* he said to himself. Somehow, though, the ale kept coming, and the air grew close as the tavern filled up with revelers.

Polly was watching the clientele closely, and shortly after nine o'clock, she nudged Myles with her elbow. "Look, ducky. There's the one we want."

He looked where she directed and saw a man sitting at a nearby table. "Who's he?" Myles asked, befuddled.

"He's the one who'll pay for the ale you've been drinking—" she laughed coarsely and nudged him again—"and for what you'll be getting afterward. Let's go."

Myles stumbled to his feet and had to catch at the table, for the room suddenly swam. She laughed at him and helped him outside, then said, "Quiet now. There's our coney." She pulled Myles along, and the boy saw that the man she referred to was so drunk he could hardly walk.

"Now then. You stay close," Polly whispered, "and when I call for you, you come in the alley." She walked away, and Myles was too woozy to understand what she had said.

Oh, *why* had he kept drinking that wretched ale? His head pounded and his stomach roiled and he was sure he would fall on his face any minute. To distract himself, he watched closely as Polly approached the man. He stopped with a foolish grin on his face when she hailed him cheerily, and the two disappeared into a very narrow alleyway between two buildings. Almost immediately, Myles heard Polly crying out. Thinking she was in trouble, he ran across the street and plunged into the dark alley—where he found Polly struggling with the man, who started to yell.

"Shut him up, boy! Are you a fool?" Polly snapped.

Instantly Myles knew he was in trouble, and he ran up and put his hand over the man's mouth and held him easily. He was a small man, and Myles's muscles were like steel from the years of hard labor. Polly reached out, and Myles saw a blade in her hand—for one horrified moment, he thought she meant to stab the man.

"Don't do that!" he cried out.

Instead, she reached out with her free hand, caught the purse around their victim's waist, and slashed at the cord that held it. When it was free, she looked at Myles, her eyes glittering. "Put him out now, or he'll tell the world what's happened!"

"What do you mean?"

"Knock him out, you fool!" With that, she turned and ran away.

In confusion, Myles shoved the man away from him and ran after her. He caught up with her just as the man began to shout. Polly cursed Myles roundly, using words he had never heard before. Finally she hissed, "Come on! If we're caught, it's Old Bailey for us, and I'd rather die than go to that place!"

At the mention of the prison, about which Myles had heard horrific tales of men and women dying from starvation and torture, he cast a fearful look over his shoulder, then began to run.

They cut through another alleyway and wound their way through a part of the city that she seemed to know well. After what seemed like hours, but in reality only took minutes, they arrived at the same house he had been in the night before.

Polly said, "Come on in, boy. Fool ye may be, but who isn't?" When Myles hesitated, she looked up at him, surprise on her face. "What's the matter with you? Oh!" she said. "You want some of the loot, is that it?"

"No, I don't want any money," Myles said abruptly. He turned to go, and she caught his shoulder and pulled him around. She had been a pretty girl once and still would have been except for the hardness in her face. His refusal to take money had thrown her off guard, and she said more gently, "Oh there now, ducky, don't be angry. Come on. You can lie down a bit until you get your wits back."

But the light in her eyes convinced him that rest was not what

she had in mind. Myles knew he should never have come here
. . . and put out a firm hand to release himself from Polly's grip
and walk away. Drunk again he might be. But that was as far as
his mistakes would take him.

He staggered down the dark London streets, his hand to his
throbbing head, and by the time he reached his lodgings, he
heartily wished he had never heard of anyone named Polly. He
washed his head in the bucket on the back side of the inn and
crept shamefacedly into the loft over the horses' stalls.

The next morning, his head pounded and his mood was surly
at best. He tried to avoid the family, but Isabella, coming out with
Percy, took one look at him and began to laugh. "Look, Percy!
From the looks of him, I'd guess Myles had a wild night. What do
you think?"

Percy grinned knowingly and said, "You'll be sorry, old boy!"

The sister and brother wandered off, but for the remainder of
their days in London, they made jokes of Myles's "wild nights"
and of his woman chasing.

Myles was glad when the trip was over. He had endured Percy's
and Isabella's teasing silently, but he grew weary of it. When the
entourage departed London and arrived back at Harrow, he went
quickly to find his mother. He found Nob sitting outside their
little shack. As Myles approached, the small man got up at once.

"I have bad news for you, Myles," he said slowly. "Your mother
has taken bad sick."

Something in the man's face frightened Myles, and he asked
with dread, "It's not the plague, is it?"

"I don't know what it is," Nob said. "Looks more like the
sweating sickness to me." Myles felt a cold fear clutch his heart,
for this was a disease that had cursed England several times with
a virulence second only to that of the Black Death. The victim,
struck down and immobile, would burn up with fever. If the
patient lasted three days, it usually meant he would live.

"How long has she had it?"

"She come down yesterday, boy," Nob said gravely. "I'm thinking we'd better get the apothecary or someone who knows healing. She's not looking good to me."

Myles's face had grown pale, and without another word he stepped into the house and went to the cot where his mother lay. She was unconscious, he saw, and drenched with sweat. He touched her forehead and closed his eyes in despair; she felt as though she were on fire!

Slowly he sank to the floor beside her, holding her hand in his, and tried to pray. But all he could think of was, *God is doing this because of what I did in London. It's all my fault.*

Six

THE BROOCH

C ome now, lad," Nob said gently, pressing his hand on Myles's shoulder. "Lie you down and try to get a little sleep." He looked over toward where the woman lay motionless on the cot. "She'll not know, and I'll stay right here beside her. Should she wake, I'll get you at once."

Myles shook his head stubbornly. He had slept little the past two days. Yet, though his eyes were grainy and his knees trembled from weakness, he said, "No. I won't."

Nob gnawed his underlip and stared at Margred Morgan's pale face. "I heard of an herb woman over in the next village. They say she does wondrous things."

Myles looked up at him. "She's no better than the one we have here. I don't think any of them are any good," he said bitterly.

Privately Nob agreed. The old woman who had come the previous day had brought some kind of nauseating concoction that she had forced down Margred's throat. As far as Nob could tell, the only effect it had was that of making her worse. She had thrown up after gagging horribly, then had lapsed back into the coma.

Shaking his head, Nob sat with Myles quietly, wishing he could think of something to do.

But there was little to do. There were no antiseptics. The only prescription that most doctors had for almost anything was bleeding, and Nob had never seen any sense in that. Studying the face of the boy, he sighed wearily. "I'll go lie down for a bit. When I get up, I'll make some soup. Maybe she'll eat a little of it."

Myles nodded silently, never taking his eyes off his mother. When the falconer left the house, Myles got up from the box that served for a chair and stretched. He walked over to the window and stared outside, marveling that somehow it was still beautiful. The sun was shining, the birds were singing, and overhead, in the azure sky, white fleecy clouds drifted by. He turned back to his mother, and the fear that had been growing in him ever since he had returned from London seemed to creep through his veins.

He slumped down on the box again, leaned over, and put his head on the edge of the cot. Once again he tried to pray. But he could not. Instead, the same horrible thought came to him that had assailed him again and again: *Your mother is dying because of you and the wicked things you did!* He tried to blot out his guilt, and bitter tears of grief rose to his eyes, but the feeling only grew worse.

The chaplain of the Bournevilles had come by early in the afternoon of the previous day, said a quick prayer, and then left. This had discouraged Myles as much as anything, for he had seen the obvious doubt in the churchman's eye. The man had already given up his mother for dead!

Unfortunately, Myles was a boy with a vivid imagination. Others of the serfs had grown to take death much as they had taken other misfortunes—sometimes they hardly seemed to grieve. But Myles could not envision a future that did not contain his mother. . . . She was all he had ever had, and the thought of losing her paralyzed him. It seemed to rise in his throat with sourness, and he quickly closed his eyes and ground the heels of his hands into them, rubbing them hard, trying to erase the image of his mother's death. Fear had become some sort of an evil, ugly monster that crept into his body and squeezed his heart with cold hands, leaving him shaky and trembling all over.

He leaned over, pressing his face against his forearm, and even in such an awkward position fatigue caught up with him and he dozed into a fitful sleep. He awakened with a start when he heard his name called, and he looked up to see his mother was awake.

"Mother!" he cried and picked up her hand. "You're awake!"

Margred's eyes were sunk back in her head, and when she tried to speak, the only sound that came from her dry lips was a rasping wheeze.

"Here, take some water." Myles got the cup and poured fresh water into it, then gently held her up. She grasped at the cup and managed a few thirsty swallows, then lay back, breathing hard. She was wringing wet with sweat. No matter what they did, the fever would not go away. "How do you feel?" he asked anxiously.

Margred looked up at him in the dim light, saw the lines on his face, and reached up one hand to touch his cheek. "How are you, Myles?" she murmured. Her hand lingered on his cheek, soothing it, then the hand seemed to fall back from lack of strength. She took a deep breath and closed her eyes.

"Mother, try to stay awake. I'll fix you something to eat."

"I couldn't eat anything," she said slowly. Every word seemed difficult for her. Then after a while she seemed to grow more alert. "Help me to sit up," she said.

He pulled her up in the bed so that she was leaning against the pillow, a sack that had been stuffed with old rags. He gently touched her face, then ran his hand down her hair, which fell down her back. She seemed to grow a little stronger, and a light came to her face. "I'm very sick, Myles," she said.

"We're going to the next village," Myles said quickly. "There is a woman there who knows a lot about medicines, and we're going to bring her here, Nob and me. She'll have something to make you well."

Margred Morgan watched her son fondly, yet with a touch of fear. She already knew that she would not live, although she did not say so. She began talking about their early days in Wales, when he was a child, and as she talked she seemed to grow even stronger.

Myles listened to her, put in a word from time to time, and tried to smile. But the fear and guilt that had haunted him for the past few days had left him raw emotionally. He hated to see her looking so wan, so weak. She had always been so pretty; now she seemed almost gaunt. And there was a strange look in her eyes, as though she were looking past him, at something beyond their world.

Oh God! Myles cried out in his heart. *Don't let me lose her!* He struggled to conceal his turbulent emotions, but he could not. With a groan he laid his head on his mother's chest and sobbed. He felt her hand, feather-light, smoothing his hair comfortingly, and he heard her soft voice saying, "Oh, my dear son, don't be afraid. You will not be alone. You have our Lord God to care for you."

At that he looked up, stricken. "No, Mother! God will not care for me, he will not hear me. Not after all the terrible things I have done!"

Margred's tired eyes scanned her son's face with tender concern. "What have you done, Myles?" she finally asked in a quiet, gentle voice.

His heart reviled against telling her, but he knew this might be his last chance to ask her forgiveness, and he could not let that go. Slowly, his head bowed in shame, he told her all about his journey to London. When he had finished, he was afraid to look up, afraid to see the pain in her eyes.

Margred reached out and touched his cheek, and at her touch his eyes flew to meet hers—and found only understanding and love there.

"Oh, Mother!" he said in a low voice filled with despair, "I am sorry! How can you . . . how can God forgive me?"

She smiled gently. "I can forgive you, dear son, because I see your repentance and because I love you. And is not God more loving and forgiving than we? Is not his love deeper and more lasting than ours?"

His eyes searched hers, a faint glow of hope beginning to burn within him. She went on, "Ah, Myles, the Lord God has promised to forgive a heart that is truly repentant, a heart that seeks his face and his grace with all that is in it. Do you believe God will do as he promised?" Myles could not speak; he only nodded. "Then, my son, let us go to the Lord together and ask him to stand by his promise."

As Margred began to pray, Myles bowed over one of her hands, and she lifted the other and put it on his head, resting it lightly on his auburn hair. As she prayed, his eyes began to burn with tears and a wave of emotion swept over him. Suddenly, he felt lighter, set free from the guilt that had been hounding him since London—as though he'd been bathed and cleansed.

Finally she said, "Amen and amen." He lifted his head and looked at her, his eyes shining.

"Thank you, Mother."

"Thank God, Myles," she replied. Then she reached up to hold his face framed between her hands, as she had often done when he was a very small boy. She held him there, looking at him hungrily, as if he were a picture of some kind that she was trying to fix in her memory. Then she said, "Always remember, my son, that God is there for you, as he has been for me. You need only to call on him with all your heart and he will answer."

"I will remember," Myles vowed softly.

She nodded, satisfied, then dropped her hands and rested them on her breast. She closed her eyes for a moment, and quick alarm filled him at the paleness of her features. He remained silent, waiting.

"You must do something for me, Myles," she said after a few moments.

"Anything, Mother. What is it?"

"Go over to that corner. Beneath all those old sacks you'll find my little box."

He knew the box well, although he did not know what was in it. She had brought it with her all the way from Wales and usually kept it well hidden, for serfs had so little privacy she was afraid someone would take it. He went to pull it out from underneath the ragged sacks that covered it. It was small, no more than six inches square and less than two inches deep, cunningly made out of some kind of wood that he did not recognize, and was almost red in color. It had been painstakingly polished and was glossy and felt satiny to his touch. He brought it over and handed it to her. "Here it is, Mother."

Margred took the box, running her fingers over it lovingly. Turning it over she said, "Look, Myles. You see this little spot right here? When you press it, it opens." She demonstrated. There was a click, and the top swung back. She smiled faintly at his look of amazement and said, "My father made it. He could make such wondrous things."

Myles looked at it curiously and said, "I wish I could do that."

Margred reached inside, and he saw several pieces of paper. Then she pulled out an object. She held her fingers around it for a moment so that he could not see it, then she slowly opened her hand. There, in her open palm, rested a beautiful brooch. It had a green stone in the center, with tiny white pearls set around it on little points of gold. Margred looked at it and said softly, "You must take this . . . to Sir Robert Wakefield."

Myles could have been no more surprised if she had told him he must take it to the moon. "But Mother! That's so far away! It would take all day to get there and get back, and I don't want to leave you."

"I'll be all right. The Lord has promised me that," she said.

"But—why? Whose is this?"

"You will know, Myles, in due time." Margred was very tired. She took his hand, put the brooch in it, and closed his fingers around it. "Now, promise me that you will show this to no one except Sir Robert. And you will somehow find him when he is alone. You will show it to him, and you will tell him where you got it. I think," she said quietly, "he may want to come and see me." Then suddenly she was overcome with weariness and her speech became slurred. "Go now! And hurry, hurry . . ."

Myles stared down at his mother and saw that she was once again unconscious. He hurried out to find Nob and said urgently, "My mother is sending me on an errand. I'll be back as soon as I can. Watch out for her, Nob."

He didn't even wait for an answer from the astonished huntsman, but turned and almost ran to the big house. He asked for Sir Geoffrey, but was told that he was not there. In desperation he sought out Thomas Ridley, the seneschal. "Please, sir," he said hurriedly, "I need to leave for a short trip."

"I thought your mother was sick," Ridley said suspiciously.

"Yes, sir, she is. She wants me to go see someone and perhaps bring them back here. But I can't go unless Sir Geoffrey lets me."

"He's gone to Hastings and won't be back for two weeks at least." The steady eyes of the seneschal studied the boy. "You'll be back when?"

"Probably tomorrow, sir."

Something in the boy's pleading eyes touched the older man, and he said gruffly, "All right, boy. Begone. I'll look in on your mother tonight."

"Thank you, sir."

Myles quickly left the village and started out on the road. He had always been active and a good walker, though he was exhausted from missing two nights' sleep. He had not gone more than three miles when a wagon came rumbling by, headed in the same direction. The man sitting on the seat examined Myles carefully. As he drew even with him he stopped the horses saying, "You there! Boy!"

"Yes, sir?" Myles stepped up to the wagon and recognized the driver. His name was Crawley and he lived on a neighboring estate.

"You're the boy what works with the dogs, ain't you? For Sir Geoffrey?"

"Yes, sir. I know you, Mr. Crawley," he said. "I remember you from the hunt Sir Geoffrey took you on, autumn last."

Satisfaction filled Crawley's eyes, and he said, "Good enough. Where you going, boy?"

"I'm going to the home of Sir Robert Wakefield."

"Are you now? Then hop up here and you can ride most of the way. I'm on a trip in that direction myself. And you can tell me some more about how to train a kestrel. I've got one and I can't do a blessed thing with her. Climb up, boy." He waited until Myles was sitting in the wagon beside him, spoke briskly to the horses, and then said, "Now. The problem is that this bird stoops before she gets to a proper height . . ."

Sir Robert Wakefield was reading in his study when one of the servants, a diminutive, dark-haired woman of twenty, came to the door and said, "My lord, there is a young man who says he must see you."

"A young man? What young man?"

"I dunno, sir. I've never seen him before. But he says he must see you just for one minute. Do you wish for me to send him on his way?" The maid sniffed disdainfully. "He ain't nothing but a common boy."

As it happened, Wakefield was tired of the work he was doing at the desk. This could prove an interesting diversion. He threw his book down, stretched, and said, "No, I will see him. It may be about one of the horses or such. You don't know him, you say?"

"No, sir. He's at the back, though. Got red hair, he has."

"All right." Wakefield headed for the back door. He was a busy man, and people often came to tell him something concerning the estate or to seek his help. So it did not seem too out of the ordinary for a poor young fellow to come to the back door. He passed through the house, stepped outside, and immediately recognized the young man. He said with surprise, "I know you. Your name is . . . it's . . ."

"Myles Morgan, Sir Robert."

"Oh yes. You're the young fellow that Sir Geoffrey brought to the tournament in London. Pulled a knife on Mr. Geddes, if I recollect rightly."

Myles nodded and said shortly, "Yes, sir." He could not think of how to approach this business and stood awkwardly, racking his brain.

"Well, what is it, boy? Speak up," Sir Robert said, not unkindly. "Did Sir Geoffrey send you with a message?"

"No, my lord. Sir Geoffrey, he's in Hastings. I . . . I've . . . I have something to show you."

"Something to show me? Something you wish to sell, perhaps?" Sir Robert said, raising his eyebrows.

"Oh no, sir. I don't want to sell it, I just want you to look at it, if you don't mind, sir."

"All right, let's have it, boy." Sir Robert stood as the boy approached and watched him plunge his hand into a small bag that he wore belted around his waist. The boy extended his hand, fist closed, then the fingers relaxed.

"What is—" Sir Robert broke off with a quick intake of breath. Myles could see a change in the man's face, and he couldn't tell if it was anger or not. Myles stood motionless, his hand held out, the brooch glittering in his palm. Sir Robert slowly picked it up, then held it in his own palm, staring at it.

There was a long silence in the yard. There was a faint noise of chickens clucking, and far away the wild cry of a hawk sounded. But there was no word spoken by either of the two. Myles was too frightened to speak, wondering if he had done something terrible, and the man stared at the brooch in his hand as if in a dream.

Finally Sir Robert looked up and stared at the boy, and when he spoke, his voice was hoarse. "Where did you get this?"

"It belongs to my mother, sir."

"Your mother?" Sir Robert looked down at the piece of jewelry again, and Myles could see that the nobleman's big hand was actually trembling. "Who is your mother?" Sir Robert asked.

"Her name is Margred. Margred Morgan," Myles answered, almost in a whisper.

Sir Robert blinked and asked instantly, "She sent this to me? Why?"

Myles swallowed hard and had to try twice before he could speak. "I think—I think she is dying," he said hollowly. It was the first time he had voiced such a thought, but he had seen enough death to recognize that it was a real possibility. "She has been sick now for three days, with the sweating sickness. And she's bad, sir, very bad. She just woke up yesterday afternoon and gave me this and told me to bring it to you. She said not to let anyone see it but you. And not to say anything to anyone except you. And so I came."

Sir Robert Wakefield was a man who was accustomed to crises. A man in his position dealt with them. He had learned to be cool under fire in battle. He had learned to deal with the various strata of politicians and churchmen and villains and workmen of all sorts. But now as he stood there, looking at the tall boy with the chestnut hair, he suddenly felt a weakness such as he had never known. He licked his lips and said, "All right, boy. How did you get here?"

"I walked some, sir, and rode a wagon some."

"I'll get two horses. We will leave in ten minutes." He put the brooch into a purse that hung at his belt and turned and disappeared into the house. Myles stood waiting, and a few minutes later, Sir Robert came back out wearing a cloak. "Come along, lad." Myles followed him to the stable, where the noble-man had the hostler saddle two horses.

As Sir Robert mounted, he looked down at Myles. "Can you ride?"

Myles said, "Yes, sir," and swung into the saddle.

"Then let us be gone," he said and put the spurs to his horse.

Myles had never ridden on such a fleet animal before. He had spent most of his time on heavy plowhorses, and so the smooth movement of the racer beneath him was a sheer joy, which he appreciated for only a few brief seconds. Sir Robert Wakefield did not look back, and Myles cried out to his horse, "Come on! Go!" and snapped him smartly with his heels. The horse gathered his muscles and stretched out into a run, and soon Myles was riding side by side with the nobleman. Sir Robert neither spoke nor glanced in his direction but kept a steady pace until they passed out of sight of his castle.

Seven

"I'VE ALWAYS LOVED YOU!"

E arly the next morning some of the light sleepers in the village heard the sound of horses outside in the street—but since it was one o'clock, those who heard were few indeed. Those who did waken did not go outside, for it was not considered safe to wander about in the dark, even in the village.

When at last they reached Harrow, Myles pulled his horse to a halt and slid to the ground hurriedly. Unaccustomed as he was to riding a fine horse, he had been hard put to stay on for the first part of the journey, and the long hours in the saddle had stretched muscles he did not know he had.

"Keep quiet, boy," Sir Robert said hoarsely. They were almost the first words he had spoken since they had left his estate. He pushed the hood of his cloak back as he turned to look at the boy, who stood waiting. Overhead a pale moon illuminated a velvety blue and black sky, and the stars were scattered like glowing bits of dust across the heavens. It was about as light as a night could be, and Sir Robert looked around apprehensively, then turned back to ask, "Where is she?"

"This way, sir." Myles took the reins of his horse and led him down the street past the blacksmith's shop toward the mews. He would have gone on, but Sir Robert halted him.

"Someone will be with her. Go get rid of whomever it is, then come back for me."

"Yes, sir." Myles handed the reins of his horse to Sir Robert and stumbled with aching legs across the way. He arrived at the shack he and his mother shared and opened the door, finding, as he expected, Nob sitting across from his mother. The feeble light of the candle threw Nob's face into angular shadows that only emphasized his weariness, but his eyes lit up when he saw Myles.

"You're back!" he said with relief. "I'm glad you've come. I don't think—"

The falconer broke off, and one look at his mother's face by the flickering light told the boy what he had most feared to learn. "She's dying, isn't she?"

Grief twisted Nob's wrinkled face, and he nodded, saying slowly, "I do fear it, boy, I do fear it."

Myles said, "There's someone to see her and he doesn't want to be seen. Go out, Nob, and when you see the man with the horses, hold them for him. He'll have his hood up and won't speak to you."

Nob cocked his head to one side, a puzzled look in his eyes. Then he shrugged. "As you say, boy." He turned and left the small shack at once.

Myles fell on his knees beside his mother, pushed the lank hair back from her forehead, and for one moment was afraid he was too late. She was so still and unmoving. Then her breast rose slightly, and he saw her eyelids flutter. "Mother?" he whispered. "Can you hear me?"

Margred's eyelids slowly opened, and her lips tried to form a word. She blinked and struggled to sit up. "Be still, Mother," he said, "don't try to get up."

At that moment, he heard a sound behind him and turned to see that Sir Robert had entered the hovel. He had the cowl over his face so that his features were hidden in shadow. He stood for one moment, still as any statue, and nothing could be seen of his face to reveal his thoughts. Then he said in a muffled voice, "Go from this place, boy. And don't eavesdrop!"

"Yes, sir." Myles rose, gave one agonized look at his mother, then rushed out the door, closing it behind him.

The candle guttered in its shallow dish, a drop of wax rolling slowly down the short length and hardening into part of the lump at the bottom. There was no wind, so the flame stood up tall and straight and perfectly formed. The room was silent as a crypt.

Sir Robert moved across the room and stood looking down at the woman, whose eyes were closed but seemed to be fluttering. He watched as they opened and she looked up at him. Then Sir Robert reached slowly up and pulled the cowl back from his head, letting it fall free. Margred studied him through eyes that were already glazed. She had had many dreams during her sickness and thought for a moment that this was one of them. Then his features seemed to clear—her eyes remained fixed on his face, and she licked her lips and whispered, "Robert."

Wakefield felt his hands trembling and thrust them behind his back to stop them. He was light-headed and there was a sickness in his stomach. He felt that he needed to sit down, and in order to have something to do he pulled the box across and sat down beside the frail form of Margred Morgan.

"Is it really you?" she asked weakly.

"It's me, Arwen," he said in a whisper. He leaned forward and peered at her closely. He had never forgotten her in all the years since he had first seen her out piling hay, her honey-colored hair blowing in the wind, her bluer-than-cornflower eyes filled with merriment. As he sat there, it all came back to him, the whole scene, the whole story.

He had been betrothed to the daughter of a wealthy family

when he encountered the woman he called Arwen. And he knew, as he looked down at her pale face, that their coming together had been his doing—not hers.

He recalled when they first met, how he had struggled against his flesh, fighting himself throughout sleepless nights during which he railed against his foolish, faithless heart. Then came the day when, upon returning from a hunt, he had found her outside, wading in a small stream. He had come upon her unawares, and she had looked up at him with stars in her eyes. Fright, too, was there, and he recalled speaking in a soothing, low tone so as to not spook her. They talked together—only talked, for he had not touched her then—and that had been the beginning.

"I've been praying you would come, Robert," Margred whispered, her faint voice drawing him back to the present. Her face was drawn, her eyes sunken, yet there was still the trace of youthful beauty that he remembered from so many years ago. He had not known her features were so clearly impressed on his memory. Now, looking down at her, he said in a choking voice, "Arwen, what have you—," then broke off, emotion stilling his voice.

At the name "Arwen" the dying woman looked up at him and a smile tugged at her parched lips. "You always called me that," she whispered, "even though it was my grandmother's name and not mine."

"It suited you better . . . ," he said in a whisper.

She smiled again, but she did not speak right away. She lay quietly, her breast barely moving under the rough coverlet, and then she reached out a frail hand, which he took at once in his large, strong ones. "You're still the same," she murmured faintly. "Still the same."

Sir Robert held her hand gently, for it seemed more fragile than glass. He remembered when it was young and strong and warm, and how he had held it like a little bird when she tried to pull it away. How they had been carried as though on a racing river by their growing friendship . . . and their growing attraction for each other. How they had laughed together, talked together, and grown in their feelings for each other.

His hand gripped her a little harder as he wondered at himself, at the powerful memories that came surging back in a tide. Those few short months he'd spent with Margred had been the happiest in his life. He had known, as had she, that they could never be married, even if he had not been betrothed. He was Sir Robert Wakefield, and as such, he could never take a serf girl to be his wife.

Margred had seemed to understand that, and yet she did not send him away. They believed they could be with each other and drink in the joy of their communion, and that would be enough. Then had come the fateful day . . . the day he had come to her in despair, torn between his duty and his heart . . . the day she had sought to comfort him in the sheltering shadows of their forest spot . . . the day friendship had turned to passion, and passion had burned out of control.

It had been wrong, they had known that. And it had never happened again. But Sir Robert could not deny that something changed between them . . . that something had been lost when they had shared what had not been theirs to share.

He thought hard of those days, then said, "I've thought of you—every day I think, Arwen. Where did you go? Why did you run away? You disappeared like a ghost." A frown furrowed his high forehead, and he went on regretfully, "Why did you leave me?"

"It was wrong," Margred whispered. "You were to be married, and I well knew it. It was my fault—I should never have let it go so far. But you didn't force me, and I was always glad of that."

He could never quite make it out, but somehow she had taken the blame for their actions upon herself . . . and then she had disappeared, like a wraith. He had sought for her, desperately riding the highways, asking if anyone had seen a girl with an oval face and blue eyes and blonde hair. He had thought that if he had found her, they might have run away together. He knew now, as he had known for a long time, that that was foolishness. So he sat with her now, the pain in his eyes evident.

"I'm glad you came, Robert. I wanted to see you before I go to be with God."

"You may get well yet," he said quickly. "Don't give up."

"No. The Lord has told me that it's time for me to go home." She glanced at him and seemed to grow somewhat stronger. A smile touched her lips as she related the story of how God had spoken to her in Wales. "We came across the mountains, and God kept us both, and he has kept us ever since. It has been a comfort to me, knowing that you were only a day's journey from here. I don't know why, but it has." She hesitated, then said, "I have something to tell you. Or perhaps you've guessed?"

Suddenly a thought came to Sir Robert. It touched his mind, and immediately he backed away from it and tried to bury it. "Why, I thought perhaps you just wanted to see me once before . . . before—"

"No, it's more than that." She glanced over his shoulder toward the door, then again her eyes met his. Her gaze was clearer now, free from the haze that had seemed to dim it when he'd first come in. And it was as though some inner strength was buoying her up. Still he held her hand and felt her fingers close around his.

The thought that had taunted him moments ago returned, and he bowed his head. After a few moments he looked back up and whispered, "The boy. He's my son, isn't he?"

"Yes."

The bare monosyllable, gently spoken, hit Sir Robert Wakefield harder than any blow ever struck him on a field of battle or at a joust. It seemed to rack his entire being, and Margred felt his strong hand trembling violently. She lay there, watching his face, knowing there was nothing she could do to make it easier for him. All she knew for certain was that God had urged her, in her heart, to tell Sir Robert what had come of their involvement. She waited, silent and unmoving. Likewise, Sir Robert said no more and did not move, except for compressing his lips into a thin, white line, his entire face stiff with tension.

The silence ran on. At length she said gently, "I have never told Myles who his father is, and I never will. I am not asking you to do anything for him." She was quiet, then nodded slightly. "But a man should know that he has a son."

"A son," Robert Wakefield whispered. He thought of the boy, almost as tall as he was, and now he recognized that his own image was indelibly stamped upon the young features. Myles was a reflection of Sir Robert's dark red hair and blue-gray eyes. All of the men in his family had those blue-gray eyes.

He sat, still and silent, for a long time. Then he said, "I'm glad you told me, Arwen. And, of course, I'll do something for the boy." He squeezed her hand and managed to summon up at least the ghost of a smile. "You have my word on that, my dear."

Margred sighed deeply, and she seemed to be looking past him. So strange was her gaze that he almost looked over his shoulder to see what she was staring at so intently. And yet he knew her eyes were fixed on nothing within this small hut. Fear ran over him as he thought perhaps it was the stare of death, and he almost rose to go call the boy. But she held him with the pressure of her hand. Finally her eyes focused and she whispered, "Yes, you will do something for the boy—and God has told me that he will do something for you."

Robert had always known that this woman was a visionary of some sort. During their time together, she had told him of the many dreams she had had. After a few moments he said, "I will do what I can for you, too. You need to be out of this place. I'll have you taken to a better place. Perhaps a hospital, even in London, they might—"

"No, Robert," she said firmly. "There is not time for that. I am at peace now that you've come and you've seen the truth." She smiled sweetly and said, "Do you know I never knew another man but you?"

Her simple words shook Robert, but he had no doubt of them. "You were always a pure woman," he said quietly. "I never had any doubt of that. And the boy," he added, "he is like you."

"The next time you look in a mirror, Robert," she said, "you will see the face of your son. He is like you as well—very like."

Robert was lost in thought for a time, and her eyelids began growing heavy. She said in a faint whisper, "Good-bye. We won't meet again. But I want to tell you one thing before you go."

"Yes? What is it, Arwen?"

She opened her eyes one more time, the pressure of her hand increased, and her lips moved very slightly as she said, "I've always loved you."

Robert Wakefield felt the hand loosen and for one moment was afraid that she ceased to breathe. Leaning closer, he saw that she still lived but had fallen once again into unconsciousness. He put her small hand down, rose, and stood for one moment, looking down at her. His face was twisted with pain as he realized there was nothing he could do for this woman who had meant so much to him. Then he turned and walked through the door.

He moved through the darkness, coming to where the boy stood holding the horses. "Give me the horses," he said and took the reins. "Go to your mother."

"Yes, sir." Myles turned to go, but then the strong hand of the nobleman reached out, grasped his arm, and pulled him around. They were almost of the same height, both near six feet tall; but where the man was bulky, the boy was slender and lean, his still-developing form giving the promise of being strong and muscular. Wakefield peered at the boy's face as it was illuminated by the silver beams of the moon.

He studied the boy long, and Myles returned his gaze with bewilderment. Then Wakefield said gruffly, "Go to your mother. I will speak with you later." He mounted his horse swiftly, took the reins of Myles's horse, and spurred the startled animal so that he took off at a dead run.

Myles waited until the sound of hoofbeats grew faint and finally faded. Then he went into the shack and sat down beside his mother's cot, wondering what it all had meant.

Eight

THE DECISION

L ady Jane Wakefield, at the age of thirty-seven, had seen little of the world. Her own world for the past five years had been the castle, particularly the suite of rooms that had been enlarged by her husband to fit her needs. She was a great reader, and books were continually brought from London by courier. She was a student of the Bible—at least of the New Testament, having learned to read Greek when she was a young girl—and her brother had been a student of Greek. Erasmus had compiled an edition of the Greek New Testament in 1516, and she had been delighted with the book.

But books were only one area in which she had expertise. The other was her husband, Robert. She knew him, she thought sometimes, better than herself. She could tell simply by the sound of his footsteps the kind of mood he was in. He might hide his thoughts from others, but to her they were as simple to read as a page in one of her books. So it was that she had known for two days now that he was going through some inner turmoil, and yet he had not discussed it with her.

Upon speaking to the servants, she had learned that a young man had appeared at the door, asking for Sir Robert. Her husband, upon going to meet the boy, had left suddenly and was gone overnight. In any other man, it might have been reasonable to suspect there was a woman involved, but somehow Lady Jane knew that was not what was troubling her husband, throwing his mind into such turbulence that he forgot even the simplest habits of his life.

It was not strange that the servants knew the goings-on of Robert Wakefield. It was one of the chief occupations of their life to study him and Lady Jane whenever possible. The servants were great gossips, of course, and it was Lady Jane's wise dealings with them that kept her home and her house servants in more harmony than was found in most fine houses.

Now she sat by the window, looking out at the road that was so familiar to her she thought she must know every blade of grass and could name every bird that came in sight. There were many, because she had given orders to provide water for birdbaths and to scatter feed for them so that they came very close to the house. Even as she watched, a goldfinch came and began to pick up the tiny seeds right below her. She followed its movements, enjoying the antics of the little spot of gold, at the same time wondering what it was that so distracted her husband.

Finally she began reading her Bible. Despite her barrenness, Jane paused to thank God for her marriage. She was a woman who had learned the hard way to praise the Lord in the face of difficulty. When child after child had been born dead, she had turned bitter and had become filled with hate for God. She felt betrayed. It had taken several years, but she had been fortunate enough to have a friend, a priest who knew more about religion than just muttering the Mass in Latin. He was a godly man and recognized the bitterness that had come into Jane Wakefield's heart, and over a period of time he had been able to show her that Jesus Christ was the all-important thing in human life. She leaned back now, thinking of that old confessor of hers, now in his grave, and she offered up a prayer for him, thankful that he had taught her the great lesson of believing God. Then she went back to her reading, but almost at once, the door opened and her husband entered.

Lady Jane took one look at him and knew that he was frightened and perplexed. She had often seen Sir Robert Wakefield perplexed, but frightened? No! Never in all of their marriage had he shown fear of anything, and those who had seen him in battle had said that he almost seemed to delight in the sound of clashing swords and the cries of war.

He came across the room, looked down at her, and started to speak. Then apparently he changed his mind, for he turned abruptly to look out the window. "Beautiful day," he said absently. "I'll take you for a ride later, down by the river. You can see the fish breaking water there . . ."

"Yes, that would be nice," she said. She waited patiently, her hands folded, and eventually he did exactly what she had known he would do.

He turned to her and burst out, "Jane, I must talk to you."

"Sit down," she said quietly, and he sat in a chair across from hers and drew it close. He seemed as nervous as a schoolboy, and she saw that his fingers were trembling. He put them behind his back to hide them. There was a tic in his right eye, something she had never seen before, and she began to grow fearful.

It must be something terrible for Robert to be torn apart like this, she thought. She offered up a brief prayer, and then she reached out and put her hand on his knee. He immediately covered it with his, then took the other hand out and held hers captive.

"J-Jane," he began, faltering and uncertain, "I've . . . we've . . . had . . . I, well, I can't say what I want to say." He dropped her hand and abruptly jumped up and began to pace the floor like a caged beast. He looked rather like a lion that she had seen once in a traveling show, pacing back and forth, his eyes glancing endlessly around the room as if looking for a way to escape.

"Robert, whatever it is, we will face it together," she said calmly. "Come. Sit down and tell me about it."

He came again to her side and sat down, running his left hand

115

through his hair in a nervous gesture. Then he gripped the arms of the chair and stared straight at her, determination written in every line of his powerful body and noble face. "I must tell you," he said through clenched teeth, "I have to tell you that I have been unfaithful to you."

He watched her warily, and sweat broke out on his forehead. Unlike many noblemen of the day, he had been faithful to his wife, with the one exception of Margred. He had buried that so deeply that he had thought he could live and die without ever mentioning it to his wife, for he knew it would hurt her to know of his infidelity. He saw something change in her face, and he dropped his head in shame. "I wish I didn't have to tell you. I should have told you before, perhaps."

Lady Jane said nothing. She had known that he was a faithful man, for she had heard enough from her married friends to know the signs of a guilty man, and Robert had never exhibited such signs. She had been almost in awe that this powerful, vigorous, and virile man had kept himself from other women during their long marriage. Now she put her hand on his, and he clasped it tightly.

"Do you want to tell me about it, Robert?" When he opened his mouth to speak, she interrupted, "But before you tell me, let me tell you this: No woman," she said plainly and with great vigor, "ever had a better husband than I have had. This is the truth, as God has let me know it."

Robert Wakefield was not a man to show strong emotion, but at her words, tears stung his eyes and he blinked rapidly to clear them. "I'm glad you can say that, Jane," he said, his voice rough. "I wanted to be a good husband, because I have loved you since the first time I saw you, and I love you now." He took in her answering smile and began to speak rapidly. He told her simply of the affair he had had with Margred many years earlier. He made no excuse for himself; indeed, he said bitterly, "If I could only live that over again, I would never do such a thing! Never,

Jane!" He looked at her, and she saw the pain that filled his eyes, for he hated to see her injured. "I've always despised men who had other women besides their wives," he said with anguish, "and yet I myself have been in their company."

Lady Jane prayed for wisdom. She knew that he had come to her, after all this time, for some reason that she had not yet discerned. But she had to make him understand how she felt. "Robert," she said gently, "it was a long time ago, and I know that you have grieved over it. I do wish you had told me about it earlier, and we could have put it behind us. I would still have married you, for I loved you even then. Why did you wait all these years? Didn't you know that I would always love you?"

His wife's words brought back the last words of the dying woman, *"I've always loved you."* Wakefield could do nothing but drop his head and sit dumbly.

"Is there something else, Robert?" she asked. "What is it that makes you come now to tell me this?"

"I saw Arwen . . . Margred . . . two days ago," he said in a muffled voice, his head still lowered. "She is a servant at Bourneville's farm. She sent for me and I went, although I had no idea who I was going to meet." He related the story of the brooch, the young man who had brought it, and how he had gone to the bedside of the dying woman.

"Is she dead then?" Lady Jane asked quietly.

"No. I mean—I don't know. I suppose so. She had the sweating sickness, and you know how quickly they go with that. She was hard hit, I fear."

"What did she say to you?"

"She told me," he began, and the words were wrenched from him, "that she had always loved me. That she had never known another man."

"Did she have long blonde hair and very blue eyes?"

He looked up startled. "How did you—?"

"I remember her, Robert. She was a servant who worked in the fields, but I often saw her as she walked underneath my window. She seemed such a happy young woman, and so beautiful!" She hesitated, then said, "She had a good face, as I remember."

"Yes, she was good. She still is," Wakefield said soberly. Then he lifted his eyes and searched his wife's face for a long moment before bringing out the words. "The boy that she sent to get me. He . . . he is my son, Jane."

Surprise caught at Lady Jane, and she took a short, sharp breath. "Your son," she breathed. "Are you certain?"

"You will be, when you look at him. He looks like me. Same hair, same blue-gray eyes. Very like me."

"The Wakefield men all bore a strong family resemblance," Lady Jane said with wonder. "How old is the boy?"

"Sixteen." Robert Wakefield looked miserable. "I must do something, I can't let him go on like this."

Lady Jane did not attempt to speak. She watched as Sir Robert got up again and restlessly paced the room. She listened as he spoke of sending the boy away, of possibly having one of his distant relatives take him in, to get him educated, to find a place for him. He was speaking almost wildly, and finally he stopped and looked down at her, asking with confusion written on his features, "What do you think, Jane? What should we do for him?"

All at once, everything seemed to fall into place for Lady Jane. She spoke positively and without hesitation. "He is our son, Robert. You must bring him home."

Robert Wakefield's hands tightened instantly into fists, and he jerked his head back as if he had been struck. Not once had he considered doing any more than simply helping the boy. Many of his friends had illegitimate sons, and some of them had done well by them. But now Lady Jane was staring at him in a strange way, and he could not believe what he had heard. "Why . . . why, Jane!" he stammered, "Of course, he's my son, but—but—"

"No, he's *our* son," she said, gently but firmly. "You are my husband, and that makes him *our* child." She waited as the idea began to seat itself in his mind and watched his face turn solemn as she continued, "He's what you've wanted all these years. And," she added quickly, "with your blood in him, he will be a fine man, I'm certain. All he needs is your help."

"But I can't take him in! I've been—I'm—," he stammered again and stopped suddenly. "I've practically promised Ralph Geddes that he will be my heir!"

"You can do many things for Ralph Geddes," Lady Jane said placidly. "You can find him a place, you can help him, you can give him money. But he is not your son, Robert." Her face grew light and her eyes glowed as she said, "This boy, he's not too old to learn, is he? He needs manners, I'm sure, since he has been raised as a serf. He will need polishing, but that will be your joy! If he has anything of nobility in him, you are just the man that will bring it out!"

The idea began to take hold of Robert Wakefield, but he still spent some twenty minutes bringing forth every argument he could think of against it, repeating himself, making up almost wild excuses.

Lady Jane stood firm. "Yes, all that may be true, Robert. But he is of your blood and your father's blood. And he will pass your blood along to his sons. Do you want your grandsons to be serfs? Or do you want them here, in this place, at Wakefield? Staying here, keeping what you have safe?"

Finally Sir Robert came to stand beside his wife. He put one brawny hand on her shoulder, and a smile came to his lips. "You are too quick for me, Jane," he said. "You know me too well."

She reached up, took his hand, kissed it, and then patted it. "Yes, I do. And I know this has been sent from God. All the prayers I have offered for a son, that we have offered, have been answered. God did not say *no*. He said *wait*. And now this boy who is so like you will be here, and we will be happy, won't we, Robert?"

"Yes!" The word exploded from Wakefield's lips, and he pulled her to her feet and held her in his arms. "Yes!" he said again, then kissed her. When he lifted his head he said with wonder, "There's not another like you, Jane. There is no other in this world!"

The funeral for Margred Morgan was simple enough, as such funerals always were. The grave had been dug. The women had come in and washed her and put her in her best dress. The funeral had been attended by practically everyone. The lord's family was there as a matter of course; they attended the funerals of all of their people.

Myles was almost in shock. His mother had died two days after the visit by Sir Robert Wakefield. She had been conscious much of that time and had spoken to him often. Early one morning, when dawn was just about to break, she had opened her eyes and smiled up at him saying, "It's time. I'm going to the Lord Jesus now. Good-bye, Myles. Follow after Jesus and be true to him." He had leaned over and kissed her, and she had closed her eyes and seemed to go to sleep. Thirty minutes later, she simply stopped breathing.

Margred Morgan had left this world.

Now, at the funeral, Myles stood between Nob on one side and Cheval on the other. Both of them had loved Margred, worshiped her in a way. Simple, plain men both, they had recognized the goodness and the virtue that was in her, as others perhaps had not. The chaplain spoke briefly, read some Scripture, and then the body of Myles's mother was lifted up from the bier as Myles watched. He followed numbly in the procession, and when they reached the graveside, tears streamed unchecked down his cheeks. He was aware that Sir Geoffrey Bourneville was looking at him in a curious fashion, but he paid little attention. Then the last rites had taken place, and he turned away so that he would not hear the clods of dirt falling on the casket.

Many spoke to him, trying to give him comfort, telling him that his mother was in heaven. He simply nodded to them. His throat was so full and he was so choked with tears that he could not say a word. He walked away quickly and moved through the town silently, staring straight ahead, until he came to the woods. For a long time, he wandered aimlessly, wondering how he would live without her.

When the shadows grew long, he turned toward home. When he reached their little house—his little house now—Nob appeared and said quietly, "Sir Geoffrey wants to see you, up at the house."

Myles said dully, "All right. I'll go now." He turned and made his way to the big house and was met by one of the servants.

"You are to go right in. The master is waiting for you," he said. "I'll show you the way."

As he entered the house, Myles encountered Isabella, who came to him. For once in her life, she was serious, her lips gentle and soft as she said, "I am so sorry, Myles. I know you'll miss her." He nodded, still unable to speak, and left her watching him.

"Right in here," the servant said and knocked on the door.

Sir Geoffrey's voice called, "Come in!" The servant opened the door and motioned with his head, and Myles walked into the large room. He stopped instantly, for there, across the room, staring at him, was Sir Robert Wakefield.

"Come in, Myles," Sir Geoffrey said. He seemed rather awkward, somehow. His fat face glistened with sweat, and he looked cautiously at the boy, then let his glance slide across the room to where Sir Robert Wakefield stood silently. "Well," he said, "I'll just leave you two here alone. You can call me, Robert, if you need anything."

"Thank you, Geoffrey," Sir Robert said, but he did not move until Bourneville left the room and quietly closed the door. He walked over to stand in front of the boy, his eyes running over Myles's face, his own features growing tense. "I am sorry about your mother," he said. "She was a fine woman."

"Thank you, sir," Myles managed to say. He cleared his throat and said painfully, "I'm going to miss her. All we had was each other."

Myles felt awkward and confused, and he didn't know what to do with his hands. The big man before him had a disturbing gaze that continually searched his face, and Myles grew even more nervous. Even so, he dared not ask any questions.

Finally Wakefield asked, "Do you know who I am, Myles?"

"Why yes, sir. You are Sir Robert Wakefield."

"I mean," Wakefield insisted, "do you know nothing else about me?"

He could only shake his head and say in a bewildered tone, "I—I don't know what you mean, sir."

The honesty in the boy's face was clear enough, and Wakefield, who had thought that perhaps in her dying moments, Margred might have told the boy her secret, was certain now that was not the case. He forced himself to relax and then said, "I have something to tell you. It is going to be quite a shock for you, I think."

Myles asked in some confusion, "Is it something wrong that I've done?"

"No, no! Nothing like that," Sir Robert said quickly. He looked at the boy and decided to speak to him plainly. He looked directly into the lad's eyes—eyes so like his own—and said firmly, "I am your father, Myles."

The words seemed to mean nothing to Myles for a moment. Then, when they began to sink in, a wave of confusion and then anger washed over him. How dare this man make fun of him, nobleman or not! He opened his mouth to give an angry retort, then he saw the expression on Sir Robert's face. He paused, swallowed hard, then dropped his head and thought. After a few moments, he lifted his face. "My mother never told me who my father was."

"I'm ashamed that I wronged your mother," Wakefield said quietly. "I blame myself for the whole thing. She was a good woman, never doubt that! I know she died in the grace of God and is now with the angels in heaven." Myles was surprised at the emotion of the nobleman's words, and wonder began to fill him.

Could it be true? Was this man his father?

"Sit down over here, Myles." Sir Robert motioned to a chair and Myles obediently sat, but he was uneasy and kept his eyes fixed on the older man. "Let me tell you how it was. . . ."

Myles listened carefully, trying to take it all in as Wakefield told the story of what had happened between himself and Margred Morgan. When the story was finished, Wakefield said, "So you see, Myles, I was betrothed, soon to be a married man. . . . I behaved very badly to your mother, but believe me, I tried hard to find her. I searched everywhere, but I never once thought of Wales. And I certainly had no idea that you even existed, not until she told me when I visited her just before her death."

He stopped then and looked searchingly at the boy. Myles's features were tense, and Sir Robert said reassuringly, "I know this is a shock for you. It was a shock for me, too." Then he leaned forward and said earnestly, "There is going to be a big change in our lives from this time on, my boy."

Myles looked vacantly at him, trying to think. "I . . . I don't understand, Sir Robert. What do you mean? What-what's going to happen?"

"What's going to happen is that you are coming to my house. To Wakefield. I am going to announce to the world that you are my son and heir. You are going to live with Lady Jane, my wife, and myself, and you are going to become a gentleman."

Confusion blanketed Myles as he sat there, struggling to take it all in. After what seemed a long time, he looked up into the face of the man who called himself his father and said haltingly, "But I . . . I could never do that! I . . . don't . . . know anything! I don't know how to live like the son of a nobleman!"

"You know enough to be an honest young man," Sir Robert said positively. He smiled then, a little tremulously, adding, "It would be my pleasure to teach you, Myles, whatever you need to know. But of course, it is your decision."

He shook his head uncertainly. "What will your family say?"

"My wife has already told me to bring you home. She's a lovely woman. I think you will find her as true as your own mother. She never had any children, and she has a lot of love to give. So there is no problem there."

"But what about—" Myles broke off abruptly, and Sir Robert understood immediately.

"Ralph Geddes has been living with us. I thought to make him my heir one day. But you mustn't worry about that—I will put things right with Ralph. I will set him up in a good fashion." He hesitated, then said, "But he is not my son. You are."

The two sat in the quietness of the room for a while. Finally Myles said in a low voice, "I have always wanted a father."

It was all the encouragement Sir Robert Wakefield needed. He jumped to his feet, pulled the boy up, and put a strong hand on his shoulder, squeezing it. He felt the firm muscle that was there, then he put his other hand on Myles's other shoulder and looked at him soberly. "It will take some getting used to. For both of us." Then he smiled and said, "But we'll work at it together. We leave as soon as you can gather your things."

"Yes, sir. I'll go get them now." He turned and left the room, and almost as soon as he disappeared Sir Geoffrey Bourneville popped back inside.

"Did you tell him, Robert?"

"Yes. He's going to get his things and we're leaving right away."

Geoffrey Bourneville stared at his friend without any comprehension in his eyes. He had always thought Robert Wakefield a man of sense, but this did not seem to prove that. He said carefully, "The boy's likely to be hard to handle. He doesn't know anything about how to live among the civilized."

Wakefield nodded and said with more assurance than he felt, "I'll teach him that. There's more to life than putting on a fancy suit of clothes. The boy's sound at heart. He can learn the rest." He grinned then at his host, saying wryly, "Well, you can start the gossip, Geoffrey. It'll be all over every county in this part of the world by morning, I suppose. So you have my blessing for telling everyone you meet—" here he paused and finished firmly— "that Sir Robert Wakefield, and his wife, Lady Jane Wakefield, and his son, Myles Wakefield, will be receiving visitors in the near future!" He laughed out loud then, joyously, and struck one fist into the other palm. "By heaven, Bourneville," he exclaimed, "life is good, isn't it! A son! After all these years!"

He left the room after clapping Bourneville on the shoulder, almost knocking him down, and Geoffrey looked after his friend. *I wonder what'll come of all this,* he mused, then shook his head. *Nothing good, I'll warrant. I've seen a lot of changes in my life, and I've been against every one of them!* Then he left the room in search of his wife, who would get the gossip started with no unseemly delay.

END OF PART ONE

The

1 5 2 2

Part
TWO

1 5 2 6

Heir

A PLACE OF HIS OWN

Myles's first glimpse of Wakefield sent a sudden stab of apprehension through him. Sir Robert had tried to make him feel at home as they had traveled that morning, but still he felt almost like an imposter. He looked down at the new clothing that his father had provided—the stout, thick boots, the fine, heavy pants, and the smooth jerkin—and he almost wished for his old rags again! However, he knew it would not do to let Sir Robert see how he felt, so when Sir Robert said, "There it is! There's Wakefield, Myles!" he looked up and took in his new home with a sweeping glance.

Wakefield, he saw at once, was like a little town that contained within its palisades all that was needed for life and sustenance, which was not unusual for the manor estates of the day. Sir Robert had told him that there were upwards of fifty people living there, in addition to other servants and retainers and half a dozen hangers-on, people with some claim on Sir Robert's generosity.

As they drew near the estate and passed through the gates, Sir Robert said, "There's the house. Lady Jane will be glad to see you, boy."

Myles swallowed and nodded. "Yes, sir. I'm looking forward to meeting her." He had seen the house once before, of course—the night he came in darkness to give his mother's brooch to Sir Robert. But he had been half wild with grief and paid no heed to what was around him.

His attention was drawn now to Sir Robert Wakefield's house, which enclosed a quadrangle on three sides, the fourth side bordered by a small river. There was a big gate by a tower, and over the gate, supported by cantilevers, was the Wakefield coat of arms: a falcon with widespread wings holding a sheaf of arrows in one claw. He stared at the coat of arms, wondering what the strange letters in a half circle over the top meant, and decided he would wait to ask.

He glanced toward the north corner of the house and saw another tower pierced with loopholes for bows or guns and tall enough to view the land approaches. All sides of the house were protected by stockades and earthworks, which made Myles wonder if Sir Robert expected to be attacked. When he inquired dubiously about this, Sir Robert gave him a quick smile.

"Probably not these days," he said, "but Wakefield has been attacked many times over the years. 'Tis an old place, Myles, and it has seen many battles in its day. Someday we might look up and see the Spaniards coming down that river or across those fields." He shrugged, adding, "If they do, we shall be ready for them."

Sir Robert led Myles to the front of the house, then dismounted. Myles followed suit. A small man with a withered, aged face came at once, and Sir Robert said, "Darrowby, this is your new master, Myles Wakefield."

The man's face twisted into a smile, and he bobbed up and down, saying happily, "Yes, indeed, Mr. Myles. And glad it is we are to welcome you to your new home. Lady Jane is very anxious to see both of you."

Sir Robert threw the reins of his horse to a tall serf standing nearby, and Myles looked at his own, then handed them carefully to the young man. As he followed Sir Robert into the house, he saw that it was built more or less on the same order as the Bourneville residence, with a great hall lined by doors leading off to various rooms.

"We go this way," Sir Robert said. "Our quarters are back here. Let's go meet—" He hesitated, then said quietly, "your mother."

A peculiar look crossed Myles's face, and Sir Robert stopped his rapid stride. "It would please her, Myles, if you could think of her in that way. Not," he added hastily, "that she is a replacement for your own mother! But she has a lot of love, my wife, and has never had a child to pour it out on."

"I'll—I'll do the best I can to be a good son to her, sir."

Myles saw at once that he had said the right thing, for a smile illuminated Sir Robert's face. He clapped the boy on the back, then turned and strode through one of the doorways. He passed through two large rooms and then finally came to a closed door, which he knocked on loudly, saying jovially, "Well, woman! We're here!" He opened the door, and Myles stepped into the room behind him, feeling very strange and rather foolish. He stopped once he was inside and watched as Sir Robert walked over to the woman who was standing at a window but had turned to face them.

Sir Robert bent over, kissed her cheek, and put one arm around her, waving the other toward Myles. "Here he is, wife!" he said proudly. "Myles Wakefield!" He gave her frail shoulders a squeeze and smiled down at her. "It sounds well, doesn't it?"

Lady Jane, Myles saw, was a small, delicate woman with dark brown hair and brown eyes. He responded to the gentleness in her smile at once. She pulled away from her husband, walked across the room, and put out her hand to him. Poor Myles did not know what to do with it, whether to shake it or kiss it or merely make the courtly gesture of leaning over it. Seeing his uncertainty and embarrassment, Lady Jane reached up and patted him on the shoulder. "My! What a fine, tall fellow you are!" she said. She turned to look at her husband. "The two of you are very alike." Her remark, Myles saw, pleased Sir Robert—and somehow it pleased him, too.

"Well now," Sir Robert said loudly, "come, the two of you sit down and get acquainted. Myles and I had a chance to talk quite a bit on our way here, but I know you would like to talk with him, Jane. Why don't I just leave you two?" He went on hastily, "I'll go find the cook and tell him that, whatever you have ordered for supper, to cook something better." He stopped on his way to the door to turn and say, a serious expression on his face, "It is good to have you here, my boy, very good." Then, as if he were embarrassed, he turned and passed through the door, slamming it loudly with his enthusiasm.

Myles shifted awkwardly and found himself wondering yet again what to do with his hands. Lady Jane understood and laughed, saying, "You must feel perfectly awful, Myles."

"Oh no, ma'am. That is . . . well . . ."

"Here. Sit over here and let me talk for a while." As he listened to her talk about Wakefield, the servants, about the routines that went on there, her gentle manner and soft voice were infinitely soothing to the young man. He saw at once that he would never have any problem pleasing this woman. She was tender and kind, and the light in her warm brown eyes seemed to bring a healing to his troubled spirit.

At length she said, "Do you have any questions, Myles? Anything?" Then she realized that he was too perplexed to question her, and her heart went out to this boy whose life had been so transformed. She considered him, letting the silence run on, and finally decided that even though they had just met and he was still full of fears, she would take a great chance.

"Myles," she said, "you loved your mother very dearly, did you not?"

"Oh yes, ma'am!"

"That is very well—a boy should love his mother. She was all you had, was she not? According to what Sir Robert has told me, you were just the two of you most of your lives."

"Yes, Lady Jane. She was always good to me, took good care of me," Myles said, nodding. Thinking of his mother, a lump rose in his throat, and he could not speak anymore.

Lady Jane leaned forward slightly and very quietly said, "You must always honor your mother, Myles, as I know you will." She searched his face earnestly and continued, "But you are Sir Robert's son, too. No one looking at you could doubt it. And I hope that you will also honor the House of Wakefield." She spoke very slowly and carefully, trying to put what was in her heart into words. Not wanting to frighten or intimidate him, she yet felt she must say, "Myles, I have never had children of my own. The Lord has not seen fit to give them to me." She leaned back in her chair, looking down at her hands, and they moved suddenly, a small gesture of pain. Then she looked back up at Myles, a slight smile turning the corners of her lips upward, "But I feel that God has given me a son now. I could never be your real mother, of course—but I wonder, would you let me be your friend? Then we shall see what happens."

Tears suddenly burned in Myles's eyes, and he could no more have spoken than he could have flown out the window. For several moments he blinked fiercely, then cleared his throat and said unsteadily, "Yes, ma'am. I would like that, very much."

Lady Jane knew that was enough. "Good. Splendid!" she said happily. "You and I are going to have all kinds of good times together! Your father will have you outside, but I will claim my time in the house." She began to outline some of the things that she had planned and was so skillful at putting the boy at his ease that he almost forgot his fright and bewilderment.

The door opened, and Sir Robert entered with Ralph Geddes by his side. Lady Jane saw Myles stiffen, and she sensed that the boy was filled with apprehension and even fear. Sir Robert noted it as well. He stopped and regarded Myles carefully, then said sternly, "Myles, you and Ralph here have had an unfortunate clash. Ralph has said that he is very sorry it happened. As it is, the two of you will be living closely together here. You are both dear to me, and I would like it if the two of you would be friends."

Geddes was more mature than Myles remembered from that terrible day. He was twenty-seven now and was still handsome with his black hair and dark eyes. There was a smile on his lips, Myles saw with relief, and Geddes stepped forward, putting his hand out.

"I hope you are willing, Myles, to let bygones be bygones." He smiled. "I was a young fool in those days. You know how young idiots are!" He laughed heartily and winked at Sir Robert, then looked back at Myles. "You'll be making a fool of yourself in a like way, no doubt, if you haven't already."

Myles almost automatically took Ralph's hand and squeezed it, though he was not accustomed to shaking hands; he had spent his life baring his head and bowing to men. He knew that Sir Robert and Lady Jane were watching him carefully. For a year, he had nursed hatred for Ralph Geddes for assaulting his mother and for causing him the shame of the stocks. After it had happened, he had lain awake night after night, thinking of ways to bring his vengeance on Geddes. But the time had passed and, looking at the smile on the face of the man and noting the apprehension in Sir Robert's eyes, he said quickly, "Of course. Let's forget about it."

"Fine, fine!" Geddes said. "Now then, you're coming with me. I shall show you to your room. We'll get acquainted, then we'll come down and see what's for supper. Come along now."

Myles did not want to go anywhere with Ralph Geddes, but he saw no graceful way to avoid it. He nodded to Sir Robert and said, "Thank you for bringing me here, sir." Then he turned to Lady Jane and smiled timidly. "And thank you, ma'am. I'll—I'll do the best I can, to be and do what you want."

When the two young men left the room, Sir Robert turned to his wife and asked a little apprehensively, "What do you think, Jane?"

Lady Jane looked at him, put her hand on his arm, and said warmly, "He's a Wakefield. He's your son, Robert. I am so happy that you found him—and that he found you." She squeezed his arm affectionately. "He will have a hard time adjusting."

"Yes, I know. It would be hard for anyone, especially for a young fellow like that. But did you see how well he responded to Ralph? I was afraid of that meeting, you know." He shook his head. "I know he hated Ralph, though he won't say much about it. I talked to him about it on the way. But it will be all right."

Lady Jane looked at the door and buried the apprehension that had risen in her. She did not want to spoil her husband's triumph, so she just smiled and said, "Of course it will, Robert."

Geddes led Myles up a stairway in the left wing of the house, and when they got to Myles's room, he pushed the door open and stepped inside. "Here it is, Myles. This will be your room." It was about eight feet wide by eleven feet long and had a tall narrow window at one end. There was a bed beside the door they had entered, with a second door leading into the rooms beyond. It was tiny, but comfortably furnished, with a bedstead, two stools, a window cushion of needlework, and a canvas to cover the window at night. On the wall there were shelves and an old map of the southern coast of England. "Think this will suit?" Geddes asked.

Myles gazed around and said, "Oh yes, Ralph. This will be fine." Then he asked curiously, "Whose place has this been?"

"Oh, it was mine," Geddes said casually. "But I've moved out, down the hall."

"No, don't do that!" Myles said in alarm. "Let me move down there. It doesn't really matter to me. I don't want to put you out."

Geddes laughed and slapped Myles on the shoulder. "Never fear," he said, "I moved into a bigger room than this. So you aren't really putting me out of anything." His words relieved Myles, and he went on, "What do you say we take a trip into London the first chance we get? Sir Robert will foot the bill, and we can see what exciting things are happening."

"I'd like that—if Sir Robert wouldn't mind," Myles said.

"Mind? Of course he won't mind! You're his son, aren't you?"

At that moment, Myles thought he saw a strange gleam in Geddes's eye—either of anger or bitterness—but it was gone so quickly that he dismissed it from his mind. "I'm glad we've made it up, Ralph," he said slowly. "I don't like to have bad feelings toward anyone."

"Of course. It will be much more comfortable if we get along." He made a dismissing gesture and asked, "So, do you want to lie down awhile? Or wander around the house? I have a few things to do, so I'll see you at supper." He paused at the door before leaving and said formally, "Welcome to the House of Wakefield."

Myles did not know what to do with himself. He stood at the window, looking out at the river and the fields, and wondered what time would bring.

Later, at supper, Myles suffered in an agony of embarrassment. He had never before seen the strange instrument that lay beside his plate, so he carefully avoided it. Ralph Geddes leaned over and whispered, "That's a fork, Myles. You stab your meat with it."

"But won't it get the fork dirty?" Myles asked doubtfully.

"They can be washed." Ralph grinned.

"Well, so can fingers," Myles said in confusion. When the others laughed, Myles smiled faintly and picked up the fork, saying to himself, *I'll have to learn about a lot more than forks before I feel at home here.*

***

Sir Robert Wakefield was a wise and experienced man, and within a few days, he had carefully gauged the strengths and weaknesses of this new son of his. He recognized the lad's expert handling of the falcons and the hawks. There the boy excelled, and he praised Myles for it until his face turned quite red. He did as well, if not better, with the hounds that were so much a part of life at Wakefield. Hunting was almost as much a part of living as eating, and few days went by that Sir Robert and Myles did not go out, either hawking or following the hounds, chasing the deer or the wild pigs that roamed the woods surrounding Wakefield.

And Myles was ecstatic with this part of his education. It was what he knew. He might not know what a fork was, along with about a thousand other things, but where the hawks and the dogs were concerned, he felt confident enough to match himself against anyone at Wakefield. He made friends immediately with the falconer, a tall thin man named Sipes, and also with the sixteen-year-old boy, Mott, who cared for the hounds. They had expected to find the new heir aloof and were both astonished and a little shocked when he turned out to be entirely different. Within a week, the three of them were deep into conversations about the birds and the hounds.

After a week passed, Sir Robert came one morning and said, "Time to begin a new part of your education, my boy. Come with me."

Myles's heart sank, for he was very much afraid that he was going to be bombarded with books and learning, something that he felt he knew very little about indeed. Instead, Sir Robert took him to a large room, stripped bare of all furniture. "This is the armory," Sir Robert said. "You have seen it before. And now we are ready to begin work." He went around, naming the various pieces of equipment, and Myles's heart sank anew when he realized what a task it would be just to learn the pieces of a suit of armor. He thought quite possibly it would require more brains than were contained in his poor head.

Under the raftered ceiling there hung a collection of weapons:

tilting lances, swords, daggers, and other things that Myles could not even guess the use for.

"First," Sir Robert announced, "we will begin with the sword." He pulled two swords out of a rack, waved them about, then handed one to Myles. "Have you ever used a sword before, Myles?"

"No, sir," Myles said. It was probably against the law for a serf to even own one, much less use one—but he held his tongue. As he looked down at the heavy weapon, a thrill ran through him.

Sir Robert said, "All right. 'Tis late for you to be learning. By the time I was your age, I was already a good match for almost any man in the county. But you are strong, healthy, and very quick, and that is what is required. *That,*" he stressed, "and one other element."

"Sir?"

"Courage." Sir Robert grinned and made a decisive slashing movement with the sword he held. "The best swordsman sometimes may be rather awkward, or not as strong as other men, or perhaps not as quick." The sword made another flashing movement through the air, and Sir Robert held it upright, his eyes on it, lit with excitement. "But a real swordsman has courage. He is not afraid." He lowered the sword casually and looked at Myles gravely. "You can build up your muscles. You can practice on your speed and agility. But courage is a different sort of thing. We'll find out if you have any."

For the next hour, Myles followed the instructions of his father, trying his best to break down the guard of the older man as they practiced. But no matter how he thrust or cut at Sir Robert, his blade was always well met. He grew almost angry with himself. Then his arm began to grow weary, and his father said, "Are you ready to quit?"

"No, sir," Myles said firmly, and there was a determined light in his blue-gray eyes. "Not yet."

His answer pleased Sir Robert, and he let the lesson go on a little while longer. Not long afterward, though, he said, "That's enough of the swords for today." He took the weapon from Myles, hefted it, and placed it back in the rack. "Now then. Let's try the lance."

If the sword had been tiring, the lance exercise was even more so. Sir Robert sat on a stool while Myles, armed with a spear, would charge against him. Sir Robert had put on a breastplate and a helmet, and he would say, "Here, strike here!" tapping his helmet or his chest. Again and again Myles charged, until he could hardly stand.

Finally Sir Robert said, "That's enough. A good beginning." He stripped off the armor, looked at Myles, and said kindly, "Give yourself time, Son. Don't be discouraged. You're young and strong, and I can see that you're not afraid. With all of that, you will not go wrong."

His words warmed Myles, and he turned them over in his mind as he made his way tiredly to his room. He cleaned himself up, then went downstairs to supper. All during the meal, Sir Robert talked about how they had practiced and how well Myles had done.

Ralph nodded approvingly and then said of himself disparagingly, "I'm afraid I'm more of a clerk than a warrior." He shrugged slightly. "Don't have the gift for it, I guess, so you'll have to be the knight of the family, Myles."

Myles blushed at the words, unsure—as usual—how to take Geddes's remarks. He turned and started to say something to Lady Jane but was interrupted.

Molly, one of the serving girls, a pretty girl of nineteen or twenty with long black hair and flashing dark eyes, had come out of the kitchen bearing a large tureen of soup. She was forced to go between where Myles sat with his back to the wall and the narrow space behind him. The table had somehow gotten pushed too close in that direction, and she saw that she could not maneuver by holding the tureen in front of her. Carefully she lifted it so that it would be over Myles's head, turned sideways, and started to edge by. Unfortunately she stepped on a branch of the rushes that twisted under her, and with a scream, she dropped the tureen of hot soup directly on Myles.

Myles was caught completely unprepared, and the soup, while not scalding, was hot enough to be very uncomfortable. He leaped up, wiping at his face, and at the same time looked around trying to find out what had happened.

Geddes, who was seated down the table from Myles, jumped out of his chair and headed toward the girl. He snarled, "You clumsy wench!" and threw his hand out, giving her a sound blow on the forehead that drove her up against the wall.

Myles saw terror leap to the girl's face. She turned to face him and threw her arms up over her head to protect herself. *She expects to be beaten,* he thought suddenly. Seeing Geddes step closer to loom over her ominously, he put his hand out and said, "It's all right, Ralph! I'm not hurt."

He saw Geddes's face grow stormy, and Geddes said, "She needs to be beaten!"

"No. It was just a little warm." Myles bent down and picked up the silver tureen, saying gently, "Here, Molly. You'll have to go get some more soup." He smiled at her. "Most of this is down my neck, so we can't eat that."

Molly's eyes blinked, and she half-lowered her arms from her face. She could not speak, so great was her fear, for she knew that if Geddes had his way she would be beaten until her back was raw. But she saw the face of young Myles Wakefield and knew that there was no danger there. "I'm so sorry, Mr. Myles!" she finally gasped.

"It's all right." He handed her the bowl, then looked at Lady Jane. "I'll just go up and slip out of this and be right back."

Molly scurried out of the room, and Myles went toward his bedroom. Geddes said, "That is setting a bad example, sir!"

"I'm not sure it is," Lady Jane said calmly.

Geddes turned to her and said, "You know how these servants are! You let them get by with one thing, then it's something else."

Lady Jane did not argue. Soon Myles came back, and they finished their meal.

Later, when Lady Jane and Sir Robert were alone, she said, "That was a strange thing tonight, wasn't it, Robert?"

"You mean the soup business?"

"Yes. Most men would have thrashed the girl. At least cursed her."

Sir Robert considered his wife. "Most noblemen, perhaps. But Myles has been where she is—" He hesitated and looked at her doubtfully. "That might be a good thing, or it might not. He may be too lenient."

Lady Jane answered firmly, "No. He did very well. I admired the way he handled it. He is going to be a young man of great poise and deportment."

The words pleased Sir Robert, as any words praising his son did, and as he considered them, his former doubt disappeared. "He is a real Wakefield, isn't he, Jane?" he said with satisfaction.

The object of their discussion had no idea the incident warranted any attention. In fact, Myles would have thought no further of the incident had it not been for Ralph. Later that night, when the two of them made their way to their bedrooms, Ralph brought it up. They passed Molly in the hallway, and she gave Myles a trembling smile.

Geddes laughed and grinned at Myles. "The wench is mooning over you, old boy. I'll wager you won her fair heart for good!"

Embarrased, Myles could think of no reply and mumbled, "Good night, Ralph."

Geddes stood there, the smile gone from his lips. He thought hard, then his lip curled with disdain, and the bitterness he'd hidden all evening swept over his handsome features. "All right, now," he muttered. "We'll just see how the dear son and heir makes out!" He whirled and went to his own room, his heart filled with a cold hatred for Myles Wakefield.

A GROWN-UP
YOUNG WOMAN

I think, dear, you need to give Myles some sort of reward."
Lady Jane had come to Sir Robert as he worked at his large
desk. When he looked up with surprise, she put her hand
gently on his shoulder. "He has worked very hard the past two
months, and he has done so well!"

Sir Robert put his turkey quill down carefully and wiped his
hands as he thought about her remark. He looked up at her with
a smile on his lips and nodded. "Yes, I believe you're right. He has
done well, hasn't he, Jane?"

"Marvelously well! In his studies and with the things you've
been teaching him, the riding and jousting. You're very proud of
him, aren't you?"

"Oh, he's done all right," Sir Robert said, trying to sound
offhand and nonchalant. When she smiled at him, he laughed
loudly and slapped the table. "By heaven, I can't be modest, Jane!
The boy is everything that a man could want in a son. I just thank
God that we found him."

"So do I. But he's looking rather tired lately, Robert. I keep him at
his books, and you keep him at swordplay and hawking and hunting.
Between the two of us, we're going to wear the poor dear out."

Sir Robert got to his feet, his face thoughtful. "What sort of
reward were you thinking of, Jane?"

"Well, I think he has all of his needs met. He doesn't particularly need clothes. I just wonder if he wouldn't like to have a bit of freedom. He has been very closely supervised here." She smiled again and put her hand on his cheek. "I wouldn't want him to get discontented and then discouraged. Why don't you offer him a little vacation? Just let him go somewhere by himself." She hesitated, then said, "He's that kind of a boy, you know. He likes to be alone."

Robert glanced at her sharply. "I've noticed that. But there's nothing sullen in it. He just seems to enjoy his own company. Not a bad thing in a young man." He thought for a moment, then said decisively, "All right. I'll do it. What's more, I'll do it right now."

He left the room at once, always a man ready to take action, and headed out of the house, going toward the mews. Myles was there, holding the new falcon. No one had been able to do much with the bird, for it seemed that all she wanted to do was hurt someone. But Myles had worked with her determinedly until finally the bird would at least sit on his gauntlet.

"Bird doing any good?" Sir Robert asked as he entered.

"She will," Myles responded quickly. He ruffled the feathers on the bird's breast and laughed as she slashed at his fingers with her beak. "She's just a little nervous right now. But when she gets used to us, she'll be all right."

Sir Robert thought, *Those words might apply to you, Myles.* But he said, "I've been thinking. It might be good for you to get away from Wakefield for a while." He noted the surprise that widened the boy's eyes and smiled warmly. "You've been working hard. Too hard, perhaps. I've been so anxious to see you do well that I've put more on you than I should have."

"Oh no—"

"Yes," Sir Robert stopped him, holding up his hand. "Lady Jane has informed me that you are deserving of a reward, and I think she's right." He waited while Myles digested this and then asked, "Would you like to get away for a while? Make a short trip somewhere?"

Such an idea had never entered Myles's head. He had not yet accustomed himself to the ways of the aristocracy, and having been bound tightly to the farm and to his work for his entire life, he was no less surprised than if Sir Robert had offered him the crown. But his thoughts began to work rapidly, and he said, "Yes, sir. There is one place I would like to go, if I could."

"Where's that, boy?"

"I'd like to go visit Sir John Walsh."

"Walsh?" Sir Robert cocked his head to one side. "I know Walsh. Why in the world would you want to visit him?"

Myles hesitated, trapped, then dropped his head and blushed a little. "Well, sir, there is a gentleman there that I admire very much. The tutor of the Walsh children. Mr. William Tyndale is his name. He's a minister."

Robert Wakefield watched his son carefully and for one moment remained silent. Then he began to smile. "Now, boy," he said, "don't tell me that a young man, being offered a vacation, is going to ride over half the countryside to listen to some dry bones of a preacher." He had seen the rosy glow on the boy's clear cheeks. "Are you sure it's not some kind of a young woman at Walsh's place who draws you there?"

Myles tried to face it out, but when he looked up and saw the gleam of humor in his father's eyes, he said, "Well, sir, there *is* a young woman there—the daughter of the seneschal for Sir John Walsh. Her name is Hannah Kemp. She's the one who taught me to read."

Sir Robert laughed and slapped the boy on the shoulder, noting the firm muscles that had developed as the result of the steady exercise and good diet Myles had been experiencing. "I like you better for it, boy! Ministers are all right, but a young lad of his age, he needs to see a pair of bright blue eyes now and then!"

"You've seen her, sir?" Myles was surprised.

"Because I know she has blue eyes? No, but when I was your age—" he smiled and winked—"I could never resist a pair of blue eyes! Tell you what," he went on, "we'll get you a fine horse, a new outfit, put some money in your purse, and you can go riding up to Sir John Walsh's like you were King Arthur himself! How will that be?"

As always, when Myles received a gift or a word of commendation from his father, he became tongue-tied. So often he wanted to blurt out how he really felt and how life had changed for him—but somehow he never could. He looked directly into his father's eyes and tried to say something. The best he could do was mumble, "Yes, sir, I'd like that a lot."

Sir Robert understood the boy's awkwardness. *He's just learning,* he thought. *Soon he will know how to put what he feels into words. And I'm glad Jane suggested this.*

"Come on, now," he said heartily. "Let's find you a horse. What about that black mare you're so fond of? Think she'd have enough style to go prancing up to your blue-eyed maid?"

Myles rode the sleek black mare up the road toward Little Sodsbury Manor. As he neared the house, he was relieved to see William Tyndale standing outside, watching plowmen with their yokes of oxen breaking up a field. For some reason, Myles felt apprehensive about meeting Hannah, and he'd hoped that he could hold onto the pretense of coming to see William Tyndale. He pulled his horse up a few yards away and, as he slipped out of the saddle, Tyndale turned to face him. Myles was surprised that there was no recognition in the man's eyes, for he thought that he might be remembered.

"How do you do, young sir?" Tyndale greeted him with a nod. "Are you seeking Sir John? Or some of the family?"

"Well, no, Mr. Tyndale. I . . . I really was looking for you." He asked almost plaintively, "Don't you remember me, sir?"

"No, I don't think so." Tyndale studied his face. "Where did we meet?"

"Right here. I visited you once before." This was awful! Tyndale could not even remember him—Myles felt his face burning. "My name is Myles. Myles Morgan, you knew me as."

William Tyndale's eyes flew open in surprise. "Why, young man! No wonder I didn't recognize you! Come, let me have a look at you." He came closer, and beneath his beard, his lips turned upward in a smile. He studied the fine, expensive clothing, the prancing horse with the fine saddle, and shook his head. "Yes, I heard your story, young man. You're not Myles Morgan any more. You are Myles Wakefield, as I understand it."

Eagerly Myles nodded, "Yes, sir! That's me! I have had a change in my life!"

"Indeed, the whole country is talking about it," Tyndale responded. "I congratulate you on your good fortune. From what I hear, Sir Robert Wakefield and his wife are exemplary citizens." He looked Myles up and down, and a mischief lit his eyes. "Well now, so you've come to see me, have you? What a fine thing! Why, most young men might be more interested in the young ladies here . . . say, Miss Hannah, for example. Of course, you wouldn't be even the least interested in seeing Miss Hannah, now would you?"

"Well . . . well . . . as a matter of fact . . ."

Watching the boy turn red and stammer, Tyndale took pity on him and nodded with understanding. "I thought you might. Come along, Myles, I think she is in the house."

Myles tied the horse to a hitching rail and followed the older man into the house. They were met by Sir John Walsh and Lady Walsh, and when William Tyndale introduced their guest, they both stared at him with avid interest.

"Why, you're Hannah's young friend!" Lady Walsh said. She was a lady of thirty-five with blonde hair and faded blue eyes. She hardly knew the correct address for the young man; Hannah had explained his station as a servant before, and now he looked like a young lord. "I expect your life has changed considerably," she said, rather foolishly.

The little group stood talking, and then a door opened and in came Hannah Kemp. At sixteen, she was a beautiful young woman. Her honey-colored hair caught the sunlight that came through the window, and her clear blue eyes flew open when she saw Myles. She knew him at once, of course, and almost ran to him. But glancing at the older people, she merely nodded and said, "Myles, it's so good to see you."

Myles had not yet mastered the graceful courtier's bow, so the best he could do was to nod and say, "It's good to see you, Miss Hannah. You are looking well." This sounded incredibly foolish to his ears—she was looking far better than well!

Sensing the young man's awkwardness, William Tyndale said, "Why don't you and Hannah come to my study, and we can have a lesson?"

"Oh, that would be fine, sir!" Myles said eagerly. Hannah's eyes lit up and she curtseyed to the Walshes. Myles sketched something between a bow and a nod, and then turned to follow Hannah and William Tyndale to his room upstairs.

For half an hour they talked pleasantly, Hannah doing most of the talking. But then Tyndale began to question Myles as to his condition, and when Myles had given him his report, he nodded with satisfaction saying, "Lady Jane is a godly woman, well known as an exemplary Christian. She will be good for you, my boy." Tyndale paused and picked up a book from his desk. He looked at it and weighed it in his hands carefully. He ran his hand over the leather cover as if it were pleasant to the touch, then looked up at Myles and said, "Learn the Bible, my son. It contains the truth we need to get us to heaven, and to keep us free from error on earth."

He began to talk about the Bible and stood up and looked out the window. "Come here," he said. When the two young people had joined him, he motioned toward a young man no more than sixteen or seventeen who was plowing with a yoke of oxen out in the field. "Do you see that young plowman?" he asked. They nodded, and the minister stared at the plowman with a visionary light in his fine eyes. "Before I am through, that young plowman and others like him, people by the thousands, will be able to read the Scriptures for themselves. In plain plowman's English."

Much of this Myles could not understand, but he had heard enough to know that having the Bible in your hands was a dangerous thing. He said rather timidly, "Isn't it enough to have the priests and the ministers teach us?"

His question seemed to grieve Tyndale, and the man shook his head sadly. "That is the argument of many, my boy—but it is not sound. God has spoken to man through his Son, Jesus Christ. But unless men are able to read that message in the written form, it is as if they are blind and deaf. No, the Word of God must go forth. It must!"

Soon after this, Tyndale looked at the two young people and said, "It is almost time for the evening meal. You'll be joining us, won't you, Master Myles?"

Myles hesitated and saw Hannah nod slightly. "Yes, sir, I'll be happy to, if I won't be in the way."

"There will be other guests tonight." A humorous light came to Tyndale's eyes, and he said, "Perhaps you will learn a little more about the nature of the ministry." He turned and left the room, leaving Myles and Hannah alone.

"Now, tell me everything, Myles!" Hannah cried. Her eyes were alive with anticipation. "Oh! People have talked about nothing else ever since you went to Wakefield! What is it like to be a nobleman?"

Myles was embarrassed by the question and frowned slightly. "I don't know what it's like," he said, then tried again. "It's—it's peculiar. I feel just the same except sometimes now I know how awkward and clumsy and ignorant I am, and I feel like a fraud!" he burst out, then took a deep breath. "But, my father and Lady Jane, they're making it easy for me," he added, and some of the tension left his voice. His eyes began to glow as he reviewed his life for her. She sat listening, her lips parted in wonder, completely unaware what an attractive picture she made. Finally Myles stopped himself and blinked with surprise. "I've become quite a talker, haven't I, Hannah?"

"I want to hear everything," she said. "Have you been back to visit the Bournevilles yet?" An uncertain look swept his face, and she went on carefully, "I'll bet you are anxious to see Isabella."

Her words pricked him a little, and he said guiltily, "Why should I want to see her any more than anyone else?" He tried to meet her eyes, but he could not. She was smiling slightly. He went on denying it, blustering, "I think she's pretty enough. But there are other people there, too, you know, that I'd like to visit. I'd like to talk with Nob and see how the hawks are doing." At the amused look on Hannah's face, Myles clamped his lips shut.

Hannah knew that he would say nothing more, so she rose and slipped her arm into his. "Come along, let's go for a walk before supper. Tell me more about Wakefield and what it's like, and about Lady Jane. . . ."

An hour later they entered the house, and Sir John came to meet them. "Come along, you two, we've been waiting for you. Some of our guests want to meet the distinguished new member of the Wakefield family."

Myles would have turned and run, but he was practically dragged into the dining room and forced into a chair. Four men fixed him with interested eyes. They questioned him carefully and closely about the transition in his life, and he answered as modestly as he could. Finally the meal started, and he was relieved he was no longer the center of interest. Myles had never seen so many high-ranking men. They all wore expensive clothes and pancake-flat berets. Two of them were lantern-jawed and stooped, one was skeleton thin, and one was plump and bulging. Their fingers glittered with jeweled rings, and ornate chains and crosses hung around their necks and flickered, giving off the light from the lamps. The guests were served on a well-filled table as the steaming food was brought in. After the meal was over, Sir John said, "Now, I believe you gentlemen have some questions for Mr. Tyndale."

Immediately one of the men, a priest, challenged William Tyndale. "Sir, you are stirring up much comment in these parts with your preaching on the Bristol Green."

Tyndale's eyes flashed. "At least I am not using the alehouse as my preaching place, as some barking curs I know of."

The priest choked on a bit of food, and another priest intervened. "Some say your views are a disturbance!" he said, his fat face red with anger.

Tyndale reached out for the salt cellar and held it up. "The nature of salt is to bite, fret, and make smart, is it not? The office of a true preacher is to be salt, and," he added, "true preaching stirs up persecution."

"But do you not fear a charge of heresy?" the thin priest demanded.

Tyndale snorted, "Heresy? The source of heresy is pride. I have said nothing that cannot be justified out of the New Testament."

Myles sat in amazement. In all of his life, he had never heard a priest challenged. In his village, priests had been the final law. Even the lords of the manor usually gave way before them, afraid of being excommunicated. And now as he looked around the table, he saw plainly the undercurrents of antagonism and even hatred that lay below the surface of the guests' demeanor. He began to hope that William Tyndale would not argue any further—but Tyndale was just warming up.

"There are twenty thousand priests in England today who mumble from morning until night and don't even know what they say! They couldn't translate Latin if they had to!"

"Why should they translate it?" the lantern-jawed priest asked, leaning forward. "Latin is the language of the church!"

"Jesus didn't know Latin!" Tyndale slapped the table with an open hand. "Why should English curates sing and say and prattle Latin with the lips only?"

Someone interrupted, "Are we to be tutored by this man?"

Voices buzzed, and finally one of the priests raised his voice to ask, "Is it true you have a heretical book in your possession?"

William Tyndale put his hand on a book by his plate. "Why, no. I don't have a heretical book. I do, however, have a copy of Martin Luther's New Testament."

A sudden silence fell over the room. One of the priests whispered in a stunned voice, "Luther's New Testament!"

Everyone stared at William Tyndale. A priest stood up, pointing a finger at him, and said, "This heretic . . . this traitor to God has in his hands a German heretic's book!"

Tyndale rose and faced him across the table. "Martin Luther is not a heretic," Tyndale said calmly. "The Word of God strips man of everything and leaves him as bare as Job. And Luther has this oneness of God from the Word of God. He has translated God's own Word into the language of his people."

"We will not knowingly consult with a heretic!" another of the priests cried out and he, too, stood. Straightaway, the remaining two priests rose, and they all walked away. Sir John followed them, trying to calm them, but no one listened. Lady Walsh watched from the doorway, her face white and strained.

Tyndale said briefly, "My time here will be short."

Sir John came back with a worried look. "I fear there will be trouble," he said.

William Tyndale nodded. "It is time for me to go, Sir John. I thank you for your kindness, but I leave this week for London."

Myles noticed that there was no protest from either Sir John or his wife—they well knew that to harbor a heretic might bring the wrath of the church down upon their own heads. There were men in the Tower now who had done less, and the relief in Sir John's face was evident.

Tyndale smiled at them with understanding. "It was inevitable, Sir John. I must thank you from my heart for your kindness—but it would be dangerous for you if I stayed here."

Later he said to Myles, "I will pray for you, my boy. Your way may be more difficult than you think." When a look of surprise came to the young man, he added, "God tests us in two ways: by difficulty and by prosperity. I think I will undergo the first, but your test may be even more difficult. Few men can stand the temptations that come with wealth and position."

He took his leave then, and Myles said abruptly, "I must be going, too."

Hannah said quickly, "Why, you cannot find an inn this late at night. We have a spare bed in the attic, and mother and father will be glad to have you. Come with me."

Myles welcomed the invitation. He went to speak his words of thanks and farewell to the Walshes, then he and Hannah left. As they walked toward the cottage where Hannah's family lived, Myles was troubled. "I never heard anyone talk like that to a priest!" he marveled. "What will happen to him?"

Hannah did not respond immediately. After a silence she said, "I am afraid for him. He's so good. I've heard it whispered that there are those in the church who are out to get rid of him. He could wind up being burned at the stake, as others have been!"

Myles stopped dead still. "Burned! Surely not! Not here in England!"

"Why should you be surprised?" Hannah asked. "Men have been burned before, and women, too, for that matter, for their faith."

"Why does he do it?" Myles asked with wonder. Puzzled, he looked back toward the Walsh's house, where Tyndale was, even as they spoke, preparing to leave. "He is such a wise man, he must see that sooner or later he will be caught."

"I don't think he minds being caught," Hannah said quietly. "As long as he gets what he wants."

"What he wants?" Myles echoed. "What's that?"

"He wants to see the Bible in English, so that people like you and me, and all the plowmen, and all the housewives in England, can read it for themselves." Her answer was simple, and her voice seemed to hang in the air.

As Myles looked at her, he realized that here was a girl who knew far more than he, and he was suddenly ashamed of his ignorance. He had always taken religion for granted, assuming that the priests would handle it as long as he attended church and did not commit too great or too many sins. He knew it had been different with his mother, but she had seemed special, as though God had set her apart for intimate communion. Myles had never known of anyone else with a faith like his mother's . . . and then the image of William Tyndale came to his mind.

He frowned. Could it be? Was it possible that there was more to religion than the church? His mind swam with thoughts and questions. And now . . . now there was this notion that there was something worth dying for in the Bible. He was troubled and said little more as they neared Hannah's house.

Just before they got there, Hannah put her hand on his arm and said, "Don't tell my parents about Mr. Tyndale. They love him very much and would be disturbed." Then she turned to go into the house, and Myles followed her. Her parents were glad enough to furnish him with a bed, and long after Myles lay in it, he thought of the strange evening.

William Tyndale isn't afraid of anything in this world, he thought with admiration. He had always thought of the courage a man might need when facing an opponent in a fight—but now he was seeing that not all battles were fought with swords. Somehow the idea frightened him, and he pulled his thoughts away. He dreamed that night of Isabella, which was not unusual. But he dreamed also of a girl with honey-colored hair and a pair of bright blue eyes.

When he left Little Sodsbury the next day, Hannah took his hand and looked up at him. "It will be terribly lonely here now that Mister Tyndale is leaving."

It was, Myles understood, an invitation, and he held her soft hand, pressing it as he smiled, and said, "I'll be back to see you soon, Hannah." Then he caught himself and added lamely, "So that we can have some more reading lessons." She laughed as the red color filled his face, and he grinned at her sheepishly.

As he rode away, he thought of what a fine young woman Hannah Kemp had turned out to be. *She'll make a fine wife for someone,* he thought and then was shocked to discover that the idea of Hannah marrying was not at all pleasant to him! He laughed at his own foolishness, saying to the mare, "She's not your property, Myles Wakefield!" He turned and looked back at her as she stood at the gate waving, the sun reflecting on her golden hair. He waved back, then rode toward home, his thoughts turning to Isabella.

Eleven

A NEW STAR
IN THE SKY

When Myles came to the fork in the road, he pulled his horse up and stared down the right-hand fork. Then, making a decision, he spurred forward, pulling the mare's head around. As he pushed forward at a brisk pace he thought, *It won't be much out of the way to go by the Bournevilles'. And after all, it's my duty to pay them a visit.*

No sooner had he finished the thought when he realized he was becoming more sophisticated. A slight grin touched his lips and he spoke out loud to the mare. "Well, Fancy, to be honest it's nearly thirty miles out of the way. But I don't think Sir Robert or Lady Jane will mind." Satisfied with his decision, he kept up a fast pace and three hours later arrived at Harrow, the home of the Bournevilles.

An odd sensation raced through him as he walked his mare, letting his eyes run over the scene, so familiar that he felt he knew every rock, every house, every human, and almost every animal that lived under the Bourneville authority. It was here he had learned what it meant to come into young manhood, and even as he looked across the open space and saw the hovel where his mother had died and where he himself had slept a thousand times, he felt a pang in his heart and his lips grew tight. He had not been able to totally reconcile himself to the loss of his mother. Deep within, he grieved silently and almost continually.

"Hi! Ho, there!"

Myles pulled up and looked around to see Nob running across the courtyard, eyes bright and a smile on his brown, wrinkled face. He slid off his horse and reached out to grab the man and gave him a fierce hug. "Nob!" he said and pounded the sinewy shoulder. "How I've missed you! But you look well."

Nob blinked his sharp blue eyes and ran his hand awkwardly through his hair. "I never would've known you," he said softly, gazing at the young man's expensive clothing and staring admiringly at the fine mare as if he could not believe what he was seeing. "I swear you've grown a foot since you left! But look at you now, a young gentleman, true enough!" The falconer suddenly became aware of Myles's arm about his shoulder and stepped backward in embarrassment. "But you'll not be wanting to show such familiarity to the likes of me," he said. "You're no longer the poor boy that I knew here."

His words caused Myles some pain, and he said, "Don't be foolish, Nob. I'm the same as I ever was."

"Aye, and it's you who shouldn't be foolish," Nob snapped, and there was an ancient wisdom in his eyes. "Someone said you can't step in the same river twice, boy. And that's even more true of life. I'm the same, no doubt in that, but you're far different from the Myles I once knew." A kindly smile lit his face. "Don't you be grieving, now. It's proud I am to see you rise in the world. And think about your dear mother, how happy she would be to see you looking like this!"

Myles dropped his head and stared at the ground. He said sadly, "I wish she could, Nob. I miss her. Every day I think about her, and at night, too."

Nob wanted to reach out and comfort Myles, but others were approaching and he knew it was no longer his place to be so familiar. "I know, I know," he said a little helplessly, "but it's proud she'd be of you."

Cheval lumbered up, looking even huger than he ever had and showing no notion of the difference in their stations. To him, Myles, for all his fine clothes, was still his helper at the lowly work on the farm. His ham of a hand clapped on the shoulder of the young man, and his gapped teeth flashed in a smile. "Well, now, you've come back!" he said superfluously. He looked Myles up and down. "You look fine, don't he now."

The other servants who had gathered around, all of them friends Myles had known for most of his life, were as awkward as Myles himself. They stood back, and though he went to each one of them and greeted them and they responded, yet it was different. He realized then that he had stepped out of one world into another. In his struggle to learn the ways of the nobility, to understand what it meant to be a gentleman, he had been looking at the world he was entering—not once had he thought that he was also leaving a world behind.

The crowd began to thin, and he looked up to see Ridley, the seneschal, standing on the steps and smiling at him oddly. "I will see you later, Nob," Myles said. "I want to see all the birds and all the dogs." He clapped the falconer soundly on the shoulder, then turned and moved across the yard to mount the steps.

"How are you, Ridley?" he asked. "It's good to see you."

Ridley looked no different than he ever had, tall and thin with gray hair and a straight, narrow line on his face that served for a mouth. He studied the young man and then mentally made some revisions. Many times in the past he had thrashed Myles, but he understood at once that this was a different time. "It is good to see you, Master Wakefield," he said, stressing the name carefully. He did not hold his hand out, but bowed shortly as he would to any of the nobility. "We have heard fine things of you, sir. And it's proud I am to hear of your good fortune."

"Thank you, Ridley," Myles said. Then he smiled a little, for he recognized the adroit change of policy that had taken place in the seneschal. He grinned more broadly and went on, "A few bits of expensive clothes make quite a difference, don't they?"

"'Tis more than that, sir," Ridley said. He studied the boy carefully. "You seem different inside as well, not just the matter of the clothes at all." Then his face relaxed and a slight smile came to his thin lips. "I am glad for you, Mr. Myles. You were always a good boy. And now you are in your proper place and you shall be a credit to the Wakefield name. Come along," he said briskly, "the family is at home."

Myles followed Ridley into the great hall and then into a smaller room that served as a dining room, where he found Sir Geoffrey and his wife, Lady Mary, waiting for him. Sir Geoffrey had gained weight, and his face was flushed as he came to Myles with his hands out. Gripping Myles's hands hard he said, "Well, my boy! Well, well, now, look at this! Can you feature it, Lady Mary?"

Lady Mary Bourneville was a woman of tremendous pride, and she was having difficulty in making the adjustment to Myles's new position. To her, this was Myles the stableboy, the servant, the serf, bound to Bourneville land, son of a serving woman. And now, to have her husband holding this boy's hands, inviting her to admire him . . . well, she felt some discomfort. Finally she nodded slightly and said, "You are looking well, Myles."

This, Myles knew, was all he might expect from Lady Bourneville, at least for the present. He smiled. "I apologize for stopping by uninvited, but I was on my way home to Wakefield, and I thought I would—"

At that moment, a movement caught Myles's eye, and he turned to see Isabella come through a side door. She was wearing a long, flowing silk gown of a light green color that exactly matched her eyes. Her hair was done up in some new fashion he had never seen before, and her eyes had a welcome that he had not expected.

"Myles!" she cried, running to him with quick little steps, holding out her hands. "How good to see you!"

He took one of her hands in his and then, feeling completely awkward, for he had never done so before, lifted it and kissed it. It may have been poorly done, but he saw approval in Isabella's eyes.

She cried, "Oh, my! You've learned the manners of a courtier already! I shall have to be on my guard against you!"

Sir Geoffrey laughed and said, "He can join the ranks of those chasing you, I suppose." He turned to his wife and asked, "Do you think we could find a bite for this fellow? And a place to put him up for the night? You are staying, aren't you, Myles?"

"If it's no trouble—"

"No, no! It's no trouble." Sir Geoffrey took Myles by the arm and said, "Come with me, I want to show you what we've done on the place since you've been gone."

Isabella intervened at once. She was a tyrant as far as her father was concerned, for he never saw anything wrong with anything she did. She stepped between the two, displacing her father's grasp, holding on lightly to Myles's arm, which sent a thrill along the young man's nerves. "No, Father! You can have Myles later, to show him the old farm—but now I am going to tell him the big news."

Myles saw Lady Mary and Sir Geoffrey exchange a swift glance. He asked, "Big news? What is it?"

"You just come along, and if you are good, I will tell you." Isabella smiled. She practically dragged Myles out of the room, saying, "Now, you tell me everything that you've done since you left. Don't leave out a single thing!"

The next hour was a pleasant one for Myles Wakefield. As they walked along, he thought she had never been so charming—or so beautiful. He had never been a young man to talk much, but she could cajole a story out of a rock, he was sure. By the time they had walked completely around the house twice and had come to one of the pastures sheltered by oaks, under which grazed a flock of sheep, he found he had talked steadily, telling her thoughts that he had not even formed completely in his own mind. "I'm talking too much," he said with some embarrassment. "I've never talked so much in my whole life."

"Oh, but it's so fascinating, Myles," Isabella said insistently. "You can't imagine how people have talked! To see a serf lifted out of the pigsty, practically, and placed in satins, wearing a gold ring!" She stepped back and looked at him, a smile on her wide mouth. "It's like a romance or a fairy story of a poor boy turned into a prince!" She examined him a little longer and then came close to whisper, "Now tell me, what are you going to do now?"

"Do now?" he asked, his eyebrows lifting. "Why, I'm going home."

"No, I mean what are you going to do with your life, now that you are a member of the nobility?"

"I never thought of it," he said ruefully. "I'm too busy learning things. It's hard, you know. I'm having to learn things that you have known all your life—how to eat properly, what to wear. I'm so ignorant!" Some of the worry he felt crept into his voice. "Sir Robert is teaching me all about weapons and the things that a man has to know, and Lady Jane is teaching me out of books. But I do seem to get on so slow!"

"I don't believe that," Isabella said firmly. She was more impressed than she cared to admit at the sight of this young man she had known practically all her life. He was fully six feet tall, and though his form was not completely filled out, the carefully tailored clothes fit him well. She noted that there was a handsomeness about him—perhaps due to the fact that his face was clean and his hair was trimmed.

Isabella liked excitement, and there was something exciting about the transformation of this swineherd into a young lord.

Determined to show him off to all of her friends, she did her best to persuade him to stay over for a few days. "You must!" she said prettily. Coming forward, she picked up his hand and held it in both of hers and looked up at him enchantingly. "I'm going to show you off," she announced. "After all, I feel like you somehow belong to me."

Her words made Myles almost dizzy. He swallowed hard, then said, "Well, I don't suppose a few days will matter." Then he remembered her teasing in the dining room and asked, "What is this news you've got to tell me?"

Isabella's eyes opened wide with excitement, and her eyebrows made beautifully curved arches over them. "Oh, Myles, you can't think!" she said breathlessly. "I'm going to London!"

"To London!" Myles exclaimed in dismay. "You mean for a visit?"

"Oh no, for longer than that. I'm to be a maid in the court of the king, waiting upon Queen Catherine!"

She could not have surprised Myles more if she had said she was going to cross the ocean. Dismay filled him, and he asked, "Why do you want to do that?" and then recognized how foolish a question it was. He had heard of the court, the glitter and the romance of it, and knew instantly that Isabella would give practically anything to be a part of such a life. To cover up, he went on, "Well, of course, it will be exciting for you. But—" he hesitated and then said, "your family will miss you."

Isabella was only seventeen but had been courted for at least three years by young gentlemen. She was a flirt by nature, by instinct, and by choice. "Well, what about you?" she asked, reaching up to touch his chin. "Will you miss me too, Myles?"

Myles swallowed and nodded, afraid to try to speak. She patted his cheek, saying absently, "But of course you would! You shall have to come to court and visit me. You'll try, won't you?"

Such a thing had never occurred to Myles. On the spot, he

decided he would begin a campaign to persuade Sir Robert to take him to London himself. *I will go there or die!* he thought vehemently. "Yes," he answered. "Sir Robert goes there fairly often. I think he will take me if I ask him."

Isabella prattled on about all the things she would be doing in London, and Myles considered some of the stories he had heard about the court of King Henry VIII. When she began to quiet down a little, he said cautiously, "The court is a pretty dangerous place, or so I've heard."

"Dangerous? What do you mean by that?"

"Well, Sir Robert tells me that King Henry is a very strange man." Then he began stumbling over his words. "No, I didn't . . . mean . . . exactly that. But he told me about several of the young ladies there that, umm . . . " He stopped, nonplussed. How to repeat what Sir Robert had said—that virtue was often lost at the court of King Henry VIII—without embarrassing Isabella . . . and himself? In fact, Sir Robert had gone so far as to say that young women played romantic games with the young nobility and that if he had a daughter, he would no sooner think of letting her go to that court than he would of letting her go to Spain!

With a sigh, Myles knew he could not say these things to Isabella plainly, and he did not know how to phrase it delicately enough for a maiden's ears. He finally finished lamely, "Oh, I don't know, it . . . just seems to be so far away."

Isabella enjoyed his evident discomfort—she was fairly sure she knew what Myles was referring to. She had heard about the vices of the court and was quite looking forward to finding out for herself if the tales were true. Her eyes sparkled and she said, "You must not worry about me, Myles. I'll be fine." Then she abruptly changed the subject. "I have heard about your many successes and improvements. Ralph has told me how you're doing."

The mention of Geddes brought a sudden gloom to Myles, for he knew that Geddes had been one of the group of young men who gathered around Isabella. While not exactly one of her suitors, he was nevertheless certainly interested in her. Ralph had told him about his visits to Harrow and about Isabella. Although Myles had said nothing, he had felt a pang of jealousy each time. Now he said, "Ralph has been a great help to me. He helped me pick these clothes out, as a matter of fact."

"Well, he did a fine job," she laughed, "but then Ralph is quite a young dandy. You just missed him, you know, he was here only two days ago." She told Myles of some of the parties she had attended with Ralph, unaware (or perhaps not so unaware!) that she was making Myles miserable. Finally she said, "Now I must take you back to Father so he can show you his old horses and things. But tonight we're having a small party. Some of the young people are coming over. And don't forget, you must stay very close to me. Don't let any of the girls take you away. Some of them are rather forward," she finished primly.

"I—I—uh, won't," Myles stammered.

As Myles walked back to the house with Isabella, he was aware of her youthful beauty and her charm and could not imagine what it would be like to be her favorite suitor. He felt himself to be a million miles beneath her—but hope springs eternal indeed in the breast of a young man who is infatuated, and by the time they reached the house he had grown hopeful. By the time the evening had come and the party was in full swing, he was able to show to good advantage just how changed he was.

Later that night, after the party was over, Isabella was talking to her father. Sir Geoffrey asked, "Well, did young Myles behave himself tonight?"

"Yes, he did very well, Father," Isabella said. There was a calculated look in her eye as she said, "It was really difficult to believe that he has learned so much. Oh, he still makes mistakes, but he is so handsome that no one really notices them. And besides, it is so romantic, the way his life has gone!" She sniffed and said, "I was almost embarrassed at the way some of those girls threw themselves at him!"

Sir Geoffrey knew his daughter fairly well and grinned at her. "Do you think he might be a suitor for you, girl? I mean, after all, he isn't Myles Morgan any longer. He is Myles Wakefield, gentleman. And one day," he added thoughtfully, "he will be Sir Myles Wakefield, master of one of the finest pieces of land in the county."

His words seemed to interest Isabella, and she paused, her lips pursed and her head cocked to one side. Then she smiled at her father. "We'll see," she said with a confident air. "We'll see how he does when he comes to London!"

She left the room, and Sir Geoffrey watched after her anxiously. *I don't know what's to become of that girl,* he thought. *First going off to the king's court, and now young Myles coming out of nowhere—!* He got to his feet and plodded from the room muttering, "Too much for me, this raising of a daughter. . . ."

Twelve

THE COURT OF HENRY VIII

As the small party approached London Bridge, Myles Wakefield turned and looked at his father, wondering if his mother had told him of his disgrace the first time he had seen London. But Sir Robert appeared to have other thoughts, and Myles was grateful. He had not found it difficult to persuade Sir Robert to bring him to London. On the contrary, Robert Wakefield had mentioned to Lady Jane that he was anxious to go show off his new son, and she had urged them to make the trip.

Now, as they approached the great city, Myles looked again at the bridge that provided the only access to London across the Thames. The nineteen irregular arches fought bravely, he noted, to stop the whole structure from toppling into the river. As he and Sir Robert threaded their way down the narrow, dark passage at the center of the bridge, Myles noted the houses along both sides of them that hung crazily over the water.

They stopped once, and Sir Robert took him to the edge of the bridge, through a narrow space between two of those houses, and pointed downward. The water rushed between the houses, and the watermen shouted and bawled at each other. Sir Robert had to shout to be heard over the racket. "They make a sport of it, trying to get through these arches at high water. Sometimes they fail, and I understand quite a few of them have been drowned."

Myles took this all in, and as Sir Robert led the way back to their horses, he thought of how his father seemed anxious to teach him everything. Not only about armor and swordplay and things of that nature, but they would spend long hours in the evenings as Sir Robert talked about the politics of the realm, the problems facing landowners and nobility, and the thousand and one aspects that made up medieval life.

When they cleared the bridge, Sir Robert waved at the wall. "Look at that wall!" he said. "Most cities have one, but not one so firm as this one." He pointed out the large turrets and the huge double gates at Aldgate, Bishop's Gate, Newgate, and others. They made their way through the city, passing through more fields and the archery range.

Sir Robert gave him a short history lesson. "Look you," he said, "the English longbow has already won the battles of Crecy, Poitiers, and Agincourt. At Crecy, the seven thousand archers did not even allow the splendid French knights to come close enough to fight! And at Agincourt, they killed virtually all the horses and left the brave knights encased in their steel in the mud, helpless as beetles on their backs. There's a law now that says every young man must become and remain a proficient bowman." He grew quiet for a time, then added with a touch of regret, "These new weapons, though, these cannons, are going to change all of that. You'll see it in your day."

They spent the day in London, where Sir Robert had business to conduct. They stayed at a tavern and were fortunate to find a room that they had to share with only three other men. The city was not busy at this time of the year, Sir Robert pointed out, otherwise there would have been at least a dozen men crowded into the room.

The next morning they arose early, and Sir Robert informed

Myles that one of the "high days" was coming. Streets were being draped with scarlet arras and carpets of every imaginable hue: cloth-of-gold, tissue, and velvet. Conduits carried red and white wines. The populace would be entertained by fireworks and pageants. As they passed Newgate, Sir Robert said, "There will be executions, probably, and public burnings of traitors and heretics. They always have such things at these holidays."

Myles could not imagine how something so terrible could be part of a holiday, although he knew they took place. He was looking at some of the costumes that the men and women passing by were wearing. Men had their hair close-cut, and their outfits were ridiculous and extravagant. Many wore fur-edged open shirts for coats, beneath which were shirts with lace ruffles, slashed breeches, long hose, and pointed shoes made of velvet, cloth, or leather. As he glanced about, Myles noted that most men wore so many clothes that the bulk made it impossible to draw a bow.

Myles noted how the women's gowns were long and flowing, though most were covered by the women's stiff hoods with lappets. Many wore their hair loose at weddings, but after marriage women covered their hair in a folded hood. Unmarried girls plaited their hair or drew it up into tussocks.

"You know," Sir Robert commented, "this dress has become so ridiculous that a new law was passed last year." He grinned at his son and explained, "It forbids any woman to wear a gown or petticoat of silk or a chain of gold on her neck unless her husband is rich enough to keep a light horse furnished for the king's service. How is that for a clever way to impose a tax!" He went on to inform Myles that citizens' wives were ordered to wear white knitted caps of yarn, and the gowns of domestic servants might not reach below the calf of the leg. Myles listened to all this, storing it away, as he did all the information Sir Robert gave him.

After a while he asked, "When will we go to the court, Father?"

He pronounced the word *Father* rather awkwardly, but his use of it drew a glance of approval from Sir Robert.

"As soon as I finish my business here. You are anxious to see the court, are you boy?"

"Well, yes sir, I am."

"It's something to see," Sir Robert admitted. "Nothing else like it this side of the ocean, I think. Though not all of it is to the good," he added ambiguously. They moved around the city as Sir Robert went about his errands, then just when Myles was despairing of ever making it to the court, they turned for the palace.

<hr />

Myles never forgot his first real encounter with King Henry VIII. He stayed as close to his father as possible when they entered the palace, and for a time, he scarcely dared lift his eyes, so dazzling were the scenes before him. The palace was made, it seemed, of gold: golden candlesticks graced every nook and cranny, gold trim shone along the tables, beautiful tapestries—the likes of which Myles had never seen before—richly adorned every wall. Even the floor itself seemed something that he scarcely dared tread upon, for it was glossy white marble.

The first event they attended was a feast. If Myles had been embarrassed the first time he had eaten at the table with the gentry, he was infinitely more so during that meal.

The first course was introduced by what Sir Robert told him was a "warner." This was a statue of wax, which was followed by spices and comfits—such as grains of paradise or dragées. Myles had no idea what to do with these and cast his eyes around the table, trying to observe. He drew little attention, for he kept quiet—quite a contrast to the men and women lining the long tables, all of whom were dressed in rich clothes, shouting and turning their silver goblets up, draining them with aplomb. At one end of the long room were musicians whose music could scarcely be heard for the laughter, talk, and shouting.

The food was brought in by a host of servants, and Myles's eyes widened at the trays laden with cuts of beef, mutton, deer, and other meats that Myles did not even recognize. Finally, after the main course was over, highly spiced wine was served endlessly around the table. Myles was wise enough to simply taste his in small sips and not gorge himself on it, as he saw some others around him do.

Sir Robert watched his son cautiously, noting with approval that the lad did not drink heavily of the wine. He spoke to him from time to time, pointing out the important noblemen and their ladies who were around the table. Some of the names Myles had heard before, but most of them he had not, and he tried valiantly to fix them in his mind.

Suddenly a slight hush came over the room, beginning down at Myles's right. Myles grew alert when his father said, "There is His Majesty . . . and the queen." Instantly Myles turned his head and watched eagerly as a small group entered the room from the arches on his right.

The leader—the one upon whom every eye was fixed—was King Henry. The king, Myles saw, was a large man, well over six feet in height, and powerful in body. He had a strange face, with small eyes that seemed to glitter, a large, powerful jaw, and a neck that was thick and already beginning to show signs of gathering fat. Henry, Myles knew, was only thirty-two years of age and at the height of his physical powers. He was extremely broad-shouldered and had very fair skin. When he spoke, his voice was somewhat high-pitched, but not at all unpleasant, and it carried over the room.

"No ceremony, no ceremony!" he cried out, waving his hand in a kingly gesture.

"That's what he always says," Sir Robert whispered, hiding his grin behind his hand. "But if we don't begin with ceremony, watch what happens then!"

Myles was not to find out that day, for the members of the nobility rose to their feet in greeting their sovereign, and Henry turned to the woman at his right, saying something to her in a low voice. Queen Catherine was thirty-eight and had been a rather pretty girl with pink skin and reddish hair—so his father informed him. She had married the king after having been married to his older brother, Arthur, who had died. Though she was only five and a half years older than Henry, she looked even older than that. Still, she looked pleasant, and Myles was taken by her air.

Everyone, of course, wanted to speak to the king, and he settled himself on the dais—a raised platform at the end of the room. Soon he was surrounded, and Sir Robert said, "I had hoped to speak with him, but we'll never get close in that crowd." The two sat in a companionable silence for a while—Myles and his father—and finally they got up and began to wander around the room. From time to time, Sir Robert would stop a man and say proudly, "I don't believe you've met my son, Myles." More than once the men he met would stare at Myles, startled, but none of them said anything that was in the least tactless or rude.

Later in the evening, Myles had drawn apart from his father, who was talking to a group of older men. A woman came by. Myles looked up and was shocked to see that it was Queen Catherine. She met his gaze and smiled, and he bowed awkwardly, saying, "Good evening, Your Majesty," as he had been taught.

Catherine, caught by the young man's sincere deference, paused and looked searchingly at him. "We have not met, young sir."

"N–no, Your Majesty. My name is Myles Wakefield. My father is Sir Robert Wakefield."

"Ah yes, we know Sir Robert, of course! But I was not aware that he had a son."

Myles was terribly afraid that he would say the wrong thing. The queen was staring at him strangely, and finally he said with some difficulty, "Well, Your Majesty, he didn't have a son—or he didn't think he did—until very recently." That sounded awkward to his own ears, but he could think of no better way to put it.

The queen blinked with surprise, and then recognition came over her face. "Ah yes, one of my young ladies who recently came to London was telling me of Sir Robert's good fortune. Isabella Bourneville, I believe. You know her, I suppose?"

"Oh yes, I do, Your Majesty. I grew up with her family."

"So she said," Queen Catherine nodded graciously. She seemed interested in Myles, and she began to question him concerning his past. Myles stumbled along as best he could. The queen, he noted, still had a slight Spanish accent despite her many years in England, and there was none of the predatory look about her that he had seen in some of the faces of the ladies of the nobility.

They were interrupted by a voice that said, "Well, my dear, who is this?"

Myles turned, and his heart almost skipped a beat when he saw King Henry, flanked by several of the court officers.

"This is the son of Sir Robert Wakefield. His name is Myles, I believe."

Myles again made his best bow, and when he rose, Henry's smallish eyes seemed to bore into his. He said tentatively, "Wakefield?"

"You remember," Queen Catherine said conversationally, "I told you about Sir Robert finding his son after so many years."

"Oh!" Henry's face grew animated with interest. "Where's your father?" he demanded loudly.

"Here, Your Majesty." Sir Robert had been watching the scene from across the room, and now he came to stand before the king. He bowed and said, "I see you have met my son."

Henry regarded Robert Wakefield with a strange look on his face, then said, "I understand he was raised as a stableboy, or something of the sort."

"Correct, sire." Wakefield nodded. "I did not even know of his existence until recently. But I feel that God has at last given me the son I have long wanted."

A spasm seemed to run across Henry's face, and Wakefield knew instantly that he had said the wrong thing. Everyone knew of Henry's desire for a son, for a male heir to his throne. So far Catherine had produced nothing but stillbirths and one daughter, Mary. But it was too late to rectify it, and he stood waiting to hear what the king would say.

A quiet fell upon the room. But Henry, looking at Myles, seemed merely a little grieved. He cast it off saying, "Well, this young fellow will make a welcome addition to our court! Is he a good hunter, Robert?"

"He is learning fast, Your Majesty. Not of your caliber, of course—but in days to come I am sure I will be proud of him."

"Good, good! We must have him on the chase with us," the king said heartily.

Henry passed along, but Queen Catherine paused long enough to tell Myles, "You will find the young lady we spoke of in the adjoining room." She smiled and said encouragingly, "Perhaps you would like to visit her."

"Oh, thank you, Your Majesty," Myles said quickly, bowing again as she left his side. His father was staring at him, and he explained, "Isabella—she's in the next room, Father. May I go visit her?"

"Go on, boy," Sir Robert said affectionately. "I'll come for you when it's time to leave."

"Thank you, sir." Myles went at once to the door that led into the adjoining room the queen had indicated. Upon entering, he spied Isabella with a bevy of young women and stopped uncertainly.

But Isabella had seen him, and she tore herself away from the group of young women, coming to him quickly. "Myles!" she said with delight. "You *did* come!" She put out her hands, and he held them fast in his. "Come and let me introduce you to the other ladies of the court."

Myles bowed to the other women, some younger than Isabella, a few older—but he could not have repeated one of their names afterward. When the introductions were over, Isabella said to the group, "And I'll not have you stealing him, as I know you would so like to do!" She laughed and pulled Myles away. "Come with me. We shall have some wine, and you can tell me what you've been doing."

The next hour passed very quickly for Myles as he talked to Isabella and listened to her in turn. She was full of the affairs of the court, mentioning the names of the famous in the land, the rich and the powerful—all of whom came to court seeking the favor of the king. Myles listened with interest to it all—except when Isabella mentioned Ralph Geddes. Though the mention was brief, Myles had to struggle to keep displeasure from showing on his face.

All too soon, Sir Robert stood by his side, saying, "It's time to go, boy. You can come back again and visit your lady."

When they returned to their lodgings, Sir Robert asked, "Well, what did you think of it, Myles? Was the court like you thought it would be?"

Myles was silent for a moment, reviewing in his mind all that he had seen. He said thoughtfully, "Queen Catherine—she's not happy, is she, Father?"

Sir Robert shot a quick look at his son and answered evenly, "No, I fear not. She never will be until she produces a son for Henry. That's all he lives for, it seems."

"What if she doesn't?"

"We must just pray that she does." Sir Robert wanted to

175

change the subject and said, "I am going to be busy tomorrow morning. Can you keep yourself occupied? Then tomorrow night, I think we will go back to the palace for another visit."

"Yes, sir, I'll look around the city."

⁂

"Can you direct me to the home of Humphrey Monmouth?" Myles asked one of the tradesmen who was standing out in front of his shop.

"Monmouth? Why, I know the man," he said. He gave meticulous directions to Myles, who at once left and followed them carefully. He had been given the name of Humphrey Monmouth in a note that had come to him from Hannah, informing him that William Tyndale was staying at the man's house in London.

He found the house without any trouble. He knocked on the door and, when it was answered by a servant, said rather haltingly, "My name is Myles Wakefield, and I am seeking Mr. William Tyndale."

"Oh yes, come in," the woman said pleasantly. "If you will wait here, I will see if Mr. Tyndale is available."

She disappeared, and Myles waited rather nervously, but shortly Tyndale himself came down a passageway, smiling and saying, "Well, Myles, my boy! I didn't expect to see you here!" He put out his hand, and taking Myles's hand warmly, said, "Come along. Let's go to my room, and we can talk."

Myles followed Tyndale down the hall into a rather large, well-furnished room. Tyndale indicated a chair, and Myles sat down, while the other man seated himself, as always, behind his desk.

"How did you know I was here, Myles?" Tyndale asked curiously.

"Hannah Kemp told me," Myles explained. "She knew I was coming to London and that I'd like to see you."

Tyndale nodded and began to question Myles closely. He was interested in the boy—partly because of Myles's new life, wondering how that would come out, and partly because he knew more than he said of Hannah Kemp's interest in this young man. Myles answered all of his questions, and Tyndale said, "I'm glad you came by. This has been a difficult time for me. I grow lonesome sometimes."

"Difficult? What's the trouble, sir?"

Tyndale shrugged and said regretfully, "I had hoped to find favor with a gentleman here so that he could finance my translation of the New Testament. But," he sighed deeply, a discouraged note in his voice, "I could hardly find a worse time to come with this sort of request."

"Why is that, sir?"

"Well, Cardinal Wolsey called Parliament in April and informed the country that the king wants a new war. Eight hundred thousand pounds must be raised somehow, and the raising of it has made Wolsey the most hated man in England."

"I heard a little about that from my father."

"Yes. As I say, 'tis a bad time. I have seen everyone I can think of who might be interested in helping me, and all of them have said they just can't afford it."

"I see. That's too bad, sir. What will you do now?"

Tyndale looked up, and there was a fiery light in his eyes. He was a determined-looking man at all times but was even more so now. "Do?" he said. "I will do exactly as God has told me to do. Do you remember," he asked suddenly, "what I told you when we looked out of the window there at the Walsh house?"

Myles thought and did remember. "Yes, sir. You said that one day every plowboy in this country would be able to read the Word of God in his own language."

"That is right, Myles. I'm glad you remembered." Tyndale fell into deep thought, then finally gave the young man across from him a smile. "I will have to leave England," he said. "It's obvious I will not be able to do my work here."

"Leave England!" Myles said, startled. "Where will you go?"

"I will have to go across the Channel. I have been thinking of late that I might go to see Martin Luther."

The very name chilled Myles, for he knew how the priests felt about Luther and what was becoming known as "Protestantism." He feared for William Tyndale, for he had come to respect and care a great deal for the man. He wished that Tyndale were not so set on what seemed to be a destructive course. "Do you have to do that, Mr. Tyndale?" he asked, a pleading note in his voice.

Tyndale considered Myles for a moment, then spoke quietly. "I wish I could put it all so simply that you would understand why this is necessary, Myles," he said. "The problem is that the church has had a few reformers who have attacked the errors of the church, but they have not succeeded. And they never will," he pronounced sternly, "until the heart of the matter is reached. Errors spring from corrupt doctrine. Until the doctrine of the church is corrected, the abuses will continue. That is why the Bible must be available to all, because only the Word of God contains the truth! All else is of man and will eventually lead to abuse, and nothing can stop it." He looked down, idly fingering a turkey quill that lay on his desk, then went on, "Martin Luther understands this. And perhaps no one else, except myself."

"But can't you do the work here? Surely my father would help you?"

"I don't think you understand, Myles," Tyndale said quietly, "how dangerous a thing this is. King Henry, at the moment, is saying little about the translation of the Scriptures. But that can change in one day. With one change of mood, he can command men like me to be burned at the stake."

Myles gasped, "Surely not!"

"Why should you be surprised? Many men have been executed for criticizing the church! And nothing makes the church more angry than talk of putting the Bible in the hands of the common people. Such an act would rob the church of its power!"

He and Myles spoke for a long time, discussing the issue, seeking solutions. Finally Tyndale said, "There is no place in England where I can safely work and translate the Scriptures. Even if there were, there is nowhere to print them. There is only one course left open to me. I must go across the Channel, to Europe."

The words seemed like a death knell to Myles. Although he did not understand much about the world, he sensed the destiny of William Tyndale was not the destiny of an ordinary man. He knew, as he got up to leave, that he was saying good-bye to a great man, perhaps for the last time.

Thirteen

A PAIR OF DARK EYES

The clash of sword blades rang out, echoing in the high-ceilinged room as the two men met and engaged, then parted to circle each other carefully.

Sir Robert Wakefield, at the age of fifty-six, was a man of great ability with the sword—a fact that had brought him pride. But now he found himself stymied at every turn. No matter how he approached his opponent, he could not break through the guard, and now sweat began to roll down his forehead. He pressed forward, grunting with the effort, and suddenly made a misstep, laying himself open to the blade of the man in front of him. Instantly he felt a sword tip at his chest. He dropped his guard and laughed loudly.

"Well, by heaven, I give up!" he said in disgust. "I haven't won a match all morning. You're too much for me, Son!"

Myles was not even breathing hard. The past three years had added sinew and muscle to his tall frame so that now he was a powerful young man of nineteen. His smooth, long muscles were not as bulky as his father's, but his reactions were phenomenal. He had been defeating all opponents for some time now, and he said almost apologetically, "You're tired, though, Father. We'll try later."

"Don't make excuses for me," Sir Robert retorted. "I may be

an old man now," he said, grinning and tossing his sword down with a clatter, "but God has given me a son to take up where I left off. I'm proud of you, boy."

It was not the first time Sir Robert had expressed his affection for Myles, but such words never failed to bring a warmth to Myles's face and a lift in his spirit. The past two years had wiped out many of the painful memories of his youth. He still remembered his mother as clearly as if she were still with him, but he thought now not so much of her death as of the thousand and one images that impressed themselves on him of her youth, vitality, life, and love. Sir Robert and Lady Jane had indeed been parents to him, the sort of which he had never dreamed he would have.

He put his sword up carefully, then picked up Sir Robert's and added it to the rack. "You're a fine teacher, sir. I couldn't have mastered any of these things if it hadn't been for you."

His praise pleased Sir Robert, and the older man clapped Myles on the back. "Well, it would take a brave pair of footpads to challenge us on the road, eh boy? Come along now and let's go see your mother. I promised her you would spend some time with her before you leave for London."

"Yes, sir." Myles followed his father gladly. The two men cleaned up and presented themselves to Lady Jane.

"You're looking mighty pleased with yourself, Robert," she observed as they came in. "Did you finally win a match?" she gibed.

Robert glared at her, then saw she was teasing him. He grinned sheepishly, saying, "No, not a blasted one! This young son of ours is a veritable King Arthur, I tell you! I don't think he has a match in all of England!" He looked fondly at Myles and said, "I hate to see you go to London, boy. Why don't you put it off for a month and then I'll go with you?"

Myles said diffidently, "That would be all right with me, sir, but you remember His Majesty invited me especially for the hunt in the Old Forest."

"Ah yes, that's so. I'd forgotten about that." Sir Robert cocked his head in a gesture now familiar to Myles and said pensively, "You've gotten on so well, boy, that even the king courts your company now."

"It's not that so much," Myles said modestly. "He uses me to find out what people are thinking. The common people, I mean."

Lady Jane looked at him curiously. "How so, Myles?"

"Oh, he knows how I grew up and that I'm still pretty close to the common people, the serfs. So he asks me things like, 'What do you suppose your old friends would think of this new tax, boy?' when he's thinking about putting a new tax on the poor."

"Do you tell him the truth?" Sir Robert demanded.

"Yes, sir. I always do." Myles grinned broadly. "He doesn't always like it. Last time he roared like a lion when I told him what the people would think. I thought he was going to run me out of the palace. But after a while he calmed down and laughed, the way he does when he changes moods. He said, 'Well, by heaven, I'm glad there's one man in the palace who's not afraid to tell his sovereign the truth!'"

"I think that is wonderful, Myles," Lady Jane said, her face alight. "You never told me that before!"

"Oh, it's not much," Myles shrugged. He was looking at his adopted mother and was disturbed. She was only forty-one but had never been strong, and the last year had been hard on her. She had fallen ill in the dead of winter, and for awhile both he and Sir Robert were afraid she would die. She had lain almost helpless for weeks while they could do nothing but worry about her. Only with the coming of spring had she seemed to improve. But even now she was very thin, and there were lines of fatigue in her fine face.

He spoke his thoughts. "You need to have the apothecary by, Mother. You need to gain weight."

Lady Jane shook her head. "I need naught that he has," she answered. Then she changed the subject by saying, "I'll miss you. How long will you be gone this time?"

"I think not more than two weeks," Myles answered. "I'm going by to visit Hannah. Would you like for her to come and stay with you for a while?"

Hannah Kemp had been heaven-sent to the Wakefields, for during Lady Jane's illness she had come from her home and waited on Lady Jane tirelessly during the long weeks. The two women had grown very close so that they were almost like mother and daughter. Myles had no idea of the long talks these two had had about him, but he had enjoyed Hannah's company. They had laughed often about his early reading lessons, and now she had decided to teach him Greek. He hadn't gotten far, but the experience had been pleasant for both of them.

"I hate to bring her away from home," Lady Jane said, "but it would be so good to have her if she wouldn't mind staying with an old woman." She smiled and said with just a hint of slyness, "Of course, I know she'd rather go to London with you."

The thought caused a furrow in Sir Robert's forehead. "I wouldn't like that," he said stubbornly. "Hannah is such a fine young woman, and the court is no place for a young girl." He glanced at Myles and knew that his son was thinking of Isabella. But he was firm in his judgment. "The chief function of those girls is to look decorative," he went on, "to provide a handsome setting for the queen on public occasions. They're there to be ornaments, and they're supposed to occupy their off-duty hours with sewing and reading. But it doesn't work out that way."

"What do you mean, Robert?" Lady Jane asked innocently.

"I mean they spend most of their time gossiping and playing with cards and flirting with the underemployed young gentlemen who seem to linger around the court."

"They aren't all like that, Father," Myles protested. "Queen

Catherine is a fine lady, and she does her best to keep the girls occupied profitably."

"I'm sure she does, boy," Sir Robert grunted. "But there's not much she can do. She's almost like a stranger in the palace. You've noticed it, haven't you?"

Reluctantly Myles nodded in agreement. "She's unhappy, and I don't wonder. She feels like a failure."

"You've talked to her, Myles?" Lady Jane inquired with surprise.

"Oh yes. She's so lonely. I've spoken with her twice when I've been there to visit. She never says anything revealing, of course, but her eyes look sad and there's not much life about her. They say she was very pretty when she was young, but she has lost her figure now, and—" He broke off, feeling unkind in what he'd been about to say.

"And she's lost the king's interest, too," Sir Robert finished for him. There was an angry look on the nobleman's face as he went on with disapproval, "The king's had many affairs, as everyone knows. The worst, I think, was that one with the Boleyn girl— Mary Boleyn, you'll remember."

"You shouldn't speak that way of the king," Lady Jane said gently. "The Scripture says we are to pray for those who are in authority over us."

"And so I do," Sir Robert protested. "But I can't close my eyes to the fact that Henry VIII acts like little more than a bull in heat! He's tired of Catherine, and sooner or later he will do something to disgrace the whole court."

Myles listened as his father spoke of the immoralities of the court and wondered if all courts everywhere were so perverse. He himself had seen some of the sad actions of which his father spoke. He knew that Ralph Geddes went to court far more often than he did, but that was understandable since Geddes had moved to London almost as soon as Myles had arrived at Wakefield. The young man had asked Sir Robert to provide for him while he made a place for himself at court. Of course, Geddes came back to Wakefield from time to time with glowing reports of how he was getting on. From what Myles heard from him, and from what his father told him, he believed it to be true.

They talked for a while longer, and finally Myles said, "I'll have to leave now, Mother, to get ready to go. I'll come and say good-bye in the morning." He leaned over and kissed her cheek. She held him for a moment, then released him.

When he was gone, Sir Robert asked her, "What do you think, Jane?"

"I think he is infatuated with Isabella Bourneville. And I think it's a bad thing for him."

Sir Robert gave her a curious glance. "Why do you say that? She comes from a good enough family. It wouldn't be a bad match."

Lady Jane looked directly at her husband. She was weak and frail, but her spirit still burned strong within her. Robert knew that she still had more strength of character than any woman he'd ever seen. "It might be a good match in some respects," she admitted, "but Myles needs a stronger woman than Isabella. She is beautiful and accomplished—but she's a flirt, for all of that. She'll never be satisfied living a normal life, not after the taste she's had of the court, and she'll drive her husband crazy, begging for new clothes and all sorts of foolish things. I hope you don't encourage him in his interest."

"I never say a word to the boy about her," Sir Robert answered hastily. Then his brow furrowed pensively. "I must admit I've had somewhat the same feeling about the girl. . . ." Shaking off thoughts of Isabella Bourneville, he said cheerily, "Plenty of time for the boy to choose a wife. Besides, I think Ralph has the inside track with the Bourneville lass. The way he's going up," he said wryly, "he'll be the one to support a wealthy wife."

"Is he doing so well then, Robert?"

"Yes, from all accounts. He has attached himself to Sir Thomas Cromwell, who is the rising star in King Henry's sky. He's Wolsey's right-hand man now, but soon or late Wolsey will make a misstep. Then there will be Sir Thomas Cromwell, ready to step into his place. I shouldn't be surprised but what he should become lord chancellor, and he seems to depend a great deal on Ralph. Or so I hear."

"I wish Ralph well," Lady Jane said. "I've never felt quite as badly as you did about the way things turned out. You don't feel that way any more, do you?"

"About Ralph? No, we've done very well for him. And I think he understands."

Lady Jane wasn't as confident of Ralph Geddes's acceptance of the situation, but she said nothing. After her husband left the room, she sat staring out the window for a while. Finally she picked up her Bible again and began to read.

If Myles's visit to the court was less a success in his mind than his previous ones, it was because Isabella seemed too busy. Ralph Geddes was very much in the picture, Myles discovered, and had made great progress in his courtship while Myles had been busy at Wakefield learning more about the management of the estate. Isabella still welcomed him, but it seemed she and Ralph had things planned on a tight schedule.

"Oh, you came at such a bad time, Myles," she lamented the first evening he was there. He had accompanied her on a walk around the palace, hoping to arrange to spend more time with her. Now she said, "If I'd only known you were coming, I wouldn't have made so many plans. You do understand, don't you?"

"Of course," Myles said, not understanding at all. "I should have let you know."

"But we'll have a good time when I get some of these obligations out of the way," she whispered. She leaned against him, and her touch seemed to riot through his veins. She knew how to stir a man, this Isabella, and he realized she had learned much in that way since she had come to the court.

But her whispered promise did not come to pass, for her "obligations" seemed to grow more numerous and more pressing. One day as she and Geddes were leaving the court for some previous engagement, Geddes had smiled, saying, "Well, Myles, we hate to part from you, but you understand, don't you?" Then without waiting for a reply, he and Isabella whirled off in a carriage.

Myles grew morose and sullen, and haunted the palace, which was almost vacant. The king was gone to hunt, and the queen was not feeling well and did not show herself, so Myles didn't know what to do with himself.

He determined to go back to Wakefield, but two weeks after his arrival the king came back and the palace grew lively again. The king noted Myles and, during another hunt, called the boy close to him. Henry was an excellent hunter, and Myles was careful to let him lead the way.

One other thing happened that kept Myles's interest. A young woman had been added to the court as a lady-in-waiting. He met her the day after the hunt. He was walking along the outer limits of the garden, wondering where Isabella was and what she was doing, when he encountered a trio. Two of the people he recognized: One was Sir Thomas Wyatt, a witty and talented courtier, a poet and diplomat often seen at court; the other, George Boleyn, whom he had never met but had seen. There was a young lady with them.

Wyatt greeted Myles pleasantly. "Oh, I don't believe you have met our latest addition, Wakefield. May I present Miss Anne Boleyn?"

Myles bowed gracefully, as he had been taught and had finally perfected, murmured his pleasure, and kissed the hand that was extended to him. Anne Boleyn was not, he observed, what one would call a beautiful woman, but she was an intensely attractive one. She had a heavy cascade of glossy black hair that fell down her back freely. Her best feature was her large, dark eyes. They were lively and curious and somehow intimate, even on this casual meeting.

"I'm happy to meet you, Mr. Wakefield," she said with a graceful incline of her head. "And what is your particular function in the court?"

Sir Thomas Wyatt laughed and said, "Oh, he's pursuing one of your fellow maids, Isabella Bourneville."

George Boleyn, Anne's brother, grinned broadly. "You're not doing particularly well at the moment, I understand." He was a close friend of Geddes, Myles knew, for Ralph had mentioned him often. The Boleyns, once wealthy and influential, had fallen on ill fortune in the last few years.

Myles studied Anne Boleyn with curiosity, knowing that her sister Mary had been the mistress of Henry VIII, but he seemed to find no signs of disillusionment or depravity on the young girl's face. She was, he guessed, less than twenty, and as he listened to the three make light conversation, he was impressed not only by her wit but by her daring.

She talks like a man, he thought with surprise as he listened to her forcefully voicing her opinions.

Not long after he joined them, much to Myles's surprise, Anne Boleyn instructed Sir Thomas and her brother, "You two run along now. I will teach Mr. Wakefield how to become irresistible to the young lady he so desires."

"If anyone could teach such a thing, it would be you, my dear," Wyatt said with a wink, then laughed and walked away.

She turned to Myles and said, "Shall we walk?" and when Myles assented, they began a slow walk around the garden. She spoke of her life in the court at France but hardly mentioned her family. She was the most vivacious woman he had ever seen, and Myles was completely taken by her. She asked him forthrightly about Isabella and about his prospects.

"Well, to be truthful, I don't have many, Miss Anne. She knows too much about me, perhaps."

"How is that, sir?"

Myles told her of his youth, of his late coming into the ranks of the nobility, and ended by saying, "She still thinks of me as a plowboy with mud between his toes. Ralph Geddes was her suitor for many years, and I feel he is the favorite."

Anne shook her head, her long hair cascading—glimmering, almost—in the bright sunlight. "Never say that! There never was a woman born that couldn't be taken by spirit and determination!" she exclaimed. She smiled and said with a conspiratorial air, "Now, let me tell you how to catch her interest. . . ."

Myles never knew how much to believe of what Anne Boleyn told him, but she was witty and charming and made him laugh. She also encouraged him. That afternoon he saw the very best side of her, for as he was to learn later, she had a fiery temper and an incapacity for forgetting a wrong.

As they drew near to the palace and the end of their walk, she smiled brilliantly at him. "A cautious heart never won a fair lady's favor!" Her eyes were almost inviting, and her tone softened somewhat. "If you need other lessons, Mr. Wakefield, I would be glad to provide them."

"Thank you, Miss Anne," Myles stammered with confusion. He thought he had seen an invitation in her eyes but convinced himself he was wrong. Surely she was not that sort of woman, at least she did not seem so.

Myles stayed on at court, waiting for Isabella, and he noticed that he was not the only man taken with Anne Boleyn. Sir Thomas Wyatt was with her constantly, and since Myles knew little about courtly romance, he thought he saw something between the two.

On the day before he was to go home, something happened that bothered him. At one of the court entertainments, there was some byplay over a trinket belonging to Anne that was flourished by Wyatt during a game of bowls with King Henry. Henry in turn produced a ring which he declared she had given to him, and suddenly the lightness of the atmosphere grew cloudy.

It had never occurred to Henry that Anne might give one of her favors to *another* man. Upon hearing this news, he could not conceal his anger, and he said roughly with his eyes fixed on Wyatt vindictively, "I have been deceived then, sir."

That was all that happened, but a friend of Myles murmured to him, "Well, that's the end of whatever romance there was between Wyatt and Anne Boleyn!"

"What do you mean by that?" Myles inquired.

"Why, the Boleyns depend on royal goodwill, and you won't find Anne doing anything to endanger that. No, you will see Sir Thomas Wyatt melt sadly and wisely into the background!"

Isabella came shortly after the incident and was very sweet to Myles. The two of them spent some time together, and once as they were talking, Isabella said casually, "I see that the king has himself another mistress."

Myles was shocked at the lightness of her manner. "What do you mean?" he asked.

Isabella looked at him, raised one eyebrow, and said, "You mean you have been here this long and haven't noticed his infatuation with Anne Boleyn?"

"I don't believe it!"

His belligerence caused Isabella some consternation. "Why should you be surprised, Myles?" she asked sharply.

"I just don't think she's that kind of young woman," he retorted.

Isabella started to pounce on him, to argue, but she saw the determined set of his jaw and changed her mind. "Well, perhaps you're right," she laughed. "Henry is a hard man to read. He does like young women, though, as I suppose a lot of older men do."

That was all she said, but when Myles went home a few days later, he realized that there probably had been truth in Isabella's idle gossip. The entire court seemed to be aware in some way he could not understand that Henry VIII was pursuing a new quarry, and that quarry's name was Anne Boleyn.

For some reason, this realization depressed Myles. When he got home his father pestered him for details of his visit, and he blurted it all out. He asked earnestly, "Do you think there can be anything to the talk, sir?"

Sir Robert hated to see his son lose his trusting heart, but he said plainly, "Henry does not burden himself with the morals of an ordinary man. He thinks he is above such things." He paused and shrugged, saying, "As for Anne Boleyn, her sister Mary was little more than a harlot. I hope that Anne Boleyn has sense enough to stay away from the king, but few young women do. And her upbringing has not been good."

"But Henry is married to Catherine!"

The remark troubled Sir Robert, and he said reluctantly, "That is true. But with King Henry VIII, that might not be the deciding factor."

"What else could be?" Myles demanded.

"His own will," Sir Robert answered grimly. "That's all that matters to His Majesty, his own will. He pays no attention to God or man. If he decides that Anne Boleyn will be his mistress, then you can be sure he will see that it happens."

Fourteen

A LESSON IN POWER

There were some men, Ralph Geddes had decided early in life, who were born to rule, to exercise power over other men. Now, at thirty-one, he was more and more convinced that his observations were true. His days at court for the past few years had done nothing to diminish this concept. At the court of King Henry VIII, power was almost a tangible thing. Men took it in, immersed themselves in it, and one could no more imagine such men as Henry VIII or Thomas Wolsey, the archbishop, as being other than they were than one could imagine a bird flying without wings.

Now as Geddes walked along the richly decorated corridors of Hampton Court, the home of Archbishop Thomas Wolsey, he was impressed again by the wealth and the sumptuous trappings of the magnificent structure that Wolsey, lord chancellor of England, had built. Hampton was one of the marvels of the age. Built entirely of brick, but in the manner of one of the older castles, it was surrounded by turrets and gave the impression of strength. It was not, of course, a castle, but it was nonetheless a mansion and the home of probably the wealthiest man in all of England next to the king himself.

Once again Geddes eyed the large paintings in gold frames, the magnificent statuary—all sculptures imported from Italy—the treasures that came from all over Europe that hung on the walls. The floor itself was paved with marble, which came straight from the finest quarries in Italy. Ralph Geddes was well aware that the palatial structure had been built with funds drained from the sweat of hundreds of thousands of peasants who lived in rude structures—structures that, in later generations, men would not even consider fit to house their cattle in. Such thoughts did not bother him, though, for Geddes had learned another thing from his time in the presence of Henry VIII and the court: Those in the lower classes existed simply for the purpose of holding up those who were above.

And Geddes, who had never been concerned greatly with the serfs or the peasants of England, was even less so now.

Suddenly Thomas Cromwell, who was striding along at Geddes's side, stopped and looked at the young man. "Did you ever wonder, Ralph," he asked with a slight gleam of humor in his eyes, "why Wolsey didn't build a real castle here, instead of an imitation one?"

"Why no, Sir Thomas. Why not?"

"Because if he had built a great medieval castle, obviously capable of being defended as a fortress against an enemy, he might have been taken as an enemy of the king. And Wolsey, above all things, knows how to stay on the good side of kings."

The humor left the eyes of Cromwell, and he turned to face the young man squarely. "It's a lesson," he said almost sternly, "that I have learned, and that you must learn."

"Of course, Sir Thomas," Ralph agreed. He had found that Cromwell did not make chance remarks. He counted himself fortunate to be in the inner circle of young men who surrounded King Henry VIII and drew their life from him. Ralph saw that Cromwell was watching him carefully and added, "I think I have learned a great deal from you about King Henry. But of course, a man never stops learning, sir."

Cromwell nodded with approval. "You're a bright young man, Ralph. And cold-blooded enough to be included among my little cadre of assistants." He observed that Geddes did not know what to think of his use of the term and continued, "You *are* cold-blooded, Ralph. If you were not, I'd have nothing to do with you." A smile came to his lips but not his eyes. "The king is hot-blooded enough to satisfy the country. It takes cold-blooded men such as you and myself to ensure that our sovereign's passions do not lead him into disaster."

Geddes watched and listened with care, then nodded in quick agreement. "Yes, sir, I see what you mean. He is a difficult man to handle, isn't he? If," he added quickly, "one can speak of 'handling' a king."

Cromwell did not disagree with the term; in fact, he approved of it. "Yes, *handle*—that is exactly the word that I might have chosen myself. We may call ourselves advisers, but we are, in effect, those who must see that the king does that which is best. All in his own interests, of course." Once again Cromwell's thick, meaty lips turned up in a cold smile.

"Let me deliver you the full truth about power, Ralph," he said, introducing the subject in a knowledgeable tone. "That is what you are interested in. I saw that when you first came here. I realized very quickly that you are intelligent enough to rise, though I had to watch for a while to see if you had the kind of mentality—what some would call 'spiritual capacity'—for rule." He settled back on his heels, swayed slightly, and went on. "I was the same sort of young fellow that you are. My father was a butcher, you know, and I had to rise above all of that. And I could not have risen to my position without learning the use of power."

"You've come a long way, Sir Thomas." Ralph nodded respectfully, with an admiration that was not feigned. Indeed, he admired Cromwell a great deal.

Cromwell appeared not to hear him. "Power . . . ," he mused.

"What is it? Power in this country is Henry. Henry VIII, the Sovereign of England. It is in his thick hands, it is in that mind that hides behind those small, guarded eyes of his. He is not the absolute monarch that other kings of England have been. He can no longer just say, 'Off with his head!' Oh no. He must go through the forms and the legal maneuvers when he wants a man sent to the block or the stake. And that is what you and I, and men like us, are for. You see, Ralph, when Henry wants something done, we see that it gets done. So the power lies in England, that is true, but the king is surrounded by the privy court, by the royal household, by officials in all areas of life who keep England going. And in some sense, Ralph, the men who control the power, which in this case is Henry VIII, well, these men are the *real* power even though they do not wear the crown."

Suddenly Ralph felt he saw more clearly than he ever had before, and he nodded slowly. When he spoke, there was a sort of shock in his voice. "Why, that is true enough, isn't it? If a man controls the king, then he *is* the power!"

"Yes, but what would happen if Henry discovered that some-one else had the power?" Cromwell's eyes burned into Ralph's. "You see, don't you? He has sent many to the block already for doing what he wanted done! Henry not only has to represent the power, he must think that it lies solely in his hands. That is why a man such as Wolsey, who had as humble beginnings as I, has been able to rise." He waved his hand at the gorgeous trappings of the corridor where they still stood. "All of this Wolsey has accumu-lated. He has made himself a wealthy man, all because he knew how to give Henry what he wanted and yet at the same time make Henry believe he had done it all himself. Oh yes. I have studied the cardinal carefully. He is my model. At least in this sense."

The two men continued their walk, and when they ap-proached the cardinal's chambers, where they were due for an appointment, Cromwell said lightly, "We will, of course, say nothing of this to His Grace. He is almost as dangerous as the king himself and quite jealous of his power."

Geddes was thinking hard and finally asked, "Will Wolsey always be able to control the king?"

Instantly Cromwell stopped again and turned to him, his eyes gleaming. "Ah, you are making progress, my boy," he said. "That is thinking as a man should. No," he exclaimed, "he will not! Sooner or later the king will want something from Wolsey that he either cannot give him or will not be willing to give. And when that happens . . . good-bye, Your Grace! Then you will discover that the Sovereign Lord King of all of England is, indeed, a carnivore." The thought seemed to please Cromwell, and he said, "That is exactly the sort of risk that we take, men like you and me. But we're willing to take it, are we not, Ralph? For we, like His Grace the cardinal, like Henry himself, crave power!"

Geddes looked intently at his mentor and nodded eagerly. "I must confess, I do have that desire within me."

"Good that you know it," Cromwell replied evenly. "Otherwise I would not have you around. Now then, the day will come when Wolsey will be shuffled off and there will be no one to advise the king. What will he do? He will reach out and take someone." He thought carefully and said, "Possibly Sir Thomas More, perhaps the duke of Suffolk. But sooner or later, those men will not do for Henry VIII. They are not—" here he smiled, showing yellowed teeth—"devious enough to get done what Henry wants done. But I am." He clapped his hand on Geddes's shoulder. "And you are the same, young fellow! You and I, we will go up in the world. I don't know what it is you want most, aside from power itself, but once you have the power, all you have to do is reach out your hand and take whatever else you desire."

Ralph Geddes smiled. He was a darkly handsome man, and there was a cold glow in his eyes that confirmed Cromwell's opinion of him. Ralph Geddes had no more scruples than Cromwell himself. "I know a few things I would like to reach out and take," Geddes said with malevolence.

"Good. Think about them. Wait patiently for them. The time is not too long until we will have our day."

The two men turned and entered the majestic suite of Thomas Wolsey, lord chancellor of England. They bowed low before His Grace, covering what was in their hearts as skillfully as actors upon a stage.

"We are honored to have His Majesty come, of course," Sir Robert Wakefield said, speaking to his wife over the remains of breakfast. "But the thing is, we may have to sell off some of our lands to pay for the expense!" He sighed and went on ruefully, "When the king of England comes to visit, he comes not alone, but with half the court."

"I know it will be expensive," Lady Jane said, "but it will be good for you, won't it, Robert? I mean, it shows that the king favors you. And it will be good for Myles, too."

"I suppose that is true. But it will be a costly visit, all the same." He had been adding up the figures in his head and recited some of them to his wife, estimating the number that would most likely accompany the king, which he believed could be anywhere from fifty to one hundred, not including a small army of servants. Food would have to be prepared for all of them—and not just boiled wheat, either, but the finest meals that could be put on the table.

Henry VIII, like all monarchs, put a great stock in ceremony and gauged carefully the gifts that his followers gave to him. He expected to be treated royally along with all of his followers. After one of his jaunts throughout the countryside, during which he stopped at various castles, sometimes for weeks, he left a wake of poverty behind him that set lords selling even their plate to pay for His Highness's pleasure.

Sir Robert rose and spent the rest of the day preparing for the arrival of the royal party. He was sharp with the servants and even with Myles, saying abruptly, "You have to help me with all this, boy! Entertaining the king is not a light matter. I've arranged for you to take him boar hunting tomorrow. He loves that, but see to it that he gets a good bag, or he won't be in a good humor."

"Yes, sir. I know where we are almost sure to get a good bag," Myles said reassuringly, and Sir Robert was satisfied, for he knew that Myles was so familiar with the area that he all but knew every deer and boar and stag within a ten-mile radius of Wakefield.

The next day the long parade drew up to Wakefield, and the inhabitants thereof were standing, waiting, dressed in their finest as Henry dismounted, threw the reins to a retainer, and strode directly to the family. "Well now, we are here, Lady Jane, to try your presence! I hope we will not be a burden upon you."

"It is to the honor of our house that you have come, Your Majesty," Lady Jane said as she made a graceful curtsey. She was still thin after her illness, but there was some color in her cheeks. "If you will come inside, we have a small meal prepared for you and the court."

Planning and preparation of the "small meal" had taken the expertise and herculean efforts of the entire staff. The great hall was packed to capacity and overflowed into other rooms.

"Why, they eat like hogs!" Molly whispered to Myles as he gave her a word of encouragement. Her face was tense, and she had already endured the maulings of several of the young cavaliers as she passed by them. "And they behave worse than a bunch of plowmen in a tavern!" she said indignantly.

Myles grinned at her, patting her shoulder in a friendly gesture. "Just put up with it, Molly. They won't stay over a week—I hope. You are doing a good job with them." He moved away, unaware of the girl's eyes upon him as he did so. He had never approached her, as so many of the young noblemen had, so he had no way of knowing that she was hopelessly in love with him.

During the meal Myles stayed busy seeing that the food and drink flowed. After it was over he walked along with Anne Boleyn, who seemed glad to see him again. "I've missed you, Myles!" she exclaimed. The spring air had brought out a fresh color in her cheeks. Once again Myles was struck with her vivacity and with the intensity in her fine, dark eyes. He knew that, while she might not be as beautiful as some of the women in the court, these facets drew all men to the woman who walked beside him.

She smiled up at him and demanded that he show her around Wakefield, which he did with pleasure. As they walked, he inquired as delicately as he could about Isabella.

"Oh, she is besieged by these young cavaliers, as you well know, being one of them," Anne said almost wickedly.

"Cavalier! No, indeed!" Myles denied vehemently. "I'll not make one of that number! Surely you know that, Miss Anne!"

She laughed—her laughter tinkling delightfully on the air— then she put her hand on his arm. "I know, Myles. I was only tormenting you." Then she went on in a more serious tone, "Your friend, Ralph Geddes, is in constant attendance on her. I almost think he is serious! Most of them are not, they are just after what they can get out of a pretty girl."

Her blunt speech made Myles blink, and he said, "Well, it seems there is little hope for me, with a crowd of aristocrats after her." He looked downcast, and she knew he was disappointed that Isabella had not come with the crowd. With a sigh he went on. "I suppose she and Ralph are together now."

"I believe they are," Anne admitted. "They went with the other half of the court, down to Surrey." She looked at Myles's face and said gently, "Don't grieve, Myles. There are other women in the world. A handsome fellow like you with such good prospects should have no trouble."

Myles gave her a quick smile and felt a warm gratitude. He had heard much about this young woman—she was becoming the talk of the court—and he was puzzled by her, for there were two seemingly contradictory rumors that were going around. One was that Anne was very interested in the "new" religion that was springing up, a religion that, as far as Myles could figure out, deviated from pure Catholicism and leaned toward Lutheranism, although not going that far, of course.

Henry's own position in this was dreadfully complicated, and Myles did not understand the politics of it at all. Cautiously he asked her where she stood, and she at once began talking with animation about it. She spoke of the "redeeming power of Christ's words in the Gospels" and said forcefully, "We are tired of the rituals and smells and bells of the old church! We need the freshness of Christ's gospel! We need the words of Christ! That's why," she went on passionately, "we have been urging the king to get the Scripture made available to the people."

"Why, that is wonderful!" Myles cried. "Have you ever heard of William Tyndale?" When she said she had not, he explained Tyndale's desire to translate the Bible and said wistfully, "But he has left England now and has gone somewhere on the Continent. It was too dangerous here."

"Well," Anne said slowly, "it is a dangerous work. I am not certain what will become of it." She continued to talk about the Word of God, and as she did, Myles tried to put this facet of the woman together with the other rumor: that the king was pursuing her as a possible mistress. Myles was relatively sure that the desire for such an involvement was all on Henry's part, and the current gossip seemed to agree. He could not, of course, ask Anne about it, and he even steered the conversation carefully away from the king.

Suddenly she waved her left hand toward the house, asking, "Is the house very old, Myles?"

Myles mumbled an answer but was so startled that he was afraid it showed in his face. Anne's left hand had six fingers! He caught only a glimpse, for she wore long sleeves, but he saw a small member just below her little finger. It was not large, but obviously a growth, for it had a small nail.

That was when he remembered what one of the young women had said at the court: *She's a witch, Anne Boleyn—she's got six fingers, and that's a sure sign of a witch!* Myles had not spoken, for he had not believed it, but now that he saw it was true, he was shaken! He made his exit as soon as possible and, later in the day, asked Lady Jane about it—not using Anne's name, of course.

"I don't believe a word of that, Myles," Lady Jane replied instantly. "People are always pointing at any variation from the normal and saying it's a sign of the devil. Such things are merely unfortunate, and it's cruel to accuse people of being under the powers of darkness for something they can't help." The answer pleased Myles and he accepted it, as he did everything Lady Jane said.

Later that afternoon, the men mounted their horses and headed for the deep woods, intent on a hunt. Henry was in a jovial mood, for he loved hunting in general and boar hunting in particular. There were two ways to hunt for boar, the safest being on horseback. This was what Myles recommended. But Henry said expansively, "Nonsense, young man! We shall fight our prey on his own ground, on our own two feet!"

"Yes, Your Majesty," Myles said reluctantly. This made his task more difficult, for the boars of old England were not beasts to be taken lightly. On Myles's own right leg was a network of white scars that gave testimony to an encounter during which an enormous boar had almost finished him off.

He passed out the spears, seeing that his own skilled huntsmen stayed close to the king. Just before they started out, he got them off to one side and charged them, "Whatever you do, do not let the king get gored. You know the penalty of that!" He held up his own spear, which was as sharp as a razor and had a crosspiece about eighteen inches away from the point. This crosspiece, or horizontal bar, prevented the spear from going too deeply into the chest of a boar. Without the crosspiece, a charging boar was capable of rushing right up the spear, even as it was going through him, and getting at the hunter. But the crosspiece held the charging animal at a spear's length. The difficulty was that one had to hold on.

As the hunting party made their way through the forest on horseback and then on foot when the shrubs grew too thick, the king spoke glowingly of the sport of boar hunting. "I've learned a lot about governing from hunting boar," he said to the small group clustered around him.

"How is that, Your Majesty?" Sir Robert inquired.

Henry laughed with delight and said, "There is only one rule in hunting boar, and that is *to hold on!* If the boar charges, you drop on one knee and present your spear. You hold the butt of it with your right hand on the ground to take the shock, and then the boar runs right onto it! And you know how they are! His one object is to heave, and weave, and sidestep until he can get at you! Isn't that right?" A wave of assent went up at once, and he said, "Then all one has to do is hold on." He looked around, a fighting light in his eyes. "So it is with kings, and with all who rule the country. Someone is always trying to get at us—Spain, or France, the bloody Scots, or the Welsh—and what we've learned to do, those who have been successful, is simply to hold on."

Henry VIII had a gift for talking and holding the attention of those listening. He spoke rapidly, keeping his listeners enthralled, until one of the huntsmen came running back to Myles. He listened briefly, then turned to Henry. "Game is just ahead, Your Majesty."

Instantly the king ceased talking, feeling, as did the others, the excitement of the coming hunt. They approached more slowly toward the boar's lair, and the hounds began to whimper and strain at their leashes. As quietly as possible, the hunters crept up, and Myles grew more and more apprehensive.

Silently, a hundred yards away in front of them, a black creature appeared and stood at the edge of a clearing. It so blended in with the brush and the thicket behind him that most of the hunters did not see him, but Myles knew instantly that this was the biggest, most fierce boar he had ever seen. Suddenly the boar turned and disappeared, and the king could not contain himself. "After him! Turn the hounds loose!" he roared.

Instantly the air was filled with the barkings and howlings of the dogs. The group, king and all, dashed through the thickets after the animal. Sir Robert hissed to Myles, "You stand on one side of His Majesty, and I'll take the other. We cannot take any chances."

He had time for no more, for suddenly the noises of the hounds grew to a crescendo of excitement, the bloodthirsty thunder of their cries pealing through the air.

"They have him, Myles!" the king cried, and he ran forward at once with Sir Robert and Myles hurrying to keep up with him.

In a small space, the boar stood at bay. He had got his hindquarters backed against a tree and stood on the defensive with his upper lip peeled back in a snarl. The hounds stood round, yowling and baying at him, and one of the dogs writhed at his feet, done to death.

As the men approached, the boar suddenly saw them. The king started to advance—and then bedlam broke loose. The boar, in a lightning-fast movement, lowered his head and charged. The dogs snapped and pulled at his hindquarters, some of them closing in, fastening on his throat or a leg, but they did not even slow the fierce animal down. The king gave a great battle cry and dropped to one knee. But as he did so, he stepped into a hole and fell to the ground with a helpless cry. Sir Robert shouted out in alarm, but he was too far to the left. So it was Myles who threw himself into the path of the charging boar.

There was no time to plant the butt of his weapon into the ground, so Myles held onto it with all of his strength. As the boar smashed into the spear, he was driven backward, the spear sliding back through his hands, the flaming red eyes of the animal only inches away from his own.

Grimly he held there, the huge, razor-sharp tusks of the animal slashing the air. As the beast slathered and foamed, Myles almost gagged from the monster's rank odor. Though their struggle seemed to last forever, it took mere seconds—too quick for intervention by the other hunters—until, inexorably, the beast pushed the man backward.

Then the force of one mighty lunge bore Myles to the ground, and the animal was upon him.

There was no defense against the tusks of a boar, and Myles had very little room to maneuver with the fallen king directly behind him. He rolled to one side and felt a sliver of fiery pain along his shoulder as a huge tusk raked him, ripping his garment as if it were made out of fragile silk instead of tough leather. The animal was grunting with rage, and Myles knew that there was no way to avoid being maimed. Then, miraculously, he felt the animal pull back a bit. With a desperate motion, he rolled over to see that both the king and his father had attacked the animal, shoving at it with their razor-sharp spears.

Springing to his feet, he ignored his wounds and grabbed the spear of a huntsman who was trying to assist him, for his own spear was still buried in the raging boar. He ran forward, but by the time he got there, the king's spear had pierced the beast's heart, and it fell over in death throes.

The king let out a cry of victory, and at once was surrounded by his followers, who were lauding the king for his bravery.

Sir Robert came to Myles and took his arm. "Let's have a look at that, boy," he said and began stripping off Myles's jerkin. As Sir Robert was treating the wound, the king came over, his eyes bright with pleasure and excitement.

"How is it, now? Not bad, I trust, Sir Robert."

"No, Your Majesty. A deep cut, but not dangerous," Robert said quickly, binding it up expertly with a kerchief. He looked at Henry and nodded. "I congratulate you, sire. That is the mightiest boar I've ever seen, and your spear went right through his heart."

Praise warmed Henry, and he was lavish with his own of the two men. "I thought I was a dead man when I fell," he said, "but this young fellow threw himself right into the monster's path!"

Myles had become enough of a courtier to know what to say. "Oh, that was nothing, Your Majesty. But you saved my life! If you hadn't speared him, he would have killed me. I owe you my life, sire."

King Henry was alive with excitement. It had indeed been a glorious moment, and truly he had saved the young man's life. "Well, now," he exclaimed, "I was glad to do it for such a remarkable lad. Fine sport, fine sport! Let's get back and have this fellow cooked for a victory supper."

They moved through the woods until they reached the horses, then mounted for the ride back. As they rode toward Wakefield, Sir Robert drew Myles aside, behind the royal party.

"That was good, my son," he said with pride. "It was you who saved the king, although we must never say so to anyone. But," he went on gravely, "you have made a mark on His Majesty. He never forgets a thing like this. I wish he loved scholarship as well as he loves hunting!"

Myles was feeling rather giddy from the loss of blood, but he was happy that it had turned out so well.

As they rode back to Wakefield and all through the victory supper that night, he was missing one thing. That was the sight of Isabella. Even saving the king's life did not quite make up for it.

THE CHOICE

Hannah Kemp was happy. She had looked forward to this trip to London for months, and now that it had arrived, her happiness was made even more complete by the fact that Myles Wakefield had come in person to escort her into the city.

She had endured many lectures from her parents on the dangers of the big city—how young girls could be led astray and lose their virtue—and she had endured them all resignedly, agreeing to take every precaution to see that she did not become a victim.

Myles had arrived, looking tall and handsome, in the best coach owned by the Wakefields. The two of them had made the journey to London slowly. The spring rains had turned the roads into mud so that they could make, at best, fifteen miles a day. More than once they'd had to get out while the coachmen and lackeys had pried the buggy loose from the thick, gummy mud. But even that had not damped their spirits, and the two of them had laughed and enjoyed their journey.

When at last they arrived, Myles paid constant attention to her. Hannah could not quite believe that she was getting, at last, the dream of her heart: Myles Wakefield all to herself.

On the day of the ball at the king's court, she spent all

afternoon getting ready. When Myles came to the door, he took one look at her and his eyes lit up with approval.

"Why, Hannah," he said, "you're absolutely beautiful!"

Hannah dimpled with pleasure and did not regret one minute she had spent on her dress. It was made of pale blue material trimmed in white, and she and her mother had spent hours putting the finishing touches on it. It fell to her feet in graceful, flowing lines. Her hair was done up in a corona about her head, making a golden glow by the light of the sun that came through the window. She smiled brilliantly but flushed slightly. Any good word from Myles always did this to her. Chiding herself for her foolishness, she asked, "Do you like my dress?"

Myles bowed and replied in a most courtly manner, "The dress is almost worthy of the wearer's beauty."

Hannah stared at him, then smiled playfully. "You've been practicing up to make that speech."

Myles laughed and confessed, "You're right. Some fellows seem to think these things up on the spur of the moment. I have to make them up and rehearse them." He then offered her his arm, and she laid her hand on it lightly. Looking down at her he grew serious. "No, Hannah, I didn't really have those words all ready for you . . . but they are true. You do look more beautiful than I could have imagined. You have quite grown up." She blushed again, and he went on. "Sometimes I still think of you as the little girl that I saw when I looked down from that balcony, in our secret place. Do you remember?"

"I remember," she said softly.

"What a dirty, impudent boy I was!" Myles grinned. "Why did you ever put up with me?"

"You *were* dirty enough," she agreed, her eyes sparkling, "but you weren't impudent. You were always very sweet and gentle."

Now it was Myles's turn to blush, and he laughed a little. "I wish you would tell that to a few people, Hannah."

"Isabella, you mean?" Hannah asked sharply.

"Well, I suppose it wouldn't hurt," Myles said absently. He did not like to talk to her about Isabella, and yet he had, time and again, bared his soul to his friend. She alone knew the depths of his feelings for Isabella Bourneville, and he shrugged almost in despair. "It looks hopeless, though. She and Ralph Geddes are seeing each other all the time."

Hannah said evenly, "I don't think Isabella would listen to any recommendations I might make." She did not like the turn of the conversation and looked up at Myles brightly. "Can we go now? I am anxious to see the court."

They left and Myles kept her amused all the way to the palace. The palace was lit up as darkness began to fall. It seemed as if at least a thousand torches gleamed outside. Inside, huge candles threw shimmering lights over the furnishings, the silver and gold that glowed almost wherever one looked, and the multitude of colors from the gowns of the women and the rich dress of the men. In all, the effect was spectacular, and Hannah felt bedazzled. She had never seen anything like it.

"Come along, and I will introduce you to the queen," Myles said after a time. He led Hannah over to Queen Catherine and her entourage and introduced her with ceremony. Catherine took the curtsey of the young girl with a gracious incline of her head and smiled at Myles.

"What a pretty thing you have brought to the court, Myles! Where have you been hiding her?"

"Oh, we have known each other for years," Myles said, the fondness in his voice evident as he looked at Hannah. "She taught me to read, Your Majesty. If it hadn't been for her, I should be as dumb as a post!"

Hannah gasped and her eyes grew wide. "Oh no, 'tis not so, Your Majesty! Myles is very bright!"

The queen was charmed by Hannah's fresh, young beauty and

stood talking to the two for a long time. Then she put her hand out and lightly touched the smooth cheek of the young girl and said almost sadly, "You remind me almost of myself when I was a child." A faraway look came into her eyes, and the sadness that Hannah had sensed in her queen became more evident. "I remember so many things about my home, before I came to England," she said softly. Then she smiled. "Did you know I met Christopher Columbus?"

"Really?" Hannah asked in delight. "You really knew him?"

"Oh yes. After his triumphant voyage, he came to my father's court. There was a jubilant celebration as the great Columbus was honored by all of Europe."

"What was he like?" Myles asked eagerly. It seemed incredible that this woman would have known the great Columbus.

"He was a wonderful man, tall and very quiet. He had time for a little girl. I remember," she said fondly, "once he took me on his knee and told me about his own family. Then he asked me about what games I played, and when I told him, he laughed and asked if he might come and play with me one day."

"Did he? Did he come and play with you, Your Majesty?" Hannah asked with wide-eyed wonder.

"Yes, he did—one time. He was on a visit to my father, of course. But he remembered, and he came by my apartments and sat down for half an hour and listened as I told him about my dolls." The queen's eyes were soft and dreamy. "He even held one of them. He wanted to know their names and where they came from. Oh, he was a wonderful man!"

The queen sighed and smiled at her two enraptured listeners, spoke a few more gracious words to them, and then moved away. Hannah said, "I didn't know she was like that, Myles. You never told me."

"Didn't I? She is a fine woman."

"But the king doesn't love her anymore, does he?" Hannah asked with a trace of sadness in her voice.

"Well, I don't . . . I don't really—"

Seeing his hesitation, Hannah interrupted sharply, "Myles, *everyone* knows it. They talk about Henry and all of his mistresses, and now how he's chasing after Anne Boleyn. Everyone knows what kind of man he is."

"Hush, Hannah!" Myles whispered fiercely. He looked around guardedly to see if anyone had heard, then stuck out his arm in a gesture that was more a command than a courtesy. Mortified, Hannah meekly laid her hand on it and allowed him to usher her over to a quiet corner in one of the nooks of the huge room.

He turned to her, his manner stern. "You must not talk like that! It could get you into trouble!"

Hannah looked around the room at the glittering jewels and the brilliant colors. She heard the cultured voices and saw the wine flowing freely. It appeared to be a room full of gaiety and laughter and pleasure, but she watched the faces of the people and her expression became disturbed. "I don't think this is a good place, Myles," she said. "Look at it. All of them trying to see how much they can drink, and from what I hear, they have no more morality than animals."

Myles was upset and retorted, "I know peasants who don't have all that much morality either, Hannah. You know that as well as I do. It isn't only the rich who sin. We all do."

Hannah realized that here she was, exactly where she had wished so much to be, with the man she so longed to be with, and she was only spoiling the evening. She put her hand on his arm contritely. "I didn't mean to quarrel with you, Myles. I just feel sorry for the queen. She's so sad."

The gentleness in Hannah's face and voice made Myles ashamed. It was only because he himself had had some of the same feelings she had expressed that he had lashed out at her. Now he said mildly, "Well, it is a dangerous place to voice such opinions, Hannah. Now, come and let me introduce you to some of the other guests."

They moved around the room, Myles speaking to everyone, it seemed to Hannah. She quickly lost track of the names, for she saw many of the famous people of the day, the dukes, the high churchmen. Cardinal Wolsey was sitting up on the dais, speaking with the king, and she studied the two carefully. She had never seen Henry VIII before and was impressed with his virility and his obvious strength. But to her, his eyes seemed cruel, and she did not like him, not as she had liked the queen. She determined to say nothing of this to Myles, however.

Myles said with a sharp intake of breath, "Look, there's Isabella and Ralph. Let's go speak to them." He led her over to Isabella, who was wearing a beautiful gown of green brocade, and around her neck, on a gold chain, was a large, clear white stone that flashed in the light. There were pearls in her ears, and she looked, Hannah admitted to herself, very beautiful.

Isabella and Ralph made much over Hannah, but they treated her as if she were a twelve-year-old child. "You must let me speak to the queen about you, Hannah," Isabella said, eyeing her. "She is always looking for attractive young women to come and be a part of her court, and I think she might look favorably upon you."

"Oh no, thank you," Hannah said hastily. "I don't think that I would—suit the court."

"Whyever not?" Ralph said. "You certainly have the looks for it. And you are a scholar, which King Henry likes."

Isabella glanced sharply at Ralph at his words, searching his face, and decided at once that he was joking. She smiled and said, "We all know what kind of *scholarship* His Majesty looks for in young women. Of course, that is not true," she added, "of Miss Anne Boleyn." She smiled maliciously and went on. "I understand that young woman is an accomplished scholar. And that is naturally why the king chases her so determinedly, so they can talk about Aristotle and Plato!"

At this, Ralph grinned and winked lewdly at Myles.

The conversation had taken a turn that Myles did not like, although he had heard it all before. He could not forbear saying, "I think Miss Anne is not only a scholar, but, in my view, a very fine young woman."

Isabella stared at him and laughed incredulously, then reached up and patted his cheek as if he were a wayward nephew. "You are such a dear boy, Myles, you never see anything but good in people. I'm glad there are a few like you around."

The group stood together talking for a few moments, then Ralph ushered Isabella away. As Myles watched them leave, a dull anger suddenly grew within him—and rapidly became white-hot. He was not a young man given to fits of rash temper, but the sight of Ralph leading Isabella away, holding her arm as if she were his possession, took away all his even temper. It was a thing he'd rarely experienced, and it took all the command he could muster to keep from dashing after them and slapping Ralph across the face. Somehow he controlled himself, but his face was so pale that Hannah inquired if he was feeling poorly. "No, I'm all right," he said quickly and turned with her to leave the scene. The party went on for a long time, but most of it was anticlimactic to Myles.

The drinking that night reached epic proportions, and Hannah noted that some members of the nobility had to be carried out by servants. She saw also that flirtations were going on that would have been expected in a tavern but hardly seemed fitting for the royal court. She was a sharp young woman, intelligent and quick to notice things. There were men taking some of the young ladies of the court out of the room, and she did not miss the expressions of lust and dissolution that marked their faces, men and women alike.

It was very late when the carriage pulled up in front of the inn where the two of them were staying. Myles helped her out of the carriage, and they walked into the inn and up to the door of Hannah's room. She opened it and then turned to him. She could barely make out his features by the flickering light of the single candle that illuminated the corridor. No one else was stirring and it was very quiet in the house.

"Thank you for taking me to the ball and bringing me to London," she said softly.

Looking down at her in the soft light of the candle, Myles felt strange. Hannah was so familiar to him, and yet at that moment she seemed different somehow. Her hair caught the amber glow of the flame, her eyes, as she looked up at him, were as clear and blue as the sky, even in the dim light.

"What did you think of the ball?" he said. He was still not sleepy, but he knew she must be tired and longing for her bed. Still, he was reluctant to leave her.

She looked up at him, noting the fineness of his features, the straight nose, the strong lips, the smooth sweep of his jawline. *He has grown so handsome, and yet he doesn't have even an ounce of conceit about it,* she thought. *I'm glad of that.*

"Well, it was different from what I expected," she answered.

"What do you mean?" he asked insistently. "In what way?"

"Oh, I don't know, Myles. It's hard for me to say," she answered hesitantly. "I'm not sure it's a good place for anyone to be."

She did not elaborate, but Myles knew what she was thinking. He had watched her expressions as some of the rawer escapades of the evening had played out before them. He remembered how he himself had been shocked at first by the adultery and fornication that went on, almost before the eyes of the king. But then, Henry himself played the role model for such behavior.

"I know it's different from at home," he said. "I don't like some of it, either."

It was very quiet in the corridor, and as she looked up at him he was suddenly conscious of the smooth planes of her jawline, of the texture of her skin, the warmth of her breath. Without meaning to do so, he reached out and put his hand on her cheek.

He had never touched her before—never—and she grew very still. He tried to think of her as a very young girl, as his childhood companion, but he realized suddenly that she was no longer a girl. Standing before him as she was, he could not deny that she was a woman.

Emotions swept through him, stirring him. Had he stopped to analyze them, he would have been greatly surprised at himself. But at the moment, Myles was not interested in analytical thought. He gazed down at Hannah and whispered huskily, "You always were so pretty, but now you are beautiful."

She did not answer, and he could not tell what she was thinking. Her eyes were fixed on him, and her lips looked very soft. He reached out slowly, waiting for her to protest. When she did not, he put his arms around her and gently pulled her close. He held her for a moment, thinking she might pull away, ready to turn her loose—but she lifted her face to him, and he lowered his head until their lips met.

Her lips were softer than anything he had ever known. Of course, he had kissed girls before, but Hannah's skin was like satin, and her mouth trembled beneath his with a vulnerability he had never known before. Her innocence revealed itself in the way she surrendered to his caress and the trembling of her hands as they rested on his breast. And yet, the firm warmth of her form as she nestled against him told him again that she was a woman and not a child.

He lifted his head, held her close for a few moments, then drew back. His arms were still around her, and he looked down at her face. "I shouldn't have done that," he whispered lamely.

"I'm glad you did," she said breathlessly but with certainty in her voice.

Her answer surprised him. He blinked and then smiled. "Then I'll do it again." He bent his head, but she put her hands against his chest and pushed him away.

"No," she said, "you mustn't." There was an odd expression in her eyes that puzzled him, and still he could not tell what her thoughts were. She stood there, her back straight, looking up at him. Her next words stunned him.

"Myles, you must get away from the court. It's not a good place for you."

"Get away from the court?" He stared at her in amazement. "Why do you say that?" Then he went on, "I know that a lot of the things that go on aren't right, but they don't have anything to do with me."

Hannah bit her lower lip in a charming way that made her enticing, somehow. Her face was smooth, but her eyes were troubled as she said, "It's a place of evil, and you cannot stay there without being affected by it. It's like a cold, heavy fog that you breathe in too deeply so that it gets into your chest. If you are in it, it will enter you." She began to speak rapidly and a little desperately. She had noticed over the past few months that Myles had changed . . . it seemed he was being drawn into the life of the court more and more, and she had seen on this night what it could do to people. "I don't want you to change, to become like these people. You are good, Myles, but this court isn't. The king isn't! You know that, don't you?"

He wanted to protest but could not. She was right. And so he stood there, struggling with himself.

Hannah knew from the expressions crossing his face that he could not deny the truth of her words, but she knew also of the temptation to rise in the world.

And then there was Isabella.

Hannah had seen men before, even in her limited experience, who had destroyed themselves over some woman who was not worthy of them. She longed to caution Myles, to draw him away from this woman who might well be his ruin. But of course, she could not. She knew instinctively that to disparage Isabella in any way would destroy the union and harmony she and Myles had shared since that first day in their secret place.

The light flickered and blew as a breeze came through the window at the end of the hall, disturbing the single sabrelike flame that rose. The flickering of the shadows seemed to make Myles's face waver in the murky darkness.

He looked at her, meeting her eyes, and a strong impulse came over him to hold Hannah again and promise her that he would flee the life of the court. But then images rose up in his mind . . . the king, the queen, Ralph Geddes, Isabella . . . and he thought, *I can't give it up now.* Shaking his head, he spoke sadly. "No, Hannah. I won't leave the court. But I will promise you that I'll be careful. I won't let it change me as it has changed others."

He saw that his words disappointed her, and her eyes grew sad. She drew back and said softly, "Good night, Myles. And thank you again for bringing me." She stepped inside the room without another word and closed the door. At the sound of the lock clicking on the far side, Myles had the fanciful notion that he was being locked out of something. Try as he might to ignore it, as he turned and left her door to go to his own room, he knew in some way that he had made a decision, the results of which would control him in the future—and possibly lead him away from Hannah.

He opened the door of his own room, went inside, and stood silently beside the window. He looked down on the dimly lit street, then glanced to the east, where the palace lay. Once again he thought of Hannah's gentle face looking up at him, her lips soft and vulnerable as she begged him to leave the court.

And then, almost savagely, he ripped off his fine cloak and threw it on the floor, trying to put the matter out of his mind. He knew, however, that he would not be able to forget. And surely enough, for long hours that night, he lay awake wondering if he was being wise. He thought of how strong and firm Hannah's lips had been beneath his, how strong and true her heart was—and then forced such thoughts from his mind.

The court won't change me, he thought stubbornly. *I'm strong enough to keep away from the wrong that's there. And I may even be able to bring some good into it all!*

But as he finally drifted off to sleep, all that was in his mind was a soft voice pleading, *"I don't want you to change!"*

END OF PART TWO

The

Part
THREE

1 5 2 7   1 5 3 0

Courtier

Sixteen

THE KING'S GREAT BUSINESS

King Henry VIII was giddy with love. He thirsted for the sight of his beloved Anne; he longed for her as he had never longed for any woman. She was his lure, his charm, the force that drew him and made him forget everything but that he loved and desired her. The power she exercised over him was—or so he would recall later—beyond seduction. It was a force so great, stirring in him a love so deep and so compelling, that he felt himself bewitched.

There were others who did not find Henry VIII's infatuation for Anne Boleyn normal. Indeed, many in the court began to gossip and spread rumors that Anne, with all her dark beauty, was no less than a witch! They argued that it could not have been her beauty that drew Henry. She was not really beautiful, not nearly so much as other maids of the court. She was wild and dark and strange and had a power over Henry that could not be explained by anything other than witchcraft. What was more, many had noticed the extra finger on her left hand, though she kept it out of sight as much as possible.

"'Tis the sign of a witch!" the whisper ran to and fro throughout the court, and many stayed far away from her lest they should fall prey to her powers.

Henry was not only giddy with love, he was giddy with hope,

and a change in attitude and approach came over him. He threw himself vigorously into the thick of his country's affairs and sent his servants rushing all over the Continent, doing his will with France, Spain, the Netherlands, and elsewhere.

Henry's avid interest in governing had little to do with his position, in and of itself. He was spurred on by a greater cause, at least in his mind, for he had made up his mind to end his marriage to Catherine. And as marriage was a sacrament governed by church law, to end it, he needed the cooperation of Pope Clement VII. But Pope Clement owed his election to none other than Catherine's nephew, Emperor Charles, and he dared not allow Henry to divorce the emperor's aunt. Nevertheless, once Henry's mind was made up, as his advisers well knew, nothing could stop him. And so he plunged full speed ahead to procure a divorce from Catherine. This was called "The King's Great Business," and though it was whispered about all over the kingdom, still Henry made no public announcement.

What of Queen Catherine during all of this? Myles Wakefield, during the three years that he had known her, had grown genuinely fond of the queen. Paradoxically, he had also grown fond of Anne Boleyn! The two women were poles apart. Anne, in her youth and slim attractiveness, was a constant reminder that Queen Catherine had lost her looks. The queen still had beautiful eyes, but her figure had thickened, and she was now a middle-aged woman who looked even older than she was.

Only once did Catherine speak to Myles of the turmoil in the family of Henry VIII. He had come to visit Isabella, of course, and during one brief interval when he was left alone with the queen while Isabella went to change, Catherine herself brought the matter up. They were walking along one of the paths in the garden, the queen showing Myles the beautiful roses, when suddenly she turned to him and said, "You have never mentioned my situation to me, Myles."

Myles was aware of her meaning, but was embarrassed and did not know how to respond to her. "Why . . . why, no, Your Majesty," he said uncomfortably. "It is not my place . . ."

Catherine looked away from him and frowned. "Everyone in England is talking about it," she said, bitterness scoring the lines of her mouth. She stared down at the ground, then she lifted her eyes, and Myles saw the pain and grief that marked her face. "I am like all foreign princesses who marry kings," she said quietly, "to produce sons and to serve as a living link between the foreign court and the husband. Now," she went on, and here again her voice took on a note of pain that was palpable, "'tis clear I will never succeed in bearing a son."

Myles wanted to comfort her. "That is in the hands of God, Your Majesty," he said gently.

"The hand of God has moved," Catherine said. There was no anger in her voice, only resignation. "My only sons have been stillborn. Henry has told me he considers this the voice of God—the judgment of God, he calls it—upon our marriage." She paused, then turned and began to walk. She was silent for a while, then stopped to reach out and touch a red rose. "A beautiful thing, is it not? Look how red, how deeply crimson it is. God makes beautiful things, doesn't he?"

"Yes, he does, Your Majesty."

"How sad that they must grow old and fade." She held the rose lightly, touching its silky smoothness. "One day soon the leaves will fade, curl, wither, and finally drop, and the rose will die."

Myles was terribly uncomfortable. He had never seen Catherine in this mood before. He wanted to soothe her, but he knew that she was exactly right. Henry's intention of divorcing her and marrying Anne Boleyn was clear. After a long silence he said, "I am sorry, Your Majesty." He hesitated, then asked, "But how can Henry do this? The church clearly forbids divorce."

"He has already informed me of how it will be." A deep furrow appeared between Catherine's fine eyes, and she went on, "He says that we have never been married at all."

"Never married at all!" Myles exclaimed. "Whatever does *that* mean?"

"He says that because I was married to his brother Arthur, the Bible says that this is incest. His priests gave him a text found in the book of Leviticus, that a man cannot uncover the nakedness of his brother's wife." Myles's eyes blinked in astonishment and his mind raced. While he was trying to find an answer she continued, "What foolishness! Even if it were so, it would not apply because my marriage to Arthur was never consummated. The king ignores this," she said sadly, "and says that he sins. That all of our marriage, almost twenty years, was nothing! We are not married at all and never were." Suddenly tears gathered in her eyes, and her voice grew thick as sobs began to rise in her throat. "I must go now. Forgive me—"

She turned and walked rapidly away, almost blindly, and Myles's heart went with her as she disappeared into the palace. He stood in silence, troubled over their conversation. When Isabella came out he at once began to speak of it.

Isabella was wearing a light silken dress of a startling blue color. Her hair was done in a fantastic style, in curls, and all built into an intricate structure on top of her head. Myles had never liked it, but he had not told her so. When he mentioned his conversation with the queen, she stared at him, then laughed. "You didn't know that? I thought everyone did. The king has made no secret of it. He called Wolsey in and told him either to get him a divorce or get ready to give up his position!"

"But it isn't right!" Myles protested.

"Right or not, 'tis what Henry is going to do. And you cannot actually blame him, can you?" Isabella shrugged. "After all, Henry needs a son and Catherine obviously is barren. She'll never give him one."

"That makes no difference," Myles said stubbornly. His lips were drawn tight into a grim line of determination, and his eyes were narrowed half-shut with the intensity of his feeling. He looked down at Isabella, adding, "When a man marries, his wife is his wife! Whether she has children or not, whether she is sick or not, none of that matters. Look at what the Bible says!"

"You don't really believe that, do you, Myles?" Isabella smiled skeptically. "Men get rid of their wives all the time, when their wives get old, or sick, or simply when they want another woman."

"Not all men!"

"Most of them," Isabella insisted.

"My father didn't. Lady Jane has been ill for years, and she has never given him a son. And he loves her just as much, or even more, than the day they got married."

Isabella looked up at him and said with a touch of smugness, "Yes, Myles. But of course, he does have you, does he not?"

With that, the discussion turned into a full-blown quarrel, and soon Isabella found an excuse for leaving him. He knew that she was leaving him to join Ralph Geddes, who practically lived at court now, and he was further angered by this. He stalked off, found some of the young courtiers with whom he had become friends, and left with them on a pleasure trip through London.

Ralph Geddes had prospered during his years serving under Cromwell . . . to some degree. He wore good clothes and had fine quarters—but Cromwell was stingy with cash. Geddes had spent his time learning from Cromwell how to rise in power, which meant in this case, how to please King Henry VIII. It was a hazardous career, the career of courtier, made fatally precarious by the ever-present power—and inclination—of the king to sweep away titles, lands, and even life at his whim. Yet some men had the shrewdness and flinty hardness to succeed at it and survive.

Ralph Geddes was clearly among those men. He well knew that the court of Henry VIII seethed with intrigue. Snakelike, the coils of conspiracy and disloyalty wrapped themselves around every courtier, powerful or vulnerable, ultimately making him sacrifice everything—his reputation, his income, even his friends and relatives—for the sake of reaching higher up the greased pole of preference.

Early in the afternoon of the same day that Queen Catherine had spoken so plainly to Myles, Ralph met with Cromwell to plan strategy. In Cromwell's apartments at the palace, in a small room that served as his office, the two men sat at a table, Ralph sipping the wine that Cromwell provided, listening carefully as his employer ran over the details of their administration. He admired Cromwell's mind, which seemed to reach like a spider-web, strands touching every part of the life and court and career of Henry VIII. As Cromwell spoke, he studied the man, noting carefully his technique and methods.

Finally the two men got to a point where Cromwell said bluntly, "Now, one more thing, Geddes. The king's mind seems to be against these new translations of the Scripture."

Geddes looked at him with surprise. "Why, I thought he approved of them!" He thought for a moment, then asked, "Did not he insist upon putting the Bible in the churches?"

Cromwell's lips puckered queerly. "That," he said succinctly, his voice sour, "was last week. This is today." He placed two fingers against his temple and went on. "And the mind of our Sovereign Majesty, King Henry VIII, has now shifted." He spoke this way so freely that Geddes was always startled. He himself knew how little respect Cromwell had for the king; the man was not afraid to show it when they were alone. Of course, Cromwell would never let the king know such a thing, for that could be fatal. But Ralph filed the comment away in his mind for a weapon to be used sometime in the future.

"What is to be done?" Geddes shrugged. "No one knows where this man Tyndale is, except that he is hidden somewhere in Europe."

"Well, someone had better find out!" Cromwell snapped. "The king insists upon bringing him to trial, and when the king insists, that means you and I must go to work. Now, I want you to find this man Tyndale."

"But—you mean go to Europe?" Ralph was appalled. He had no liking for being sent on such a mission as this, particularly since it was apparently a hopeless one. Men had been sent before, trained agents, to ferret out the whereabouts of William Tyndale. All had returned reporting utter failure, which had enraged Henry.

"Oh, I think something might be done here," Cromwell said. He leaned forward and spoke rapidly. "There is a man here in London. His name is Humphrey Monmouth. Several years ago, before Tyndale left the country, Monmouth was taken by him. He took him into his house for a time. We have reason to believe that he is still in contact with Tyndale."

"Then what is the problem?" Geddes demanded. "Why hasn't the man been forced to talk?"

"Because up until now, it has not been an issue with Henry," Cromwell retorted impatiently, his eyes growing hard. "But now, Ralph, it *is* an issue. So I want you to have this man arrested, and it will be up to you to find out what he knows about Tyndale." He rose suddenly and studied the young man across from him. "You are an ambitious fellow, Ralph." He smiled grimly, but the smile did not touch his eyes. "You would like to have my place, wouldn't you?" He held up a hand at Ralph's sudden protest, saying, "Do not be ashamed of it. I would like to have Wolsey's place. Wolsey would like to have the pope's place. As for Henry—"

he shrugged—"I don't know whose place he would like." Then he added grimly, "Pick this man up and take him to the Tower. Find out where Tyndale is." He left the room abruptly and Geddes followed him, his mind busy with this new plan.

The Tower of London had been, for hundreds of years, one of the most impressive sights in the city. It had begun as a fort and had become also a royal encampment, where kings had their quarters, and a gathering for assemblies, for the making of treaties. What was more, it became the only place of coinage in all England, and it housed the armory of the nation, with its warlike provisions. It also became the storage house for the jewels and treasures of the Crown.

Some of this Ralph had seen, but he had only heard of the grimmer aspects of the Tower: the dungeons where prisoners were tortured. As he passed through the yards leading to the torture chambers, he glanced over to the block where traitors were beheaded. He had attended more than one execution here and had never become inured to the sight of heads rolling into the straw, the crimson blood spurting like fountains. He averted his face quickly and tried to control the sweating of his palms, wiping them surreptitiously on his jerkin.

"This way, master," the Tower guard said as Ralph hesitated. He led the young man through the stone archways, then down a series of corridors, which were dank, cold, and airless. They passed through a room where he saw several men chained to the wall, their faces pale from lack of sunlight. The look of hopelessness on their countenances depressed Ralph and sent a strange thrill of fear through him. He was not a man of action. Rather, he was a man of thought, of planning, of intrigue; and it was times like this, when he had to enter into the actual dirty business of the court, that he felt himself lacking in something.

"Right in here," the guard said, and Ralph entered a room where there was a man sitting at a desk. The man looked up questioningly. "Mr. Ralph Geddes?"

"Yes, I am Ralph Geddes."

"My name's Harkins." The tall, cadaverous individual wore a somber suit of black. He was so thin he appeared almost skeletal, and his face resembled a skull, with his eyes sunk far back into the sockets. "You are here to question the prisoner Monmouth?"

"Yes."

"Come this way then. Guard, bring Monmouth to the rack."

Harkins rose and walked out of the room, and Geddes followed him down a long hall and through a door. When he stepped inside, his eyes fell at once on what he knew to be the rack. It was a raised bed made out of wood, at one end of which were wheels with handles that allowed them to be turned. There was some sort of a ratchet arrangement, he saw, that would lock the wheels into place. Quickly his eyes ran over the leather thongs and chains, presumably for binding the ankles and wrists of the unfortunate wretch to be racked.

Harkins asked dispassionately, "You shall be putting the question to him yourself, Mr. Geddes? Or do you prefer that I do it?"

As it happened, Geddes would much have preferred that the torturer do it. But he knew that word of this "questioning" would get back to Cromwell, and he was sure it would not do to show squeamishness. "I will handle it myself, Harkins," he said brusquely.

"You have experience in questioning men?"

"No, not actually," Ralph admitted. "But we only need to know one thing from Monmouth, the location of a certain individual, William Tyndale." He was nervous but tried not to show it. "Do you think the man will be stubborn?"

Harkins's face took on a death's-head grin. "Not for long, Mr. Geddes," he answered. There was an awful quality to the man.

Anyone who made his living creating pain for other human beings, in Geddes's eyes, was less than human. But he gritted his teeth and waited, determined to show nothing of his feelings.

Moments later the door swung open, and two burly guards half-carried a man in. He was small, no more than five feet five or six, Geddes saw, and his eyes were blank with terror. He was trembling in every limb, and his face was pasty white.

"All right, put him on the rack," Harkins ordered in a business-like voice.

"Please! Don't! Don't!" Monmouth cried. He had been arrested without warning and had not been allowed to speak to anyone. Now the sight of the torturer in his black clothing, with his burning eyes, brought terror to him. "What is it? What—what do you want?"

Instantly Geddes said, "We only want one thing from you, Monmouth." He shrugged, eyeing the small man closely. "There's no point in a man suffering for nothing. If you will just give us one little bit of information, we will release you and you may go back to your family."

Monmouth licked his lips, his eyes darting from Harkins to the rack, then back to Ralph. He shuddered and pleaded desperately, "I don't know what you want!"

"We only want the location of William Tyndale."

Monmouth blinked. He swallowed hard and said, "But Mr. Tyndale has not been at my house for years now! He has left England! He's gone somewhere across the water!"

"We know that," Geddes snapped. "We need to know where in Europe he is."

"But I can't—I—I don't know!" Monmouth moaned. "I don't know. I cannot tell you what I don't know!"

Geddes glanced at Harkins and nodded slightly. "Go ahead," he muttered.

At a sign from the torturer, the two soldiers grasped Monmouth and stretched him out on the rack. One of them fastened his ankles into the irons, the others his wrists, and then they stepped back.

"If you will stand directly there, Mr. Geddes," Harkins said calmly, "we will begin the questioning." He stepped back beside the large wheel located over the head of the prisoner, put his hand on the handle, and gave it a short turn. There was a clanking sound as teeth fell into prelocated crevices. The chains took up their slack, and Monmouth's arms and legs straightened with the first tug of the rack. Harkins experimentally moved the wheel again and then again. With each turn there was a clicking sound until Monmouth's body suddenly grew tense.

Ralph moved to stare down into the man's face. Hurriedly he said, "There is no point in this, Monmouth. Tell us where Tyndale is and you may go home."

"I don't know! I don't know, I tell you!" the man moaned.

Ralph looked up at the torturer and signaled again, noting that Harkins's face had a fixed grin. His hand tightened, and the wheel moved slightly. He turned it several times until Monmouth was stretched tight. Ralph saw the chains biting into the man's ankles and wrists, and as the clicking and clanking continued, Monmouth's chest arched and he began to scream.

"Why, we have hardly begun!" Harkins said in surprise. He paused and looked over the poor wretch with obvious pleasure, waiting until the moans had died down. Then, leaning on the wheel, gave it two or three very quick turns. It was harder now, and he put his strength to it.

As Monmouth's arms were pulled mercilessly over his head, Geddes saw his face contort with a terrible pain. Then he heard a sudden snapping sound and saw that the man's shoulders—or some part of his body, Ralph thought with a shrinking feeling—had dislocated. Monmouth's eyes widened with shock and then closed.

"He's fainted!" Ralph exclaimed.

"We will wait, then," Harkins said. "We have plenty of time." He glanced down at the unconscious man's taut body. "You won't have any trouble, Mr. Geddes," he said, his tone conversational. "We may have to dislocate a few more bones, but he will tell you what he knows. 'Tis my professional opinion."

But Harkins was not altogether correct. On and on, the torture went on, seemingly for hours, with Monmouth fainting and the two men waiting until he came back to consciousness before beginning again. He screamed and he begged and he pleaded— but he denied over and over again that he knew the whereabouts of William Tyndale.

Finally the torturer said, "I must admit, I believe he is telling the truth." He glanced over Humphrey Monmouth's torn body and shook his head. "He is too much of a coward to endure this much. He would have told you if he knew anything. Is there anything else you would like to know? Maybe he can answer something else."

A thought came to Geddes, and he said, "Yes, there is one more thing." He turned back to Monmouth, who was drifting dazedly back and forth between consciousness and unconsciousness, and said, "All right, Monmouth. You don't know about Tyndale. But you do know some of the names of people he is in contact with. Tell me that, and we'll send you home."

The poor wretch muttered weakly, "Lady Jane Wakefield. She . . . knows . . . Mr. Tyndale. He . . . writes . . . to her . . . some-times."

Ralph straightened up, a light of astonishment on his face. "Lady Jane Wakefield!" He looked at the torturer and said, "All right. You may let him go now. I shall see that he is taken back to his home."

He left the grim chambers of torture, emerged into the bright sunlight, and shuddered. He would not soon forget what he had just gone through. Yet as he walked across the green grass toward the entrance to the Tower, there came a smile to his face.

"Lady Jane Wakefield! Now that is most curious," he murmured softly to himself. "I wonder if Sir Robert is aware that his wife is trafficking with a heretic!" The smile grew broader, and he took a deep breath of satisfaction. "It will be interesting to find out about that, won't it now?"

Seventeen

MESSAGE FROM LADY JANE

"Come along, Myles," Isabella said with excitement flashing in her eyes. "We'll miss the bullbaiting!" The two of them were standing off to one side by a tall, gray building, but the crowd was streaming past them, headed for the arena where the event was to be held. Isabella was wearing a new dress comprised of a bodice and a skirt, which Myles had learned was called a *kirtle*. The neckline of the bodice was low and square-cut and set her figure off to the best advantage. Ordinarily she wore a hood, but on this day she had broken with tradition by letting her hair flow freely down her back. It sparkled in the sun, and she looked very beautiful, Myles thought, as he stood holding her hand.

Isabella looked at him and gave his hand an impatient tug. "Oh, don't be so stubborn!" she coaxed. "I'm told it's going to be a fine spectacle!" She moved closer, pressing the curves of her body against him. Reaching up with her free hand she stroked his cheek and murmured, "Come along now, Myles, don't be a bother." There was something suggestive in her movements and in her eyes, and she did not pull away, but stood still, caressing him. She saw him relent and laughed, "Let's go. We have time later for such as this."

Myles gave in—as he always did—and followed her as they became part of the crowd pressing forward, arriving shortly at the arena where the bullbaiting was to take place. They stopped at a vantage point for viewing, and Isabella talked brightly, first to this young courtier, then to that young woman.

As for Myles, he felt very much left out. Isabella knew everyone at court, it seemed, while he knew only a few.

Before he could ponder this thought too long, a young ox was led into the arena and fastened by a long rope to an iron ring in the middle of the field. The handler disappeared, and instantly some of the men who had brought dogs loosed three of them. The animals rushed toward the bull, with horrible growls coming out of their throats, and leaped to attack.

The dogs were large, two of them black and one brown, with massive jaws. One of them scored a deep gash in the bull's flank but was caught immediately by one of the horns, which ripped him open and flung him to one side. He was cut to the death but, even in his dying agony, tried to pull himself back toward the fray.

The other two dogs were leaping at the bull's throat, but soon they, too, lay dying. Instantly other dogs were released so that the bull had no respite. Always, one had a grip on the bull's throat or an ear, and from time to time the handlers would have to come and pry them loose with poles when they were all but dead. Finally the bull, after having killed several dogs, became so slashed and mangled that he seemed to be covered with blood. And, as was inevitable, some of the larger animals finally pulled him to the ground, where they finished him off.

"Oh, that was a fine bull, wasn't it, Myles!" Isabella exclaimed breathlessly. Her eyes were wide with excitement, her lips parted in an entrancing manner.

Myles looked at her in wonder. "I can never understand," he said, "how anyone can get any enjoyment out of seeing animals, especially dogs, mangled."

Isabella rounded on him, clearly irritated. "You and your old dogs!" she said in disgust. "You act like they're little babies! They are made for our sport, aren't they?"

Myles sighed deeply. He knew almost everyone shared this view, but he himself loved dogs and considered bullbaiting depraved. He could never stand to look at the fierce, bloodthirsty faces of the observers. Standing quickly, he said abruptly, "I'll leave you here. I don't care to watch such butchery." He turned on his heel and walked away quickly.

"Myles! Myles, don't go!"

But he had had enough. Even as he left, he saw the handlers bringing out a bear and fastening him to the iron stake, preparatory to letting the dogs go at him. Disgustedly he left the arena, knowing that by doing so he would leave Isabella to the attentions of others who were always glad for such an opportunity.

Isabella was almost ready to run after him. She had tormented him on purpose, finding pleasure in manipulating him, but she had not meant to go so far as to make him leave. Just as she started to go after Myles, a hand grasped her arm, and she turned to find Ralph grinning at her.

"You had no luck with Myles, sweetheart," he said. "Perhaps you will find my company more agreeable."

Instantly, a flirtatious smile curved Isabella's lips. "Oh, he is so—so—irritating! You know how he is, Ralph. He feels so sorry for the stupid dogs that he wouldn't stay."

"Yes, he is a tenderhearted fellow, all right," Ralph said with a nod. He well knew Myles's sympathy as far as dogs were concerned. He himself took every opportunity to taunt young Wakefield for this particular tendency. "Or perhaps I should say chickenhearted." Then he moved closer and whispered, "At the ball tonight I shall have something for you. A present from France."

"Oh, what is it, Ralph?" Isabella asked at once. She leaned against Ralph as she had leaned against Myles, pleased with the power of her persuasion. She had learned that a woman could control men as easily as men controlled the hawks. Surely men did not realize this, she thought, or if they did, they chose to ignore it.

Ralph laid a finger on her lips and said, "Later, Isabella. At the ball." He turned and said, "Now, let's watch and see how the dogs do with this bear."

Myles paused at the edge of the field, beside the gate, to take one last look. He saw Isabella and Ralph standing close together. Ralph's arm had slipped around Isabella's waist, and the sight of it depressed Myles. He left and went at once to his room, where he worked for two hours on some bookkeeping that he was doing for his father. He had become almost a seneschal for Wakefield, taking over many of the duties that Sir Robert once had seen to, and had found that he enjoyed it. He now knew every foot of the manor and had learned the intricacies of managing a large estate, although he was still only a young man.

He was interrupted by a knock at the door. Startled, he rose and opened the door. A servant of the lodge where he was rooming stood in the corridor. "A message for you, sir," he said, bowing respectfully. He held out a sealed paper, took the coin offered him, and pulled at his forelock. "Thank you, sir," he said cheerfully and disappeared.

Myles held the paper in his hand, wondering whom it could be from, and moved over to the window. Breaking the seal, he opened the folded paper and saw it was the handwriting of Lady Jane:

My dear son,

   I hesitate to disturb you, but if it is possible, I have need of seeing you at once. If you can, come to Wakefield quickly.

With all my love,
Lady Jane

Myles stared at the short note, puzzled greatly, for Lady Jane had never summoned him from town.

It must be important, he thought. *She would never send for me like this unless it were.*

Immediately he threw a few items into a bag, left his room, and stopped to see the innkeeper. "I shall be gone for a time, Francis," he said. "I don't know how long." Then he left and made his way to the stable. He kept a horse in London, and he had the hostler saddle the animal. He tied his bag onto the horse, swung up into the saddle, and rode out of the stable at a fast pace.

He made good time that day. The sun was shining brightly, and he enjoyed watching the laborers out in the fields after he had left the city. By now, he knew the road from Wakefield to London as well as he knew his own backyard.

He stopped that night for a meal at an inn and considered spending the night there but decided against it. His horse was still fresh in spite of the miles they had come, and he decided to ride on through the night. He did so, arriving at Wakefield the next morning just as gray dawn was breaking in the east. A surprised hostler appeared, and Myles tossed the reins to him, greeting him cordially, then walked toward the manor house.

Entering, he was met by one of the maidservants, who exclaimed in confusion, "Why, Mister Myles! We weren't expecting you—"

Mother didn't tell anyone, Myles thought. *Perhaps I shouldn't say anything.*

"Is my mother up yet?" he asked.

"I . . . doubt it, sir," the maid said hesitantly. "She were up late last night, with her guest."

"Who was that?" Myles inquired.

"Miss Kemp, sir."

"Oh, indeed?" Myles said, not greatly surprised. Hannah had come often to Wakefield, especially when someone was ill. The thought that perhaps his mother had become ill again stirred him, and he said, "Is Miss Kemp in her usual room?"

"Yes, sir."

"Then go see if she is awake and ask her to come down, if you will."

He went into the kitchen and found that the cook had already begun his day's work. He was hungry but waited until Hannah came down before he ate. He saw her coming down the long stairs and went to greet her. She was dressed in a simple tan dress that became her. She moved as if she were tired, and her face looked worried.

Myles asked anxiously, "Is anything wrong, Hannah? Is Mother ill?"

"Oh no, Myles," Hannah said hastily. She reached out her hand and he took it, and she squeezed it affectionately, smiling at him. Her hands were firm and very strong, and she kept her hands conscientiously so that they were always clean and the nails well cared for. He thought now, as he had many times before, that they were the hands of a musician.

Amused at his appraisal, Hannah drew her hand back, folding both in front of her. "You haven't seen your mother yet?"

"No. She sent for me to come at once." He looked at her searchingly. "Do you know what is wrong?"

Hannah hesitated, chewing her lower lip thoughtfully. She half-turned from him, and Myles could see that she was disturbed. Then she turned back to face him and said haltingly, "I—think so. But I would rather that your mother told you herself."

Myles was certain then that it was serious. "This must be worse than I suspected," he exclaimed, "if you can't even talk about it! I'm going to go up right now and see if she's awake."

He started toward the stairway but turned back to Hannah. "You are looking well," he said. "And your family, they are well?"

"Yes, they're fine."

Myles could see that she did not want to talk and said, "I'll see you later, Hannah."

He turned and went to his mother's room, knocking on the door gently. A voice said quietly, "Come in."

Myles entered the room, and Lady Jane Wakefield's eyes lit up like stars when she saw him. She was sitting in a chair by the window, reading as usual, and he walked over, leaned down, and kissed her cheek. "Myles!" she said warmly, holding his head down, her thin fingers running through his thick hair. "You got here much more quickly than I had thought you would."

Myles had grown tremendously fond of Lady Jane. She had indeed become a real mother to him. "I was worried," he said gently. He pulled a chair closer and sat down beside her. "What is it? Is there something wrong with Father?"

"No, it's not that," Lady Jane assured him quickly. She clasped her hands together in her lap and turned to look out the window. She had a habit of pausing before making an important statement, and he had learned that pause came because she was uttering a quick prayer. She had taught him to do likewise, though she had not made him a man of prayer. Still, she had been another strong woman in his life, who lived from day to day on a talking basis with God, as had his mother. But where Margred's relationship with God had been visionary and somewhat mysterious and awesome to a little boy, Lady Jane talked with God, Myles thought, as a man talked with his friend. This was equally wondrous to him and made him understand that something in his own life was missing.

He waited impatiently, and finally she said, "It's about Sir William Tyndale." She always gave the teacher the title *Sir*, as was often done, applying the rank to a scholar and a tutor. She watched her son's face as she spoke, and when she saw only a sort of relief in his eyes, she smiled. "I know you are fond of him, aren't you, Myles dear?"

241

"I have nothing but admiration for him, Mother."

"He is in great difficulty," Lady Jane said. She sighed and stared out her window, a faraway look in her eyes. "Of course, he is always in difficulty, is he not?"

"Where is he, Mother?"

"In a small village in Germany. Marburg, it's called. In hiding, of course. The king's agents have been more active of late. They are determined to hunt him down and drag him back to England. He will be burned at the stake if they find him, you know."

"I don't understand it," Myles said moodily. "What has he done? As far as I can tell, he has done nothing but translate the Scriptures into English."

"That's all it takes to offend the king," Lady Jane said calmly. She reached over and picked up the Bible she had laid on the table when Myles came in and handed it to him. "This is what he has done. Put the Bible into English. In a language that, as he says, even the plowboys can read."

Myles took the book, filled with curiosity. He knew that Tyndale's Bibles had been circulating in England. Hannah had told him that the work was finished, but he had not yet seen one. The book was rather poorly bound, he thought as he opened it. He began reading the first line his eyes fell upon. "'And as Moses lifted up the serpent in the wilderness, even so must the Son of Man be lifted up, that whosoever believeth in him should not perish, but have eternal life.'" He read the words aloud, then looked at his mother, his brow wrinkled. "What does that mean? 'As Moses lifted up the serpent in the wilderness.' I don't understand."

His words seemed to grieve Lady Jane. "My dear boy," she said, "I have neglected your education. You should have had your own English Bible long before this!" She quickly explained about the Israelites, how they had been bitten by vipers and were suffering and dying. She related how Moses had made a serpent out of brass and put it upon a pole, being commanded to do so by God. Then she said, "And if anyone was bitten by one of the fiery serpents God sent, all he had to do was just look at the brass serpent, and he was healed of the bite and did not die."

"I never heard that story," Myles said with wonder. Lady Jane had read from the Bible to him many times, but he had no recollection of this story. He read the line again and said, "I'm so ignorant of the Bible. I need to get one of these for my own. But," he added, "I think it's illegal to own one."

"It's certainly illegal to bring them into England. That is the work that William Tyndale is giving his life for. And that is why I have sent for you." She stopped and looked directly into his eyes. "He is almost destitute, Myles. Someone must help him."

"What is it that you want, Mother?" Myles asked gently. "You know I will do it, whatever it is."

His words pleased Lady Jane, and she said, "I have some money. If you will take it to Sir William and see that he gets it, I would be so relieved. It will mean that he won't starve and he can live decently while he does his work."

"Why, of course I'll do it, Mother," Myles said instantly.

Lady Jane held up her hand. "It won't be easy," she warned. "Even I don't know exactly where he is. All I know is the name of one who can take you to him. It will be very dangerous. Spies are everywhere. Sir William has to move, very often, and several times he has almost been caught. And anyone who helps him, if they are brought back to England, can be hanged for treason." She took Myles's hand and went on anxiously, "I hate to ask you to do this, Myles, it is so dangerous. But I have no one else." Then she said in a low tone, "Hannah was going to do it."

"Hannah!" Myles stared at her incredulously.

"Yes. You know how she feels about Sir William and his work. She has always revered him, and she even helped raise some of the money. But when I heard that she was planning to take it herself,

I was petrified! It's so dangerous, and she has never made a journey alone. For a woman, it would be a disaster, I think."

Myles at once said, "Of course she can't go! But I will." He drew a sigh of relief and said, "I spoke with Hannah downstairs and she was very troubled. I didn't know what it was. Now, though, it will be all right."

"Not as all right as you think," Lady Jane said. "I told her my plan to ask you to go, and she was against it."

"Against it? Why should she be against it?"

"She knows you are not really a believer, Myles," Lady Jane said, regret in her fine eyes. "She says that only those who believe in the cause, in the Word of God, should risk their lives for it." She saw the shock on her son's face. "I think if you will just go with her, she will allow that. You can go with her, look after her, make certain that she is all right. But you will have to persuade her, I'm afraid."

Offended, Myles wanted to defend himself to his mother. But he held his tongue and said only, "Well, of course, Mother. I'll go to her right now. How soon do you think we should leave?"

"As soon as possible. I'm really afraid that the poor man is in dire straits."

Myles bade his mother good-bye then and left her chambers. He went at once to find Hannah and finally came upon her standing outside, watching the dawn light the sky. "Why didn't you tell me what was happening, Hannah?" Myles demanded without preamble. "You must have known that I'd be willing to help."

Hannah turned to him, and a smile turned up the corners of her lips. "I knew that, Myles," she said warmly, "but I don't want you to go. It is very dangerous. Anyone caught helping William Tyndale will be executed."

"All the more reason why I should go," he said recklessly. His eyes grew rather cloudy, and he said half-angrily, "I'm afraid I don't take this kindly, Hannah. After all, it is only right that I should help the man." She put her hand on his arm, and seeing the gentleness on her face, he shrugged and said more calmly, "Don't mind me. I just have a quick temper. But understand this: I don't think that you should go at all. But I suppose you're determined."

"Yes, I am. I must do it."

"Very well. But I will go with you," he said firmly. "And Mother thinks we should go at once. I will wait and talk to Father. We'll make our plans and get away as soon as we can."

"Oh, Myles," Hannah said, and now her voice did tremble, and her lips as well. "I'm so glad! I didn't tell your mother, but I was terribly afraid of going alone! With you there, it will be all right."

Myles took her hand again, looked at it, and said gently, "Such a small hand," then squeezed it. He looked into her eyes, laughing quietly, and said, "And such a determined woman! The man that marries you will have his hands full!"

She blinked at him, caught by surprise at his words, and said spiritedly, "And the woman that marries you will have all she can say grace over!"

Then they both laughed, turned, and walked away, talking excitedly of the adventure that lay before them.

A week after Myles had rushed home, he stood beside Hannah on the deck of the *Amaryllis,* a small trading ship. It was dusk, and the two of them had just boarded the ship, been shown to their small cabins, and then had come back up on deck. A fog was rolling up the Thames, and they heard shouts on the dock as the rest of the cargo was loaded onto the ship.

"I can't believe we're really going!" Hannah marveled. She pushed the cowl of her cloak back, and her hair shone like spun gold in the fading light of the afternoon.

Myles smiled at her. "I can't believe it, either," he agreed. "It's like some sort of dream. I feel like a pirate or a smuggler!"

"Well, I suppose we are smugglers, aren't we?" Hannah said soberly. Her oval face took on an intense look as she gazed down the river, and Myles noticed how her hair caught the flickering red gleams of the sun as it sank into the river. Hannah went on, "We're helping a smuggler, at least. That's what they call him sometimes. Sir William, I mean. 'The Lord's Smuggler.'"

"You mean he is smuggling the Bibles into England," Myles said. He thought about it, then nodded. "Yes, I suppose that's true enough." Looking around the dock, he searched for a sign of anything unusual. All he saw was the laborers carrying their loads up the gangplank, and the usual loafers around the pubs that lined the docks. "I don't think anyone will pay two voyagers a bit of attention," he said confidently. "They would think we're husband and wife, getting on a ship together. Maybe I'd better look a bit more attentive to my bride." He put his arm around her waist and drew her close. "Now, wife, what think ye of this trip we'll be making?" he teased.

Hannah blushed furiously and giggled but did not attempt to pull away. "Myles, you fool," she said playfully. "You always were a forward one, though."

"Never miss an opportunity to hug a comely woman, that's my firm policy," Myles boasted. Impulse took him, and he leaned over to kiss her cheek, admiring the smoothness of her skin. Then he pulled her around to face him. "I don't know if I have ever told you," he said quietly, "how much it meant to me, all that you did for me when I was a boy. Teaching me to read and all that."

Hannah's face was turned up to him, her eyes searching the strong features of his face as they were drawn into angular lines by the dying rays of the sun. He looked so solid and strong, his skin tanned, his eyes very bright as he looked down at her. "Oh, Myles, it wasn't all that much," she said.

"Yes, it was. And I shall never forget it. I think about it all the time," he said. "You were the first person in the world, aside from my mother, to take any interest in me." He was holding her lightly, aware of her nearness. He released her suddenly and turned, putting his elbows on the rail. "I'm sorry, Hannah. I didn't mean to manhandle you. I guess I've gotten some of those infernal 'court manners' since I've been going to London." He frowned and said gravely, "They are altogether too free, men and women, in that place."

As she watched him, Hannah knew he was thinking of Isabella. She said nothing but put her hands on the rail next to him, a wave of resentment washing over her. She had known Isabella Bourne-ville all of her life and was well aware of the shallowness of the girl's affections. She wished she could tell Myles what she thought, that Isabella wasn't worth even a thought from him, but she knew she could not.

And so the two of them stood quietly, watching the sun go down, a huge red wafer, into the Thames, and the darkness came rushing out of the east.

In the corner of a dark, low-beamed pub called The Eagle and the Child, two men stood. Both were cloaked and stayed well in the shadows of the room. They had been watching the pair on board the *Amaryllis,* and one of them now chuckled, saying, "Now, sir! I told you true, did I not!"

The other man nodded. "You've done a good job, Sackville. Did you have any trouble then, keeping track of them?"

"None at all, sir. I done just what you said. I went to Wakefield, and as soon as young Wakefield came home, I knew something was up. The girl, she had come a day before. There was something suspicious about the whole thing. When they left together, I says to myself, 'Ned, ol' boy, they're up to something.' I knows 'tis no good to watch Lady Jane; she never goes anywhere. So I follows them all the way back to London. When they books passage on the *Amaryllis* is when I came to you, Mr. Geddes."

"You did a fine job," Geddes said again. He took a small bag that clinked as he handled it and gave it to Sackville. "I don't care how you do it," he said, and a warning note came into his voice. "You will have to get on that ship, but you mustn't let either of them see you because you must follow them when the ship lands. Wherever they go! You have plenty of money there to see to your expenses, but do not let them see you," he warned again.

Sackville was a small man with sharp features and a bristling mustache. "See me? You don't understand, Mr. Geddes. You do my vocation wrong. If Ned Sackville chooses not to be seen, then he might jus' as well be invisible, and that's all there is to it, sir!"

"I believe you," Geddes said briefly. "Now, remember, when you discover where they are going, you will report at once to Sir John Offley. I have written his name and where you can reach him on this paper. Get word to him. But you stay with those two. I want to know everywhere they go. They will lead us to William Tyndale, I am certain. And if we net that bird," he laughed suddenly, as if delighted by the thought, "the king himself will have a nice, fat reward for you!"

Avarice gleamed in the smaller man's eyes. "Never you fear, sir." Jingling the coins in his hand, he put them into his pocket. "The bird is as good as taken. I'll be going now. But they'll never see me, not Ned Sackville."

"Success to you, Ned," Geddes said, and the small man slipped away. Ralph stood motionless, watching, until it grew too dark to see, then he left the pub. His thoughts raced ahead. *If I get my hands on Tyndale,* he thought exultantly, *that will be something to catch the attention of King Henry! Of course, Cromwell will try to take all the credit, but there is a way, I am certain, to get around that.*

He smiled in the darkness and strolled on. He thought of Sir

Robert Wakefield, how the man had cheated him out of his rightful place, how he had promised to make him his heir and then given it all to that upstart Myles Morgan! A nobody! As he made his way back to the court, he had no doubt that he had found the key to take his rightful place in life—and to get his revenge on the family that had so humiliated him.

Eighteen

AN OLD ACQUAINTANCE

Sackville had not achieved the distinction of being one of the best secret agents in the employ of the English govern-ment for nothing. He made the passage over the Channel completely hidden from the eyes of the two he was sent to follow, and when they disembarked in Belgium, he crept behind them at a distance.

They slept that night, in different rooms, he took note, and the next morning, when they left by carriage for Germany, Sackville himself was a passenger. No one, however, would have recognized him, certainly not Myles nor Hannah, even if they had seen him before. He was a master of disguise, Sackville was, and the two young people saw only a very elderly man, so feeble that Myles had to assist him into the coach.

"Why, thank 'ee, young man," Sackville muttered feebly.

"You are welcome, good sir," Myles said, then sat back beside Hannah.

As the coach made its way across the country, deeper and deeper into Germany, Sackville kept up his excellent charade. When they stopped that night for a rest at an inn, it was Myles who helped him down, and the old man leaned on him so feebly that Myles insisted, "Let me help you in, sir. You are worn out with the journey." Myles received the wan thanks of his fellow traveler and saw to it that the old man was given a comfortable room.

That night Myles was fortunate, although he did not know it. He and Hannah had agreed before leaving England that, when in public, they would say absolutely nothing about their mission, and their talk that day had been totally innocuous. As a result, Sackville had been able to glean no information, although he sat right across from them and greedily listened to every word.

The journey continued the next day. Late in the afternoon, they arrived at Marburg, which was some fifty miles north of Frankfurt. The driver asked, "Sir, will you be going on to Frankfurt tomorrow?"

Myles turned and replied, "No, we are stopping here for a while."

Stopping here for a while! Sackville thought, and a sort of desperation seized him. *Why would they be stopping here? There is nothing at Marburg. If Tyndale is anywhere in this area, he should be at Antwerp or Worms. We are certain of that.* He hobbled into the inn, leaning on his cane heavily.

Myles asked in a friendly way, "Will you be going on, sir?"

The old man answered in a shaky voice, tugging on his earlobes. "No, my daughter lives here with her family. I shall be staying with them. You shan't see me again, so I'm thanking you now for the help you've given me on the way." He held out a thin hand and Myles took it gently, shook it, wished him well, and watched as the old man went outside and sat on a bench, evidently waiting for someone.

"Hope the old fellow's daughter comes to get him soon," he remarked to Hannah. "He's not strong enough to be out alone." Then he went with her, first to her room to make sure she was comfortable, then to his own for a good night's rest.

As soon as the two had gone up, Sackville scurried around busily, going to the inn across the street. He purchased a room for the night, insisting on one that looked out over the street so that he might watch the inn where Wakefield and the young woman were staying. As soon as the door was closed and he was alone, he threw off the clothes he had been wearing and began to cleanse his face of the oils he had used to disguise his rather youthful skin, and scratched his head. *Now I can get this confounded powder out of my hair,* he thought. *I'm sick of being a gray-haired old man!* He dusted his mustache, which was also powdered, and that night washed from head to foot.

He laid out the clothes he would wear next morning, which were the clothes of a prosperous merchant. He threw the old clothes away, saying, "Good-bye, old father, I won't need you again!" He went to bed early, for he intended to be up at the break of day to keep a careful watch on the two across the road. "You'll be going to William Tyndale soon or late!" he muttered, looking over the street. "And I'll be finding him when you do!"

The next morning, Myles and Hannah rose early, dressed, and had a good breakfast in the dining room of the inn. As they ate, Myles asked, "Do you have the paper that my mother gave you?"

"Yes. I keep it always with me," she answered, and she touched her breast, indicating that it was hidden in her bodice. "I hope we aren't questioned. But if we are, Myles, you mustn't be implicated. Get away and save yourself."

"Not likely," Myles said with a grin. "But let's not think about that." They ate for a while in companionable silence, and Myles thought about Lady Jane. "That was quite a prayer my mother prayed before we left, wasn't it? Think of it! She asked for angels to be all around us and to keep us from harm!" He looked around the dusky old inn, which was now filled with the smoke of many pipes and the smell of cooking meat, and looked back at Hannah, his head cocked to one side in a most

253

attractive way. "I don't see any angels," he said, "unless there's one across the table from me."

Hannah glanced at him rather sharply. "None of that, now. We have important things to do. Are you ready?" She rose, and the two went out.

A carriage driver was outside the inn, and Myles asked, "Do you know where Strober Lane is? Mr. Schultz's shop?"

The cabbie nodded slowly and said in a thick, guttural accent, "Ja. I know." Myles handed Hannah into the carriage and climbed in beside her. At a word from the cabbie, the horses started at a fast clip.

Neither Myles nor Hannah bothered to look out the windows of the cab, being amateurs in this sort of business. If they had, they would have seen a small man with a sharp, pointed face exit from the inn across the street, wave another carriage down quickly, gesture toward their disappearing carriage, and get inside.

The city of Marburg was not large. Before long the carriage stopped, and the two got out. Myles paid the fare, and they turned and looked at the shop that simply said *Bucher.*

"I think that means 'books' in German," Hannah said. "Let's go inside."

They stepped inside the door and were met at once by a corpulent, cheerful man, his round face wreathed in smiles. "Ja?" he said inquiringly. Then, identifying them after a quick perusal, said in careful English, "Can I help you?"

"Oh, you speak English," Myles said with relief. "That's good, because I don't speak any German." He glanced quickly around the small shop and asked, "Are you Mr. Schultz?"

"Ja," the heavy man answered. His eyes narrowed thoughtfully, and he inquired, "How can I help you?"

Myles was certain they were the only people in the shop, but he lowered his voice nevertheless. "We are from England. We have been sent by Lady Jane Wakefield."

"I do not believe I know the name." Schultz's eyes narrowed even more, but he scratched his head and said thoughtfully, "Lady Jane Wakefield? No, I do not know her. Does she wish to purchase some books? I have a fine supply here."

Hannah turned slightly, reached inside her bodice, and pulled out a slip of paper. She handed it to Schultz, saying politely, "Would you examine this, please, Mr. Schultz?"

Schultz unfolded the paper, his gaze fixed on the young woman for a moment, then he dropped his eyes and read the words:

> Please admit the bearer to my lodgings at once.
> William Tyndale

Schultz appeared to turn to stone for one moment, then he looked up and shrugged his powerful shoulders. "I am sorry," he said regretfully. "I do not believe I know the gentleman."

Despair settled on Hannah's face as she studied the German's face carefully. "Please," she said, "we must see him. It is vital."

Schultz spread his hands wide in a gesture of helplessness. "I am truly sorry, Fräulein, I do not know the gentleman. If you would care to leave a message . . . people do come in from time to time, and this gentleman might perhaps come in and wish to contact you."

"No, we cannot do that," Myles said hurriedly. He did not want their names attached to that of William Tyndale in any way. "Come along, Hannah."

As the two turned to leave, Hannah said, "Wait. I want to buy a book while I am here. Do you have a copy of Martin Luther's New Testament?" she asked.

Schultz looked puzzled, then nodded, "Yes, I have one. Do you read German?" He went to a shelf, picked up a small book, and handed it to her. He named a price, and Myles paid him. Schultz went on, "I wish there were an English translation of it."

Myles glanced at him sharply, but there seemed to be no artifice in the eyes of the big man, so the two turned and left. They walked along the street, talking in low voices.

Hannah said in anguish, "What shall we do? Schultz was the only name that Lady Jane gave us!"

Myles answered thoughtfully, "I know. And I can't help but think he knows where Mr. Tyndale is. There was a flicker in his eye when he saw that note—but something seemed to shut down his words."

"I expect he's afraid," Hannah said. "Even here in Germany, it is dangerous to know William Tyndale. As it was dangerous to know Luther, and perhaps still is. So what are we going to do, Myles?"

Myles thought hard, searching desperately for a solution, trying to make a decision. Then he shrugged and said, "We shall take a vacation." He smiled slightly at her expression and went on, "There's nothing else for it. We'll stay here in Marburg for a few days. I'll rent a carriage, we'll see some of the sights, and we'll just be travelers out enjoying Germany."

"But we can't stay here forever!"

"No, but I think in a few days we should have another talk with Herr Schultz. Perhaps one not so public as his shop. Hopefully, by that time he will have checked with Mr. Tyndale, and we shall get a different answer."

They followed that plan—and in doing so, almost drove Ned Sackville crazy. He had tremendous difficulty following them. Every day he had to don some sort of a new disguise. He could not afford even one slight chance of being identified. His prey went on long, solitary drives out in the country, so he had to rent a horse and follow, staying just out of sight. He was not a horseman, and his muscles ached the next day.

And then the two wretches went to the small entertainments that the town provided, and he almost despaired, becoming convinced that the pair was on an innocent mission.

On the fourth evening of their stay, Myles and Hannah returned from another long drive in the country and ate a late supper. They went to their separate rooms, both of them discouraged, and undressed and went to bed. Myles did not sleep well, and he was suddenly startled out of his fitful, dream-filled sleep by a sound—a very quiet knock on the door. It was so soft that he doubted at first it was real. Then he heard it again. Slipping out of bed, he moved silently toward the door.

When the tapping came yet again, he whispered, "Who is it? Who's there?"

"A friend you have been seeking," came the faint whispered answer.

Alarms went off in Myles's head. He reached over and picked up the short dagger that he always carried, slipping it out of the sheath. Holding it in his right hand he unbolted the door with his left and slowly opened it a tiny crack. A man stood outside with a broad hat on. There was only one small candle in the passageway, so the man's face was hidden in the darkness and shadow of the brim of the large hat.

Myles whispered fiercely, "Who are you? What do you want?"

The man's head tilted back, and he said quietly, "Why, Mr. Myles Wakefield! So harsh with an old acquaintance are you?"

"Mr. Tyndale!" Myles cried, then he yanked open the door and pulled William Tyndale inside unceremoniously, his face aglow with excitement. "Here, let me light another taper!" he said excitedly. He rushed over and lit several candles, and soon the room was illuminated with the warm glow. He turned to Tyndale and started, "What are you—why, we—its—"

He could hardly speak for excitement, and Tyndale held up his hand. "Now, don't get so excited, lad. I'm glad to see you, too."

Myles's head was swimming, and he could barely catch his breath. "We've looked all over for you, Mr. Tyndale!"

"Yes, I know, you and Miss Hannah." He looked at Myles with

a light of amusement in his eyes. "And the gentleman that follows you everywhere you go."

Myles stared at him and said blankly, "Gentleman? There is no one with us."

"Oh yes, there is," Tyndale said with a nod. "You have a spy. I doubt you've seen him, for he is a clever one. Right now, he is in his room, asleep." He smiled gently and said, "I have my own informants, and he is being carefully watched. Schultz came to me the same day you came to his shop, but we had to check to be sure that we wouldn't be revealing ourselves."

"Let me get Hannah," Myles said. "She needs to hear this."

"Very well. I shall wait while you go get the young lady."

Myles started for the door, and Tyndale said dryly, "Don't you think, my lad, that it would be wise to put some clothes on before you go to get her?"

Myles looked down at the bare necessities he wore while sleeping, flushed a bright red, then laughed ruefully. "I guess you're right!"

He quickly dressed, then went and tapped on the door of Hannah's room. She must have been awake, or almost so, for at once she whispered through the door, "What is it? Who is there?"

"It's me, Myles," he whispered excitedly. "Get dressed, you must come to my room at once!"

"Yes, I'll be there!" Hannah answered instantly.

Myles hurried back, and the two men talked until Hannah came to the door. When she saw William Tyndale, her smile seemed to light up the room. "Sir William!" she said, her voice alive with pleasure. "How good to see you!"

Tyndale took both of her hands and leaned over to kiss her cheek. "My daughter," he said gently, "I can't think of anyone on the face of the earth I would rather see than you."

Hannah said, "I was so afraid that we wouldn't find you! How did—"

"There's no time for long explanations," Tyndale interrupted.

He explained, as he had to Myles, how he had been forced to exercise caution because of the spy.

"A spy? I can't believe it! How could they have known?"

"I'm afraid Lady Jane has become suspect, my dear." Tyndale shrugged. "Now you have been searching for me. Is something wrong?"

"Indeed, no!" Hannah said. "We brought you a gift. Myles has it." It had been agreed that Myles would carry the money. He walked over to the bed and reached under the pillow, where he always kept it while he slept, and pulled out the bag full of heavy gold coins.

"A present," he said, "from my mother, Lady Jane Wakefield. And from Hannah."

Tyndale's eyes went to Hannah, and he bowed deeply. "Two beloved sisters," he breathed. He took the bag and, feeling its weight, looked up with surprise. "Why, this is a great deal of money!"

"Lady Jane has been very worried about you," Hannah said. "She insisted that we get to you as soon as possible. She wants to be sure that you at least have no monetary problems on top of all your other burdens."

"That is like Lady Jane," Tyndale mused. He looked at the pair fondly and said, "We must talk. But it will have to be at times like these, when your 'friend' over there is asleep. You must not come to my dwelling place, not ever. The man over there—even he may have a follower. They sometimes put spies to watch spies. They are clever fellows, those agents of Cromwell." He took a deep breath and squared his shoulders. "But sit down," he said. "We have plenty of time tonight." A light of humor came into his eyes, and he said mischievously, "Tell you what we must do. We shall sleep all day, and let that busy fellow over there stay up watching. And then at night, I shall come to you here. That way we'll get to see each other more." And that was what they did. Myles and Hannah would sleep sometimes until noon, the hapless Sackville watching ceaselessly, afraid he would lose them. They would go out eventually and spend the afternoons leisurely touring the countryside, visiting the tourist sites as they had been accustomed to, then go back and take their time with a fine supper, finally retiring to their rooms. Sackville watched by his window until past dark, until past midnight sometimes. Then he would put out his taper and go to bed.

As soon as that happened, Tyndale would appear and slip into the inn where Myles and Hannah were waiting for him, always in Myles's room. They did not even tell the innkeeper what was happening, so that no one knew of their meetings.

On the third night, however, Tyndale said as he was preparing to go, "This must be our last meeting for a while. And you two must go back to England. Sooner or later, something will be suspected. Besides, I have my work, and I must get back to it."

"Is there anything we can do for you?" Myles asked. His love for this man had been rekindled. During these nights, Tyndale had told them about his time spent with Martin Luther, about his finding a place to get his books printed, and about the terrible struggle he had had until the previous year, when he had been able to get the complete New Testament translated and the first volumes of it smuggled into England. Myles's heart was filled with admiration for the tenacity and the unbending integrity that marked the carriage and face of this wonderful man. "I'll do anything I can," he said firmly.

Tyndale inexplicably shot a quick glance at Hannah, then answered Myles with some hesitation, "Well, there is one thing. But it might be a little dangerous. In fact, I should not let you do it."

Instantly Myles straightened his shoulders, and his eyes gleamed with excitement. "What is it? Just tell me," he said insistently.

"Our big problem," Tyndale said slowly, "after the Bibles are printed, is getting them into England. We have been smuggling them in using a rather clever method." He smiled.

"How have you been getting them into England?" Hannah asked curiously. "They are for sale there, but no one seems to know how they got into the country."

Tyndale sat back in his chair, still smiling. "Well, I might ramble on telling you how it's come about. I think," he said, "the hand of God has been in it all. You are aware that last year, Suleiman the Magnificent—the powerful ruler of the Muslim world—swept through Hungary with an army of more than one hundred thousand men. That will probably be remembered in history. But more than that," he said earnestly, "I think it will be remembered as the year the first printed copies of the English New Testament were smuggled past the vigilance of the royal agents. And they fell into the eager hands of student and peasant alike."

He stood up and began to pace the floor of the room. His face was that of a visionary—worn and tired and lined with the years of his labor but with eyes that burned with excitement. "God had prepared the way in England. The previous winter was terrible, and the disastrous harvest of the previous summer brought a near famine to England."

"Yes," Myles said, nodding with sadness. "We have seen people almost starving to death. Only the goodness of my father and mother has kept our own people alive."

"Yes. So Wolsey attempted to stockpile the dwindling corn stocks. When there were riots, he lied, saying France had promised to send grain to England. Of course, they didn't. However, this was part of the plan of God, for during the very time that grain could not be bought in London for any price, the men from the shipyards began importing wheat so fast that it became cheap and plentiful." He clapped his hands together with evident delight and laughed. He was not a man who laughed often, but now there was such pleasure in the sound that both Myles and Hannah looked at him in amazement. "With the cargoes of grain," he said gleefully, "another seed was smuggled in. A seed more precious and more necessary to England than all the wheat in the world!"

"Bibles! There were Bibles in the grain!" Hannah exclaimed.

"Yes, my dear. That's right. And that seed has been spread all over the country. Now Wolsey has discovered this, so that that source of—um—'shipping' Bibles has been shut down. We must find other ways."

"You want us to take Bibles back with us?" Myles exclaimed. "Is that what you'd like us to do, Mr. Tyndale?"

"I would like it more than anything," he admitted, "but you must pray about it. It is not a thing to be done lightly. Will you do that, my son?"

Myles flushed and looked quickly at Hannah. "Well, Hannah will pray about it," he answered. "I have already decided." He looked down at the floor and mumbled, "I am not on such good speaking terms with God, Mr. Tyndale."

The older man's face filled with compassion, and he went to Myles, putting his hands on his broad shoulders. "You will be, my boy," he said softly. "Heaven's hound is on your track. Jesus will find you, and you will find him." Then he turned and said, "Hannah, you must pray and ask for God himself to give you a clear, direct word. There are two ways," he said firmly, "for us to know the will of God for our lives. If it is so stated in the Bible itself, then we may rest assured that we are on solid ground. But in cases like this, where the Bible is not specific, we must rest on the Holy Spirit. He is able to bring us the certain knowledge of the will of God."

"How shall I know it?" Hannah whispered, eyes wide.

"That I cannot explain," Tyndale said, meeting her gaze forthrightly. "But I think, my child, after all our talks, that you know the voice of God when it comes to you, not with a roar of thunder, but in a still, small way. Pray about this thing, and we shall talk once more. I must have your answer by tomorrow, for I will be taking a journey on the following day." He turned and walked to the door, bade them good night, and melted into the darkness.

"Well," Myles said, taking a deep breath, then expelling it. "It looks like it's up to you to decide."

"Oh, no! I can't do that!"

"Mr. Tyndale thinks you can," Myles said sturdily. "You and Lady Jane are closer to God than anyone I know. I can't help you with this, but if you think that God is telling us to do it, I will do everything in my power to move those Bibles to England!"

Hannah walked slowly to the door, going to her own room without another word. When she was inside, she fell on her knees beside her bed and for hours prayed earnestly.

The next morning she met Myles for breakfast. He took one look at her face and said, "We're going to do it, aren't we?"

"Yes," she said firmly. "The Lord has assured me that it is his will for us to carry the Word to our brothers and sisters back in England."

"Let the will of God be done then," Myles said gently. He suddenly felt humble in the presence of this slight girl. He towered over her—was much more powerful than she was—but there was a strength in her that he realized far exceeded anything in his own heart. All that day he studied her, mentioned once that it was a dangerous proposition, and saw that, if anything, she had less fear than he did himself.

"God will be with us," she said calmly. "Whatever he does is right."

In the final stages of the plan, there was one difference between that which Hannah had envisioned from listening to William Tyndale and the manner in which it finally transpired. She was utterly against it at first. Tyndale came to them and said to Hannah, "My dear, we feel it would be safer if you and Myles traveled separately. Obviously the spy has traced you from Lady Jane. There could be no other way, I think. Therefore, you will get on one ship and return to England. The spy will be forced to make a decision, and he will most likely follow you. Then, in a few days, Myles will take another ship with his 'cargo'. In this case, we have decided to hide the Bibles within bundles of clothing."

"No," Hannah said vehemently. "That is not fair! I want to be with you, Myles!"

"It's better this way, Hannah," Myles answered gently. "It wasn't my idea," he added hurriedly, "but it does make sense. This way both of us will be safe."

Hannah disliked it intensely and felt that it was somehow wrong, but she was forced to agree. The next day, she said good-bye to Myles as he helped her into a carriage. She leaned out the window, holding out her hand. He grasped it and smiled at her. "In just a few days," he said, "I shall be at Wakefield. With the Bibles." He grinned. "As soon as I get back, I'll come to you."

"God keep you, my dear!" Hannah said. Her lips trembled, and her eyes filled with tears, which she dashed away. "I mustn't be silly about this," she said, and forced a quavering smile. "Come to me as soon as you can, Myles."

"I will."

The carriage moved off, and Myles watched it go. He kept his eye out for anyone following the carriage, but he saw no signs of such. *Maybe Tyndale was wrong,* he thought as he turned back to the inn. *Maybe the man has already given up and gone back to England.*

But such was not the case. Ned Sackville watched as luggage was loaded on and saw the young woman put into the carriage, then leave after bidding farewell to the young man. Instantly he had to make a decision, and it was not difficult. He turned to a tall man standing close by and said, "Ben, I must follow the girl. You stay with Wakefield. Do you understand that, Ben?" An unholy look came into his eyes, and he rubbed his hands together. "If we can net this bird," he said gleefully, "there is nothing— nothing!—that we can't have! We'll be set for a lifetime!"

"Don't worry, Sackville," the man called Ben said. "I'll stick to him closer than a flea on a dog!"

The two parted, and Sackville rushed across to his room, gathered up his things, and rented a carriage. He followed the woman's coach until it reached the coast, then, changing into the disguise of a roughly dressed peasant, made the same voyage Hannah Kemp made. She never looked twice at him. When she disembarked and got into a coach, it was another change of clothes, and Sackville followed her all the way to Wakefield. She stayed there for one day, then returned to her father's house.

Sackville sent for one of his hirelings and set him to watch the girl. Then he went at once to London, where he made his way to his master.

Geddes listened carefully as the agent made his report, and he asked pointedly, "Are you certain that this agent of yours is clever enough to keep up with Wakefield?"

"Oh, Ben's a right leech," Sackville assured him. "Never fear. We'll know when he leaves and when he gets back to England. Shall I watch the girl, Mr. Geddes?"

"Yes. Whatever else happens, even if your man loses Wakefield, he will go back either to Lady Jane or to this girl. Put someone to watching both places, and you stay on top of it. You hear me? Don't fail!" Geddes said ominously. Then he relaxed a little and went on, "You have done well, though." He reached into his desk, pulled some gold coins from a beautiful carved box, and poured them into the agent's hand. "Do well with this—" he smiled— "and we both shall be rolling in gold!"

When the agent was gone, Geddes thought over what had happened. *Perhaps I should tell Cromwell,* he thought, then discarded the idea. No, he would take all the credit for it. *Better if I catch the bird, then hand him over to King Henry myself! Then there would be nothing Cromwell could do, save to wish he had thought of it!* The idea pleased Geddes. He laughed aloud, closed the drawer, and went back to his work.

Nineteen

DEATH OF A CARDINAL

O n the day that Myles Wakefield left Germany, his precious cargo of Bibles cleverly concealed in bales of what appeared to be cloth, Wolsey fell.

No one knew better than the cardinal himself how dangerous it was to be close to Henry VIII, but he had always been able to maneuver the king adroitly. Now, however, he had failed Henry in The King's Great Business. He had done all that a man could do to persuade the pope to grant an annulment to Henry, but the pressures on the pope had been too great, and Wolsey had been forced to confess to the king that there would be no help from that quarter.

Henry VIII would not endure failure in anyone—not a woman, not a man, and certainly not in the lord chancellor of his realm. Instantly he was finished with Wolsey and he was finished with the pope. He decided, almost in the space of a twenty-four-hour period, that he himself would become head of the church in England.

And while the Protestant Reformation—and the subsequent fall of Catholicism—that Henry unwittingly sparked with this momentous decision could not and did not occur overnight, the fall of Thomas Wolsey did.

The king gave orders, and Henry Percy, a former suitor of Anne

Boleyn, was assigned the task of bringing the cardinal to the Tower. Wolsey had, some time before, been sentenced to the wild moors of Yorkshire, a terrible punishment for one who could not bear to be disassociated from power. The cardinal was a creature of civilization and artificiality, and he longed for the courts, for the satins and silver, for the golden goblets and intrigues and spies. Judging himself to be still of worth in those high places, he dreamed of rising again in Henry's esteem.

When Lord Percy and his company came to Cardinal Wolsey in his receiving quarters, Percy found himself totally confused. There was no fire in the fireplace, no wood, and the cardinal was dressed in old clothes. Yet he roused himself in the old manner and bid them welcome as if they were at Hampton Court.

He came forward to embrace Lord Percy as a friend of long ago. He gestured to Percy, chattering, "I plan to do all the confirmations in York diocese next May. And perform all the weddings. There are many in the summer, and, of course, I shall enjoy my simple life in the country."

"My lord," Percy said in such a low voice that Wolsey scarcely heard him. He simply continued babbling. "My lord," repeated Percy, tapping him on the shoulder. Then he said in a voice that was almost a croak, "I arrest you for high treason."

Wolsey whirled, and the two men stared at each other. Wolsey swallowed and seemed unable to speak for a moment. Then he nodded, saying, "Ah, so you are come at last!"

Percy did not understand. Not at the moment. But later, he did. He told one of his followers, "Wolsey knew this would come. All those that grow too close to our sovereign feel his deadly hand at last." He led the party away, Wolsey with his head down, saying nothing.

Halfway on the first day's journey, Wolsey began to complain of pains in his stomach. By nightfall he could scarcely sit a horse. Lord Percy stopped at Leicester Abbey to rest for the night.

As Wolsey went in and was met by one of the brothers, he said, "At the eighth hour of the eighth day, I have come." His face assumed a peculiar expression, and he added mournfully, "I have come to lay my bones among you." The good brother was greatly impressed and hastened to tell his superiors that the great Wolsey was there to spend the night.

Wolsey was given a simple pallet in a stone cell and was well cared for by the monks. His ailment grew worse and worse, and finally Lord Percy was called by the abbott. "I fear for his life," he told Percy. "He surely is dying."

"Dying!" Percy exclaimed. He rushed to the cell where Wolsey was kept. When he went in, he saw at once that the cardinal's illness was not feigned. He sat beside the man for over an hour, and Wolsey thrashed on his pallet the entire time, filled with pain, clutching his stomach.

He spoke only one time before he died. His body arched convulsively, lifting free from the bed, and when the spasm had passed, he turned his head to stare at Percy. Then he whispered in a voice filled with pain and sorrow and grief, "Had I but served my God with half the zeal I served my king, he would not in mine age have left me naked to mine enemies!" Then his body sagged, he turned his face to the wall, and grew still.

Percy pulled the limp body over, saw the life had departed, and a chill of fear went over him. He muttered to himself, "Everyone this king touches dies miserably!" He rose and left the dreary cell. The next day, he took the body of the banished cardinal to London.

***

The death of Cardinal Wolsey left a vacuum which was rapidly filled by Thomas Cromwell, one of Henry's most important advisers, almost before Wolsey's bones were placed into the ground.

Anne Boleyn rejoiced over Wolsey's downfall. She and her

friends celebrated his death by staging a masque, "Cardinal Wolsey Descending to Hell," in her private quarters. She persuaded Henry to place her private household chaplain, Thomas Cranmer, who had been a scholar and a theologian at Cambridge, in a place of prominence. Cranmer was not a man for court; he was a gentle sort, unaffected by pomp, yet Henry liked him and agreed to accept him.

He spoke of this to Cromwell. Henry spoke casually of the cardinal's demise almost as if he had had no part in it. "He was an excellent administrator, Thomas," Henry said, carelessly studying the rings on his fingers, "but he failed me in the one matter where I had real need of him."

"Ah yes, the annulment." Cromwell knew that this was his great opportunity. If ever the king were open and suggestible it was right now, and he must seize the moment. "Your Majesty," he said quickly, "I have made an extensive study of this question. And in my humble opinion, there is a much greater issue than the marriage itself. The marriage is merely God's way of opening other ideas to you, of leading you to ponder heretofore unthinkable things."

"What things?" Henry asked, his piggish eyes fixed on Cromwell.

"That some of Your Majesty's subjects are but one-half your subjects," Cromwell announced. When Henry's eyebrows lifted, he continued, "The clergy. They take a vow of obedience to the pope. How then can they be your loyal subjects?"

"Yes, of course." Henry cut him off sharply. "But then there is the heavenly kingdom and the earthly kingdom, and they are separate." He was listening carefully, for he had already decided to do the very thing that Cromwell was suggesting. All he needed was a method—and he knew that Cromwell was crafty enough to provide that!

"Are they, Your Majesty?" Cromwell asked, holding his meaty

palms upward. "If, upon pain of death, a subject chooses to obey a foreign ruler over his king, what is heavenly about that? It would be treason in any other man. Is this not so?"

Henry nodded slowly, the idea beginning to take hold in his mind. As Cromwell went on explaining his theory, that the ruler of every realm was empowered by God to protect his subjects, both bodily and spiritually, Henry's body grew tense, his face avid and intent.

"It is as God wills," finished Cromwell smoothly. "He is displeased with this state, it is a perversion of the truth. That is why prophets like Wycliffe and Huss and Luther have been sent! That is why Rome has been laid low, the pope reduced to a shivering prisoner by the emperor! They are signs, Your Majesty," he said, nodding sagely, "Signs that you must act to restore the rightful order of things."

"Words, words," Henry grunted. "Wolsey was full of words also. What of deeds?"

Cromwell was at the precipice. He was fully aware of the fact that, should he make a mistake now, he would be gone forever. But he had lived for this moment, had thought about it for years, and he did not hesitate. He said firmly, "The people groan beneath the weight of the monstrous burden of the papacy, but they are powerless to help themselves. Only one person can break their bonds: the king."

Henry leaned forward, his mouth drawn into a tight line. "How?" he demanded.

"They will follow you, like the children of Israel followed Moses," Cromwell said persuasively. "The church must be left intact. It must retain all the outward semblances of the past. It will be as always but with one exception." He now leaned forward, holding the king's eyes, and spoke with great emphasis. "The king, not the pope, will be the supreme head of the church in England! And the people," he insisted, "will follow like sheep, as they always do." Cromwell leaned back and held his breath.

Henry sat still, thinking and considering. He was a scholar, an artist, a man born to rule, a man who had known nothing but power. His mind now was filled with one thing: Anne Boleyn. And Catherine, of course. And how to replace Catherine with Anne.

These things . . . and the fact that he had always despised the power of the pope. He always had had the feeling that he, as ruler of England, had more right to rule the people than any man far off in Rome.

"A pretty picture," he said thoughtfully. "And how is this to be achieved?"

Cromwell immediately felt the seed of triumph and began to speak rapidly. He outlined the plan: Parliament would give Henry the power, then he might do as he pleased.

"You may grant yourself an annulment, sire," he said with a dismissing gesture, then went on decisively, "To a man, the Parliament resents the privileges of the clergy. Let this be a wedge to separate you from Rome. In the meanwhile, you can reduce the church to subservience. Take over the monasteries! Once this is accomplished, you will have the country, the nation, the people, and perhaps all of Europe, in your hands, my lord."

For one moment, Cromwell thought that the king meant to dismiss and deny the entire exchange. A strange expression came to his face, but finally Henry nodded and Cromwell released his breath.

He knew now that he was safe.

"We shall speak of this further," Henry said slowly.

In spite of the vague words, Cromwell understood that the king's mind was made up. And this meant that it must appear that the idea, the entire theory, came from Henry himself. So he merely smiled and said, "Your Majesty, of course, will be given the wisdom of God to do his will."

Henry waved him away, and Cromwell left with his heart racing. He was not an emotional man, and he could never remember a time in his life when he felt so exalted. "It is all here," he said to himself as he walked out of the palace. He noticed that his hands were trembling, and he stared at them in wonder. "I didn't think anything in the world could make me do that," he mused. With an effort, he clamped down on his feelings and went to his office. He gave orders to his assistants, setting the wheels in motion for what he knew was coming.

Cromwell dismissed all of his assistants, but Ralph Geddes remained behind. "A word with you, Sir Thomas."

"What is it, Ralph?"

"It concerns the Wakefield affair."

"Oh? Was it successful?" This was typical of Cromwell. He wanted no details, simply to know if it succeeded or failed. He had absorbed this principle from his sovereign, King Henry VIII.

Geddes shifted a little uncomfortably and shook his head. "Not entirely, sir, but soon, I think." He outlined what had gone on, having now decided that it would be wise to advise Cromwell. That way in case of failure, he would not be caught off guard. He ended by saying, "We know that the girl is back. And one of our men overhead that young Wakefield was to board a ship." He slapped his thigh with an angry gesture saying, "I know they contacted Tyndale! I know! But they were clever."

Cromwell listened to him impassively. "Excuses will not do, sir," he said tersely. "Should you capture the man, let me know. If not, I am not interested." He waved his hand in an abrupt dismissal.

Ralph scrambled to his feet, said, "Yes, sir!" and, with a quick bow, left the room. Anger raced through him. He stalked the halls of the palace, trying to think of some way to hurry things along. But it was not until the next day that he got a clue.

Sackville came rushing in, his face alight. "We've got him!

We've got him!" he exclaimed. Hurriedly, his words tumbling over one another, he went on, "He was supposed to leave Germany on a ship, the *Grey Falcon*. Fancy name for an old tub. And he won't be coming empty-handed!"

"What does that mean?" Geddes questioned sharply.

"He's supposed to be bringing a shipment back with him, so my agent tells me. Now, what are we guessing that it is, sir?"

"Bibles! New Testaments!" Geddes slapped the table, his eyes glittering. "It must be!"

"Exactly," Sackville grinned. "They were able to avoid us and make this arrangement somehow. But I'd stake my reputation on it! He's bringing New Testaments from Tyndale back to England, make no mistake."

Geddes clasped his hands together, squeezing them hard. It was almost as if he had Myles Wakefield's neck between them as his knuckles turned white.

"When does the ship dock? Come, man, give me the details!" He listened carefully as Sackville gave him the information, then said, "Let him unload his precious cargo. In fact, let him deliver it. That way we shall find out who is receiving the goods, and we shall have them in the Tower, too! But," he warned sternly, "no matter what else, I want Myles Wakefield caught. Do you understand, Sackville?"

The agent smiled toothily. "Never fear, Mr. Geddes. I'll have plenty of handy fellows about. Handy with a sword, that is."

"Do not kill him!" Geddes said with emphasis. "I want him taken alive!"

"Yes, sir, I'll instruct the men. Any more orders?"

"No. When you capture him, bring him directly to me. Then we'll take him to the Tower."

"Yes, sir."

Sackville left and Geddes, unable to sit, walked the room, his mind racing. He had it all in his hands now. There was no doubt but that Myles would go straight to Wakefield with the Bibles. He would allow them to reach there, and then he would have them all . . . Sir Robert Wakefield *and* his precious son!

Twenty

THE TRAP

The *Grey Falcon* docked just outside London early on a Thursday morning. The crossing had been rough, and Myles had spent most of the time below deck trying not to think of his stomach. As soon as the harbor was cleared, he went topside and asked one of the seamen, "How long do you think it will take to get the ship unloaded?"

The sailor, a squat, hairy fellow with one blue eye and one brown eye, squinted the blue eye at him. "Well now, sir, that's depending upon where your goods be. If they be on top, it may be two hours. If they be on the bottom. . . ." He shrugged eloquently and turned back to his work.

As it developed, Myles discovered that his "goods" had been stored in an inconvenient part of the ship's hold. The first mate informed him that it would be late in the afternoon, perhaps even dark, by the time they were uncovered.

Myles took him at his word. As soon as the ship docked, he went ashore. His first impulse was to go straight to Hannah and to Wakefield, but he knew that his responsibility was to get his cargo delivered safely. Tyndale had warned him that, despite the fact that the Bibles had been carefully concealed in what appeared to be bales of clothing, this would not necessarily keep him from being discovered. "If they suspect for one minute that you have a

Bible," Tyndale had said ominously, "they will rip the bales apart." He added in a gentler tone, "If you get trapped, save yourself, Myles. We can print other Bibles—" and here he placed a friendly hand on the young man's shoulder—"but only God can make a young fellow such as yourself."

His first task was to find something to transport the Bibles in. He had no intention of committing them to anyone else's hands. Fortunately, his time in London with his father had familiarized him with several hostelries, and he went at once to a place where he was able to rent a rather small cart pulled by a single horse. The horse he eyed doubtfully, but the owner of the stable assured him, "He is slow, but faithful and strong. He'll do the job for you, sir." Myles relented and paid the fee then drove the rig back to the docks.

It was still early when he arrived, so he pulled up outside one of the pubs that lined the harbor, got down and tied the horse, then entered.

The food on the *Grey Falcon* had been pitiful! He had felt sorry for the sailors who had to eat it. But now that he was away from the pitching of the ship, he felt hungry. Sitting down, he waited until the innkeeper came in, wiping his hands on his white apron. "What shall I bring you, sir? We have some fine kidney pie today and fresh baked bread. Do you smell it now?"

Myles did smell it, and his mouth watered. "Yes, bring me some of that. And some good ale, if you will, innkeeper."

Soon the food was brought, and as Myles was eating with relish, a man entered the dining room. He was a smallish man, dressed in sailor's garb, with a black cap on his head and a pair of sharp brown eyes. He sat at the large common table with Myles and pulled on the brim of his cap, saying, "Good day to you, sir. Warm today."

Myles nodded briefly and asked presently, "You are a sailor? Have you just got in from a voyage?"

"That I have. Came in just this afternoon." He began to tell Myles about the voyage he had just been on, and the two talked idly for a while. The sailor ordered plain food and ate it as they talked. Myles was actually paying him little attention, although he kept up the conversation pleasantly enough.

Myles finished his food and his ale and paid his bill. Lingering in the dining room, he looked out the window and saw that afternoon was dimming and night would soon fall. He hesitated, considering taking a room for the night.

"Going to be a bad night, I'm thinking," the sailor volunteered. "If it don't rain cats and dogs, I'm no sailor." He sniffed the air almost like a dog and told Myles, "I was going on into London, but 'tis not wise to be on the streets of London with the rain coming down. I'm thinking I'll take a room and wait for the morrow."

Myles was halfway inclined to do the same, but he was in a hurry to complete his task. "Maybe it will hold off." Nodding at the sailor, he left the pub.

He briskly drove the cart to where the *Grey Falcon* was docked and went to find the mate. Inquiring about his goods, the mate nodded, "Sir, we are down to them now. If you should care to pay a few coins, I'll see the men load your goods right onto the wagon for you, sir."

"Yes, fine, do that." Myles nodded. He stood beside the cart, and soon the sailors emerged from the hold, carrying the bundles on their shoulders. They had been packed in rather small bales so as to be easily handled, and they fit snugly inside the cart. When they were loaded, Myles paid the men off, giving the first mate something extra for his trouble. More gentlemanly than truthfully, he said, "Thank you. It was a pleasant voyage," then jumped nimbly into the cart and drove off down the now-dim street.

The wheels clattered on the cobblestones, and Myles knew that dark was overtaking him. Innkeepers were lighting the lanterns that threw off a pale, feeble glare through the shadows, so that he could trace the street as it wound around, headed for London Bridge. The air was muggy and damp, and he could sense, as the sailor had said, the smell of rain as he drove.

There was a strange click in his mind, and he began to think of the sailor almost involuntarily. There was something about the man that nagged at Myles, but he could not put his finger on what it was. As the cart rumbled along, he thought, *What was it about the fellow?* He could not define it, but Myles had a lively mind that would not let the thing alone. He worried it, like a dog worries something he has caught, shaking it, looking at it. Over and over in his mind he turned it, remembering the entire conversation.

I have seen that fellow before. The thought came clearly to him, almost as though it were spoken aloud. *But where was it? Think, man, think!* He narrowed his concentration to it, though noting subconsciously that rain had begun to fall.

The rain came in single, huge drops that splattered loudly on the street, and he pulled his hat down over his eyes and hunched on the seat. As he approached the bridge, the rain fell harder until it became visible sheets that swept across the road in front of him. The feeble light of a lantern flickered, and Myles could hear faint hisses as the rain came down. The garbage that was in the streets began to wash down the gutter, and still Myles could not think where he had seen this man. Finally he shrugged and thought dismissively, *Probably he looks like someone I know.*

There was something almost frightening about the streets. The chattering of the rain as it swept across the cobblestones was the only sound; most people had taken shelter to avoid it. Still, as he drove along in the gloomy darkness, he thought he heard the sound of hoofbeats behind him, not those of his own plodding horse, but something else. Immediately alarm ran through him, and he pulled the horse to a halt.

"Whoa," he called softly. He listened hard for a moment,

almost certain that he heard the sound of horses on the cobble-stones, but then they seemed to stop.

He stayed motionless for a moment, listening, then said, "Giddup!" and the cart started again. But the incident had made him alert and wary. He glanced about and knew he was not far from the Tower, where his head could be removed summarily from his body if he were caught with the load that was packed so neatly behind him. Anxious to finish his mission, he spoke a sharp command to the horse, slapped the reins, and the animal broke into a feeble trot.

They approached the bridge, which loomed suddenly out of the darkness, and he drove the horse down the middle of the way. He had always been fascinated by London Bridge, but now all he wanted was to pass over it. He glanced at the houses that were built on both sides and wondered again why they had permitted people to build houses on a bridge. If they had not been there, the bridge would have been wide and easily passed. But the houses were jumbled together, built in no order whatsoever, and rambled haphazardly along the length of the bridge, some of them two, and a few even three, stories high.

As he started across, he glanced up, knowing that the heads of traitors were stuck on poles on the bridge, but it was too dark to see, and the rain beat onto his face. So he ducked his head, wiped his eyes, and spoke again to the horse.

He had gone no more than halfway across the bridge when suddenly he had one of those moments of insight that come on rare occasions to a man. He had experienced such a thing a few times in his life, usually after thinking for a long time on a matter which he was unable to resolve; and suddenly, after finding no answer, it would pop into his mind, inexplicably and without warning.

That sailor fellow! He pulled his earlobe and squeezed it with his fingertips the same way that old man did in Marburg!

Instantly Myles knew that this was no coincidence. The man that had made the journey with him and Hannah in the coach to Marburg had done this over and over again . . . and now Myles could see vividly in his mind the sailor doing it exactly the same way.

"He's an agent!" Myles exclaimed, and he began to feel the first tremor of alarm. Peering backward, he could see nothing through the darkness—but his senses were heightened, and he could again faintly hear the sound of horses following. Hastily he tried to form a plan.

If I cross over and go into London, he thought, *they'll have me trapped with no way to leave the city except this bridge. They'll be waiting for me to deliver the Bibles. Then they'll arrest me and the man I have to deliver them to. I can't let that happen!*

His mind spun with ideas, all of which he considered and rapidly discarded. Then he saw an alley between two of the houses that lined the edge of the bridge. Impulsively, he turned the horse sharply. The animal grunted in protest, then moved where he was directed. There was just room enough, Myles saw, to admit the narrow wagon—a full-sized one would not have made it. Ahead he saw the end of the bridge, or thought he could, and he could hear the sound of the Thames rushing along underneath. He spoke to the horse, who pulled up, and he leaped to the ground. Silently gliding to the edge of the short alleyway, he pressed himself against the side of the building and waited.

Across the way, a single lantern sent out slight yellow beams that picked out the slanting path of the falling, fat drops of rain. Within a few tense moments he heard it: horses coming from the far end of the bridge. He peered through the darkness, keeping well back in the shadows. Then he saw them, eight or nine riders. The forms emerged gradually in the darkness, moving slowly along. When they were even with him, he heard one of them say, "We must move closer when he leaves the bridge—we'll lose him in the dark streets of the city."

It was the same voice of the sailor that he had met in the pub!

Myles waited until they moved on. Then he leaped back in the cart, knowing what he had to do. He pulled the reins tight, jerking on them lightly, and spoke briskly to the horse. The horse reluctantly started backing up, pushing the cart with his hind-quarters awkwardly into the street, but when he cleared the alley, the horse uttered a shrill neigh of protest. Myles snapped, "Shut up, blast you!" and sawed the reins to turn him around.

Then he heard a cry from down the bridge. "He's cut back! Look! There he is!" Myles knew he was caught in the yellow light that hung over his head, and he lashed at the horse with the reins.

"Giddup! Get on!" The frightened horse reared, and then began to fight the reins and traces. Myles, having no whip, could do nothing but curse through clenched teeth, struggling to keep hold of the reins. He could hear the sound of hooves clattering on the cobblestones at a run, and suddenly the horse lowered his head and began a wild gallop. The cart careened down the bridge between the buildings, but Myles knew that the old horse would never outrun his pursuers.

Then a rider appeared beside him. Myles had time only to lift his hand before the rider threw himself onto the cart. Myles caught him and then threw him to the back of the cart, all in one almost graceful motion. He dropped the reins and turned to reach for his dagger, but he had no time to use it. His assailant, uttering a loud cry, threw himself again at Myles from behind. At the same moment, the wheel of the cart dropped into some sort of a cavity, and Myles felt himself losing his balance. Then the man had him, and the two of them fell over the side to the street. Fortunately Myles landed on top, and he heard the breath rush out of the man with a fierce whoosh.

Scrambling to his feet, Myles started to run, but a hand darted out and gripped his ankle, and he went down like a felled tree. He fought desperately and again got to his feet. Like lightning, the agent whipped out a sword and started toward him.

In one smooth motion, Myles drew his own blade, and as the tip of his opponent's sword cut the air in front of him, he parried with a simple, barely discernible motion of his blade. Then, knowing that others were coming, he did what he had hoped he would never have to do. He ran the blade into the man's chest. The man uttered one soft, pain-filled cry, and Myles pulled the blade out as the man slumped to the ground, writhing like a cut worm.

But Myles had no time for remorse. The air was already full of the cries of the rest of the company, and then the horses were swarming around him. Myles whirled and ran down the street. Instantly the "sailor" yelled, "Head him off! Stop him, there!" Two horses flashed by on either side of Myles, then wheeled, and he could see the glint of swords as they blocked his path. Myles glanced over his shoulder and saw that several other men had dismounted. Three of them were coming straight for him, blades gleaming in their hands. The leader cried out, "Put your weapon down, man! You are under arrest in the name of the king!"

All motion seemed to cease for Myles. It was one of those frozen moments when one must make an instantaneous decision. He had noticed before, sometimes in the midst of a duel, that it was as if the action would just stop, then go into a very slow, sleepy movement, while his brain raced madly. That was the way it was now as he stood in the driving rain on London Bridge, the yellow light picking up the blades that surrounded him. He knew that he was a dead man if he allowed himself to be taken, and a fierce determination suddenly steeled him.

Almost a blur, he threw himself to his right. He had seen a slight break in the facades of the houses that lined that side and hoped that it was a way of escape. As he rushed toward it, he could see the narrow crevice, no larger than one man could walk down, and he shot into it. He knew that if it came to a dead end, there would be no escape.

"After him! He's gone in there! We have him now! Spread out!" the sailor bawled.

The narrow way opened out suddenly until it was at least six feet wide. Then despair came over him when he saw that the alley came to a dead end against some sort of a small building that covered the edge of the bridge. He whirled, and two men were upon him. One of them had a sword in his right hand and a dagger in his left. "Give up now!" he growled, and the two advanced steadily.

Myles knew that he had no choice. He had glimpsed something to his right, a ladder of sorts, fastened to the side of one of the buildings. The buildings here were high, going up three stories. It was his only chance.

Without thought he engaged the second man, who had a sword but no dagger, and the blades rang shrilly in the darkness. This man was an expert swordsman and defended himself well, but the other agent could not get at Myles because of the narrowness of the alley. So Myles and the swordsman engaged furiously, blades clashing loudly, the rain hissing as it hit the ground.

It was a scene that Myles would never forget. His opponent's glittering eyes caught and reflected the feeble light of the lantern, and the smile on the man's lips was full of confidence. Myles then took a chance. He dropped the tip of his sword, pretending to stumble, and the man lunged at him, uttering a wild cry. Myles rolled to his left, his sword materializing straight and gleaming in front of him, parried the blow, and allowed the man to simply run onto his blade. Awareness leaped into the man's eyes, and his mouth opened in a large O. He tried to speak, but only blood came from his lips as he fell backward.

Myles whipped his sword out, almost too late. The other man had jumped over the body of his companion, and Myles rather awkwardly deflected the blow. But he was not able to parry the strike of the dagger that slashed out at him and caught him along the ribs, raking a fiery line of pain across his abdomen. There was no room for Myles to make a pass with his sword, so he did instinctively what he had never learned. He deftly twirled his sword around, laying his right hand flat against the handle, and then struck upward toward the man who stood so close. The blow smashed into the man's right temple, the butt of the sword making a dull thudding sound with the power of Myles's right hand behind it. The man grunted and dropped to the ground, unconscious.

Myles felt warm blood running down his side but could not take time to examine his wound. Others were coming down the narrow passage. He leaped to the ladder—which was simply a series of boards tacked to a wall—and scrambled madly upwards. Pain shot along his side, and he knew that he had been badly cut by the dagger. He had dropped his sword, so there was no hope for him unless he could hide. And he knew, too, that they would be after him, for he heard the outraged cries of his pursuers when they found the men below.

His breath was gone when he got to the top of the ladder. He discovered that it led out onto a roof that was flat. He scrambled out upon it and made for the other side. Below him he heard feet scrabbling against the building, and he desperately looked around for an escape.

Then he saw it. There was no way down! He was on top of a three-story structure, and the next house was more than thirty feet away and at least ten feet below him. If he tried to jump, he would miss and smash to the cobblestones below. He ran around the outline of the roof. Nothing.

The first agent topped the ladder, struggled to pull himself to the roof, and then cautiously got to his feet.

The rain had slowed now but was still falling in a filmy sheet that reflected the light of the man's sword as he approached cautiously. Others came up behind him, and finally the sailor's head appeared as he pulled himself upward. Myles backed to the edge of the roof. The sailor came forward, a smile gleaming under his mustache.

"All right. Come with us. You are under arrest in the name of the king."

Myles was standing with his back to the edge of the flat roof. He glanced behind him, but there was only blackness. He could hear the rushing of the Thames, though, and he knew it was floodtide. The waters of the Thames at floodtide rushed between the arches of London Bridge at a frightening speed. Anyone caught in the turbulence of the river ran the chance of being battered to death against the sides of the massive arches.

And Myles had no idea exactly *where* on the bridge he was. He might be over one of the sections that had been built up with rock and rubble, upon which the arches stood. Even if he took his chance of jumping, he might land on one of those and break every bone in his body.

"Come along, man, you're caught," the sailor said insistently. He motioned to the others, who spread out into a half-circle and then began to close in.

It was hopeless. As they tightened the circle, centering slowly and inexorably on him, he thought of throwing himself on them and trying to wrestle a sword away, but he knew that he would be doomed. He stood motionless, thinking.

Then, without a word, he turned and launched himself out into the darkness. Feet first, he plummeted down. He heard the cries of the men above, the leader cursing, then bellowing, "Now he's done us in!" He heard the whistling of the wind.

He spread his arms and half bent his knees. Downward he plunged through the darkness, and his mind raced. He knew that within seconds he might well be dead, and one thought etched his mind, *And I'll be in hell.* A cry was wrung from him, and he reached out in a prayer such as he had never prayed: "Oh God, save me, that I might give my foolish life to you!"

He only had time for those few words, and then the darkness swallowed him.

Twenty-One

"I'LL BE BACK!"

Somehow it always seemed to soothe Hannah's spirit to work in the rose garden. It was the pride and joy of her mother's life, and she had learned early how to nurture the beautiful flowers. She came out into the sunshine and entered the garden, noticing in the manicured beds the roses blooming, such heavy loads of flowers on the stems that it seemed the branches might break from sheer color, weight, and profusion.

The south and west exposures of the walls were one mass of climbing roses so that each brick had some twenty blooms spread out upon it. There was a sweet blush in every delicate shading between red and white.

Perhaps it was the scent that drew her here so often. There was so much in her world that smelled unpleasant: garbage, waste, fetid rushes, and unwashed bodies. But here the sweet fragrance of a multitude of blossoms was like balm to her spirit.

Reaching out, she touched one of the velvety blooms and whispered, "Where is he, Lord? Where can he be?" A slight breeze stirred the roses, and it seemed to her they nodded in sympathy to her question.

She donned a pair of heavy gloves and began to work among the budding plants, thinking all the while, as she did each day, of Myles Wakefield. It had been many days now since she had made her uneventful trip home from Germany. She had expected that Myles would accomplish his mission and be back within a few days of her own arrival. But he had not come. Every day she watched the road, and at night she lay awake, listening for the sound of a horse riding up. But she had heard nothing.

At last a message had come: Myles had indeed left Germany. But where *was* he? So far as anyone knew, the earth might have opened and swallowed him up.

She looked up and saw her father coming down the road. He came to her side, a troubled look on his face. "I just heard from Judson. He says Sir Thomas More has been appointed lord chancellor."

Hannah calmly patted the dirt around a tender young plant and asked quietly, "This is not good news, is it, Father?"

"Not for us. More has a deadly hatred of anything that smacks of Protestantism. Wolsey didn't care. He was whatever the king wanted him to be. But More will influence Henry, and I fear the persecutions will begin in earnest now."

Hannah continued to tend to the small plant, and her father watched her with compassion in his dark blue eyes. "You are worried about the lad."

"Yes, I—I am, Father."

"So am I. I'm afraid he has come to grief. He's had time—more than enough—to get here from Germany."

"I pray every night for his safety. And Father, I have assurance that he is all right." Concern creased her forehead, and she closed her eyes for a moment. *Lord, I want to trust you. . . . Help me to leave Myles in your hands.* Her expression grew calm, and a serenity seemed to settle over her. Her father watched her, admiration in his eyes. He recognized her prayerful posture and the peace that now graced his daughter's face. It was the same serenity that he had seen first in Hannah's mother, and now he was glad to see that his daughter was of the same spirit.

"Well," he said with a shrug, "we shall have to wait, that's all. But I must warn you, it will be dangerous now to be even seen with one of Tyndale's New Testaments. Any person carrying one is under suspicion, and with More directing the persecution, it is bound to grow even worse."

"We will trust God," Hannah said quietly. She got up, took off her gloves, and put her arms around her father. "He has always taken care of us. He always will."

"There's my good girl," John Kemp murmured, stroking her hair. He loved this daughter of his, and it had grieved him to see what he thought was a secret attachment to Myles Wakefield. He had said to his wife, "That young lad will marry upward with one of the wealthy ones, I'm afraid. That's the way it is with aristocrats. Very seldom will they stoop down to find a wife."

But to Hannah he said only, "I will pray with you for the lad. You are right, God is in control." He squeezed her affectionately, then went across the garden toward the barn.

Hannah worked all afternoon in the garden, only taking time out at intervals to go to the well for a cool drink of water. She wished to weary herself, to grow tired, so that she would sleep better that night.

It was about three or four in the afternoon, when the sun was well down below the low-lying hills and shadows were beginning to grow long, that Hannah looked up, shading her eyes, and saw something moving down the road.

It was a man, walking.

He was coming down the road that wound around and eventually led to London. Even a brief glimpse showed Hannah that he was bent, making slow work of the walk because of a bad limp. *It must be a beggar,* she thought, and worry lined her forehead.

There was always trouble with beggars. The authorities had grown concerned with the issue of beggars and rogues and vagabonds. Some of them refused to work, roaming the country-side or congregating in the city streets, begging, stealing, defying all authority. While many strict laws were passed during the time of Henry VII, the church viewed kindness to beggars as one of its good works, and so granted them considerable freedom. But the present king had replaced those laws with more stringent edicts: Old or infirm beggars who could not work were to be allowed to beg, but only in their own parishes. If they went outside of those boundaries, they were to be punished as if they were able-bodied vagabonds.

The local justices of the peace were ordered to draw up lists of all aged or infirm beggars and give each a license. A man without a license who was fit to work but who owned no land, was apt to be severely punished should he be caught begging. Hannah had seen for herself the punishment such men in her own village received. Stripped of clothing, they were beaten and then tied to the end of a cart that slowly paraded them through the town.

The strict laws had made it harder on the beggars, for those who would have helped them before grew afraid to do so. Hannah and her family had been more generous than most, and sometimes she wondered if there was some sort of a secret code among those people, for many of them came directly to the Kemp family after passing by many other homes.

The man very slowly drew closer. When he was within a hundred feet of her, Hannah saw with horror that he was not just a beggar. He was terribly disfigured by some sort of ravaging disease. His face was covered with a rash; the skin seemed to be peeling off. His eyes were hooded by lids that were being slowly eaten away. The word *leper* immediately seared Hannah's mind.

Leprosy had been a serious problem in England at one time. Now the disease had, for the most part, disappeared, but there were still those who bore the marks of its terrible disfigurement.

She stood still, resisting the impulse to turn and flee into the house. The bent figure stopped ten yards away from her, and she managed to say in a strained but courteous voice, "Good day. Have you traveled far?"

Her greeting seemed to surprise the beggar. He wore nothing but rags, the arms that stuck out of them ending in claws. His fingers seemed to be twisted and held in place like the talons of a huge bird. His forearms were scabbed over in places, and there were patches of raw flesh. His head lifted a little at her words, then he bent in a grotesque parody of a bow. He spoke with a voice that was raw and had a ratchety note in it, similar to metal grinding upon metal. It sounded as if he was not accustomed to speaking.

"Thank 'ee, lady," he said. "Yes, I have come a long way today."

Hannah waited for him to ask for something, but he simply stood in silence. Then she realized that he was probably as afraid to ask for aid as she was of his disease. Immediately she said, "You must be very thirsty. Let me get you a drink. Come this way." She turned and walked to the well, and he followed her in a crablike motion. *His feet must be damaged like his hands,* she thought. *And he keeps that one arm clutched close to his side, as if he's holding himself together.*

When they reached the well, she got the bucket, then hesitated. There was only one cup. The beggar reached into the old bag slung across one shoulder, pulled out a battered pewter cup, and held it out timidly. Hannah carefully filled it to the brim, noting that his hand shook terribly as he lifted it to the gaping wound that was his mouth. He drank it down thirstily and then croaked, "Please, more?" Hannah filled the cup again.

It took three refills before he sighed and lowered the cup. He wiped his mouth with the rags that made up one sleeve and said, "That wor mighty good, lady. I thank 'ee."

Hannah was repulsed by him, yet she well knew the admonition of the Scriptures to be kind to those who had no help, and she asked gently, "Are you hungry?"

"Yes," he said simply and stood there, waiting. There was a stillness about him that was almost stonelike—as if he would move no more than he had to. His poor decayed body seemed to tremble in the afternoon breeze. But he said no more.

"Here, sit in the shade of this tree," she said, "and I will go get you something to eat."

"Thank 'ee, lady," he said in a whisper, then made his slow way to the tree in the painful crabwise gait. Once underneath the tree, he abruptly slumped to the ground as if his legs had failed him.

Hannah turned and hurried into the house, going right to the kitchen. Quickly she gathered leftovers from the noon meal: bacon, potatoes, and bread baked that morning. She added to the food one of the apples of which her father was so proud. Looking around the kitchen, she spotted a large mug of cider and reached out to carry it in her free hand. Balancing her load, she went back to where the man rested and placed the nourishment on the ground beside him.

She stifled the urge to warn him not to get her dishes contaminated and was thankful she did so when he showed his consideration by pulling a battered pan out of his bag and holding it out gingerly. Feeling slightly ashamed of herself, she put the food on it. He sat cross-legged, and she saw that the legs that poked out through the tatters were indeed as misshapen and blotched as his forearms and hands. Wordlessly he held out the battered pewter cup. She poured it full of the fresh cider and then stood uncertainly.

He ate slowly—as though even his teeth hurt him—and without looking up, clutching the food closely, much like a dog that expected a bone to be snatched from him. Hannah stood watching, feeling terribly awkward.

Soon he finished, all except for the apple. He held it up before him, looking at it. His eyes were almost hidden under the floppy brim of the old hat that covered his head and neck, and the white tufts of hair that covered his forehead shadowed his eyes even more. "I ain't had an apple for a long, long while," he whispered. His hands trembling, he began to gnaw at it.

Hannah heard a voice and turned to see George Fenton, who worked for her father, striding up. He was frowning, and he barked, "Get that beggar out of here, Miss Hannah! You know what the law says. I'll wager he has no license, do you, old man?"

The beggar shrunk back and shook his head. "No," came faintly from beneath the dirty, gray hat. "No license."

"There, you see!" George said. "Now, be off with you!"

Hannah was angry. George sometimes overestimated his own importance. "Go on with your business, George. I shall take care of this," she said sharply. He glared at her, but she looked back at him steadily, and he wheeled and went off, muttering darkly.

Hannah turned to the beggar and said, "It is almost night." She bit her lip doubtfully, but felt impelled to ask, "Do you have any place to stay?"

"No. Just under the sky," he answered. "Got a blanket." He patted the bag and pulled out the edge of a tattered, torn, and very dirty blanket. His voice was weak and shaky, and his eyelids were fluttering. Hannah thought he might be on the verge of passing out.

She said, "Go into that barn over there. I will see that you have a place." She ran into the house, found one of their older blankets, and returned to the barn.

The man was standing in front of the barn as if he were afraid to enter. Hannah opened the door and said gently, "Come in." She went into the barn. It was already growing dark, so she lit a lantern and hung it high upon a nail. It was a good-sized barn, filled with hay and corn and feed for the animals. Her eyes swept it, and then she moved over to a small platform that had been built some time ago for holding equipment. She pulled some hay over it, smoothed her blanket over it, and said, "There, you may sleep here tonight."

He looked down at the bed, then he turned to face her. "The blanket. It will na' be clean if I sleep on it," he whispered.

"It's all right. You take it with you when you leave tomorrow. I will ready you some breakfast early and a little food to take with you."

He stood just a few feet away, close enough for her to see the skin peeling off in flakes from his cheeks and around his mouth. The lips moved, and she thought she could see the gums exposed as they drew back. "Your people won't like it."

Hannah knew that he was right. Her parents were good people, but they were very careful about who they helped. This man, she knew, would give them both cause for alarm. Not only was he diseased, he was unlicensed—but she determined that she would make them understand.

"It will be all right," she said. "Don't touch the lantern," she cautioned. "If you should drop it, the barn would most likely burn down. I will bring you some water so you won't be thirsty."

She picked up the milking bucket and went to the well. Carefully she washed out the bucket and filled it with water, then returned to the barn, placing it on the floor close to his bed. He was still standing in the same place, looking down at the floor. Suddenly he lifted his head and said, "Lady—" and stopped.

Hannah said, "Yes?"

"Can I . . . kiss your hand?"

The voice was grating, and Hannah at once was repelled. *He should not ask such a thing,* she thought, cringing inside. But then a feeling crept over her that this was somehow, in some obscure way, a test of grace. Unbidden, the thought flitted through her mind: *What would Jesus have done?*

Of course she knew the answer at once and faced it squarely. She held her hand out.

The old beggar bent over, his hat still low over his face, his ravaged features hidden. She felt a light touch, almost like the brushing of a butterfly's wing, on the top of her hand.

"'Tis the sweetest hand in all of England!"

The voice was young and strong. Hannah's heart lurched with shock as the beggar straightened up to his full height. He was very tall. He swept the hat off his head, and blue-gray eyes bored into her startled ones.

"Myles!" she cried. "Oh, is it really you?"

He laughed and made an elaborate, courtly bow and said, "Lady, it is I. Myles Wakefield, fugitive."

The barn seemed to blur and fade in Hannah's eyes, and for the first time in her life, she was afraid she was going to faint. She reached out her hand blindly, and he took it. She felt the strong flesh of his hands and forearms as she held onto him desperately. She said breathlessly, "Myles . . . I don't . . . I don't . . ."

"Sit down," he said with concern and self-recrimination. "I'm a fool for doing this to you." He led her over to the platform, eased her down, then sat down beside her. He kept her hands covered with his. After a few moments, he looked at her sheepishly. "Are you better now, Hannah?" he asked quietly.

She drew a deep breath and stared up into the brilliant, blue-gray eyes. Small wonder he'd had to hide them with the brim of a hat and with hair down in his face. They were the eyes of a young man and could not be disguised.

"Myles, I never would have known you," she said faintly. "Are you all right?"

"Oh yes," he said with a smile. He gestured eloquently at his face. "Not a bad bit of makeup, is it?" Holding one arm straight out, he pulled up the tattered sleeves. Whatever makeup he had on his forearms to make them appear white and scaly and raw ended abruptly just above his elbow; she saw his biceps, tanned and corded with muscle.

"I thought . . . we all thought . . . ," she stammered, "that you might have been caught . . . or—" She broke off, unable to finish.

"Or dead," he said, nodding. "It almost came to that. I want to tell you about it, Hannah. And about something else that has come into my life."

She listened with wonder to Myles's story. He told her of getting off the boat, of beginning the journey, and of the encounter with the king's agents. When he got to the part where he leaped off London Bridge, he said slowly, "I was frightened, Hannah. I thought I was going to die. And I knew that if I did there was no hope. I would spend eternity in hell." He took a deep breath. "So I cried out and asked God to help me. And I promised to serve him." Running his fingers through his dyed hair, he looked at Hannah gravely. "I landed in the river, and the current took me down. It turned me over and over, and I was sure I would drown. But God took care of me. It was dark, but I made my way to the bank. Fortunately, I had gold in my pocket and bought myself a hiding place."

Myles looked around the barn but he did not see it; his mind was filled with the events of that fateful night. He grew quiet for a while, and Hannah waited patiently, content merely to drink in the sight of his face, to clasp his firm, warm, and oh-so-alive hand.

Then Myles continued. "There was an old man who lived in a deserted-looking hut. I think he knew I was in trouble—I know he knew I was badly wounded. Yet he asked no questions. I offered to pay him if he would let me stay, and he agreed. For days the hunt went on, and as I slowly healed, we grew to be friends. He's an old actor. That's all he'd ever done. I didn't tell him who I was, but he knew the men roaming all around were hunting for me."

Myles squeezed her hand, and Hannah clasped her other hand over his. Myles met her eyes, and she saw his feelings reflected in their depths as he continued. "He could have gotten a reward if he had turned me in, but he never did. And he did something for me."

"What's that, Myles?"

"He taught me how to do this," he said, indicating his face and arms. "He'd been on the stage all his life, and it was amazing how he could make anyone look old, or young, or just—different. He could do anything. I've been with him all this time while he taught me. But that's not the only thing that happened while I was there," he said slowly.

She saw his hesitation and encouraged him, saying, "Yes, Myles? What happened?"

He looked at her and said simply, "I learned to know God."

Hannah's eyes shone and a joyous smile lit up her face. Myles went on, his own eyes filled with wonder. "When I called on him as I was falling into the river, thinking that I was going to die, all I knew of God was that he was real. But when I lived, I realized that there must be more to it than that. So I began to pray and seek God, and do you know what? That old man—his name was Edwards—was a Christian! A real believer! He knew much of the Scripture, though he couldn't read, and he quoted it to me over and over. I don't know where he learned it."

"But how wonderful!" Hannah cried. "Tell me all about it. Everything! Don't leave out a single word."

They sat close together, and for over an hour Myles recounted the past days, how the old man had helped him, how he had called upon God, and how God had revealed many things to him. Myles said quietly, "God came to me, and I put my faith in Jesus. It was all I knew to do. I had made all kinds of promises, but Edwards knew a Scripture that said, 'It is not by works of righteousness which we have done, but according to his mercy he saved us.' He quoted that to me time after time, until finally I began to understand it. And then I knew what I needed to do, and I came to God."

Myles sighed deeply and smiled at Hannah. The smile looked grotesque on his ornately made-up face, but the joy was un-mistakable. "And God came into my heart. And he's there now, the way he's been in yours for a long time, and in Lady Jane's, and in your parents' hearts. All my life I've seen people that had peace with God. I watched my mother, you, Mr. Tyndale, and I envied you all. I wanted what you had, but I didn't know how to find it. And now . . ." He shook his head in wonder. "Now I know that all I needed to do was ask the Giver and he would answer in love. Hannah, God has shown me his heart and drawn me to his side, and I will serve him all my life."

Hannah's eyes overflowed and great tears ran down her cheeks. She made no attempt to stop them; she just reached up, her hands trembling, and put her arms around Myles's neck and rested her head on his chest and cried with joy. The rags scratched her cheek, but she held to him tightly.

Myles was shaken by the depth of her emotion. He felt her body trembling and heaving with sobs as she wept and wept and wept. Before long, he felt moisture in his own eyes and blinked rapidly to forestall the tears that smarted there. After a while he felt her sobs abate, and Hannah pulled back. When she smiled at him, Myles thought her tears looked like diamonds in her eyes, and her smile was the sweetest thing he had ever seen on earth.

"I am so glad, Myles," she whispered fiercely, "so glad! Now you know what it is to love God."

They talked more and it grew late. He said, "I can't go to Wakefield. They'll be watching everything, everywhere. I suspect they know that Lady Jane has been in contact with Mr. Tyndale. Hannah, you must go and tell them that I'm safe."

"But where will you go?" she asked.

He stood up, and even in the wisps of rags, he now looked powerful and strong. She stood before him and repeated, "Where can you go?"

He put his hands on her shoulders. "I'll go help William Tyndale. That is what God has told me to do—to be a servant of that man. And I am going to do what God says."

His words came to Hannah as if from a great distance. She had a sense, though, of the rightness of it all. Without conscious thought, she again put her arms around him and clung to him tightly, her body pressed against his. She said softly, "Oh, Myles, I will miss you so."

Myles looked down at her, and his heart swelled with emotion. Tenderly, he lifted her face and leaned down to kiss her soft lips. He let his lips rest on hers, drinking in the peace and a joy that he could sense within her. Theirs was not a kiss of passion or ecstasy—rather it was a pledge, an act for both of them that sealed something.

Hannah clung to him, and he drew her even closer, and the strength in his arms was a comfort to her.

Long, silent moments passed before Myles drew back. He looked off into an unseen distance, staring as if he could see through the barn, all the way to Germany. When he spoke, his voice rang with joy and certainty.

"I have to leave England. But I'll be back, Hannah. Many times I'll be back, and always I will bring with me the Word of God!"

END OF PART THREE

The

1 5 3 0   1 5 3 4

Fugitive

Twenty - Two

A TERRIBLE BLOW

The old decade dragged on throughout England. The king's divorce wasn't settled, so Henry diverted attention from himself by declaring a war that no one wanted upon Charles V. Though Henry never intended to take action, the stance made him feel good. Trade ceased because of the threats of war, and the sweating sickness returned to decimate the population. Even the elements seemed set on laying waste to the country as first a drought and then floods devastated the land.

Henry saw it all as the wrath of God against his marriage to Catherine.

He was having great difficulty with the queen. She cried and pleaded and obstinately refused to be divorced. It became ever clearer that she had no intention of retiring gracefully into a convent. Henry could handle foreign ambassadors, his ministers, and even Parliament, but he was never quite able to manage Catherine of Aragon. His case had been taken to Rome and then passed back. The charade of a trial had been enacted to prove the king guilty of sin in marrying Catherine, widow of Henry's brother. The only man who remained silent was the pope, because whichever way he jumped, he would fall into great difficulty.

Through all this time, William Tyndale, with his new disciple, Myles Wakefield, lived under the shadow of arrest and the stake.

Moving from town to town, he and Myles evaded the agents that unceasingly scoured the countryside for them. It was during this period that Tyndale turned his attention to the Old Testament. And so the disciplined, lonely scholar—with Cromwell's pack baying for his blood—calmly set himself to master Hebrew.

Myles was amazed at how quickly William Tyndale learned the language he was studying. Tyndale had learned some Hebrew at Wittenberg during his time with Martin Luther, and now he simply obtained an old manuscript of Hebrew grammar and began to study. If Myles had had any doubts about the scholar's dedication—which he did not—they would have disappeared during those long months when Tyndale labored over the Pentateuch.

Day after day, with a head that ached and eyes that rebelled against the constant attention to small letters in the half-light, Tyndale labored on. After hours and days hunched over his desk in a small spare room that had been lent to him by a friendly merchant, his cramped body ached in every limb and cried out for exercise.

Finally, though, the task was done. When the manuscript was ready for the press, Tyndale and Myles set out on a new search for a printer.

Hamburg had been invaded by the sweating sickness in June of 1529. This mysterious and frightening plague swept the Continent during the latter half of the fifteenth century and the first half of the sixteenth. It wreaked its most deadly devastation in England, where it was thought a great blessing if even half of every town escaped. The boiling fever claimed men, women, and children without warning within a few hours. People fell down in the streets, and general panic was widespread.

"Are you certain it's wise to stay here in Hamburg, Mr. Tyndale?" Myles asked doubtfully one day, as they were waiting for the press to finish the printed editions of the Pentateuch.

Tyndale was now thirty-six years of age, but he looked more than ten years older. His clothes were worn, and there was a continual fatigue lining his fine features. He put down his pen and smiled at Myles, forming a temple with his long sensitive fingers. "Do you think that God does not know we are here, Myles?" he asked quietly. "Remember Jonah fleeing God? And yet God found him, in the middle of the ocean."

Myles grinned back at him. "I'll never learn, I suppose. All these months you have been teaching me how to believe and trust in God, and it seems I never learn anything."

"That's not so, my boy," Tyndale answered sturdily. "You have grown in grace, and Christ Jesus has been formed in you since you have come to me. It has been my joy to see you become a faithful and devoted servant of the Lord Jesus."

Myles flushed at the praise, feeling it was undeserved. "I only wish I might do more," he said.

"You've done much," Tyndale said. "How many trips is it now you've made to England, carrying the Word of God? Five? No, six. And each time God has kept you safe." He laughed lightly, which was unusual for the scholar. "Those disguises of yours! I never know what you'll look like from one day to the next!" He leaned back and relaxed, eyeing the young man in front of him.

At twenty-three, Myles Wakefield was in his prime. The life he had led had been hard, so he had slimmed down until there was not an excess ounce of flesh on his body. He was firm and muscular as well as agile.

Tyndale studied the bright, blue-gray eyes set in the squarish face, the short English nose, the wide lips and small ears that lay flat against Myles's skull; he noted the pugnacious chin and was again grateful, as he had been many times, that the young man's quality of fierce tenacity had not been left out. Myles was stubborn, did not seem to know the meaning of fear, and would never stop once he had set his mind to a task.

"That last disguise of yours," Tyndale said with something akin to mischief, "was not to be believed. Dressing up as a Catholic priest! That was a dangerous one! If you had been questioned, you would have been found out at once."

"Yes, if it was by another priest or a high-ranking official of the Catholic church," Myles retorted. He had made his way to England in the priest disguise, delivered his Bibles, and returned to the Continent with no problem whatsoever. "Most people don't question priests, they just obey them." He smiled and added, "It was rather a pleasure to be obeyed so completely. I almost envy those fellows in the black robes."

They talked amiably until the printer's helper brought out a wheelbarrow full of printed copies. Myles loaded them into the buggy that he had brought, and he and Tyndale made their way down the street to their lodgings. They worked all afternoon packing the Bibles, disguising them to pass the eyes of the agents of the king.

Myles had grown adept at finding ways to conceal the Bibles and this particular time felt he had achieved a sure success. The printer had had a supply of a favored book of the time: *In Praise of Folly* by Erasmus. Myles packed the Bibles in crates, then placed two layers of this innocent work on top. Then the crates were sealed and labeled plainly with the title of Erasmus' work.

"Anyone opening these cases will find plenty of folly, but no Bibles," he commented with satisfaction to William Tyndale. "So, I am off again, sir."

"And what disguise is it to be this time? Make it a good one, Myles."

"I may as well use this smattering of German I've learned. I shall go as a prosperous German bookseller. I'll introduce you to the Reverend Hans Mueller before I leave."

The following afternoon Tyndale was interrupted by a man who threw open the door to his small study and entered unceremoniously. "Hans Mueller, at your service," Myles said in German. "How do I look? Prosperous enough?"

Tyndale stared at the young man, who was dressed in the rich attire of a wealthy merchant. He had found some jewelry that looked good—a large gold chain hung around his neck and rings twinkled on his fingers. Somehow his face looked much fatter and his eyes smaller. His auburn hair was dyed a light gray. He looked to be a man of around fifty and was well padded out so that he seemed corpulent.

"I don't see how you do it, Myles," Tyndale said with wonder. "I wouldn't know you if I passed you on the street two feet away!" He rose from his desk and embraced the young man. "I hate to see you go," he said. "I shall be in prayer until your return. God go with you, my son."

Myles made his farewells and went to the carriage he had hired to take him to the coast. The coach trip and the voyage went smoothly and uneventfully, and two days later Herr Mueller had delivered his cargo safely into the hands of a bookseller on the edge of London.

For some reason, Myles did not return immediately to the pier, as he had planned. He had thought often about his family and friends in England. And yet, the one person who had most occupied his dreams over the long months had been Isabella Bourneville. He had heard nothing from her, which was not surprising since he was in hiding, but it bothered him nonetheless. He frequently received letters from Hannah Kemp and his family, and he scanned them for word of Isabella. But they knew nothing of the affairs at court.

He had longed to ask after Isabella, but he knew neither his mother nor Hannah would be pleased at the question. Day after day, he had scolded his foolish heart, telling himself to forget Isabella, that she was not of his world. Day after day, he prayed, asking God to free him from his love for Isabella. But neither his heart—nor God, it would seem—paid him any heed, for his feelings had not lessened, and with each passing day, they became more acute until her image filled his mind and hindered his ability to concentrate.

Now he paused for a moment, looking in the direction of the court. He was so close . . . all he wanted was to see her, possibly to speak to her. That would be enough. Then he seemed to make up his mind. He would go to the court.

He made his way there cautiously, alert to all that was going on around him. One slip and he would be a dead man. He had manufactured an excuse for coming to court: a proposal to sell books printed in Germany to King Henry at a great discount. Henry, of course, saw himself as a man of learning and kept his great library well stocked. Myles was well aware of this, for he had spent many happy hours there at the king's own request.

When he arrived and asked for an audience with the king, he was told by one of the minor officials that Henry was not available. Myles asked tentatively in broken English, "Might I zee the queen?"

The servant stared at him, then shrugged. "I will see," he replied. Myles waited restlessly until the servant returned, saying, "The queen is not well. Come back another day."

Defeated, Myles thanked him, then began to wander about the court. He had not the faintest idea of how to find Isabella, but he knew that if he could stay long enough without arousing suspicion, it was possible he might encounter her. He knew her favorite haunts: the garden, and the large dining room where the ladies of the court often went between meals for sweets and gossip.

On a guess, he sought out that part of the palace and saw a group of the young women of the court gathered there, laughing and talking. Drawing closer, his heart beat faster when he saw that one of them was Isabella.

The young women stopped abruptly as he approached and made an effusive bow.

"I beg pardon," he said with a thick German accent, "but is it possible to zay vord vith young ladies?"

All of them stared at him, uncomprehending, and it was Isabella who asked, "What is it you want, sir?"

"I am Hans Mueller, bookzeller from Germany. I haf come to make a present to the king, but I cannot zee him. Would one of you young ladies—" Myles paused and bowed his head to Isabella—"you, perhaps, Fräulein, gif me one moment? I vill explain. The king vill tank you for it, I am sure."

Isabella considered him for a few moments, then, perhaps more from boredom than anything else, she dismissed the other women with a wave of her hand, saying, "We'll talk about the ball later." She waited until the young women had left the room—very much like a gaggle of geese as they chirped and giggled and simpered—then turned to face Myles squarely. "Now, sir, what is this about a present for the king?" she demanded impatiently.

For a moment Myles could not answer. Isabella was twenty-four now, one year older than he, and she had only grown more beautiful. Her long blonde hair fell down her back, and her green eyes were still bright and shimmering—although bolder and harder than he remembered them. Her lips were touched with some cosmetic, and he saw that her skin also bore some traces of artifice. She was dressed in much finery, and the bodice of her dress, which was cut lower than was customary in England, exposed the curves of her figure.

"May ve valk in ze garden?" Myles asked. "Then I vill tell you."

"Oh, very well." Isabella usually had no time for the elderly, which she considered anyone much older than herself to be, but this man had caught her interest.

Myles did his best to keep her attention, explaining in faltering English that he was a bookseller in Germany and that he had heard of King Henry's scholarship. As he spoke, he took quick glances at her, and the longing deep within him to tell her he loved her suddenly overwhelmed him. Surely, when she knew the depth of his love, she would realize that her own feelings for Myles went as deep, and she would love him, too.

But discretion won out over desire, and he held his tongue. It was enough for now merely to be with her. And so he went on, telling her that he had purchased a great stock of books and now wondered if the king would be interested in adding to his magnificent library, at a great discount, of course.

Isabella came to an abrupt halt, startling Myles into silence. She turned and faced him with impatience. "I thought you said you had a gift for the king," Isabella said sharply. "King Henry is not interested in seeing tradesmen."

Myles's heart dropped at the frustrated tone in her voice. His mind raced, seeking the right words to catch her interest again.

But Isabella had had enough of the prattling old fool. She turned to leave . . . and then she heard a deep voice say simply, "Isabella."

She froze in her tracks. She knew that voice, knew it as well as she knew her own.

"Be careful, Isabella, don't show any surprise."

Turning around slowly, like the good actress she was, she showed only mild interest on her face. But her whispered words were filled with apprehension. "Myles! What in the world—"

"I had to see you," he said in a low voice. He looked around surreptitiously and saw that people were wandering about the garden. "Come, we must be alone for a moment."

"This way," she whispered and led him to a secluded spot in the garden, fenced off on three sides by six-foot brick walls. The other side had a low hedge with a view of the path, and no one was in sight. She turned to face him and said, "Now, what are you doing here? Don't you know you'll be sent to the Tower if you're caught?"

He ignored the question, reaching out and pulling her close. "I had to see you, Isabella," he said huskily. The feel of her in his arms and the scent of her perfume seemed to drug him. He clasped her tightly and kissed her, almost roughly. She surrendered to his embrace, wrapping her arms about him, and the old hungers stirred within him.

Then, suddenly, she pushed him back. "Not here, Myles! What are you thinking of!"

"I had to see you," he repeated, his voice ragged. "I was about to lose my mind. . . . I *had* to come."

It was hard to see Myles through the skillful disguise he wore—only his eyes seemed the same, and Isabella stared into them. She had thought about Myles, too, over the last several months. Her stay at court had not been what she expected. At first, it had been wildly exciting and thrilling, what with the king and Anne Boleyn and Catherine of Aragon and all the great lords and ladies. She had loved it all, even thrown herself into it, learning the art of seduction as it was so often played here. But she had always refrained from giving herself away.

Sooner or later, she had thought, *I will find the man who'll give me everything I want.*

Now as she stood, staring into Myles's intense blue-gray eyes, she realized suddenly that in truth she had not found the man. Many had sought her out, most of whom, she knew instinctively, desired only the momentary pleasure she might give them. But she was aiming higher than that. Much higher.

As she stood there, pondering her life and gazing at this man who had loved her for so long, it came to her suddenly and quite clearly that she had to make a decision. She was older than many of the young women in court. Several younger than she had married and now lived on their own estates or manors while she kept on, seeking a man that did not seem to exist.

Suddenly she knew, as clearly as if it were printed on a page, what she must do.

"Myles," she said urgently, "you must leave here—and you

must stop thinking about me. There will never be anything between us."

He looked at her as though she'd struck him. "What are you saying, Isabella?"

"Oh Myles, there never was anything between us," she answered, an almost kindly note in her voice. "You've had some sort of boyish dream about me all this time." She laughed and said, "I know, I can see it. I've had the same sort of dreams about young men. It's all part of growing up." Then her eyes and her face grew harder, and she went on. "But we are grown up now, you and I. It's time to face reality."

Myles reached for her again, saying, "You are my reality, Isabella! I want you!"

"No!" she protested and pushed him away, hard. She looked at him and said, "I'm marrying Ralph!"

Myles stepped back, stunned. She couldn't mean what she said! "You can't! You can't marry him!" Myles said wildly. He made a dismissing gesture and said, "You don't love him!"

Isabella raised her chin and regarded him haughtily. "And what do you know about who I love? I haven't seen you for months! And besides, even if I did love you, what would we do? Where would we go?" There was a world of scorn in her voice. "Can you give me an estate for my home? Can you provide for me and our children so that we will always know this," she looked around her at the grandeur of the gardens. "This is my world, Myles. Not that of a fugitive. You should know that by now. We have to take what we can get, Myles, and I am taking Ralph!" She lifted her head defiantly, eyes blazing. "He's become very successful, you know. He's Sir Thomas Cromwell's chief lieutenant now. Cromwell is in Parliament and he will go even higher—and he will take Ralph with him when he goes."

Myles could not believe what she was saying. A croquet game was going on somewhere, and he could hear the faint clicks of the balls and the cries of excitement and pleasure floating on the summery air. They were surrounded by the opulence, wealth, and trappings of royalty, yet Myles saw only the face of the young woman who had filled his dreams for years—a face that he suddenly felt he'd never really seen before. "It sounds like a fine business deal," he said bitterly. "I hope you are holding out for your best offer."

Rather than the indignation Myles expected, Isabella seemed lost in thought. Truthfully, she had been moving toward this decision for months. It was nothing new to her. Of course, she had weighed the possibility of getting a better offer than Ralph Geddes at least a thousand times in her mind. He was not an exciting man—not to her at least, for she had known him too long. But he did care for her, he did have money and position, and—most important of all—he was rising in the world. Now that she had asserted her intention to marry Ralph, she had had a revelation: She needed to modify her behavior a bit and make Ralph fall all over himself to marry her. He had become discouraged of late, and she must rectify that immediately before he found someone else.

'Tis a miracle, she thought with new anxiety, *that he has not married another woman.*

Myles watched the expressions that flitted across her face, noting the faraway look in her eyes, and the old desperation almost overcame him. "You can't do this, Isabella! Listen to me!"

Isabella snapped out of her thoughts and fixed him with a cold stare. "Myles, forget about me," she said tersely. "Leave this place." Impulsively she put her hand out and laid it on his arm. In a softer voice than she had used before, she said, "You are a fine boy, Myles. Get away from here. Go back to wherever you are hiding out, and don't try to come back to England. It will be death for you if you do. Now, go at once." She gave him one last look of farewell, then turned and walked away.

Myles watched her, then he turned away from the palace and made his way across the gardens and grounds. The croquet match was still going on, and several of the players looked at him curiously, wondering at the corpulent, gray-haired figure with sloping shoulders who moved as if he were carrying a heavy burden.

One of the players whispered, "Who is that?"

Another whispered, "I don't know. Nobody important, I think."

And with a shrug of their expensively clad shoulders, they went back to their game.

On the ship that carried him back across the Channel, Myles stood looking down at the gray water as the prow of the freighter cut through the waves. Seagulls screamed, and when a sailor threw some garbage overboard, they fought viciously, their harsh cries rending the air.

Myles watched them blindly, going over and over in his mind the scene with Isabella. His jaw was clenched, his mouth a taut line. He knew he had lost something, and there was an emptiness in him. Or rather, he had realized for the first time that the empty place that had been in him ever since he had laid eyes on Isabella Bourneville was now permanent—it would never be filled. He did not know how he felt any longer. For so many years she had been his dream; a wild dream, he knew, impossible from the beginning. Yet some deep romantic streak in him had kept him holding onto it. Hoping, dreaming, imagining the impossible . . .

Now he knew. The impossible was not going to happen. He would never have Isabella Bourneville as his wife.

The darkness closed in, and still he stood looking out as the boat nosed through the dark waters toward Europe.

Twenty - Three

"LOVE IS FOREVER"

All of England was aware of Henry VIII's besotted, obsessive attachment to Anne Boleyn. The King's Great Business was discussed not only in the palace by dukes and princes but also in the taverns and bawdy houses all over the land. By now Henry's determination to divorce Catherine and marry Anne became obvious to everyone not only in England but in Europe. The kings and princes of those lands kept a careful watch on the amorous activities of King Henry VIII and Anne Boleyn.

But one man did not seem even the least interested in the situation. Myles Wakefield was too engrossed in his own crisis of the heart to ponder the doings of royalty. His encounter with Isabella and what he perceived to be her callous rejection had cut him so deeply he could not bear to speak of it. His dreams shattered, Myles went about his duties mechanically, made several trips to England, carried out countless daily tasks for William Tyndale—and perhaps performed even better than before, for his whole mind could be fixed upon the work of Tyndale. And so it was that Myles's work kept him busy—and gave him time to heal.

William Tyndale was not unaware of his assistant's emotional struggles. He had, of necessity, grown to be a man of great sensitivity. Every face he met he had to scan carefully, for it might be the one to betray him. That being the case, it was not difficult for him, after Myles's return from that fateful trip, to see that something was amiss. At first Tyndale thought it was something to do with Myles's parents, but a casual question proved that was not the case. Tyndale, wise and compassionate, knew what it was to be a vital young man. He knew also that Myles had an attachment to some woman in England, a woman of high position, he had discerned. So it was not a difficult thing for a man with his insight—and with the evidence of Myles's hangdog expression and depressed demeanor—to conclude that the young man had suffered some sort of rejection.

Myles never knew that William Tyndale had guessed his secret. He worked closely with the older man, seeing to his comfort and caring for him as a dutiful servant. He continued his trips to England, of course, smuggling Bibles by the thousands, and before long, this was what gave him the only satisfaction he felt in life. He took pride in doing more than was expected, and it gratified him to know that he had become necessary to the older man.

As the months went on, Myles's emotions began to mend, but his lightness and cheer were gone from him, and William Tyndale missed that side of the young man's personality. One evening, after the two had been working hard on one of the editing chores of a manuscript, Tyndale pushed the books back, rubbed his aching, gritty eyes, leaned back in his chair, and said abruptly, "Myles, I feel I must talk with you."

"Why—yes sir," Myles answered promptly. He had learned much about William Tyndale's manner and knew this must be something serious. "Have I done something wrong?"

"No, indeed, quite the contrary," Tyndale replied quickly. "I don't know what I should have done without you, Myles. You've been God's gift from heaven, my 'Timothy,' if I may phrase it so. Every day I thank God for you." He smiled warmly at Myles, while noting that the young man's cheeks had grown hollow and his eyes were sunken. "However, though you have grown in the Lord and in usefulness to me, I am aware that you have been unhappy."

Myles, who had thought that he kept his emotions fairly well concealed, asked in surprise, "But why do you say that, Mr. Tyndale?"

"Why, it's obvious," Tyndale said with a shrug. "When you first came here, you were like a bird, waking up every day with your eyes bright and cheerful. Everyone noticed it. No matter how hard the work was—or how dangerous—you never changed." There was a silence in the room, and Myles leaned forward, resting his elbows on his knees, staring down at his clasped hands. Tyndale's voice was quiet and calm. "Not until that trip you made last year, the one when you went disguised as a bookseller. Something happened on that trip, didn't it?"

Myles was trapped. He still did not meet Tyndale's eyes, just continued to study his hands. Idly he thought that they were brown and looked strong but were somewhat thinner than before. He sighed, wishing he were anywhere but under the knowing gaze of William Tyndale. With a resigned sigh, he said, "You are too perceptive for me, Mr. Tyndale. I'll tell you about it. . . ."

Tyndale listened carefully, not interrupting or commenting, as the young man went through his tale of woe. When Myles seemed to have run down, his voice trailing off, he asked curiously, "And you still love the young woman, Myles?"

Myles immediately opened his mouth to answer indignantly that he did—then he stopped in sudden confusion. *Did* he still love Isabella? He turned his thoughts inward, seeking his heart, at first confused and then wondering. Something amazing had happened over the past months! Though he still thought of Isabella, it was not the same. At first his thoughts had been full of anger and bitterness, but that soon had changed to a dull pain at his loss. He remembered the day he had heard of her marriage to

Ralph, and it had again struck him like a blow that a part of his life was gone forever.

But now . . . now, spurred by William Tyndale's simple question, he began to examine that part of him that had been hidden beneath the surface. And he was shocked to discover that the dull pain had now passed into something else.

"Why—," he said with something almost like shock, blinking his eyes rapidly, "I . . . I don't think I do!"

William Tyndale hid a smile behind his long fingers, and the tired eyes that peered over them were glad. Myles was looking at him, unseeing, gingerly examining this revelation. Finally he turned his eyes on the older man. "But I thought a man was supposed to love a woman forever."

Tyndale's face grew a little solemn then, and he said earnestly to Myles, "I think that is God's plan. But there are two things I must ask you. The first is: Are you absolutely *certain*, Myles, that you loved this woman in the first place? Many men admire women, feel affection for them, and are drawn to them. All sorts of things happen between men and women, but few of those things are really love. True love, love as God intended it, is a thing not only of the flesh, but of the spirit. Did you know that?"

"Umm . . . well . . . I never thought of it," Myles said hesitantly. Weighing Tyndale's words carefully, he mentally went back over his times with Isabella, examining the feelings he had experienced. Tyndale watched him, waiting patiently. At length Myles shook his head. "No. There was never anything spiritual about my love for her. She was beautiful and rich and way above me, and I looked at her as a man looks at a star, I suppose."

Tyndale's warm, glad smile returned. "It is very common for a young man to go through a thing like that. It is not, however, the sort of emotion on which to build a marriage. Although I, myself, have never been married, I have studied the Scripture on this subject. A man and a woman must love one another more than anything on earth, except God. Even more than their children." Myles again looked surprised, and Tyndale continued patiently, "Children will leave, but the man and wife remain together, made one by the curious alchemy of the spirit! Two bodies, one soul." He gestured toward Myles. "And that was not the case with you and this young woman, was it?"

"No, never!" Myles said, feeling as though he had suddenly awakened in a room he didn't recognize. *Something has happened to me,* he thought. *Somewhere along the way I changed.* Aloud he said with some relief, "Well, Sir William, this is all new to me."

"It is new to most people. Men are drawn to women, and too many go to them and marry them without ever asking once if God is in it."

Myles sighed, feeling a lightness come into his spirit. He smiled. "Well, what shall I do with myself now?"

"I think you need to seek the Lord. Ask him about this important matter in your life. You are a young man, but you are growing older." Tyndale looked around the room and shook his head. "This is not a life for a man considering marriage. A man could not ask a woman to share this."

"If she were the right woman, he might," Myles answered with spirit. He needed to think. "I leave the day after tomorrow to take the Bibles to Bristol. While I'm gone, I'll pray. And you pray, too, sir. Perhaps God will give some insight." He got up to leave, then turned at the door. "Thank you, Sir William. I'm thinking I have been a fool."

"Young men generally are," Tyndale remarked dryly. "But even a fool will not be deceived, if he looks to the Lord. So we will agree to seek God on this."

With a nod, Myles left the room, amazed at the lightness of his spirit. "What a surprise you are at times, Lord," he whispered with a smile.

A week later Myles set foot on the English coast. He was disguised as a French aristocrat, adorned in an expensive suit of clothes, a cape of black silk, and a broad-brimmed hat with a huge sweeping plume. He had grown a mustache and let his hair grow long, then dyed both jet black. His heavy tan gave him a swarthy complexion, and he tried to keep his eyes downcast as much as possible. He knew enough French to pass, having learned much of it at court.

As he left the ship, he remembered how Tyndale had come to him the night before he was to leave. "My boy," he'd said, that light in his eyes that always shone when he'd been in prayer, "I want you to know that I have been praying for you since we talked."

"Thank you, sir," Myles said with a smile. "I have been doing so as well."

"Fine, fine," the older man said with approval. Then he flashed his rare smile. "I thought you should know, too, that I have been given a most amazing assurance." Myles looked at him curiously, and Tyndale went on, his smile growing wider. "God has impressed upon me that you will find your answer soon." He reached out to place a hand on Myles's shoulder. "Go forth now and do your work on God's behalf, my boy, and know that your God is at work on your behalf as well."

Remembering those words, Myles felt again the wonder—and the peace—that had come to him as Tyndale spoke. He disembarked, then gathered his cargo and went to deliver the Bibles at Bristol. All went smoothly, and before long Myles found himself with nothing more to do. Standing outside, leaning against a building, he decided it was time to see his parents. He rented a sleek black horse from a stable and rode through the countryside, stopping at inns, flirting with the tavern maids, noting more than once Cromwell's agents as they stood watching those seated at the tables. England appeared to be swarming with agents, and one evening Myles even played a game of cards with one of them, a muscular, blond man named Simpkins.

Simpkins did not, of course, actually admit that he was an agent for the Crown, but he began to drink and soon grew careless. Myles himself drank little. As the night wore on, Simpkins began to boast of some of his exploits.

"I've caught three of them Bible-thumpers just this week!" he boasted. "And more I'll have before week's end! God's eyes," he swore, "they're getting thicker than fleas on a hound's back!"

"Your king, then, ees still determined to stamp out ze Bible in England?"

Simpkins laboriously managed a wink at Myles. "Well, monsoor, this year he is. But who's to know the king's mind year next? Once he had Bibles put in all the churches, you know. Besides," he added, "he ain't thinking Bibles now so much as he is that Boleyn wench."

"Ah yes. Do you sink he weel marry her?"

"Marry her? He's bedded her, ain't he? Waiting for old Catherine to die, which she won't. The old heifer will most like live forever! An ugly wife always does." He took a huge gulp of wine, wiped his lips, and went on with an air of great consequence. "There will always be work for us, no fear of that!" He peered at Myles suspiciously. "And you, Monsoor? French fellow, are you now?"

"*Oui,* from Normandy. I am here to see about a property I am thinking of buying." He moved his hand casually, letting the rings on his fingers glitter in the candlelight. The jewels were not real, of course, but this lout would never know. Wiping his mustache daintily, he asked innocently, "Do you know zis country well, *m'sieur?*"

"Do I know it? Well, I guess I know every inch of it," Simpkins said expansively, waving one hand.

"The property I am thinking of is owned by a family named Wakefield."

"Wakefield?" Simpkins blinked stupidly, then nodded. "Yes, I knows it. And a good property it is, as I hear it. Old man Wakefield's getting a bit long in the tooth, but that's neither here nor there. Can't tell 'bout these old duffers, live a hundred years sometimes." Downing another generous swallow of the wine, he belched mightily, then leaned over closer to Myles. "I'd be careful if I was you, monsoor. The Wakefields are Protestants. That's all right with the king right now—he's in that line himself, sort of—but his mind might change one day. Wakefield's one of the spots we've been ordered to watch. You might be keeping that in mind before you lay down hard cash."

As Myles rode to Wakefield the next day, he thought of the conversation with Simpkins, wondering what was to become of his parents. A life of intrigue was difficult enough when one was young.

He rode into Wakefield, worrying if anyone there might recognize him. The first man out to meet him was Darrowby. He was a relic now, at least eighty. He had served the Wakefield family all his life, and he and Myles had been good friends. Now Darrowby merely bowed and said, "Yes sir? What may I do for you?"

Myles said in heavily accented English, "I am 'ere to see Monsieur Wakefield."

"How shall I give your name, sir?"

"Just say Monsieur Fugitive," Myles answered slyly, and in the heavy accent it sounded like "foojeeteef."

"Yes sir, Monsieur Foojeeteef."

Darrowby bowed stiffly and made his way slowly into the house, leaving Myles holding the reins of the prancing, high-spirited horse. After what seemed a long wait, the door opened and Darrowby appeared. "Come this way, Monsieur Foojeeteef," he said with great dignity. "Master and Mistress asks you to come in promptlike."

Myles followed the aging butler down the hall he knew so well. When they reached the door of the chambers shared by Sir Robert and Lady Jane, he handed Darrowby a coin saying, *"Merci, monsieur. You are a good servant."*

Darrowby's eyes flew open at the sight of the gold coin. He took it with trembling fingers, bit it carefully, then said gratefully, "Why, thank 'ee, monsieur. I have never had no gold coin before."

Myles said warmly, "But you deserve it, do you not?" He patted the old man on the shoulder, which also drew a surprised look from Darrowby, then slipped inside, closing the door softly behind him.

Sir Robert came toward him, beaming. "Well, Sir Fugitive!" He laughed and embraced Myles heartily.

Myles returned the embrace in kind, saying, "You're sharp enough to catch me, aren't you, sir?"

"Go give your mother a kiss, you young rascal!" Sir Robert commanded. He watched, his eyes a little misty, as Myles quickly moved across the room to Lady Jane's usual chair by the window. She was in poor health now and did not rise often. Myles dropped to one knee and held his arms out, and she leaned into his embrace, murmuring endearments.

Sir Robert thought of the years that had passed. He and Jane had been lonely for the boy, and their one prayer had always been that he would come back safely and take his place as master of Wakefield.

After a few minutes of joyful reunion, Sir Robert ordered food and drink to be brought, and the three of them sat gathered closely around Lady Jane's small table, eating the impromptu meal. At least, Myles ate. Sir Robert and Lady Jane were too excited.

"You look like a brigand!" Lady Jane smiled. She reached out and touched a black curl, then caressed it. "Not nearly so pretty as your own hair." She could not seem to tear her eyes away from him and murmured softly, "Oh, Myles, it's so good to see you."

He swallowed hurriedly and said, "It's good to be home. I wish I never had to leave here."

Robert Wakefield fidgeted with some grapes on the table in front of him and sighed heavily. "We'd all like that, to be sure. But with the way it is in England now, no one knows. England is like a drunk walking a narrow ledge. Every step may be the last." He talked about Henry's propensity for doing whatever came into his head. "The man," he said with finality, "is not quite sane. He's throwing his kingdom away for a trollop like Anne Boleyn!"

"It's that bad, is it?" Myles asked anxiously. "No hope of the king changing course?"

"Always, there is hope," Lady Jane put in. "Robert, leave him alone and let him finish his meal! Then he can tell us what he has been doing."

Myles spent the evening with his parents, the three talking for hours. As it grew late and Myles was preparing to leave, he said tentatively to his mother, "I would like to go see Hannah."

"Of course you will go see her!" Lady Jane said, as if it were not a question to be discussed. "What are you thinking, to be this close and not go see her?"

Myles was embarrassed. He tried to think of a way to explain to his mother, but he simply couldn't find the words.

Lady Jane said shrewdly, "You are thinking of Isabella? That Hannah will be upset with you because of her?"

Relief washed over Myles, and he nodded. "That's exactly what I was thinking, Mother." Laughing a little, he said sardonically, "You always did know what I was thinking. My head may as well be made out of glass."

"She'll not chide you," Jane said, ignoring his wry remark. "My dear," she went on tenderly, "were you terribly broken up when Isabella married Ralph?"

"I suppose it hit me hard, Mother, but I've gotten over it now."

"Truly? Have you, Son?" Robert inquired, searching Myles's face. "I knew your heart was set on the girl, but somehow it never seemed as if she was the right one for you. She and Ralph are more suited, I've always thought."

At first Myles was a little surprised at his father's discernment, but, of course, Sir Robert knew people well. After a moment, he nodded. "Yes, I think you're right, Father. But why didn't you ever tell me?"

Wakefield answered with some asperity, "You can never tell a young fool in love anything!" Smiling at Lady Jane, he said, "Why, if someone had dared to tell me to leave you alone, I would have run the blackguard through!"

His exuberance amused Lady Jane, and she said, "Hush now, Robert. Don't torment the boy." Then she turned to Myles and said, "Hannah is a fine woman. She's cared for me so often, I feel as if she is my own daughter."

"Yes . . . well, I'll go then, if you think it's all right," Myles said thoughtfully. Then he took a deep breath, smiled brilliantly at his parents, and went to his room.

The next morning, he rose very early, before the household was stirring, curled his hair patiently, donned his French costume, and rode out again on the black mare. He was surprised to find himself filled with a great anticipation at the thought of seeing Hannah. "Well, of course I'm eager to see a friend," he told himself with some disdain. But a voice deep within him mocked him: *Oh, indeed? A friend? And Hannah is nothing more than that, is she?*

"Well, what else would she be?" he muttered to himself impatiently, and the answer that flew to his mind so startled him that he jerked up short, earning a protesting whinny from the horse. He sat there a moment, considering. And then Tyndale's words came to him, echoing in his mind, *"You will find your answer soon. . . ."*

His eyes widened and he sat as though stunned—then a smile broke out on his face. With a deep laugh, he urged the horse forward. He pictured his meeting with Hannah and found that being dressed as a dashing French aristocrat made him feel rather daring and romantic. He daydreamed a little as he rode, then said aloud, "You fool!" The horse pricked up her ears, and he laughed at his own antics, gibing at himself, "You're old enough to know better! Settle down now."

He rode slowly along the familiar road, his eyes drinking in all the sights he had dreamed of a thousand times. He knew every tree, almost every flower that bloomed, he had pictured it in his mind so often. When the Kemp cottage came into sight, he pulled up the mare, and they stood still in the middle of the road, Myles drinking in the sight. He had amazing eyesight and could see, even from this distance, that the roses were in bloom. It reminded him sharply of the last time he had seen Hannah in the rose garden when he had come disguised as a beggar. The memory of that night now flooded over him, and he lived it over and over again, thinking of what she had said, how she had come to him and held him, how she had felt in his arms, with her soft lips beneath his own.

"How could I not have realized. . . ?" he muttered, then shook his head at his own blindness. He touched the spurs to his horse and rode toward the cottage at a fast gallop, suddenly consumed with desire to see Hannah again.

He swung off the horse in a smooth motion, tied her to a sapling, and was at the door in a few long strides, knocking firmly. Almost at once Susan Kemp, Hannah's mother, came to the door. She was forty-five now but looked much younger. She had reddish hair and the clear blue eyes that Hannah had inherited. Always Myles had been a favorite of hers.

The inquiring look on her face changed to a close examination of the man standing before her. "Yes? What is it, sir?" she asked in a carefully guarded voice.

Myles could not help but grin. "Why, Susan! I'm surprised you don't recognize me!"

Susan Kemp gasped and her eyes flew open wide. She reached out and rather unceremoniously yanked him inside, then hugged him fiercely. "Myles!" she cried incredulously.

He held her for a few moments, then asked eagerly, "Where's John?"

"Gone to town, he won't be back until late. What are you doing here? How long will you stay?" She bombarded him with questions, but before he could answer any of them, she put up her hand as if to stop *him* from talking. "But wait! You must go to Hannah, she'll be so glad to see you! You will stay the night, of course, and maybe longer?" she pleaded.

"Maybe a little." Myles grinned. "Now, where is Hannah?"

"She is at the Burkes, taking them some soup. They've had illness in the house. But she will be back soon. Perhaps you should wait here, and I'll go get her." She looked out the window and ordered, "Yes. And hide that expensive horse in the barn before someone sees her!"

"No," Myles laughed, "let people see her. That's part of wearing a disguise. The more blatant you are, the less you are questioned. I'll go fetch Hannah myself, Susan. And I shall make certain everyone in the village sees her walking with a French aristocrat!"

He left the cottage and rode swiftly to the Burkes. Pausing in a grove of trees some distance away, he tied his horse, then slipped a little closer to watch the house, hoping that Hannah would come out.

Soon enough, she did and started walking along the lane leading back to her home. When she drew near Myles, he stepped out in front of her and made an elegant bow, sweeping his hat off, the plume dusting the ground. *"Pardonnez-moi, mademoiselle,* but I believe you might have a kees for a lonely Frenchman, *n'est ce pas?"*

Hannah gasped, then dropped the bucket she was holding and,

at a dead run, threw herself into his arms and held to him, calling his name. She smelled clean and warm and fresh, and she embraced him with an eagerness he had not anticipated.

"Hannah," he whispered, "you're even more beautiful than I remembered!"

She drew back a little, her face glowing from the compliment, and said with some confusion, "Oh, Myles, you are forever coming out of nowhere and surprising me!" Her face flushed a rosy color. "I didn't mean to throw myself at you like that, I was just so glad to see you!"

Myles said warmly. "Well, I don't mind at all. In fact, I'm glad you did it. I don't get to hug many pretty young girls, these days."

"I should hope not," she retorted indignantly. Then they both laughed, and Hannah rested her hands on his arms and said simply, "I've prayed that you would come back safely. Are you all right?"

"Yes, I'm very well. Come along now, we have a lot of talking to do." Myles retrieved the mare, and they walked along the shady lane, the huge oak trees overhead making a quiet, cool tunnel. They came to a little brook where they had often sat and talked when they were very young. He had made little sailboats for her and often carried her across the water so her shoes and hem wouldn't get wet.

He reminded her of those days and said firmly, "And I think it is time for a repeat."

"Oh, no," she protested, but he swept her up and waded across the creek. When he got to the other side, he didn't put her down, he just stood there holding her and looking down at her face.

"Are you trying to guess my weight?" she said impishly. Her eyes were such a bright blue, burning in the sun, and they reminded Myles of the hottest part of a flame. She blushed, realizing how closely he held her. "Put me down," she insisted, "someone will see us!"

He did not, however, do so. Instead, he held her even more

tightly, and a laughing tenderness filled his eyes. "It will do you good, Hannah. Every girl needs a rumor circulating about her that involves a dashing Frenchman. So let's just stand here for a while until someone comes along."

"You fool!" she giggled. Then she laid her hand on his cheek and breathed, "You haven't changed a bit, Myles. But really, put me down."

Regretfully he set her on her feet, and the two walked. They spent all afternoon together, oblivious of the time passing. They sat under an oak tree, Myles idly skipping stones in the brook that meandered by. It murmured sibilantly, and he grew silent.

"What are you thinking about?" Hannah asked.

He skipped a stone expertly, watching it intently as it hopped four times before disappearing. "I'd like to stay right here, under this tree, beside this brook, with you, for the rest of my life."

"We'd get awfully hungry," she said mischievously. Still he didn't look at her, he only smiled wistfully across the brook. Realizing how serious he was then, she said in a chastened tone, "I was sorry to hear of Isabella. I know how you felt about her."

He turned to her, surprise on his face. "No, I don't think you do, Hannah. I really don't think *I* knew how I felt about her." He explained how he had idolized Isabella and then shared his talk with Tyndale.

When he finished, she said quietly, "He is a very wise man. Marriage is a spiritual thing." She got to her feet, dusting off her skirt. "I must go home. Come along, Myles."

He rose and caught her hands for a moment. He looked at them, admiring the soft skin, the underlying strength, and thought of all the years he had known this woman. In a low voice, he said, "Hannah, do you know the one memory that is more real to me than any other?"

"No, Myles." Her answer was almost inaudible.

"It is of the day I looked over that balcony and saw you

standing there with your book, looking up at me. I can see that just as clear, right now, as I can see you."

"We were children. You can't remember all that so clearly."

"Oh, but I can! You have the same amazing blue eyes, and your skin is still as white and soft as it was when you were a child." He lifted his hand and traced her smooth cheek, then he caressed her hair. "And your hair . . . still like raw gold."

She stood silent, trembling at his words and his touch. A quiet had fallen over the glen. The shadows had grown long while they talked, and the wild things had hushed for the night's coming. The birds settled in the trees, making very faint cooing sounds.

But Myles noticed little of this, for his senses were filled with an awareness of the woman who stood before him. He knew now that his heart was responding to her in a way it had always done, but he'd never quite understood. As he held her hand, he began to think of all she had meant to him, of all the years they had known each other so well, and how important she had been in his life.

Hannah watched him, almost fearfully, and waited.

"I have been thinking of what Sir William said," he murmured, "about marriage being a spiritual thing."

"Yes." Hannah said simply and surely.

"He's right, you know . . . ," he said, almost as if to himself.

"Yes, Myles?" she whispered. She had never felt so vulnerable. His hands held her lightly, and yet they were suddenly like bands of iron around her heart. She knew that she could not have broken away, no matter the struggle. Hannah had loved Myles for years, yet she had never felt free to say a word of her feelings, not to his parents or hers—and certainly not to him. His fascination with Isabella Bourneville had been a barrier, and she had known it was not one she could break through. Now as he stood so close, so tall and strong, looking down at her so warmly with those piercing blue-gray eyes, her heart cried in agonized silence, *Why didn't you turn to me, Myles? Why?*

It was as if her thought burned its way into his head, for at that moment Myles blinked, looking down at her with widened eyes. He studied her face, examining her features closely in the soft, gray light. Her hands were soft and warm in his, her clasp firm and strong—as always, she was a delightful mix of pure femininity and solid strength.

Emotions flooded Myles as he stood there so that he could not speak. He shook his head, as though dazed, thinking, *I have been blind! I've been dreaming about a woman that I really didn't love, and certainly didn't need, all these years. And all the while, the one woman I truly needed was right here!*

The silence flowed over both of them, and their emotions were almost a tangible thing. As if in a dream, Myles looked down at her hands again. "You're trembling. Are you cold?" he asked softly.

"N-no."

Her voice was uncertain, and looking into her eyes, Myles knew with a certainty that God had proven faithful and his answer now stood before him. *Oh God, what a wonder you are!* his heart sang out gratefully. *Now let me say this as you would have me say it.*

He took a deep breath and said very quietly, "Hannah, all the years I have known you, I have loved you." She started to speak, and he gently placed a finger against her lips, halting her words. "Wait. Listen to me for a moment." She stilled, and his hand moved to cup her face tenderly. "At first, I loved you as a sister. And then I loved you as my first and only true friend." He hesitated for a moment, and when he spoke again, his voice was full of grief. "And all these years I took what you offered and gave nothing back."

Hannah could stand it no longer, and she leaned her cheek against his hand, breaking in. "That is not true, Myles!" her whispered words were passionate. "You've given me many, many things!"

"No. I have given you nothing," he said painfully. He dropped his hands, then turned to look again at the brook as it sang in shadow. "I have been a fool!" Bitterness tinged his voice.

Hannah could not speak. Her eyes stung with unshed tears, and her heart ached for him. She knew what was in Myles's heart, she had always, somehow, known it. In the last few moments, his eyes had shown a sudden, shocked awareness of his true feelings for her. Slowly she reached out, took his arm, and turned him to face her.

"Myles . . . ," she began, then hesitated, much in the way a gambler does when he stakes his very last coin in the very last game. If what she said now frightened him, it would all be over. Even so, she knew that now was the time—the first and the only time—to speak her heart. She stepped closer to him, looking up into his face.

"Myles, I love you."

She saw his eyes grow wide with astonishment, and for one heart-stopping moment, she thought he would push her away. She went on with determination, "I think I have always loved you. At first, like you, I loved you like a brother, and then as a friend. But . . . that is not . . . how I love you now . . . ," she faltered, then whispered, "Now I love you as a woman loves a man!" She dropped her eyes.

Myles uttered a soft cry of amazement. "Hannah!" His voice choked, and he swept her into his arms. She looked up, startled, and without conscious thought, he bent and their lips met.

The world seemed to stop for both of them. They held each other, his hands tightening around her back, her hands slipping around his neck. And they were lost in the wonder of what they had found.

Over and over, Myles savored the sweet taste of Hannah's lips, the eagerness of her touch. When at last he lifted his head, he saw tears in her eyes. "Oh, Hannah," he muttered, "I didn't know. I didn't know! How could a man love a woman and not even *know* it?"

She gave a gasping laugh, and the tears in her eyes spilled down her cheeks. "I don't know, Myles. But I know that love is forever, and I'll never love any man but you!"

"That's what Sir William said!" Myles exclaimed. He held her for another moment, savoring her nearness, and then said quietly, "I don't know what to say. I can't ask you to marry me."

"Why not?"

"Why not!" he repeated incredulously. "Because I have nothing to give you!"

Hannah reached up to stroke his cheek, then held her hand still, letting it rest lightly against his face, warm and gentle. "You have yourself, Myles," she whispered. "That is all I have ever wanted."

The words were like a swift arrow, going straight to his heart, and he stood transfixed. He had never known such love existed, never dreamed it could be so freely and willingly given to him. What he had felt for Isabella was a pale imitation of what he now held in his hands and his heart—and his spirit soared with thanksgiving that God had brought him to this place of glory.

He met her eyes, placed his hand over hers, where it still rested against his cheek, and asked gravely, "You'll have me then?"

"Yes." Not one second's hesitation, not a trace of doubt was in Hannah's voice. "Where you go, I will go. Where you lodge, I will lodge. And our God will go with us. We'll be one, Myles, one in him. Nothing will be too hard as long as we have that."

"We must go back to Germany, you know that, don't you? It will be hard," he warned.

"No harder than it has been living here without you. Besides, I've always felt God meant for me to go back to Germany, to help you and Sir William with the work. And now I may do so with the joy of going there as your wife." Such boundless joy as she had never known welled up in her, and she threw her arms around him, laying her head against his chest, holding him tightly. "Oh, Myles," she mumbled almost incoherently against the fine black silk, "I am so happy!"

He held her and thought about the future. There was nothing he could give her, and he could not know what would happen. To many, it would look impossible. And yet he knew without a doubt that God had brought them together. That made anything, and everything, possible.

He held her tightly and remembered what Sir William had said, then repeated it as she rested in his arms, "Love is forever."

Twenty-Four

THE TOWER

Anne Boleyn began to suspect that she was pregnant during the Christmas festivities of 1532, yet for several months no one knew. No one, that is, but the few family members and friends who had gathered on January the 25th of 1533 to witness the simple, secret wedding of Henry and Anne.

The wedding took place in hiding and haste, a furtive meeting of the bride and groom, the bride's parents, her brothers, and two of her women. Tudor wedding ceremonies were always brief, but this one was merely a few whispered vows by the bridal couple, followed by a rapidly pronounced blessing and prayer, then the swift scattering of the witnesses to other parts of the palace.

Henry and Anne exchanged rings in private, but did not dare to wear them. Everything had to be as before, save that now the parents-to-be were husband and wife and their child would be born legitimate.

It had been imperative, quite some time earlier, to remove Catherine from the vicinity of the court. She had been shuffled from one residence to another and finally was informed that the king had made a new marriage. Far from yielding, Catherine said plainly that she intended to go on regarding herself as queen.

Henry struggled to find a way to announce directly that Anne was now queen. On Easter Eve, she appeared in royal state, loaded with jewels, a mantle of gold about her shoulders, and a suite of sixty waiting maids to attend her on the way to Mass. Thus, her circumstances spoke for her. She was escorted to and from the church with all the solemnities—if not more—formerly accorded to Catherine, and she was addressed as "Queen." The priest offered prayers for Queen Anne as he had once said for Queen Catherine.

Henry rushed to have Anne's coronation take place, and he raised loans every day to cover the bills. The cost would be huge, for he intended that the whole kingdom know without doubt that the son Anne was carrying was to be the next king of England.

However, to many people, Anne's coronation was the symbol of the triumph of evil over good. Catherine, their virtuous and embattled heroine, had been destroyed by Anne, a vice-ridden wench and England's nemesis! Public opinion was clear: Catherine was a saint, Anne was a witch. The witch was to be crowned, and the people were almost unanimously opposed.

Isabella Geddes took no part in the coronation that shook the entire country. She was aware of the ear-shattering booms that echoed through the city, rattling the frames of old houses, reverberating back and forth across the city, until it seemed the world was coming to an end. It was the sound of the Tower guns and the guns of the warships moored at Greenwich, thundering out a welcome to the new queen as she stepped off her barge at Tower Wharf.

Isabella, watching from her apartment window on the second floor in a third-rate district of London, turned to Ralph, her face marred with anger. "Just think!" she spat, "I could have been part of that ceremony! I could have been beside Anne!"

Geddes, working at his desk, looked up somewhat wearily. Their marriage had been unhappy almost from the start, for Isabella had demanded more than he had to give. Truth was,

Geddes, though high on Cromwell's list of agents, was but meanly paid. He had gone to Cromwell several times concerning this, but Cromwell merely put him off with excuses. Now Ralph said briefly, "Best that you are not with that woman, Isabella."

Isabella tossed her hair defiantly and came over to stand beside her husband, looking down on him as he worked on the papers littering his desk. "We never have a penny to spend! At least when I was in the court I had plenty of new dresses. I haven't had a new one since we married." She glared at him angrily. "And why shouldn't I be with Queen Anne?"

"Because," Geddes said deliberately, putting his pen down and massaging his fingers, "she will not last with Henry."

Isabella put her hands on her hips and asked coldly, "What exactly do you mean?"

"I mean that Henry is already sick of her. The only reason he is having her crowned queen, as you should know, is that she is carrying his child, which Henry hopes is a son. Henry would give his immortal soul for a boy to carry on the Tudor line. If you don't realize that, Isabella, you do not know Henry VIII."

Isabella flounced over to the window and looked down again at the crowds milling about on the street. The procession would pass this way, and she stood waiting. Soon she saw Anne, nearly six months pregnant, borne along in a swaying litter down the reeking, narrow pathway. Isabella's eyes widened with surprise at the hostile reactions of the crowd below. Still, she knew she shouldn't be shocked. Even before Henry had taken Anne publicly for his mistress, she was widely disliked.

Marshals rode ahead to divide the people to make way for the new queen, yet she had no real protection. The people, Isabella knew, were curious to see for themselves if she was carrying a child. She had heard one woman call out tartly, "And is it the king's, or the devil's?"

Ralph came over to stand beside her and watched in silence

until the procession wound its way out of sight. "Did you see how they hate her?" he asked Isabella pointedly. "The people will not have her for a queen. They love Catherine and they hate Anne."

"Henry will keep her," Isabella argued, "if she has a son."

"*If*," Ralph said enigmatically. "The chances are only fair. And that child is the only thing that will stand between Anne and another divorce—or something worse."

Isabella looked at him, intending to sharply question him. But when she saw the expression in his eyes, she did not ask what might be worse than being divorced and put out. Turning impatiently from the window, she began to pace the room and complain again, her voice strident.

Ralph seated himself at his desk and took it as long as he could. At last he shouted, "Will you shut your mouth, woman! In God's name, what do you want out of me?"

"A decent life! Some new clothes! A nice place to live! Is that too much, Ralph?" Isabella stood stiffly in front of his desk, her hands clenched tightly at her sides. All of her dreams had dissolved into a dreary gray mist within a few weeks after their marriage, and though she knew it did no good, sometimes she could not—or simply would not—stop herself from screaming at him. But Ralph was still in love with her, and she could still manipulate him in many things.

Drawing a deep breath, she decided on a change of tactics. She rounded the desk and put her arms around his shoulders. "I am sorry, my love. I don't know what possesses me. You are doing the best you can."

Ralph reached up, pulled her head down, and kissed her passionately, stroking her hair. He drew back and sighed deeply. He did love this woman, and the pride of his life was that he had taken her from Myles Wakefield. But he was bitter about their circumstances and said so. "I don't like it any more than you. But we are at the mercy of Thomas Cromwell. Until something happens, until he sees fit to put us in a higher place," he shrugged, "there is nothing else to do."

"There must be something," she said tightly. "What about Wakefield?"

"Sir Robert already gave us the cash settlement, you know that."

"I know, but he was going to make you his heir!" Isabella moved behind him, draping her arms about his shoulders again. Leaning down close she whispered, "He cheated you out of Wakefield. It belongs to you. And Myles—why, they don't even know that he *is* the son of Robert Wakefield! He's just a waif that they picked up. Besides . . ." She kissed his ear lightly. ". . . he's gone anyway and will never be able to come back. Isn't there some way that you can get Sir Robert to make you his heir again?"

"No," Ralph said flatly, but he grew silent, lost in thought. Isabella didn't react, she just gently ran her hands over his shoulders. Then he muttered, "Not . . . a way that would be . . ."

There was a pause, and Isabella prompted gently, "Not a way that would be what, my love?"

"I have thought about it," he admitted. He had not spoken to Isabella, or to anyone else, of Wakefield, but for some time a scheme had been forming in his mind. "You know, Lady Jane is thick with William Tyndale," he said thoughtfully.

Isabella straightened and moved to stand beside him. "Can you prove that?" she asked sharply. "And what if you did?"

The ideas that had been swimming somewhat aimlessly in his mind for months now began to coalesce. His lips grew tight, and his eyes half closed. "If," he said slowly and deliberately, "it could be proved that Lady Jane and her husband, Robert, were guilty of giving aid to William Tyndale, and of being his agents here in England, it is possible that Cromwell . . ."

He halted, but Isabella had already worked it through. "He

would give you Wakefield, Ralph? In exchange for delivering them up?"

Ralph looked up at her, a curious half-smile on his face. "I think he might," he said slowly. "I think he might."

Sir Robert heard the sound of heavy footsteps outside his study but thought it was the servants coming to remove a heavy chest he'd ordered taken to another room. When the door opened and he saw Lady Jane enter, her face pale, followed by Ralph Geddes and three strange men, he stood up at once. One of the men was well dressed. The other two were armed soldiers.

"Ralph, what's wrong?" he demanded, moving to stand beside his wife. He met her eyes and saw they were filled with fear.

Geddes said loudly, "This is your man!" He tried to meet Robert's eyes but faltered, allowing his gaze to drop.

"Sir Robert Wakefield, I am an agent of the Crown. My name is Stokes." The speaker was a thin man with pale skin and the burning eyes of a fanatic. He was not unknown to Sir Robert, for everyone had heard of "the king's bloodhound," as Herbert Stokes was called.

"And what is the purpose of this visit, Mr. Stokes?" Robert demanded.

Stokes smiled thinly. "We are not here on a personal visit, Sir Robert. We have reason to believe that you and your family have been engaged in treasonous actions."

"That's a lie!"

The official didn't flinch. "I certainly hope so," he said smoothly. "Still, we must do our duty, you understand, which means that we must search your house."

"For what?" Lady Jane asked at once. "What crime are we suspected of?"

"Treason, as I said." Stokes gave a nod to the two armed

soldiers. "You will see that Sir Robert and his wife remain here."
Then turning to Geddes, he said, "Now, sir, I must ask you to
direct me."

"Of course, Mr. Stokes." Geddes wheeled and left the room,
followed by Stokes, leaving the two soldiers standing erectly, their
eyes fixed on the couple.

"Robert—what does it mean?"

Wakefield put his arm around his wife and stared at the door,
a growing apprehension in his gaze. "Trouble for us, I fear."

"Whatever happens," she said quickly, "We know that God is
with us."

They moved to sit down and wait . . . there was little else they
could do.

After what seemed a long time, Stokes and Ralph returned.
Stokes halted in the middle of the room, a pleased look in his
hooded eyes. Holding out a black book, he asked formally, "Does
this book belong to you?"

Robert took the book, looked inside, then shook his head.
"No. I've never seen this before."

"Ah—? But it was found in your quarters."

Wakefield shot an angry glance at Geddes. "Then someone
must have placed it there, Mr. Stokes!"

"And the cases of Tyndale's Bibles, and the heretical tracts in
the storage room in your cellar . . . you deny any knowledge of
them as well?"

Sir Robert felt a touch of fear, a tightening in his throat—not
so much for himself as for Jane. He glanced at Geddes, and when
he saw the look of triumph in the sly eyes of the young man for
whom he'd done so much, he knew he was lost.

"Ralph—," he said, hoping that even now Geddes might turn
the tide.

But the younger man only said loudly, "Do your duty, Mr.
Stokes—and I hope you will report to the king that I am grieved

at the wicked behavior and traitorous action of my former benefactor!"

"I shall so inform His Majesty," Stokes nodded, then snapped, "I regret to inform you that you are under arrest, Sir Robert." He motioned to the guards. "Put the irons on him."

As the soldiers produced the fetters and bound Robert's wrists and feet, he tried to offer some comfort to Jane. "We'll fight this, my dear. Have Mr. Tyrone come to the Tower at once. He must stand for us at the trial. . . ."

But Mr. Tyrone, for all his expertise in the arts of law, could do nothing. The trial was held exactly six days after Sir Robert's arrest, and it lasted less than half an hour.

"They're anxious to do away with you, Sir Robert," Tyrone whispered as the judges rushed with furious haste to summon witnesses for the Crown. He looked up at the next witness, asking, "Who is this fellow?"

"He's a wine seller," Robert said. "His name is Jacob Isen. I've done some business with him." His eyes narrowed, and he grew pale. "He's been to the house several times, restocking the wine cellar."

Jacob Isen, a bulky man with heavy features marked by dissipation, stared straight at Robert Wakefield and testified how he'd found the heretical Bibles and tracts. "I know where *my* loyalty lies," he said loudly, "so I went at once to the authorities—"

"You lie!" Sir Robert leaped to his feet, his face livid with anger. *"You* put those books there yourself!"

But his rage did no good, and a half hour later the Chief Justice had Robert Wakefield brought before his bench. "You are found guilty of treason, and are remitted to the Tower until your execution."

Stunned, Robert stared at the stony face of the judge—but again his thoughts were not of himself. "What in God's name will happen to Jane?" he muttered as they led him away.

Robert was not to see it, but the next day as he sat in the foul cell into which he was thrown, Lady Jane faced the new lord of Wakefield Manor. She had been too ill to go to London for the trial, and when Mary, her maid, came to say, "Lady Jane," there was such grief in the girl's eyes that Jane knew something dreadful had come.

"What is it, Mary?" she asked, and when told that Mr. and Mrs. Geddes were demanding to see her, a sudden strength came to her.

Walking out of the room, she found Ralph and Isabella standing in the great hall. Ralph said at once, "I am sorry for your misfortunes, but you must know how things now stand."

Jane gazed at him, and a silence fell that seemed to frighten Ralph. He blurted, "Now, I don't want to be unkind—"

"I will be out of this house in one hour."

Isabella moved forward, saying, "Oh, there's no need for such untimely haste, Lady Jane."

"Oh, I quite disagree." Jane held their gazes, and something about the frail woman kept them silent. "God forgive you, Ralph," she said after a moment, then turned and left the room. One hour later she left, carrying a small bag and accompanied by her maid. Getting into the carriage, she looked at Wakefield's massive front and wondered, *Will I ever pass through that door again?*

"Oh, be careful, Myles!" Hannah called out anxiously. "You'll drop him!"

Myles laughed and threw the chortling, fat baby high into the air again. "Drop him? What if I did? He'd just bounce, this fat fellow!" He caught the baby under the arms easily, held him up, and rolled him from side to side as the infant laughed deep in his throat with delight. Myles loved to hear that sound. Now he

moved the baby close, kissing him on the fat cheek and murmuring, "There's a fine boy. You like your old dad, do you?"

"Give him to me! He's hungry," Hannah fussed.

Myles surrendered the baby to her reluctantly, then sat down
to watch as she nursed him. It was a sight he never tired of, and
he said with certainty, "That is without doubt the most beautiful
baby on earth! Look at that hair, those eyes! Those legs!"

Myles reached out and poked a finger between the chubby
creases on William Wakefield's leg, and the baby kicked and
squealed. "Stop that, Myles!" Hannah ordered, but she was smiling. She turned away slightly to protect the baby, then looked
down at him. For long moments she and Myles admired the crest
of red hair—redder than his father's own chestnut color—and
appreciated the unmistakeable blue-gray eyes and the way that
Myles Wakefield's strength of features already were evident in
William's face, even at the tender age of six months.

William's arrival had changed Myles and Hannah's life. They
had lived happily enough after their marriage, though sometimes it was in a room no larger than a good-sized crate. But
they were deeply in love, and their only regrets were that they
had to be separated during the times Myles left to take Bibles
to England. This had gone on for almost two years, and Myles
and Hannah had borne the separation and the danger bravely,
but the arrival of William had made it much more difficult.
Now Myles was more reluctant than ever to be absent from his
little family.

He watched his wife and son with tenderness. "I don't want to
go and leave you and the boy," he said suddenly, leaning forward
to put his chin on his hand. He studied his son, adding, "I just
don't want to be separated from you."

"That's good to hear," Hannah smiled saucily. "And would it
be leaving me, or William, that grieves you so?"

"Both of you," Myles protested. Then he grew thoughtful.

"Hannah, I've been thinking that maybe I will give up taking Bibles back to England. There are others who could do that."

"What would you do here?" she asked. "That's what we came here for, to get the Word of God back into the hands of the English people."

"I don't know . . . but I could do *something*," Myles answered restlessly.

The answer satisfied neither of them, and all day the conversation was repeated in one form or another. For a week Myles stayed around the house, spending most of his time taking care of William. He loved to play with the baby, took him for long walks, and was already teaching him to say words, or trying to. He was deliriously happy, happier than he ever thought he could be. He missed England, and he missed his parents and worried about them, for times were hard there. But he was in love with his wife and deeply loved his son, and all he wanted was to be with them.

Scarcely a week had gone by when Myles came in one afternoon with William under one arm, held like a sack of feed. Hannah was horrified. "Don't carry him like that! You'll hurt him!"

"He loves it! Don't you, William?" Myles grabbed the baby, tossed him in the air until he squealed, and then handed him to Hannah.

Hannah took him and said, "There is a letter for you. It's addressed to you and not me, and it's from my father."

Myles glanced at her and saw that her face was tense. She looked at the table, and he picked up the envelope, which was carefully sealed. "What can John be writing to me about?" he wondered, then opened the envelope and took out a single sheet of paper. He read it quickly, then looked up at Hannah and said tersely, "Listen, Hannah." His face was sober, even stern.

"My Dear Son,

"I regret being the bearer of ill tidings, but I know you would want to hear as soon as possible that Sir Robert has been arrested and placed in the Tower. The charge is treason. The details I do not know, except that it has something to do with the smuggling of Scripture, and possibly an accusation of being an agent for a foreign power. Susan and I, and all of us here, take that to mean that he was arrested for being an agent for William Tyndale.

"Lady Jane has been forced to leave Wakefield. We have her here with us and she is being well cared for, so do not trouble yourself on that account.

"I think you should come to England at once. I know it is dangerous, and you must come well-disguised. They will, no doubt, be expecting you to come. I do not know what you can do, or what any of us can do, except pray.

"I must tell you the rest. Wakefield, apparently, has been taken from Sir Robert and given to another. His name perhaps you may guess: Ralph Geddes and his wife, Isabella. How Geddes convinced Cromwell and the king that he was deserving of Wakefield I cannot say.

"You must do as you think best. I ask only that you remember you are a married man now, with a child. If you were single you might throw yourself into the fray without fear, having only yourself to care for. But there are others now. So do nothing hastily, and we shall pray for God in his wisdom to guide you.

"John Kemp"

Myles put the letter down slowly on the table and sat down blindly, feeling for the chair. "I can't believe it," he whispered.

"I can," Hannah said quietly. She came over and stood beside him, holding the baby in her right arm, putting her left around his shoulder. "Ralph has always hated you because Isabella favored you and, before that, because you robbed him of his inheritance, or so he thinks. He has been planning for a long time, no doubt, to do something to hurt you. He hates your father, too. I always knew that."

"I have to do something!" Myles exclaimed. He smashed his fist into his palm, the blow making a loud, meaty noise. He struck it several times, saying, "I must! I must do something, Hannah! I can't just sit here and let Sir Robert stay in the Tower. Or perhaps be executed!"

"But what can you do, Myles?"

"I can go to England, that is what I can do. If they put him in the Tower, they had to have some evidence. I will find out what it was then I'll run it into the ground."

"Who will believe you? You are a fugitive from justice yourself!" Hannah said sharply. Fear was filling her thoughts, for like Myles, she had been as happy as a person could be in her marriage. William's birth had only made her happiness complete. Now she saw grim darkness clouding the future, and it was frightening her.

"I'm afraid, Myles."

He stood and put his arms around her. "You know what Sir William always says. 'God has not given us the spirit of fear, but of power, love, and a sound mind.'" He held her for a moment, then said, "We must tell him of this."

They went to William Tyndale, who had a small room in the same inn. He listened with grave concern in his eyes. When they had finished, he said, "I grieve to hear this from you, Myles. Sir Robert and Lady Jane are God's children. They have been generous beyond their means."

"What do you think I should do?" Myles implored him desperately.

Tyndale said, "Let us pray for one moment." They all bowed their heads, and silently each began to pray. William gurgled happily, playing with the simple necklace that hung around

Hannah's neck. He looked around and saw that no one was paying any attention to him. So he doubled up his fist and struck himself in the eye, then cried out happily.

Finally Tyndale raised his head and said, "I believe God has spoken to me, but not just about this situation. I have been praying for some time about you two, or rather, you three." He paused, sighing heavily, and continued, "Myles, it is time for you to go home. You have a family now."

"But I came to serve you! And I am bound to you, Sir William."

"That time is passed," Tyndale said gently. "You came in God's timing. He needed men to get the Word into England. Now the Bible is there so that every plowman can have a Testament. And I know somehow in my spirit, that God is calling you to go home to declare the truth that is in the written Word."

"But what will happen if he goes home?" Hannah asked, still with a trace of fear in her. "He's an outlaw!"

William Tyndale looked at her, as he had so many times, with eyes full of compassion and understanding. "Daughter, God does not call us without going with us. He can open a door for Myles. I understand your fear, but I know that it's time for Myles to return to England." He turned to Myles and said firmly, "You must go first and make a way. Find the door that the Lord has provided. Let God speak to you, and act accordingly, as you hear from heaven. Leave Hannah and William here with me, and when God has made the way clear, come back and take them home to England."

❦

It was a dreary day, some weeks later, when a monk with a cowl over his head came to the Tower to visit a condemned prisoner. The guard barely took notice of the priest as he listened to his request.

Nodding, the guard said, "Come along now, Reverend Father. I'll take you to the prisoner."

"I thank you, sir," the monk said, his voice low and calm. And so Myles Wakefield followed the Tower guard through a maze of hallways, down to the lowest levels. He watched as the guard slid the bolt and creaked the door open, the rusty iron hinges groaning in protest, and Myles stepped inside the dank cell.

"Call the guard when you are ready to go, Father," the guard said. Glancing over at the prisoner, he said more harshly, "See if you can get him to tell the truth. If not, he'll be without a head before it's over!"

The door clanged shut, and the bar slammed home with a grave finality. Myles stood silently, looking at the man who sat on the bunk, his face illuminated by the light of the single candle that burned on a small table. At sixty, Sir Robert Wakefield's hair was white, and the firm, supple presence of youth was gone. He looked almost frail as he sat there, and yet there was defiance in his fine old eyes as he looked at the monk.

"What can I do for you, priest?" he asked, his voice rusty with disuse.

Myles stepped closer and went down on his knees, which caused Sir Robert's eyes to fly open with shock. "What are you doing?" he cried, flinching back almost in fear. They had sent priests before to try to convert him or get information out of him, but none had done anything like this.

Myles swept the cowl back. "Father, it's me—Myles."

Sir Robert's eyes blinked several times, and he licked his lips before he answered, his voice filled with incredulity, "Myles! Myles, my boy!" He reached out and touched his son's cheek with a hand that trembled.

Myles threw his arms about his father, and they held each other for a long time. Robert finally drew back and wiped his ragged sleeve across his eyes, snorted loudly, and cleared his throat. "Well now, here's a fine thing! You risking your life like this—"

"Don't worry," Myles broke in hastily. "Chances are almost

nonexistent that I'll be questioned. They don't question priests, and certainly not monks. Now," he commanded, "tell me everything!"

"No! Tell me first. My grandson, tell me about him."

A smile of delight came slowly to Myles's lips. "He's better looking than either one of us ever was!" Then he began to tell about William's antics. He watched his father as he spoke and could see the words sink into his father's mind like drink to a thirsty man. He talked about William eagerly for some time, then said spiritedly, "You will see him, Father. I promise you!"

"Not likely," Sir Robert said, slumping his shoulders a little. "They have me, Myles, and they never turn a man loose from this place."

"You have William Tyndale praying for you. And me and Hannah and Mother. That is more power than all of King Henry's armies! Now, what are the charges, and what evidence do they have?" Myles spoke with assurance and calm.

Sir Robert looked at his son with admiration. "You always were the cool one." He smiled. "All right. Here is what happened. . . ."

Myles listened carefully, and when his father's story was done, he summarized it. "So, Ralph charged you with being an agent for Tyndale. He dredged up a witness from somewhere. Then they found some Bibles at Wakefield. Is that it?"

"That was enough. It was all planned, and when Cromwell is behind something like this, it rarely goes awry," Robert said bitterly. "There is nothing you can do. I want you to leave here, go get your mother immediately, and take her back to Germany with you."

"I won't do that," Myles said gently, but with firmness. "Tell me again about the man that gave evidence."

Sir Robert looked stubbornly at his son for a moment. Slowly his face changed as he seemed to come to a decision, then he began to give clear, concise details of his accuser to Myles. He gave him the name of the man and every detail of his appearance and countenance that he could think of. Then with a trace of despair he asked, "But what can you do? Suppose you prove that I didn't do it? To whom would you submit the evidence? The proper man would be Sir Thomas More, lord chancellor. And you know how he despises Tyndale and all Protestants! He would do nothing." Robert took a deep breath. "The next would be Thomas Cromwell. After that, his assistant, Ralph Geddes."

"An unholy trio," Myles reflected grimly. Then he placed his hands on his father's bent shoulders and looked directly in the blue-gray eyes that mirrored his own. "Father, I am going to leave now. But I want you to know that I believe God has told me he will deliver you from this place. If I have to corner Henry VIII like a hunted fox, he will hear the truth of this matter!"

"And what would Henry do? He is so caught up in trying to produce a son to pass his crown along to that he has no time for trivialities such as this. Even if he knew an injustice was done, you know as well as I what the man is like. He will not be bothered."

Though Sir Robert's words spoke defeat, Myles thought he could see the merest glimmer of hope in his father's eyes, and he quietly said, "I must go now. But remember, God knows our ways. He has not forgotten us!"

Half an hour later, he was free of the Tower, his face set with purpose. As he walked along, he whispered, "God, you must do it all. It's in your hands and not mine."

Twenty - Five

THE EVIDENCE

The world of 1533 went about its business as usual. On the frozen plains of Russia, Ivan IV—one day to be called Ivan the Terrible—acceded to the Russian throne at the age of three. In Europe, Suleiman began to push the Ottoman Empire to its greatest extent, conquering most of Hungary and much of Europe. In Peru, Francisco Pizarro captured and murdered Atahuallpa, ruler of the Inca Empire, thus completing Pizarro's conquest of Peru. Jacques Cartier, the French sailor, reached Labrador in his attempt to find a northwest passage. And Ignatius of Loyola, a Spanish priest, founded the Jesuits in Paris for the purpose of defending Catholicism against heresy. In Rome, Michelangelo began the immense "Last Judgment" on the altar wall of the Sistine Chapel, and Hans Holbein arrived in England to become the court painter.

But all of the activity of the world, to King Henry VIII, Sovereign Lord of England, was as nothing on the late afternoon of September the 7th. On that day he roamed the gardens at Greenwich, which was Anne's favorite residence and the spot she had chosen for her royal confinement.

For months, the fear that he might have a female heir or another stillborn son had scrambled like a rat through Henry's brain, and he had thrown himself into doing what man could do to prevent any harm from coming to Anne. One month earlier, he had secluded her here with a few trusted women. It was a velvet prison, designed to prevent any possible counterfeit babe from being switched with the true prince. It was also for the queen's protection.

Anne, however, did not see it that way. "To be shut up during high summer," she lamented. "Kept secluded like a Turk woman! No man to see me except the physician! 'Tis cruel, sweet Henry."

"'Tis custom." Henry mustered a smile. "We have broken so many large ones, we are bound all the more to observe the small ones. I will never be more than a half day's ride from your side. I wouldn't leave you, not for all the jewels in Becket's tomb. We will be together until the day you take to your chamber with your women."

"Women!" she snorted. "A lot of dull, boring creatures."

"You do not care for the company of women?"

"No, I do not. I want wit and music and poetry about me. Give me that! My brother George and his friends. Tom Wyatt. They are amusing. But a gaggle of gossiping, stupid women!"

Anne spoke truly, for she always surrounded herself with men and had no close women friends. Her closest companion was her brother George, not her sister Mary.

Henry at this point was determined to do nothing to disturb Anne. He soothed her as best he could and made his escape as soon as was possible. He was walking now about the garden, although the fall freeze had blasted most of the flowers, when Cromwell came striding up, a worried look on his face.

"What is it?" Henry said.

"From the pope." Cromwell handed Henry a sheet of paper, saying almost tonelessly, "Your formal damnation, sire."

"I am excommunicated, then?" Henry said. He took the paper and glanced over it carelessly.

The average Catholic would have been riddled with fear by the dire threat of being cut off from the church, but Henry had long ago passed the point of being frightened. "I am not a man to be intimidated by that old man in Rome," he snapped.

"Of course," Cromwell readily agreed. "It means nothing."

"When my son is King of England, he will fear him no more than I!" Henry boasted, and Cromwell nodded his agreement.

Cromwell had, Henry knew, no fear of the pope in Rome, and at times Henry even suspected him of having Lutheran tendencies. Handing the paper back to Cromwell, he shrugged and left him, walking the rest of the morning in the bleak garden. Then he returned to his room to study.

Anne lay back against the pillows, exhausted. The birth had been terrible, but now she was almost in a state of euphoria. During the worst of the labor, when the pain almost blocked out everything, one thought was never quite lost.

You will have a son—and Henry will be happy.

It was not a new thought, but had been the foundation of her very existence for months. For all his power, Henry was helpless in this matter. He had shaken a kingdom—nay, the world!—to rid himself of one wife who could not bring this to pass. And every day Anne had prayed for a son, a healthy son, so that her life would have meaning—and the monarchy would be safe.

Now in the shadows, a figure moved, and as she blinked the form of the physician came into focus.

"How are you feeling, Your Majesty?"

Anne did not like Dr. Manning, but he was accounted the most able physician in matters of childbirth. Anne tried to speak, then, finding that her lips were dry, licked them.

"A little wine for the Queen—quickly!"

Anne struggled into a sitting position, swallowed the contents of a small golden cup, then lay back. "Very well—" She nodded. "Let me see the child."

Dr. Manning hesitated, then turned to nod at the nurse. "Bring the infant," he said. He had a dry, dusty voice, and there was an odd light in his pale blue eyes as he watched the nurse lay the baby in the arms of Anne. He was a silent man by nature, his head filled with knowledge that physicians accumulate. He knew enough to have dozens of men and women thrown into the tower, but all was entombed in his skull. Now as he watched the Queen push the blanket back and soothe the hair of the child, his face was expressionless, but for once he felt a twinge of pity.

"A healthy child—very strong, Your Majesty."

Something in Manning's voice alerted Anne. Glancing up, she studied the thin features for a moment, then a thought came to her. A touch of fear caused her eyes to widen, and she asked, "What is it? Something is wrong!"

Manning gave a slight shake of his head, but when the Queen continued to stare at him, he knew he had no choice. Clearing his throat, he said in a flat monotone, "Your daughter is very well-formed and perfectly healthy, Your Highness."

His words dropped into the silence of the room, then seemed to spread out, like the waves created by a stone dropped into a still pond. He saw Anne's eyes close and her lips tighten—as if she had bitten into bitter fruit.

"My . . . *daughter?*"

"Yes, Your Majesty."

Anne turned her head and looked down at the tiny morsel that lay in the crook of her arm. Something in her seemed to freeze, and her hands trembled almost violently. Looking up, she said, "Does the King know?"

"No, Your Majesty. I have sent for him."

"Very well."

When Dr. Manning saw the Queen shut her eyes, he asked quickly, "Shall I have the nurse take the child?"

"No."

"Ah—well then, I shall—"

"Leave me—and take the nurse."

Manning was startled. "But, Your Majesty—!"

Anger seemed to leap out of Anne's eyes, and her voice rang loudly. "Leave me—do you hear?"

"Yes, of course."

Quickly Dr. Manning motioned to the nurse, then the two of them left the room. Anne paid no heed, but lay with her eyes closed, her spirit dulled. She lay very still, willing herself to think about the future—but there was a torpor in her mind, and she was conscious only of an emptiness that seemed to draw her mind down into a tiny fragment. Nothing seemed important—nothing had meaning for her.

She was roused out of this trancelike state by the creaking of the door. Looking up, she saw Henry approaching, his smallish eyes bright with anticipation.

He leaned over, kissed her, and then stroked her cheek gently. "The child is healthy, Manning tells me."

Anne stared up at him, despair in her dark eyes. It took all the will in her to whisper, "Yes, your daughter is very healthy."

Henry blinked, and he looked as though someone had dealt him a sharp blow. "A girl?" he whispered. He did not show anger—but a futile light in his eyes showed Anne what he was feeling. He put his hand out and touched the red hair of the sleeping infant. For one long moment, silence filled the room, then he said quietly, "God has sent us a daughter, but you will bear sons, Anne."

Hope sprang up in Anne at once. Reaching up, she seized Henry's hand and kissed it. Her tears fell on it, and she nodded, scarcely able to speak. "Yes! We will have a son!"

Henry stayed only briefly, then walked from the room, his back stiff, his face wooden. Over and over in his mind ran the bitter awareness that the son for which he had longed so desperately, of which he had been so certain, had never even existed.

All that night he drank heavily, wondering how such a disaster could have been wrought upon the Lord's chosen sovereign. *How did this happen?* his mind cried in silent agony. *Who has brought this debacle upon me?* Slowly, after many hours and innumerable cups of strong drink, he found his answer: *Anne has failed me.*

At the advanced age of forty-two, Henry had come to a place of physical and emotional crisis. The voice that had brought him consolation, that of Wolsey, was silenced. And Henry had neither the fortitude nor the knowledge to govern his people without this trusted advisor at his side. There had also been growing support for Catherine, which only amplified his fears and weaknesses, until they never seemed to leave him, taunting him especially when he strove to sleep. And he had since given up even that endeavor, as insomnia was a constant companion—one that made him vulnerable to illness.

In addition, a chronic and painful varicose ulcer on his thigh made it impossible for him to walk comfortably. The activity he most loved in the world—riding—was a source of excruciating pain, and so his magnificent horses stood idle, a silent testimony to the great king's increasing debilitation.

And now, the fact that his damnable divorce and remarriage had failed to produce a son only added to his torment. His long-awaited child, the supposed heir to his throne, to his legacy as king of England, was a girl. A useless girl! The gall of this disappointment sat heavy in the beleagured king's heart, and every day the certainty grew stronger within him that only one person could possibly be to blame for all his troubles: his beloved Queen Anne.

❦

Jacob Isen opened his eyes painfully, turned his head, and a ray of golden sunshine struck him almost like a red-hot iron, passing from temple to temple. He moaned softly, held his head, and thought of the previous night. Or tried to think. All he could remember was that he had been enormously drunk and a harlot had appeared from nowhere. It was not an unusual sort of evening for Isen.

Rolling out of the bed, he went across the room to where he kept his scanty store of cash behind a loose board in the wall. Moving the board, he found the small leather sack there and breathed a sigh of relief. He straightened up, emptied the coins out, fingered them a moment, then replaced them. "I've got to do *something!*" he muttered.

He dressed, cleaning up as well as he could, sneaked out the back way so the innkeeper would not see him, and made his way to the court. He was hungry but had no money to spare for food. Upon arriving at the court, he took his place among the men who waited outside Cromwell's office. Hours passed, and Isen's stomach rumbled and his head ached.

Finally the door opened, and he was relieved to see Ralph Geddes come out. He walked up to him, saying brightly, "Well, Mr. Geddes. Haven't seen you lately."

Geddes frowned at him and said succinctly, "It has been awhile."

The brevity of the reply told Isen much of Geddes's feeling. The man was cold as a wedge, never a kind word for anyone. But Isen forced himself to be pleasant. "I will tell you, Mr. Geddes, I am in need of employment." He winked and went on. "Sure and there must be something in which you might find me of use."

Geddes sized him up thoughtfully for a moment, then half turned in dismissal. "There is nothing right now, Jacob. I will send for you should I need you."

The words were like a dash of cold water, and anger welled up inside Jacob Isen. He wanted to snap, "You wasn't so cool when you needed me!" But he knew it was useless, so he turned and left the court, returning to his lodgings on the seedy side of London.

He spent the day trying to borrow money, with no success at all. The money that he had received from Geddes on the last job had vanished somehow, and he was quite mystified as to how it had happened. Late that afternoon he went to a pub and began to drink. By the time it was dark and he left with a bottle, he had only two coins left in his flat purse and had not eaten a morsel.

To make things worse, when he got to the inn, he was caught by the innkeeper, a man half a head taller than himself, who said, "This is your last night here. Be out come morning, or I'll be putting you out!"

Isen wanted to smash the man's face, but the innkeeper was too burly for that. So he merely ducked his head, mumbled in agreement, and stumbled to his room. He sat in the single chair, trying desperately to think what to do. Now that Geddes had refused him, the only choice he had was to return to Germany, where his brother had a small iron works. He hated his brother, and the feeling was returned with interest. But he knew his brother would take him in for the simple pleasure of tormenting him, putting him to dirty, hard work, and forcing him to live like a pig.

He took another drink and thought rebelliously, *But what else can I do? I'll starve if I stay in this cursed England!*

A knock sounded and he looked up, startled and wary. He put the bottle down, picked up a knife from the table, and pulled it from the sheath. Opening the door a small crack, he peered out to see a well-dressed man standing in the dim hallway.

"What is it?" Isen growled. "What do you want?"

"A matter of business," the man answered evenly.

His visitor was no more than twenty-seven or twenty-eight, Isen saw, and had a pair of steady blue-gray eyes. The thought crossed Isen's mind, *Geddes has sent him. He's changed his mind.* The finery the man wore signaled that he was someone high in the social realm, and Isen pulled the door open quickly. "Come in," he said and stepped back.

The tall man entered, turned, and waited as Isen shut the door and walked back over to the small table, tossing down the knife. "What can I do for you?" he asked.

"As I said, it's a business matter."

"Business? Did Ralph Geddes send you?"

A smile touched the man's wide lips, and his eyes grew watchful. "You may say that," he said.

"Well, sit down. Will you have a drink?"

The man sat on the bed, and Isen picked up the bottle, waving it toward the man slightly in a "Here we are" gesture, and poured two drinks. The visitor took his but merely held it with both hands, down on his lap.

There was something in the man's manner that baffled Isen. He could not place him, had never seen him as far as he knew . . . he took a deep drink, his eyes watchful over the edge of the glass. Licking his lips, he put the glass down and asked defiantly, "Well? What do you want. Is there a job in it?"

The man set the glass down by the bed, untouched, leaned back slightly, and folded his arms. The sword at his side spoke wealth, too. He said, "You didn't do too well on your last venture with Ralph Geddes, now, did you, Jacob?"

Instantly alarms went off in Isen's head. He was a crafty man, sly and alert, and his body tensed at the casual words. "What's that to you?" he demanded warily.

"How much did he pay you for inventing the evidence and testifying against Sir Robert Wakefield?"

Without preamble Isen's hand darted out, and he grasped the dagger. This was danger! He had known when he had assembled the false evidence and lied in court that he was taking a chance, but Geddes had assured him there would be no defenders and there was no way the plan could go wrong. Now, this fellow was here, who could well be an officer of the court!

"Get out of here," he said hoarsely. "I did my duty and that was all."

Myles Wakefield stared at the man's face, totally ignoring the threat of the dagger. "Couldn't have been more than forty or fifty crowns for a job like that, am I right, Jacob? And that's been fair spent, has it not?"

Myles had the satisfaction of seeing the man's heavy face drain fishbelly white. Isen was not a bad-looking fellow, although he was running a little too fat. He had a heavy German face and a burly body to match, but now drink and dissipation were taking their toll. Myles had found him after a long search. He was certainly not a well-known man, and it was only through a woman who had been his mistress for a while that Myles had learned where Isen was lodging. She had demanded money for the information, but now Myles knew it was worth it.

"I don't know what you're on about, man. Get out of here!" Isen growled. But there was a trace of fear about him, and the hand that held the knife shook ever so slightly. Isen made his living by doing the bidding of those above him, usually doing the dirty jobs they didn't care to touch with their dainty, white hands. As Myles was making no threat, Isen began to wonder if there might be something in it for him. Myles remained silent and unmoving, and Isen finally demanded, "What do you want?"

"My name is Wakefield."

He's come to kill me! Isen's mind immediately responded. *For lying about his father and putting him in the Tower!* He slashed out with the knife, intending to put it against the man's throat. Then two things happened, and Isen never actually saw either of them—he just saw the end results.

The man was holding steady a long, thin dagger in front of his face. Isen had not even seen the man move. Next he felt a powerful, sharp blow on his arm, and his fingers went numb, his own knife falling to the floor. Then the cold steel of the man's blade was against his own throat.

"Don't—kill me!" he begged. "Don't kill me!"

"It would be easy enough to do," Myles answered almost pleasantly. "And, to be honest, that was in my mind when I came here." But Myles's thoughts were racing. Now, having trapped the one man who could help him free his father, he considered his options. *I could threaten him with death, and he would tell me the truth. But as soon as we went into court he surely would lie again. It'll have to be bribery.*

The dagger disappeared, and Isen thought stupidly that he hadn't even seen how he did *that*. Myles leaned back and appeared to relax again, nonchalantly placing one booted foot over Isen's dagger and crossing the other leg over his knee. "It wouldn't profit me to see you dead, Jacob," he said in a conversational tone. "So how would you like to have five hundred golden crowns?"

Jacob Isen stopped breathing for a few seconds. The fear that had paralyzed him before was now replaced by avarice. "Five hundred golden crowns!" he whispered. "For doing what?"

"Why, for helping me get my father, Sir Robert Wakefield, out of the Tower and back in his rightful place."

"I can't help you with that," Isen whispered uncertainly.

"You are the only one who can," Myles said mildly. "It was your testimony that put him there, along with your evidence. You did plant that evidence, didn't you, Jacob? You know and I know that you put those Bibles in place, to be found by the officers, so there would be something to charge my father with."

"I never! It's a lie!" Isen said fearfully.

"Oh, come now, Jacob. It's just the two of us here. No matter what you say, you can't be charged with it," Myles said earnestly, leaning forward a little. "I could kill you. That is what many sons would do to a man who's done what you've done to my father. But I'd rather discuss another way." Myles could be very persuasive. He had learned during his time of smuggling Bibles to deal with men at almost every level.

In the same offhanded tone, Myles remarked, "Geddes didn't treat you too well, did he? Didn't pay you very much, and now all of it is gone. And there he is, sitting in the middle of one of the finest estates in the country, wearing gold rings, eating the best food, sleeping in a fine soft bed." Myles's low tone, enumerating these grievances, echoed Isen's feelings exactly. "And you got your forty or fifty coins, while he gets all of that. No justice in it, is there, Jacob?"

Jacob Isen was almost mesmerized by Myles's reasonableness— by the spectre of five hundred gold crowns. He looked around the room, thinking that the man was right. "All right. I'll say this here, but nowheres else. Geddes hired me to do the job. But," he added plaintively, "he told me that it wasn't all a lie, that the Wakefields do have some connection with William Tyndale. So I just fancied the story a bit when I testified."

Myles thought that, to Isen, the "job" was just that simple. The man obviously had no morals, but that might actually work in Myles's favor. He leaned forward and said, "If my father should be released from prison and his properties returned to him, he could do a great deal for you."

"A great deal! Fah! He'd have me hanged, and wouldn't that be doing it up right, now!"

"Hm, yes, I see your point. But suppose," Myles said meaningfully, "I explained to my father that it was due to Jacob Isen that he had been released from the Tower and had regained his rightful place. That it had all been a terrible, but honest mistake. My father would be very grateful, and he might even go better than five hundred golden crowns." Myles cocked his head and smiled benevolently at Jacob. "You're not getting any younger, Jacob. You are in need of a profession."

Jacob had been listening acutely, and he asked sharply, "What kind of profession?"

"Oh, I would think marrying a wealthy widow might be along your line," Myles told him airily. "You're not a bad-looking fellow, but there's no courting a widow wearing those clothes." Myles gestured disdainfully. "And with your hair like that, well, a man must have appearance to make an impression. I would even wager you most likely know such a woman, do you not?"

As a matter of fact, Isen *did* know such a woman. She had outlived three husbands and was plain almost to the point of ugliness—but she had the coin! Furthermore, she seemed to be open to a bit of romancing. Why, with a fine suit of clothes, maybe riding up in a fine carriage, a little sweet-talking, Widow Hoskins could be his! After he was married there would be ready money for girls and drink, and the woman would just have to keep her mouth shut. That was how it was with wives. He had thought of Widow Hoskins more than once but had seen little chance of winning her when other suitors had more with which to tempt her.

Now he said craftily, "I might be knowing a woman such as that. But naught of good it'll do me if I be hanged for giving false evidence!"

A tremor of excitement ran through Myles. Here, at last, was a chance. He smiled reassuringly and said, "Do as I say, Jacob, and you will be all right. You shall have your widow, I will have my father out, and he will have Wakefield." Myles paused, and Isen watched the blue-gray eyes narrow and turn ice cold. "The only one that will lose will be Ralph Geddes."

Jacob Isen grinned a sharkish grin, his own eyes full of malice. "I wouldn't mind that," he said wolfishly. "Now, Mr. Wakefield, tell me all about this plan of yours."

Twenty-Six

IN THE WORD OF A KING, THERE IS POWER

The wind was shifting. The courtiers, ever alert, sensed it and began to trim their sails. After the birth of Elizabeth, they watched carefully. One of the leaders said, after weeks of observation, "The king is no longer satisfied with Anne."

This was a dangerous thing to say, for during her pregnancy, Henry had had laws passed—very strict laws—that penalized anyone who spoke against the queen. But now he obviously had other interests. The quarrels that had broken out between Henry and Anne were not lover's quarrels but were outbursts of pure enmity. Those in the inner circle began to think that Henry, who had rammed his way clear of a constricting marriage once before, would extricate himself from this one as well. "It's only a matter of time," they said sagely to one another.

For a time, Myles moved around London, seeking a way to present the new evidence. He had Jacob Isen primed, although he had paid him only a small portion of what he had promised. Isen had been suspicious at first but was gradually won over as Myles convinced him that the entire fee would be paid. Isen had tried to raise the price but had finally agreed with the original terms. He was nervous, however, and kept asking, "But how will you keep me clear of it? How can we get Wakefield out unless I change my story? And should I do that, they'll be asking me why, for certain!"

Myles was asking himself the same questions. He simply could not find a way. It was Cromwell's business, and his alone, to summon another trial. And immediately behind Cromwell was the shadow of Ralph Geddes, who, if he got wind of such a scheme, would crush it out of hand.

He was struggling with this one morning as October winds scoured the countryside and a wolf-lean winter began to creep over England. A knock at his door startled him out of his chair, where he had been bent over for hours, alternately praying and trying to think. He cautiously opened the door, and his eyes widened. "Nob!" he said, "What—what—"

Nob, smaller and leaner than ever but with the same sharp blue eyes, came in at Myles's bidding. "Ran you to ground, didn't I." He grinned. "And a hard job it was, too. Be glad when the day comes you can live under your own name."

Myles had chosen the name George Rochester to cover his identity. His disguise this time was somewhat simpler than most. He had cut his hair short, dyed it almost white, and wore a large black eyepatch over his left eye. He was surprised at how much that one item had changed people's reception of him. Anyone who wore an eyepatch became a stranger, even to people known for a lifetime. It was almost as effective, he discovered, as putting a mask over his face. People unerringly looked at the patch and not at the rest of his features.

"What's wrong, Nob?"

The older man's eyes grew hard. "I've left the Bournevilles," he answered.

"Left the Bournevilles? But you've been with them practically all your life!"

"Sir Geoffrey and me had a bit of a run-in," he said blandly. "And I'll not go back."

He would say no more, though Myles tried his best to find out the reason Nob had left. Finally he gave up and asked, "What will you do now?"

Nob looked down at the shabby gray hat he was holding and shrugged. Myles thought of the first day he had seen him, when he and his mother had staggered, almost unconscious, across the fields in the cold, searching for a river. His first memory was of sitting on the floor of the mews and being handed a bowl of something hot to eat by a man with a lean brown face. It had been a stern face, almost as hawklike as some of the falconer's charges, but Myles had learned over the years that this man was his friend, faithful unto death.

"Maybe I can find you a place with one of my friends—" Then Myles stopped and said wistfully, "but of course, I have no friends now."

"It's not for that I've come," Nob said sturdily. "I'll make out fine. But your mother, she's not doing well."

Myles looked up, startled. "She's ill?"

"That she is. I stopped at Mr. Kemp's to see if I might get a few days' work, and so it's been two weeks now. Your mother took bad with the cold weather. I thought you needed to know."

Myles had already tossed a cloak around his shoulders and was throwing his things together. "Yes. Come with me, Nob," he ordered. "We'll rent a couple of horses."

Soon the two were on the road, riding fast and steady, and reached the Kemp household in record time. Before Myles's horse came to a full halt, Myles jumped down and tossed the reins to Nob, saying, "I'm going to Mother at once." He walked to the front door and was admitted by Susan, who seemed glad to see him but had a distracted and worried air.

"How is she?" Myles asked anxiously.

Susan Kemp said haltingly, "She is some better now, but she's had a hard time of it. And I'm thinking it's not just the cold in her head—she's missing Sir Robert. She's in the small bedroom, Myles. Go on in to her."

Myles hurried to knock on the door softly. There was a faint answer and Myles went in. His mother was propped up by pillows in the bed, the covers pulled up high, and the ever-present Bible was on her knees. "Myles!" she said, her voice faint but her eyes alight.

He sat down on the bed beside her and kissed her gently. She smiled and said, "What an outlandish garb you have on! How are you? Tell me everything."

Myles talked with animation of Hannah and William and William Tyndale, all the time studying his mother, trying to assess her condition. He did not like Lady Jane's color, which was pallid with a slight grayish tinge. She seemed very weak and had lost weight.

He had not seen her since running Jacob Isen to ground, so he began to relate his meeting with the man and what he proposed. He ended the story by saying, "So I have Isen ready to change his testimony, if I can find a way to do it without getting his neck stretched."

"Oh, that is wonderful! I knew you would think of something like that," Lady Jane said.

"Not quite so wonderful, Mother," Myles said wearily. "If he tells the truth now, he may be hanged. But if he doesn't, we lose our only chance of clearing Father." His face was long and his shoulders sagged with defeat. "So the bird is penned down, but I dare not let him fly."

"God has led you to do this much," Lady Jane said with equanimity, "so we shall pray about it and see what more is to be done."

He smiled involuntarily. "That's always your answer, isn't it Mother?"

"What else, Son?" she asked with innocent surprise. "What

372

good is our feeble human wisdom? We need God's wisdom, of course, for a thing like this." She settled back into the pillows a little and went on, "And you know, we cannot go up to heaven, bang on God's door, and demand that he give us what we want."

"No, I've tried that often enough," Myles said ruefully. "Doesn't work very well, does it?"

"Well, Son, sometimes God gives us what we ask, even before we ask. But there are other times he seems to try our faith." Her eyes focused on a far-off distance that Myles could not see, and her voice was soft, introspective. "Our faith is precious in his sight, like a diamond. And when we own a diamond, we hold it up to the light, turn it so that it reflects the colors. We hold it in different positions in the palm of our hands and admire it and place it here and there, just so, to see the beauty of it in different settings. And that is what God does with us as we make our pilgrimage, I think." Though her face was marked with illness, she looked peaceful and serene, and she went on in a dreamy voice that enveloped Myles with warmth. "He puts us in difficulties so that he can watch our faith. He turns us this way and pulls us that way, and it sometimes seems capricious to us. But then, as our faith holds fast, my! How God must smile!"

There was silence in the small plain room. Lady Jane's calm voice and the images and meaning of her vision were to Myles almost a caress. "I never thought of that," Myles said with wonder. He had never seen anyone with the vivid imagination and wealth of expression his real mother had, except for Lady Jane. Like Margred Morgan, she had always seen her walk with God as a great adventure that was not only spiritual but also a tangible, visible, exciting daily experience. She was totally confident that, no matter how dark the day, God's sunshine lay just beyond, and waiting until the day came was of no consequence, for God was in the shadows as well.

Myles smiled at her. "I am staying until you're better. I was doing no good in town anyway. Oh, how I miss Hannah and William!"

He stayed for a week, then began to grow restless. He would say to his mother a dozen times a day, "I've got to do *something!*"

Lady Jane's reply was always calm and reassuring. "You are doing something, you are praying."

"Well, it doesn't seem like enough to me!" he would complain. "I can't see that anything is getting done!"

"Nothing is ever done on earth until something is done in heaven. Don't you know that, Myles?" Lady Jane chided him gently one day. "We are simply waiting until whatever God decides in heaven will be done here on earth. You remember that Jesus said he was doing the work of his Father, that whatever he saw the Father in heaven doing, that is what he did." She found the place in her New Testament and began to read aloud passages of faith, and Myles listened quietly. Slowly, the dark cloud of doubt that had hung over him was blown away by the refreshing wind of truth.

After a while, Myles reached out and took his mother's hand and said, "I believe, Mother, that it will all come out right."

It was two days after this when Lady Jane sent Susan to get Myles from the stable, where he was grooming his horse and talking with Nob. He went to her room and she told him, "Myles, I have something to tell you."

His eyes lit up and he became excited. "What, Mother?"

"You will never be able to get Robert's case reversed in court, not by yourself," she said firmly. "Ralph is too powerful, and even if somehow it came before the court, he would step in or have one of his hirelings step in. He has Cromwell behind him, and Cromwell is the second strongest power in the land."

"But, Mother, it must be done in court!" Myles protested. "There is no other way!"

"That may be so. But the court may be swayed."

"They aren't *supposed* to be," Myles said rather abruptly. "They're supposed to be above influence and mete out justice. But . . ." He shrugged. ". . . it seems they never do."

Lady Jane continued patiently, "Well, there is one way, and only one. If the court must be swayed, then the one man who can sway it must step in."

Myles was bewildered and then thought that perhaps she had lost some of her keen intelligence from the long illness. "The king?" he asked incredulously.

"Yes. The king."

"But, Mother," Myles said desperately, "that's even more impossible than the first course! Why should the king step in? He only does what is good for himself. He is the most selfish human being on the face of the earth." He shook his head. "I am sorry to talk of my sovereign this way, but his record is evident."

"He has become that way," Lady Jane agreed, "but he was not always so. As a young man, there was generosity in him and a desire for justice. 'Tis the power of the throne that has possessed him and corrupted him. But it may be," she said spiritedly, "that that which was in him as a young man may still be there, though buried and forgotten. You must go to Henry." She held up her hand at the objection she saw forming on Myles's lips. "I know he is surrounded by an army."

"Yes. No one can get through his guards. And Cromwell has his own little corps there. After all, he wants no one who may be dangerous to himself speaking to Henry. He weeds the king's visitors out carefully."

There was a silence in the room for a few moments. Then Lady Jane said with finality, "That is what the Lord has shown me. You will never get to see the king as long as he's at court. But when he goes to hunt, he is not so well protected then, is he?"

Myles lifted his head, his eyes becoming alert. "Why—that's

true! Many times he'll carry only two or three men with him, sometimes not even men of office or of the court. Maybe just his royal hunters or the servant in charge of the dogs."

"That is what you must do. Wait for him until you can speak to him alone, or as near as possible."

Myles looked searchingly at her. "You do realize, Mother, that I'm a fugitive myself? When I tell him who I am, he may simply call for my arrest. Then I would be with Father in the Tower."

"We must leave that to God," Lady Jane said with all the firmness she used whenever she spoke of her Lord. "God never contradicts himself, Myles. If it is his will for you to speak to the king, even if you go to the Tower for it, it is the right thing to do."

Myles knew then that there was no other choice, although it seemed suicidal to him. He leaned over and kissed her cheek, saying with determination, "I'll be leaving then, Mother."

She held to him for a moment and whispered, "God be with you, my dear. I am a weak old woman, but in our weakness, God is shown to be strong and all-powerful. As you go, Susan and I will be here praying for you. And Hannah, too. Though she knows nothing of this, I know that every day she sends up prayers for you. Go, my son."

Myles straightened his shoulders and left the room, and already his mind began to fill with ideas and plans. He went to the stable and told Nob, "Saddle the horses, Nob. We're leaving."

Nob calmly began to gather saddles and bridles and blankets and asked, "Where are we going?"

Myles gave him a quick, peculiar glance, then started picking up gear himself. "The first thing we're going to do is to steal some of the birds from Wakefield."

"The hawks? The falcons, you mean?" Nob's eyes grew open wide, and he froze in his tracks, holding Myles's saddle, looking at the young man as though he had gone totally daft. Stealing a falcon was a hanging offense.

Myles continued to bridle his mount and went on grimly, "And as soon as we've done that, we're going to show them to a man who loves good falcons."

Henry's quarrels with Anne had reached epic proportions. Knowing that her only hold on him had been the promise of a male heir to the throne, she felt him slipping away. If she had managed to control herself, it might have ended better. But it was not in Anne Boleyn to give up. She grew more aggressive, and even as she lost her leverage, her voice became shriller, at times literally driving Henry from the palace.

This happened one bleak December day. Henry rose early that morning, and Anne immediately started trying to convince him—for what seemed like the thousandth time to the king—to rid the country of Catherine. Always before, Henry merely replied to her urgings that Catherine was no longer a threat. Anne, however, knew otherwise. She knew also that Catherine's daughter, Mary, who was now seventeen, was the next heir to the throne. If something happened to Henry, Mary would be queen, and her mother, Catherine, would have her claws into Anne Boleyn as her first act.

At least, this was how Anne perceived it.

She followed Henry around that morning until he lost his temper. "Wench!" he shouted, "Leave me alone! I will not hear this anymore!" He stormed out of the room and went out into the dreary, cold gardens, leaning heavily on his cane and muttering darkly.

One of the butlers appeared in front of him and said timidly, "Sire?"

"Well! What is it?"

"A—a message. From the mews, sire."

"Message? What sort of message?" No matter how upset or

busy Henry was, any news of his dogs or his hawks gained his immediate attention. He was unable to ride with the hounds as much as he once did, but he still went out with the hunting birds at every opportunity.

"They say, sire, that there is a gentleman here who wishes to give you a gift. I mean," the butler added nervously, "two gifts, actually. A peregrine and a tiercel, I believe, Your Majesty."

Henry brightened a little. Surely this would be more interesting than listening to that screeching woman in the palace. "Yes, I'll go see the birds. No, I'll go fly them," he said decisively. He went to his quarters and changed quickly to his hunting clothes. While he was changing, he saw that the ulcer on his leg was bleeding again. He changed the dressing himself, staring at the raw wound and wondering why God had allowed this to happen to him.

When he was dressed, he headed for the mews, and three young courtiers joined him along the way. "No," he said, waving at them imperiously, "not this time. I wish to be alone for a while." They bowed, their disappointment evident, but backed away without argument.

When Henry reached the mews, he saw two men waiting for him. There was a small, older man dressed in the customary garb of a falconer. The other was a tall, broad-shouldered man with white hair and a black eyepatch. Both of them bowed low as he approached.

Henry waved a dismissal at their humble greetings, saying, "Yes, yes, what are your names?"

"George Rochester, sire," the larger of the two men answered. He was a fine looking man with a youthful face, despite the white hair, and a fit, strong body that Henry envied at once. He had long given over to drink, and especially to food, and was now swollen out of most of his clothes.

This young fellow looks like I did twenty years ago, he thought almost resentfully. *But he's brought me a bird, so I'll not begrudge him.*

"Rochester? Any relation to Sir Edward Rochester?"

"No, sir. I am not of nobility, only a gentleman and your humble servant." Myles made a small, smart bow.

"Nothing finer than an English gentleman!" Henry said heartily, and at the moment, he meant it. "I understand you've brought me a gift," he said with almost boyish eagerness.

"Yes, we heard of Your Majesty's love of hunting birds, sire," Myles said and then paused. He was trying desperately to form a plan. His first mission had been to get Henry away from his handlers, and he had succeeded with amazing ease. Now he was wondering what to do next. "I do have two birds that I wish to give you, sire, should you find them acceptable."

"Well, let's see them," Henry said, his eyes bright. "We'll go out and try them. There ought to be hares stirring this morning."

A stroke of fortune, Myles thought exultantly, *to get the king away from the palace and out into the fields!* No doubt they would be followed by his bodyguards, but perhaps they would stay beyond hearing distance. They would also, he reminded himself more soberly, be near enough to arrest him and take him to the Tower if his scheme did not work.

"Yes, Your Majesty." He moved to Nob, who was standing slightly behind, and said in a low voice, "The tiercel."

Nob bent and opened one of the cages as Myles pulled on a gauntlet and squatted down to thrust his arm into the large cage. The tiercel—the finest falcon from Wakefield—perched on his arm, and Myles stood, turning proudly to the king. "This one is simply called Lightning, Your Majesty. He is not as beautiful as some birds, but he seldom misses his strike."

Henry came over and began to examine the bird. He held up his arm, without a gauntlet, and prodded the tiercel's claw to make her step forward. The talons fiercely gripped Henry's naked arm. "Looks aren't everything," he said, avidly examining the bird. Just being there, dealing with the birds, had calmed his spirit.

He expertly pointed out the good points of the tiercel and handed him back to Myles, nodding with approval. Myles handed him back to Nob and then bent to the other cage. "And this, sire, is a bird *almost* worthy of Your Majesty's talent." He stood up holding Hector—the pride of Nob's life—on his wrist. As he turned, he kept his eyes steadily on the king's face.

When Nob had seen the tiercel from Wakefield's mews, he'd known that, as fine as he was, Myles would need a better falcon to impress Henry. And so, despite Myles's dismayed protests, he'd volunteered his treasured Hector—for as precious as the bird was to the old falconer's heart, Myles was of far greater value.

As Nob had been sure would happen, Henry's eyes flew open and he almost shouted, "By heaven! I've never seen a finer bird!" His eyes darted to Myles, and he asked shrewdly, "And how is it you've come by this bird, Mr. Rochester? You know, I suppose, that by law one must be at least an earl to fly a peregrine."

"Aye, that I know, sire," Myles said, and grinned wolfishly. "And I know also that that law is probably broken more than any law in your kingdom."

Henry did not smile, though he wasn't exactly frowning. He merely raised one eyebrow, staring at Myles speculatively.

Myles grew a little nervous, though he didn't let it show. He went on with a mocking air, "And I, being the English gentleman that I am, decided to rescue this bird from the pernicious commoner that broke this noble law and present him to royalty, sire, as I do not believe even an earldom is deserving of this bird!" Myles offered the bird to the king and held his breath.

Henry had not moved, and his expression had not changed during this speech. Now, suddenly, he laughed loudly and Myles found he could breathe again. "I can't argue that!" he said gleefully. He took the falcon and began to preen him, turning him slightly from side to side, admiration in his eyes. "I'm of a mind to try him, Rochester," the king said. "Come along. You and I will have a hunt."

Shortly after, Myles found himself walking along in an open field filled with old brush, left deliberately that way for the hares to nest in. The grooms even put food out for the animals, so they proliferated almost wildly. Close to the castle, this spot was a favorite hawking ground of the king's.

The hawking went well, and the king was obviously delighted with both birds. When the bag was full, he turned to Myles and said, "Rochester, 'tis a magnificent gift! Seldom have I seen better!"

The wind was keening slightly, and the king's face was ruddy and filled with pleasure. As he watched the king, Myles suddenly knew that he was at a turning point in his life. Never would there be another moment such as this. So he breathed a quick prayer and said, "Your Majesty, my name is not Rochester."

King Henry blinked in surprise, then his face grew hard with suspicion. "What's this?" he growled. "A trick?" He was always aware of the threat of assassination, and his eyes flew to his bodyguards standing a hundred yards away.

"I am Myles Wakefield, Your Majesty," he said quietly. "The son of Sir Robert Wakefield."

Surprise washed across Henry's face. He had been grieved at the treachery of Sir Robert Wakefield. He had never been close, exactly, to Wakefield, for he was rather far down the list of courtiers that Henry spent personal time with. But Sir Robert had proved himself over the years to be an excellent soldier, an invaluable military adviser, and—until recently—a most loyal subject.

Memories began to surface in the king's mind as he stared at Myles, and he repeated slowly, "Myles Wakefield . . ." He had a keen mind, Henry Tudor, remembering minutiae and particulars that always amazed his followers. The parts formed a whole in Henry's mind, and he said, "You fled overseas. You were forced to leave the country, though I've forgotten the cause." The king's face darkened and his voice grew ominous. "Surely you know the penalty for returning to England without our royal invitation?"

"I know, sire," Myles bowed humbly, but as he rose, his gaze was direct and unflinching. "And I stand ready to pay the penalty. But I ask Your Majesty one boon: Hear what I have to say first, before you call the guard."

At that instant, a hare started. Henry, born a hunter, whirled and threw the peregrine he held into the air. The great bird's wings beat the air as he rose majestically. The falcon wheeled sharply, spotting the fleeing animal, and dropped like a stone. It struck, wings flung high, talons outstretched, and killed the rabbit instantly. Henry turned and said, "Well, man, don't just stand there! Let's go get the blasted hare!"

The moment had broken Henry's severity, and he began to think of long ago. When Myles picked up the hare and put it into the bag, Henry said abruptly, "I remember! I couldn't rightly see you beneath that silly disguise you're wearing! You're the young fellow that went with us on the boar hunt the time we stopped at Sir Robert's!"

"Yes, sire."

The memory was flooding back, and clear images of that day flitted past his mind as though they were in a painting. He had that kind of memory, to bring back the past, and it was both a blessing and a curse. This memory was a blessing, and Henry smiled very slightly. "I remember that day," he said. "It was a day much like this one. The air was sharp, the dogs were excellent. And that boar—the biggest one I'd ever seen!" He turned again to Myles. "The boar charged. And I fell."

"Yes, you did, Your Majesty."

"And you threw yourself at him to save me, didn't you?"

"Well, yes, Your Majesty—but you remember, I was the one that was saved. You leaped up and charged right into the fray. I was practically under that boar—I could smell his breath, and his little red eyes were staring me right in the face! I had given myself up for dead, but there you were, with your spear. One stroke to his heart!"

"Yes, that's the way it was. I remember it all."

The king conveniently forgot to remember that Sir Robert had been at least partially responsible for killing the boar, so Myles gently reminded him. "I've never forgotten that day, sire, and the way you and my father kept that beast from killing me." He said no more, but he saw that Henry's first anger upon learning of Myles's deception was now gone. Instead, the king's face was flushed with pleasure, the brisk December wind, and the excitement of the hunt, so that he looked almost peaceful.

Myles had difficulty remembering that this was the same man who had been the youthful king. Then, his face had been clean and eager and earnest, but now it was rounded unhealthily from a life of dissolute indulgence. As he considered his king's face, he knew that he was over the first hurdle, the one that he had so feared: that the king might preemptively throw him into the Tower without listening to him.

Henry took his fur cap off and rubbed it in his hands. Made out of black ermine, it was a beautiful piece. "I got this from the Emperor Charles," he said absently, running his hands over the glossy fur. He seemed to have forgotten Myles, but of course, he had not. Finally he lifted his head and said softly, "Yes, I remember that day, Wakefield. It was a good day. There were many good days then, when I was young. And I've always remembered that one particularly." He looked out across the gray, barren field and went on, speaking almost as if to himself, "I wish I could go back." The cool wind moaned a little, and there were tiny little droplets of cold water in it now. Myles could smell the woods and the smoke of cooking fires. Henry shook himself and said briskly, "Now, what's this all about?"

Calmly Myles said, "My father has been unjustly accused, Your

Majesty. The court was not at fault," he added hastily, when Henry opened his mouth to protest. "But they had improper evidence. I have come to ask you to reconvene the court and reconsider the verdict."

"What evidence?" Henry demanded. It was a serious matter to meddle with the work of the court. Once you began, there was no way to stop it. He listened closely as Myles put forward his case.

Myles told Henry the whole story, slightly altering it so as to keep Jacob Isen from being hanged. He told the king that Isen had been misled, though he did not name the culprits. He spoke concisely and with clarity, and when he finished the story, he did not implore the king but stood simply waiting.

Henry chewed his lip a little, frowning with thought. "This Isen, Jacob Isen. He is ready to go before the court and give new evidence?"

"He is, Your Majesty."

"Is he such a friend of justice, then?" Henry demanded. "Does he realize he could be arrested for perjury?"

"There are few men who seek justice fervently," Myles answered. He decided to take yet another chance with his king's indulgence. "I had to help him remember things and to see . . . to take another look at the evidence and the testimony he gave," he said with great care. "And now he's ready to do it, sire."

Henry was no fool. Though he could not recall the case, he had the sudden notion that the final outcome had not been just. What he did recall was that Cromwell had inveigled him into assigning the Wakefield estate to one of his retainers, whose name he could not even remember. His lip curled. Cromwell was more than capable of manipulating such things in the favor of those who served him. Ordinarily, Henry would have paid no attention to such an injustice, but the memories of that day, so long ago it seemed, when this young man had so willingly thrown himself in front of that monstrous boar to save his king, continued to flit through his mind. He wondered how many of his subjects would be willing to do that to save their sovereign.

With a pensive look at Myles, Henry said, "I shall see to the matter. Have your man in the palace tomorrow. I will leave word that you are to be brought for a private audience." His eyes went to the falcon, and a wry grin touched his thin lips. There was humor in Henry at times, and he asked, almost humbly, "And am I to be allowed to keep the birds, Wakefield? If I see that your father gets a new hearing?"

"The birds are yours, Your Majesty," Myles said and bowed low. "This is the man who has trained them," he said, motioning to Nob. "Tell the king about Hector, Nob."

Nob raked his cap off and tugged his forelock. "He's a kingly bird, Your Majesty." His mouth tightened, and he added stubbornly, "I know Your Majesty has many fine birds. But, my life on it, this one will be the finest of them all!"

Henry laughed and acknowledged Nob with a slight, quick incline of his head. "Well, Wakefield," he said, "I'll take the birds."

Myles's heart leaped, for he knew the king was saying in effect: "I will see that justice is done."

"Your Majesty is merciful, indeed, and gracious," Myles said, adding, "and just."

Henry gave him a sour look, but his eyes were drawn again by the great falcon, and his face softened. He looked again at Myles and inclined his head. "I am used to hearing so much flattery that, when an honest man speaks, I hardly know how to respond." He lightly ran a finger along the bird's chest, still not looking at Myles, and said almost inaudibly, "Forgive me, Wakefield." He turned and walked across the field, headed for the palace.

Myles watched him go, his heart alive with praise. *Thank you, God, for preserving me. Now, be thou my help and my father's friend.*

Twenty - Seven

HOMECOMING

As Jacob Isen stood before His Royal Majesty King Henry VIII and the tiered row of judges, he thought of a picture he'd once seen. It had been a painting of a group of Christians being thrown to the wild beasts in the Colosseum in Rome during the days of Nero. He could remember the vivid details—such as a black-maned lion tearing at the leg of a slender woman who was trying to escape.

As he stood sweating before the somber-faced panel of men, his sturdy legs shaking so badly he could hardly stand, he thought, *I'd stand more chance with the wild animals than with these men!* He had just given his testimony in a voice that trembled, and now he stood there, enduring the heavy silence as the small eyes of the king seemed to bore deep into his very breast.

"And so you planted the *evidence* in the home of Sir Robert Wakefield and then perjured yourself before the high court!" Henry swelled up, rage flooding his fat face. "You'll be hanged for that, you scurvy dog! I'll have no man attacking men of honor in this land!"

"Oh—please, Your Majesty!" Isen threw himself on his knees, folded his hands in a beseeching attitude, and whimpered, "It wasn't *me* as thought of it! Mr. Geddes—he told me that Sir Robert was guilty—and that we *had* to do it—it was for *you.* Your

Majesty—that's what he told me!" Isen's face was contorted, and he pulled at his neck as if he could feel the sharp edge of the headsman's axe. Frantically his gaze ran around the room, but he saw nothing but death in the faces of his judges. Then his wild eyes fell on Myles, and he cried out, "Please! Mr. Wakefield—!"

Henry glanced at Myles and, after a moment's hesitation, asked, "Are you speaking for this man, Mr. Wakefield?" He spoke his lines well—only he and Myles knew that he had already decided the scenario that the trial would follow.

Now Myles followed the direction his king had given him earlier and rose at once. Henry noted how the young man made an attractive picture—his tall, athletic form richly clad in a new suit of blue silk, a velvet cloak tied at his throat. The king had insisted that young Wakefield dress for the role and was pleased at how Myles had complied. Now Henry listened with interest as Wakefield spoke clearly, "The man has been dishonest, Your Majesty, but I feel he has learned his lesson. I pray you, be merciful to him."

Henry glared ferociously at Isen, as if he wished to eat him alive—then slowly nodded. "Very well. He shall have his back scratched with the cat and spend a few months in a cell."

"Oh, thank you, Your Majesty!" Isen gasped in relief and was hurried out of the room by two of the guards.

Henry looked down the line of stern faces that made up the court and said, "I see no profit in prolonging this matter. It's plain to me that Sir Robert Wakefield has been falsely accused. Does anyone here see the matter differently?" Henry did not even bother to look surprised when the judges all nodded their agreement. Instead, he turned to Myles and smiled. "The court will give you the papers that will set your father free."

Thomas Cromwell, his smallish eyes glinting and his steel trap of a mouth opening just enough to speak, said, "Also, Your Majesty, the necessary papers for the arrest of Ralph Geddes, I think?"

"Yes! See to it, Cromwell!"

The darkness had become so familiar to Robert Wakefield that he no longer paid heed to it. When he had first been put into the cell, he had almost gone mad, for he was a man who loved the outdoors, the open skies, the winds caressing the face of the earth. He loved the beating of the sun on his face and often had revelled in the force of it.

When all that was taken from him and he was cast into the tiny cell with only a single candle for light—and sometimes not even that—he prayed for death.

Now as he sat alone on his hard bunk, he allowed his mind to slip back to the days that preceeded his arrest. It had been his only salvation for months now—that and the books that had been allowed him by a kindly jailer. He had read one over and over: a small Gospel of John, translated by whom he did not know, for there was no acknowledgment on it. He hoped at first that it might be by William Tyndale, but he was certain it was not because William Tyndale defiantly labeled his translations.

The book had contained that single Gospel and no more, but he had read it a hundred times and the words had soaked into his soul. Now his eyes were weary, and for the past three hours, he had retreated from his cell and the darkness, leaning back and thinking of happier days.

He thought of the days of his youth, growing up in the midst of a busy and prosperous estate, of his father and his mother. He relived those days constantly, grieving sometimes over his actions. He remembered his marriage, and often he thought, with pain and regret, of Margred Morgan, whom he always recalled as Arwen. But thoughts of Arwen always led to thoughts of Myles, which filled him with gladness. Most of all he now thought of Lady Jane, knowing that she was praying for him, and dreamed of Wakefield and the life they had known there.

He knew now that his home belonged to Ralph, had in fact been deeded to Ralph by the court and lost forever to him. Never again would he walk across his broad acres or counsel with his seneschal. All was gone.

Sir Robert Wakefield returned to his home often, though, in his mind if not in body. He would shut his eyes, closing out the damp unpleasantness and the cold, the filth, and the bad food, the mind-numbing monotony of life in the Tower, and think on other things. Only by doing so had he managed to survive throughout these long, weary months.

As the image of his wife came to his mind, he frowned slightly. He worried about Lady Jane, knowing that she was frail, and he again thanked God, as he had many times, for the Kemps, who had taken her in.

His mind then moved to Myles. He thought of the time Myles had first come to him, young and fearful and bewildered, but staunchly determined to do his dying Margred's bidding. He remembered the hour he had learned that Myles was his son, the flesh of his flesh, bone of his bone. It had been the joy of his life to have a son, to pass along what he had learned from life. And few pleasures matched that of knowing that Wakefield would belong to Myles, that what had been his father's would be his son's and then his grandson's. The thought of that grandson, so far away in Germany, who was now never to have a hope of being part of this land as his ancestors had been, grieved Robert sorely.

So he began to pray. He had been a man of infrequent prayer, but long months of imprisonment had taught him much. Once he remembered saying, "I don't know how anyone could pray for an hour! I could say everything I need to say to God in ten minutes!"

In the darkness of the cell—for his candle had again burnt out hours before—he smiled at that thought. Now it was nothing for Robert Wakefield to pray for ten or twelve hours. He hardly called it praying, though, for he had always thought of praying as presenting God with a list of needs and then saying a routine prayer of thanksgiving. This was different. He had learned that, if he lay quietly, stilled his mind and his thoughts, and lifted his spirit to God, sooner or later there would come that inexpressible sense of the presence of the Almighty. He had hoped, for a while, to hear voices or to see visions. Such had never happened. And yet, in his spirit he began to know God. Slowly came the realization that this was better than a vision, better than an audible voice, for he had come to take by simple faith the things of God.

That realization had brought with it joy he never imagined. He had never understood how Lady Jane could be so peaceful, even joyful and happy, having been robbed of the desire of her heart: having a child. But she had constantly been filled with a joy that he had never been able to explain, nor had she.

"Now I know how it is," he whispered, "when God is within. Those hard and terrible things outside cannot destroy you."

He started suddenly as the bar of his cell screeched and the door swung open. The light outside in the corridor was not brilliant, but it was so much brighter than his own gloomy cell that it hurt his eyes, and he quickly covered them. He put his feet over the edge of the cot, squinting and trying to identify the jailer.

"Is that you, Jim?" he asked.

"Aye, 'tis me, Sir Robert."

"What is it? Time for a little exercise?" From time to time, this gentle, kindly guard—the same one who had brought him books—took him out to a small courtyard to enjoy an hour's pleasure. He knew that Jim was breaking his orders to do this, and he was always extremely grateful for it.

"Not this time, Sir Robert." There was a strange note in the guard's voice, and he moved closer. "Get yourself cleaned up, sir," he said, "and you'll be needing your cloak, for certain. Bring all your things with you."

Sir Robert was not possessed of many things, and even as he spoke, Jim was raking them all together, putting them into a small bag that he had brought with him to the cell. Sir Robert put on his cloak, fastening it with trembling fingers. It was one of his few personal items, and he had been surprised when they had mercifully left it with him. Made of thick and heavy wool, it had kept him warm during the long days and nights.

"What is it?" he asked anxiously. "Is this the end, Jim?"

"The end!" Jim was shocked. He was a tall, thin man, not at all suited for being a Tower guard. There, cruelty was the norm—in fact, the rule—and Jim had a gentle spirit. "No, no, not a bit of it!" he exclaimed reassuringly. "Come along, sir, you don't have much time."

That sounded strange to Sir Robert, who for so long had had all the time in the world. He hurried along, stopping and groping blindly when the full light of the sun slanted through a high window and fell full upon his face. He had not seen the sun for days, and his eyes watered painfully. He felt a hand under his arm, and Jim said gently, "This way, Sir Robert, that's it—you'll be fine now!"

Almost blinded and much weaker than he realized, his legs trembling from lack of exercise and poor food, Sir Robert followed the guard. He was placed in a cell with a single window that looked out over the courtyard, and Jim said, "Wait right here, Sir Robert." Wakefield smiled at Jim's persistent use of his title, since they both knew he no longer could legally claim it. It was just one more kindness Jim offered the imprisoned man.

Jim stepped outside, and the cell door slammed.

Instantly Sir Robert made his way to the window. Standing upon a small chair, he could see out. It was a bright day, the sun touching the tops of the white towers. Below in the large courtyard, people were walking purposefully, guards and noblemen, for the king had quarters here.

He watched avidly, taking in the colors, which, gray as they were on that December day, looked rich and varied to him after the days of darkness. After what seemed a long time, there was a noise behind him, and he stepped off the chair, looking at the cell door expectantly.

In shocked amazement, he saw Myles come in—without a disguise! A horrible thought filled his mind, and he said, "Oh, Myles, have they taken you, too?" He stumbled forward and would have fallen, but his son's strong hands caught him. Robert felt the young man's arm about his shoulders, holding him steady. He looked up at Myles with fear but then saw the clear eyes and the smile on Myles's lips. "What? What is it, Son?" he asked.

"You are free, Father," Myles said huskily. His own eyes suddenly swam with tears as he looked at his father's worn face, but they were tears of joy. "You're going home. To Wakefield."

"But—but—how can that be?" Robert gasped. Myles's words were rather like being doused with cold water, and Robert's head was swimming. After so much time alone, he began to fear that he had lost his mind and now was imagining things. He stared wildly at Myles and managed to say, "Tell me what has happened."

Myles squeezed his father's shoulders, reassuring him, and told him the story. The king had simply called together the court that had condemned Robert Wakefield and told them there was new evidence. "I went in with Isen," Myles said, "and his testimony proved you innocent." He shrugged and went on, "Cromwell tried to protest, but the king gave him a look that could have killed an ox! When Cromwell saw which way the wind was blowing, he shut up. That was it, of course. The judges would no more think about going against Henry's wishes than they'd think about flying to the moon."

"And the verdict?" Robert asked in a stunned voice.

"The verdict is that you are innocent of all charges, and Wakefield is restored to your hands."

Sir Robert began to tremble. His mouth moved, but no words came. He took a deep breath, steadied himself, and said in an astonished voice, "God has done this, Myles. God himself has done it."

"You're right about that, Father," Myles agreed. "Now come with me, I want to get you out of this place."

The two of them left the Tower. As they passed by the famous block, where so many had lost their heads for crossing King Henry VIII, Robert looked at it and said softly, "I had thought to come to this place someday, Son."

Myles stopped, and they both stared at the block, stained darkly with the blood of the enemies of the king. It was a gloomy place, and even though the sun shone brightly, they began to feel chilled. "Let's go, Father," he urged. "I don't like this place."

They walked as quickly as Sir Robert could, and when they were outside the Tower grounds, Myles led his father to a waiting carriage.

"Sir Robert!" a voice cried out.

Robert looked up to see his coachman, Percy, standing at attention by the carriage, and there were tears running down the servant's cheeks. "Sir Robert!" was all he could say, over and over. When Robert put his hand out, the man took it, and his tears fell on it as he bent over it.

Myles's own eyes grew misty, and he said, "Take us home, Percy."

***

"I still can't get over it, Hannah!" Lady Jane exclaimed. She was holding William in her lap, delighting in her grandson and in the strength he displayed trying to get away from her.

"Let me have him, Mother," Hannah said. "He's too big to

be held, or so he thinks." She took the baby, put him gently down on the floor, and he squealed with delight. She turned and told Lady Jane, "I had to come. It was too awful, being in Germany, not knowing what was happening here. And Sir William insisted on it." She had arrived only that morning, and now that she was here, she vowed never to go back. Lady Jane had been astonished to see her but was overjoyed, and they had been together, talking eagerly since Hannah had walked into her parents' house.

Lady Jane had been rejoicing in the news of her husband's release and was making glad preparations to return to her home, Wakefield. Now it only increased her delight and thanksgiving to have her much loved daughter-in-law and her precious grandson there to share in Sir Robert's homecoming.

Hannah asked Lady Jane imploringly, for the fourth time, "How did it all happen?"

"'Tis a miracle of God, that's true enough," Lady Jane said triumphantly. "The king himself attended the hearing. He listened to the evidence, and according to Myles's letter, he commanded that Robert be set free that instant. And he granted Myles pardon for the charges against him as well. Two days ago, Robert and Myles went to see what they could do for poor Ralph. We are to return to Wakefield tomorrow."

"Do Ralph or Isabella know what has happened?" Hannah wondered quietly.

Lady Jane shook her head. "No, I don't believe they do. But they will know before the day is out." A small frown creased her forehead. "I pray God will be merciful to them."

<hr />

Isabella paused as she passed by the large mirror that adorned the east wall of Wakefield's dining room. She admired the diamond brooch on her bosom as it glittered like cold fire. She had taken possession of all of Lady Jane's personal things, and now as she moved toward her place at the large table where a sumptuous feast was laid out, she smiled at Ralph, saying, "I think we must go to London this week." She touched the brooch, saying playfully, "I can wear Lady Jane's jewelry but not her clothes."

"Again?" Ralph shook his head, took a drink from the heavy silver cup, then set it down. "You've bought enough clothes to last you a lifetime, Isabella."

"Ah no, my dear!" Isabella looked over the gold and silver vessels that loaded the table. "There *aren't* enough clothes to last me a lifetime."

"We're not made of money, you know." Ralph took another pull at his wine, wiped his lips with his sleeve, then shook his head. "The way you've spent money, you must think the Wakefield money is endless!"

Isabella lifted her head haughtily, knowing that no matter what Ralph said, she *would* go to London—but she also knew that he held the purse strings. So she laughed and said, "I'll get a few trifling things, and you can buy that horse you wanted so much."

At her words, Geddes's eyes brightened. "Ah! Lord Scurry's mare! Yes, I do—" He broke off, for the butler had burst into the room, a rather wild look on his thin face. "Well, what is it, James?" Geddes demanded.

"Sir . . . you have . . . visitors!"

"Visitors?" Geddes glanced toward Isabella. "Did you invite someone?"

"Why no. Not for this evening, Ralph."

"Who is it?"

"Sir . . . you'd best come to see—"

But James never finished his sentence, for the large double doors swung open without warning—and at the sight of the "visitors," both Ralph and Isabella leaped to their feet.

"Well, Ralph—" Sir Robert smiled grimly—"I trust we don't come at an inconvenient moment?" His face was thin and pale, but there was a bright glint in his blue-gray eyes. He stood there, dressed in a suit of brown wool, letting his eyes run over the pair, who had grown white as paper.

Myles stood to the right of Sir Robert, his eyes fixed on the face of Isabella. He had long understood that Ralph was no more than an opportunist, but Isabella?

She's so beautiful—and I loved her for so long, he thought, tracing the smooth beauty of her face. *Or did I ever really love her?*

He had no chance to ponder the question, for Sir Robert said, "I believe you are acquainted with my friend, are you not, Ralph?"

Geddes's eyes had been fixed with shock on Sir Robert, but when the man who'd been standing behind Wakefield stepped forward, he gasped, "Stokes!"

"Ah—we meet again, Mr. Geddes." The man's cold eyes seemed to glitter, and he rubbed his hands together as though he were washing them. "I fear the circumstances are somewhat different on this occasion."

"What does this mean?" Isabella burst out. She moved across the room—but strangely enough, not to stand behind her husband. Instead she placed herself in front of Myles, asking, "What has happened, Myles?"

Stokes answered her. "It's quite simple, my dear. I have a warrant for your husband's arrest." His skinny hand disappeared into the inner pocket of his coat and emerged with a sheaf of papers tied with a black ribbon. "Of course, you may read them for yourself. There is plenty of time on the way to the Tower."

"The—the Tower?" Ralph whispered. His eyes were fixed on the papers in Stokes's hand, but he shifted his gaze toward Robert Wakefield.

"Ah yes." Stokes caressed the parchment lovingly, adding, "You will be imprisoned there until your trial."

"On what possible charge?" Ralph demanded, doing his utmost to fill his voice with contempt. But the tremor in his words gave him away.

"Basically, the charge is perjury—but our sovereign liege, Henry VIII, has indicated that treason might be a more . . . ahh . . . *equitable* charge."

Ralph stared at Stokes, then licked his lips. His left eye suddenly developed a nervous tic, and he stepped toward Robert Wakefield, holding up his trembling hands in a gesture of importunity. "Sir, surely you won't allow the king . . ."

For the past months, Wakefield had dreamed of—indeed, had lived for this moment—but now that it had come, he found no enjoyment in the sight of Geddes groveling. He felt pity for the younger man and wanted only to be free of the entire situation. Now he said gruffly, "I have already asked the king to show mercy on you, Ralph. He was not willing to listen. But I promise you I will do my best to speak to him again before your trial."

"Ahhh, very *gracious* of you, Sir Robert," Stokes said, nodding. Then he called out, "Sergeant, come in here, please." As two men entered, he said, "Mr. Geddes, I . . . ahhh . . . *regret* to ask it, but would you allow these men to prepare you for your journey to London."

Myles watched as the soldiers put the fetters on the trembling man and wondered if they were the same chains that had bound his father when he'd been taken away. He felt a sudden surge of pity for the couple and said, "Isabella, I'm sure my mother would offer to let you stay until things are . . . settled."

Isabella cast one desperate look at her husband and knew that her life was over. But she had enough pride to lift her head and say, "No. I will go to my family." She laid a hand on Myles's arm and whispered, "Will you see me there, Myles?"

He smiled gently at her, suddenly grateful that all he felt at her touch was a fleeting pity. "I think not, Isabella," he answered quietly. "But we'll have a carriage take you there."

She recoiled as though he had struck her. "No! I'll ride with you, Mr. Stokes—if you will be so kind!" Anger and humiliation pulled at her lips, twisting them into an ugly shape, and she walked out of the room with her head high, following the soldiers who led Ralph away.

Stokes bowed, once again rubbing his hands together. "Ahhh . . . I will see the lady to her home. Good day to you."

Father and son watched the small procession depart, and after the door slammed shut with a sort of grim finality, Robert Wakefield bit his lip and looked at Myles. "I can't help but feel sorry for the man!"

Myles nodded. "He is a tragic and lonely figure—as all men are who don't know God. We must pray for him."

Robert laid his proud gaze on his son and suddenly threw his arms around him, saying, "God be thanked—for giving me such a son!"

The next morning, almost at first light, Lady Jane and Hannah returned to Wakefield. They entered the huge front doors with a great gladness and were met by the butler, who informed them that Myles and Sir Robert had gone for an early ride.

"They weren't expecting you back so early—," he said apologetically, and Lady Jane cut him off with a happy laugh.

"It's all right, Darrowby. We'll just surprise them when they return. Tell the servants to keep a watch for them and let us know when they come back. Come, Hannah, let us wait in the parlor."

She and Hannah rejoiced together, talking animatedly, playing with the baby. Lady Jane sighed happily and said, "Oh, he is going to be Myles all over again! And Robert, too." She laughed with sheer joy. "These Wakefield men all look alike, don't they? So handsome, every one!"

They were interrupted about an hour later when a maid came running in without ceremony and cried, "They're coming! They're coming! Peter has just run in with the news. He ran all the way to tell us."

Lady Jane turned to Hannah in delight. "It will be the surprise of Myles's life to see you here, Hannah!" She turned to the servant and ordered, "Let no one mention that my son's wife and baby are here. Do you understand?"

A broad grin lit the maid's plain face. "Yes, m'lady. 'Twill be just as you say."

Jane returned the smile and said, "Good. This time, *we* shall have something to surprise that son of mine!"

They heard footsteps in the hallway, and then the door of the room opened and Sir Robert strode in. He took two steps inside, then stopped dead still. Lady Jane was standing by the window as he had seen her do a thousand times before. She held out both hands and he went to her, tears filling his eyes, and threw his arms around her. She could not utter a word, and they stood together, holding each other tightly.

Myles stood watching, a smile on his face, tears in his eyes.

"Myles!"

He whirled and saw Hannah standing there, holding William. The room swam in front of his eyes, and for a moment he thought he was having a vision. Then he gave a great whoop and ran to them, picking them both up and swinging them in wild circles, shouting their names over and over.

Hannah breathlessly protested, "Myles! You'll hurt William!" She was laughing, and tears were rolling down her face at the same time. Myles set her down but grabbed William and tossed him high in the air, and William squealed and chortled and gurgled. "Oh, Myles," she cried, "I had to come! You're not angry, are you?"

"Angry?" Myles shouted joyfully. He tucked William under one arm in the flour-sack way he carried him and grabbed Hannah with the other arm, kissing her soundly. "How could a man be angry to see a beautiful thing like you! And a beautiful thing like you, too!" he said, lifting William with one strong arm and kissing his rosy cheeks. William promptly started protesting, since he obviously enjoyed the tossing more than the kissing.

And then they all came together. Myles held William and took Hannah's arm, walking over to stand beside his parents. Sir Robert looked at Myles and smiled. "I never thought to see this day. It's God's own mercy."

"Yes, it is, Sir Robert," Hannah said. "God has brought us this far. He will never desert the Wakefields. Not as long as we trust in him."

"Amen!" Robert said heartily. Then his eyes went to William. "Let me get my hands on that young fellow," he demanded. Soon he was over in one corner, playing with his grandson with as much enjoyment as if he himself were only two years old.

Hannah pulled Myles a little aside, and they watched as Lady Jane joined the two, determinedly tossing a fat pillow to the floor and slowly lowering herself onto it. "They have their heart's desire now, haven't they? Look how happy they are!" Hannah whispered.

"No happier than I," Myles said with his eyes on her. He hugged her again and stole another kiss, and they contentedly watched his parents and their son.

"What will happen now?" Hannah asked.

"Happen? We will live here at Wakefield, we will raise William—" he grinned slightly and pulled her closer—"and the others, of course. Can't let William be the only Wakefield to carry on the family name, now can we? What do you say, my dear? Wouldn't a little brother or sister be a fine gift for our son?"

Hannah blushed, smiled prettily, and pinched Myles playfully.

Then she grew serious and asked, "But what about Sir William? What will happen to him?"

"He is in God's hands," Myles said. "He has done a work that no other man on earth has done." He pulled her over to the window and pointed out. There was no plowing now, but he said, "Do you remember when Tyndale pointed at the plowboy and said, 'Before I am through, every plowboy in England will be able to read God's word for himself'?"

"I remember," Hannah said softly. They stood, remembering for a few moments, then Hannah turned to him, pulled his head down, and kissed him thoroughly.

Myles again marveled at the softness of her lips. He pulled his head back slowly and asked in surprise, "What's all this?"

"Tell me some more," Hannah said firmly, though she was blushing furiously, "about this little brother or sister that you have on your mind."

She looked at him mischievously, and Myles kissed her again. "It is a matter that will have my utmost attention, you may be sure," he said solemnly. His blue-gray eyes twinkled, and he turned again to watch his son as he played with his grandfather and grandmother across the room.

EPILOGUE

On July 6, 1535, Sir Thomas More was informed that he would die before 9 A.M. He replied, "For your good tidings, I most heartily thank you." He was taken to the scaffold, and when the old structure seemed to totter, he said, "I pray you, Master Lieutenant, see me safe up, and for my coming down, let me shift for myself." When he reached the top, he looked out over the crowd, and his last remark was, "I die the king's good servant—but God's first!"

Anne Boleyn, convicted of adultery and incest, was brought to the place of execution on the 19th day of May, 1536. According to one eyewitness, she said with a smiling countenance: "I humbly submit me to the law, and the law hath judged me, and as for mine offenses, God knowing them, I remit them to God, beseeching him to have mercy on my soul; and I beseech Jesus save my sovereign and master, the king, the most goodliest and gentlest Prince that is, and long to reign over you."

She then removed her headdress and kneeled at the block. The executioner from Calais, who had been brought over for the occasion, drew his great two-handed sword from its hiding place under a pile of straw and cut off her head with one stroke. Head and trunk were bundled into a makeshift coffin and buried that afternoon in the chapel of St. Peter-ad-Vincula, which overlooked the execution ground.

Through early 1535, one question often plagued Henry VIII: "Where was William Tyndale?" But that was a question to which the king could find no answer. After Henry had thrown off any hope of persuading Tyndale to return to England as a penitent subject, he determined to gain his person as a pestilent heretic. But every effort to discover the whereabouts of Tyndale failed.

If they had looked in Antwerp, they would have discovered the great translator living in the home of an English merchant there named Thomas Poyntz, for it was there that Tyndale quietly continued to work on his New Testament, editing and improving the text.

All the powerful agents and the impressive secret service of Henry had failed to discover Tyndale, but in one of those grim ironies that often are seen in human affairs, a rather dull man named Henry Phillips played a remarkable starring role.

Born of wealthy parents, Phillips had managed to waste all his substance and was finally branded as a traitor and a rebel. When he was destitute, a friend asked him, "Why don't you capture this fellow Tyndale whom the king is so eager to apprehend? You'd be paid royally and have the king in your debt."

On no more than this, Phillips left England and sailed for Antwerp, arriving there in early 1535. More by blind luck than skill, he managed to discover that a famous scholar was living at the home of Thomas Poyntz, and from then on the fate of William Tyndale was sealed.

Phillips managed to meet Tyndale and somehow gained his trust. Then, on May 21, 1535, he led the agents of Henry VIII to their long-sought quarry. Going into the Poyntz house, Phillips persuaded Tyndale to accompany him on an errand. When they left the house, Tyndale saw two officers and then, before he could wheel and flee, was shoved into the hands of the king's officers—and it was over.

"I have finished my course," one of the agents heard him mutter.

He was taken to the grim castle of Vilvorde, just six miles north of Brussels, where he was thrown into one of the foul-smelling, damp dungeons with nothing for company but the lapping moat and the scurrying rats.

For one year and one hundred and thirty-five days, he was kept in that foul place, and during that time, he toiled mightily. As the autumn of 1535 faded, his chest and head labored with heavy catarrh, but he penned one of his most compelling works, *Faith Alone Justifies before God*. He was not alone, for he was allowed to have visitors. Many came, and his conduct and his testimony were so strong that his keeper, the keeper's daughter, and others in the castle were brought to know Christ as Savior.

It was late afternoon in September of 1536 when a solitary visitor was admitted to Tyndale's cell. The prisoner looked up, the light from outside blinding in the semidarkness. The door closed, the bar rattled into place, and Tyndale courteously nodded. "Good day, sir. Will you sit down?"

"Sir William!" The man moved to bend down, and the feeble light of the single candle illuminated his face, causing Tyndale to cry, "Why, it's Myles!" He rose hastily, and the two men embraced. Tyndale held the younger man fast, then drew back, his eyes bright. "I'm so glad you've come! Now, tell me everything. . . ."

The two men sat for hours, talking endlessly. Tyndale wanted to know every detail—first, about Hannah and the child. He drank in Myles's words, exclaiming, "What a treasure for you, my boy!" Then he wanted to know about the Bibles. Were they being read? Were they available? How much did they cost?

Myles reached out and squeezed the thin shoulder of the prisoner fondly, "Didn't you say that the day would come when every plowboy would read the Word of God for himself? And you have done it, sir! Everywhere, all over England, the Bible is in the hands of the people!" He spoke warmly and with enthusiasm of the great movement sweeping the country, and finally he said quietly, "God has used you mightily, Sir William."

"To God be the glory, then!"

"But—cannot we do *something!*"

Tyndale shook his head, and a faint smile touched his pale lips. "Do not concern yourself, Myles. God has allowed me to complete my work. Now . . ." He hesitated, and the silence seemed somehow alive in the dark dungeon. "Now there is something else my Lord requires of me, and he will get glory from it."

Myles came every day for two weeks. Then, on the morning of October 6, 1536, he forced himself to go to the field where executions took place. The sun had barely risen over the horizon when William Tyndale—who had been tried, found guilty, and condemned as a heretic—arrived at the open space. Myles stood close to the spot where the condemned man would pass—and when Tyndale was five feet away, Myles said in a choking voice, "God be with you, Mr. Tyndale!"

Tyndale turned to look at the young man, noted the tears flowing down his cheeks, and said with a calm smile, "Bless you, my boy. You have been a blessing to me!" And then he was gone, hurried by the guards to the center of the open space.

He had been led out wearing his priest's robes and was forced to kneel. His hands were scraped with a knife as a symbol of his having lost the benefits of the anointing oil with which he was consecrated to the priesthood. The bread and the wine of the Mass were placed in his hands and at once withdrawn. This done, he was ceremoniously stripped of his priest's vestments, clothed as a layman, and handed over to the attorney for a secular punishment. The church would condemn but always left it for the secular offices to stain their hands with murder.

A circle of stakes enclosed the place of execution, and in the center was a large pillar of wood in the form of a cross and as tall as a man. A strong chain hung from the top, and a noose of hemp was threaded through a hole in the upright.

The attorneys and the priests arrived first and seated themselves in state nearby. The prisoner was brought in, and the final appeal was made that he should recant. Steadfastly Tyndale stood, immovable, his keen eyes gazing at the common people, whom he pitied for their ignorance. He met the cruel and merciless stare of his judges and pitied them also.

A silence fell over the crowd as they watched the lean form and the thin, tired face of the prisoner. His lips moved with a final, impassioned prayer, and every person heard it clearly. "Lord, open the king of England's eyes!" That was all.

Tyndale moved toward the cross. His feet were bound to the stake, wire and chain fastened around his neck, and the hemp noose placed at his throat. Only the Anabaptists and heretics were burned alive, so Tyndale was spared that ordeal. As piles of brushwood and logs were heaped around the condemned man, the executioner came up from behind the stake and with all his force bore down upon the noose. Within seconds, Tyndale was strangled.

Then the executioner came forward, placed a lighted torch to the tinder, and the commoners sat back to watch the fire burn. Finally, the charred form hung limply on the chain. An officer broke the staples with his halberd and allowed the body to fall into the glowing heat of the fire. More brushwood was piled on top, and the crowd began to move away.

William Tyndale had paid the final price exacted by man.

A week later, Myles arrived at Wakefield at sundown. When his family greeted him in their private quarters, they saw at once that he was weary and filled with sadness.

"Is it over, Myles?" Sir Robert asked quietly.

"Yes. He was executed last week."

"Tell us, Son," Lady Jane urged, and they listened quietly as Myles related the last days of the man they all had so loved and respected.

When he ended, he leaned back and covered his face with his hands. "I could do nothing—nothing!" he groaned.

"No, nor could any man under heaven," Lady Jane said softly. When Myles glanced up at her with surprise, she added, "It was in God's hands, Myles. The blood of the martyrs is the seed of the church."

"I think that is right," Robert said thoughtfully. "God does not allow men like William Tyndale to die uselessly."

Hannah had remained silent, but now she rose and came to sit beside Myles. She stroked his gaunt face, saying, "It was said of Abel that, being dead, he yet spoke. Through his translations, Sir William is speaking to thousands. And that voice will never cease until the Lord Jesus comes back!"

Myles brightened at her words. "You always have the power to lift me up, Hannah, and—"

But he never finished his sentence, for a small but sturdy figure came rushing into the room, yelling, "Father!"

Myles rose and met his son, holding him fast. "Look at this big boy!" he exclaimed. The others watched with smiles as the toddler chattered incessantly. Finally Myles asked, "Were you a good boy, William, while your father was gone?"

"No."

Myles bit his lip to keep from smiling at the blunt answer. "No? And why not?"

William Wakefield had the same blue-gray eyes of his father—and the same sort of spirit! "It's hard to be good," he said, nodding.

At that, his grandfather lifted his hands and uttered a cry of mock despair. "Heaven help us, Jane! We've got *another* stubborn one to raise!"

Soon Myles's parents moved from the room, taking a very unwilling boy with them. When the door closed, Myles at once put his arms around Hannah, holding her close and whispering into her hair, "I am only half a man when I'm away from you!"

Hannah's eyes dimmed with tears, but she blinked them away fiercely. Pulling his head back, she kissed him thoroughly, then put her lips close to his ear. "Half a man, is it? I've no use for such a thing!"

Myles laughed aloud and suddenly spun her around the room until she pleaded for mercy. Then he set her down, and looking into her eyes, he said, "He spoke of you—of what a good woman you have always been."

"I think he was not unhappy to go, Myles."

Her words caught at him, and they stood there, thinking of the days so long ago when they had sat at the feet of the man who had loosed the Word of God over England.

The night was coming on, and as the darkness fell over Wakefield, the two went to watch out the window. Myles said, "No matter how dark it gets in this England of ours—or in the world—there'll always be the light of God's Word."

"And it was Sir William that made it shine on us, wasn't it, husband?"

He nodded, and they turned and left the room, joining the family and looking to the days to come. Wakefield would stand, for untold generations. Likewise, the Bible would stand—and never again would England be the same as it was before William Tyndale gave the Word to all the plowboys.

And all over England, the Bibles one man had translated were circulating, in the homes of the rich and powerful, in the homes of the poor—in the homes of the farmers, the tradesmen, the plowmen—everywhere the Word of God was stirring.

THE END

In addition to this series . . .

THE WAKEFIELD DYNASTY

. . . look for more captivating historical fiction from Gilbert Morris!

THE APPOMATTOX SAGA
Intriguing, realistic stories capture the emotional and spiritual strife of the tragic Civil War era.

RENO WESTERN SAGA
A Civil War drifter faces the challenges of the frontier, searching for a deeper sense of meaning in his life.

Just for kids

THE OZARK ADVENTURES   (New! Fall 1994)
Barney Buck and his brothers learn about spiritual values and faith in God through outrageous capers in the back hills of the Ozarks.